SHELTER

JUNG YUN

SHELTER

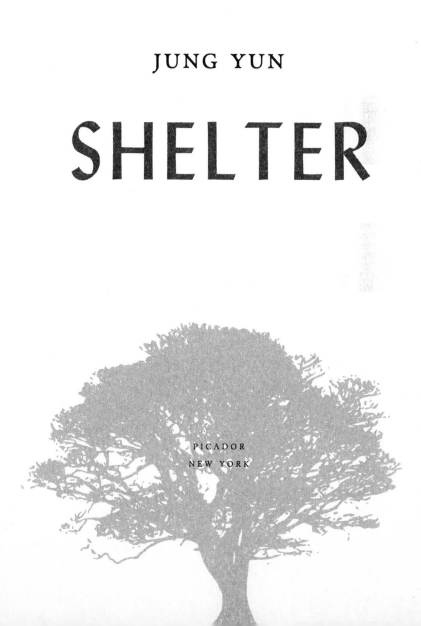

PICADOR
NEW YORK

picadorusa.com • picadorbookroom.tumblr.com
twitter.com/picadorusa • facebook.com/picadorusa

Picador® is a U.S. registered trademark and is used by St. Martin's Press under license from Pan Books Limited.

For book club information, please visit facebook.com/picadorbookclub or e-mail marketing@picadorusa.com.

Designed by Jonathan Bennett

Library of Congress Cataloging-in-Publication Data

Yun, Jung.
  Shelter : a novel / Jung Yun.
    pages cm
  ISBN 978-1-250-07561-1 (hardcover)
  ISBN 978-1-250-07564-2 (e-book)
  1. Korean Americans—Fiction. 2. Family life—Fiction. I. Title.
  PS3625.U53S54 2016
  813'.6—dc23

                                                      2015029507

Our books may be purchased in bulk for promotional, educational, or business use. Please contact your local bookseller or the Macmillan Corporate and Premium Sales Department at 1-800-221-7945, extension 5442, or by e-mail at MacmillanSpecialMarkets@macmillan.com.

First Edition: March 2016

10 9 8 7 6 5 4 3 2 1

To my husband, Joel,
who changed everything

No man steps in the same river twice,
for it is not the same river,
and he is not the same man.

——HERACLITUS

PART ONE

DAWN

ONE

The boy is standing in the doorway again. He's smiling, which hardly seems right. A smile means he's not sick. He didn't have a bad dream. He didn't wet the bed. None of the things he usually says when he enters the room uninvited. Kyung nudges his wife, who turns over with a grunt, face-first into her pillow. He sighs and sits up, rubbing the sleep from his eyes.

"What's wrong?" he asks. "What's the matter?"

Ethan, still smiling, takes a step forward, holding a remote control in his outstretched palm. "Battery," he says, pronouncing the word "buttery."

"You want batteries now?"

He nods. "To watch cartoons."

The curtains in the bedroom are open. The sky outside, a pale silvery blue. It's early still. Too early to be thinking about batteries, but Kyung resists the urge to say so out loud. At this hour, he doesn't trust himself to do it nicely. He kicks off the sheets, grazing Gillian's leg as he gets out of bed.

"Five minutes," she says. "I'll be up in five."

The night-lights flicker as they make their way downstairs,

past floorboards that creak and sigh under their weight. Kyung finds a dusty package of batteries that he doesn't remember buying. He swaps out the old for the new and hands the remote back to Ethan.

"You want some breakfast now?"

Ethan climbs onto the sofa and turns on the TV. "Okay," he says, flipping from one channel to the next.

The boy always agrees to eat and then doesn't. If given the choice, he'd probably subsist on a diet of grapes, popcorn, and cheese. The kitchen is down to the dregs of the week's groceries. A spotted brown banana. A cup of cereal dust. Half a cup of almost-expired milk. Not much to work with, but enough. Kyung slices the banana into the cereal with the edge of a spoon, making a face with the pieces because Ethan is more likely to eat something when it smiles. As he tosses the peel into the trash, he notices the calendar pinned to the wall. There's a circle around today's date. Inside the thick red ring is a single word that disappoints him. *Gertie*. Weekends are best when there's nothing to do and no one to see. A visit from Gertie is the exact opposite of nothing.

"Did your mom mention someone was coming over today?" he asks, depositing the bowl of cereal in Ethan's lap.

"She said I have to clean my room."

"I need to go talk to her for a minute. Will you be okay here by yourself?"

"Dad, shhhhh." Ethan points at the screen as a bright blue train speeds past. "I'm missing Thomas."

Upstairs, Gillian is making the bed. The realtor is coming at ten, she says, confirming what he hoped wasn't true. He wishes she'd mentioned this the night before, but he knows why

4

she didn't. Selling the house is her idea, not his. Kyung glances at the ornate paisley comforter, the expertly arranged pillows and bolsters, piled high like a soft hill. He wants to climb back into them, to pull the sheets over his head and wake up to a day that isn't this one.

"I'm not canceling again," she says.

"I didn't ask you to."

"But I can see it on your face."

What she actually sees is surprise—surprise that Gertie would agree to another meeting with them. At his insistence, Gillian canceled their last three. It was dishonest of her to plan it this way, but he realizes he gave her no choice.

"Come on," she says, taking his hand. "We have a lot to do before she gets here."

They eat their breakfast standing up—a stack of dry toast on a paper towel. Kyung searches for something to moisten the stale bread, but finds only a thin pat of butter, flecked with crumbs, and a jar of crystallized honey. He misses the pancakes and omelets that Gillian used to make before Ethan was born, the lazy meals they shared after waking up at noon. These days, breakfast is what they consume in large, distracted bites while attending to other things. Gillian is leaning over the counter, reading him the to-do list on her computer. *Sweep floors, clean up laundry room, vacuum carpets, take out trash.* It seems odd to go through so much trouble for a realtor, he thinks, someone they're paying for a service. Gertie Trudeau is supposedly the best in town. She should be able to price the house whether they do these things or not.

"What about the garbage disposal?" he asks.

"What do you mean?"

"Don't you think I should fix it?"

"We'll just tell her the sink's clogged. It's more important for everything to look clean."

"I think I'll try to fix it," he says, because trying is his only means of protest.

Gillian puts on her shoes and opens the door to the garage. "Fine," she says, in a tone that suggests just the opposite. "I guess I'll start with the trash, then."

Kyung has never fixed a garbage disposal before. He has only a vague idea of how it works—blades, motor, plumbing, pipes. He's not handy like some of the other men in the neighborhood, the ones with toolboxes as big as furniture, always borrowing and lending the contents as if they were books. Kyung isn't friendly enough with any of them to ask for help, although he sometimes wishes he could. The sink is half-full with foul gray dishwater—it has been for days. He's not sure what to do about it except plunge his hand into the murk. An inch shy of elbow-deep, he finally touches the bottom. There's a thick layer of grease in the chamber, solid like wax.

"Well, no wonder it's clogged," he shouts.

From the garage, a muffled "What?"

"I said 'no wonder it's clogged.'"

Gillian doesn't respond. He's about to remind her that cooking oil settles in the blades, but his wife is a selective listener. If she didn't hear him the first time, she's not likely to hear him now. He loosens the edge of something with his fingertips and removes a jagged shard of congealed fat. The air suddenly smells like rotten meat, the remains of a thousand family dinners. He feels an urge to gag that he traps with his fist and then a tug on the hem of his shirt.

"What are you doing?"

Ethan is standing behind him, still dressed in his pajamas. Around his waist is a tool belt with multicolored loops, most of which are empty. From the original set, the only pieces that remain are a bright yellow hammer and a miniature tape measure.

"I'm trying to fix the garbage disposal."

"What's wrong with it?"

"Things just break sometimes. Have you cleaned your room yet?"

"I can fix it with you." Ethan gets up on his tiptoes and bangs away on the chipped Formica.

Kyung pinches the bridge of his nose, massaging the dull rings of pain around his eyes. Every time the cheap plastic hammer hits the counter, he feels a little worse. "Stop," he says, placing his wet hand over Ethan's. "Please stop."

Although he barely raised his voice, Ethan's lower lip starts to tremble and his crusty brown eyes well with tears. Kyung doesn't understand why his son is like this, so quick to cry. He's not the source of it, and Gillian, who comes from a family of policemen, hasn't cried once in the half decade he's known her.

"It's okay," he says quietly. "But it only takes one person to fix a garbage disposal. Maybe there's something upstairs that you can fix? Or outside, with Mom?"

Kyung watches carefully, waiting for the threat of tears to pass. He's grateful when Ethan slips the hammer back into its loop and runs off to his room. The banging resumes almost immediately, still annoying and persistent, but less so with distance. He turns his attention back to the sink, throwing lumps of grease in the trash until the pileup resembles a tumor, opaque and misshapen and thick like jelly. After scraping the chamber clean, he runs hot water from the tap, hoping to see some improvement, but the water level doesn't drop. Instead, the surface shimmers with a slick, oily residue in which he catches his reflection. He looks disappointed, as he often does on weekends when a minor household task unravels into something that resembles work. He imagines the rest of his day wasted on this project—driving to the hardware store for a new tool, disassembling things that he shouldn't, searching the Internet for a clue. Nothing in his house works anymore, which is part of the problem.

By the time the realtor arrives, Kyung has completed exactly zero tasks on the to-do list. The garbage disposal, still broken, might even count as minus one. He watches from the window as Gertie rolls up in a silver Mercedes, sleek and recently washed. She parks in the driveway and surveys the lawn before ringing the bell, wrinkling her nose at the weedy flower beds. She looks different from her photographs, the ones posted on every other bus and billboard in town. Older, he thinks, and heavier too. When he greets her in the foyer, he notices that her teeth have been whitened, and she's wearing diamond solitaires the size of erasers on her ring finger, in her ears, and around her neck. He distrusts her immediately, the way she screams *sales*.

"Pleased to meet you," she says, shaking his hand as if pumping water from a well. "I'm glad we could finally make this happen."

Gillian and Ethan join them in the foyer. They've both changed clothes. A pair of blue denim shorts and a button-down shirt for him. A yellow sundress for her, dotted with orange flowers. Kyung is still wearing the T-shirt and shorts he slept in. His feet are callused and bare, outlined with dirt from the sandals he wore the day before.

"Now, who is this precious little boy?" Gertie asks.

Ethan steps backward, hiding behind Gillian's leg.

"Say hello to Mrs. Trudeau," Kyung says.

Ethan extends his small hand to her, which she takes between her thumb and forefinger.

"How old are you?" she asks.

"Four," he whispers, retreating behind Gillian again. She makes no effort to stop him, which they've discussed in the past. The boy is shy because they coddle him.

"What a gorgeous child," Gertie says agreeably. "Biracial children are always so beautiful. The best of both parents, I think. You two are what? Chinese and Irish?"

"Korean," he corrects.

Gertie quickly depletes her reserves of small talk and asks for a tour, which they start in the living room. Gillian takes the lead and tries to point out the nicer features of the house, describing even the smallest things too cheerfully, as if the person she needs to convince is herself. Kyung brings up the rear, occasionally stealing a peek over Gertie's shoulder as she jots down notes in a leather-bound legal pad. The brick fireplace in the living room receives a check-plus, along with the bay window, the wood floors, and the size of the adjoining dining room. The kitchen appliances, the worn carpets on the second floor, and the water stains in the bathroom all receive a check-minus. Pantry and garage, check-plus. Wet basement and old boiler, check-minus. He isn't insulted so much as impressed by the skill and speed with which she catalogs the good and bad. Gertie sees dollars, not disappointment, which is exactly what he needs right now.

After the tour, they sit down at the kitchen table while Gertie removes a manila folder from her briefcase. The label on the tab reads MCFADDEN—Gillian's last name, not his.

"I pulled up some sales data on comparable houses in the neighborhood." She flips through a few sheets of paper, frowning as if she left something behind at the office. "Of course, you know the market's down right now."

Under the table, Gillian taps nervously on Kyung's leg. Get to the point, he thinks. Get to the point already.

"I'd say your biggest selling point is the neighborhood. The taxes are a little high here, but you're in an excellent school district, and the commute to Boston is pretty reasonable. As for the house . . ."

He wants to cut her off and tell her about their plans. They had so many of them—a new kitchen, a sunroom, replacement windows, and a deck—but what does it matter now? It's obvious they couldn't afford to do any of it. That's the hesitation he hears in her voice.

". . . the house could use a fair amount of remodeling. And that boiler will have to be replaced soon, which won't be cheap. Ah, here it is." Gertie pulls out a piece of paper from the bottom of the stack and adjusts her reading glasses. "I'd probably suggest a list price of three hundred and sixty-five thousand dollars. Maybe you could go as high as three ninety if you're not in a hurry to move, but I wouldn't necessarily recommend that route."

It doesn't matter what she would or wouldn't recommend. Even the higher price is less than what they hoped for, less than what they owe. Kyung forgets himself for a moment and rests his forehead in his hands. This is exactly why he put off the meeting for so long.

"I'm sorry. Is that not what you expected to hear?"

He can't quite bring himself to answer the question. Although he knew Gertie wouldn't be able to save them, at the very least, he thought she might throw them a rope.

Gillian sends Ethan into the living room and tells him to turn on the TV. "Can we be completely honest with you?" she asks.

"If you expect me to sell your house, you shouldn't be anything but."

"Well"—she picks at a line of dirt under her nail—"we're kind of embarrassed about this, but you might as well know . . . my husband and I refinanced at the height of the market and took cash out against our mortgage, so we actually owe the bank about four hundred and eighty thousand for this place."

The books and Web sites that Gillian always asks him to read refer to this state as "underwater" or "upside down"—terms he actively dislikes. It's bad enough that everything in the house keeps breaking. He doesn't need to imagine himself drowning too.

"So it's a short sale," Gertie says. Her expression gives away nothing. "They're much more common these days. The trick is getting your bank to take a loss on the difference between what you owe them and what you can sell for."

Her matter-of-fact tone should encourage him, but it doesn't. He already knows their bank won't agree to a loss unless they fall behind on their payments. By some sort of miracle, they haven't yet, although they're behind on everything else. Gertie fails to mention that a short sale would be disastrous to their credit rating, almost as bad as a foreclosure. No one would be willing to lend to them for years. Kyung can't stand the idea of being reduced to a renter at his age, asking a landlord for permission to paint a room or hang up some shelves. He was raised to believe that owning a home meant something. Losing a home like this—that would mean something too.

"An alternative to selling now is renting this place out until the market picks back up. You could easily get twenty-five hundred a month, maybe even as much as three thousand." Gertie turns to him. "Would you have somewhere else to go if I found you a good tenant? I actually know of a couple. They're relocating to the area and want to get acclimated for a year before they buy."

They do have a place to go, a place that makes sense financially, but it would wreck him to exercise the option, to explain why he had to. His parents live three miles away, just past the conservation land that separates their neighborhood from his own. As Gillian keeps pointing out, they have plenty of space, they could live there rent-free, and it's what his parents wanted all along—to spend more time with their grandson. He just can't imagine living any closer to them than he already does.

"Kyung's parents own a six-bedroom up the hill," Gillian says.

"Marlboro Heights." Gertie is impressed. "Well, this will be perfect, then. I'll call my clients and schedule a showing the next time they're in town."

The conversation is moving ahead without him. Kyung

hasn't even committed to the idea of renting yet, and already, Gertie and Gillian are making plans.

"How do you know these people will even want to rent our house? What if they don't like it?"

"What's not to like?" Gertie stands up and walks to the kitchen window. "Second to Marlboro Heights, this is the best neighborhood in town. And look at this view. Trees as far as the eye can see."

Their backyard abuts twenty-six acres of pine and spruce. The locals on both sides of the conservation land refer to it as the "green wall." It was the feature Gillian fell in love with when they first started house hunting, that sense of being surrounded. The three-bedroom colonial was at the top of their price range, but he could tell how much she wanted it, and he wanted it for her. Now their decision is ruining them. He shakes his head and glances at Gertie, who hasn't said a word since she turned toward the window. Her eyebrows are angled sharply into a frown, and her mouth is open as if she means to speak, but can't.

"Is something wrong with the yard?" he asks.

Slowly, she lifts her finger and taps on the glass. "I think that woman out there—I think she might be naked."

Kyung and Gillian gather around the window, craning to see what she does. Their backyard is empty except for the swing set and clothesline. The neighbors' yards too—all empty. He looks out toward the overgrown field of weeds and wildflowers where their property line ends and the conservation land begins. Kyung's eyesight isn't what it used to be, but when he squints, he thinks he can see someone wading through the tall grass.

"Is she actually naked?" he asks.

Gillian leans in closer, fogging the glass with her breath. "Jesus, Kyung. I think that's Mae."

He narrows his eyes, trying to sharpen the blur of lines and colors coming at them. The woman's hair is black like his, but with the sun parked behind a cloud, he can't make out her face. It's not her, he thinks. She's limping. Mae doesn't have a limp.

"You two know this person?" Gertie asks.

"I think it might be Kyung's mother."

He continues staring as the woman approaches, holding one hand over her breasts, and the other over her privates. Neither hand can obscure what Kyung realizes is not an optical illusion, not some crude misunderstanding of distance and light. His mother is completely naked.

"I'm sorry," he says. "I don't understand. . . ." Half of him wants to tear out of the house, but the other half wants to salvage the meeting by making up excuses. "She hasn't been well lately. She's . . . forgetful, I guess you'd call it."

"My mother had Alzheimer's too," Gertie says. "It's a sad way of losing someone. Why don't I leave you two alone now?" She collects her papers and puts them back in the folder. "When I hear from my clients, I'll give you a call."

Kyung restrains himself, clutching the back of his chair as Gillian tries to show her out, but Gertie stops just before she reaches the door.

"I know you probably hate the idea of renters in here. Most people in your situation do, but it might not be the worst thing in the world to spend more time with your parents right now. I wish I had."

Mae is fifty-six years old. She doesn't have Alzheimer's. She doesn't have anything. But Kyung doesn't bother to correct her because dementia is the only reasonable explanation for what she's done. As soon as Gertie leaves, he runs out the back door toward the field, the same way he did when he saw Ethan turning blue at a neighbor's birthday party. He was choking on a piece of candy, a thumb-sized chocolate that he wasn't supposed to eat. Kyung was terrified at first, and angry later. Now he feels the full force of both. He rips a beach towel from the clothesline, and a plastic pin snaps off and hits him in the face, missing his eye by almost nothing.

The grassy field comes up to his knees, littered with things that he never noticed from a distance. Everywhere he steps, there's broken glass and pieces of metal and thick patches of thistle that sting and scrape his legs. Even if the ground were free of obstacles, he wouldn't look up. He can't. His mother is so conservative, so timid about her body. She's never even worn a bathing suit. He doesn't understand how that woman became this one. As they meet near the middle of the field, Kyung turns his head and hugs her with the towel, covering the parts of her that he doesn't want to see.

"What?" he shouts. But his thoughts are too scattered to finish the question. "*Why?*"

Mae's face is filthy. Her skin is covered with dark brown streaks. He worries that it's excrement, a possibility no stranger than wandering naked from her house to his.

"Where are your clothes?"

Mae's expression doesn't change, not even when he shouts the question just inches from her ear.

"Help," she says, followed by something in Korean—so low, he can barely make out the words.

"English. Speak English. I can't understand you."

"Help," she repeats.

"I'm *trying* to." He pulls the towel around her tighter, embarrassed by the sight of Mae so diminished, wrapped in hot pink sea horses and neon green stripes. "Where's Dad? Can we call him to come get you? Can he bring you some clothes?"

"Aboji ga dachi shuh suh."

"What? What are you saying?"

"Aboji ga dachi shuh suh."

Korean is no longer the language he speaks with his parents. They retired it from use years ago, when Kyung was just a child. Like a dog, he sometimes recognizes the sounds of certain words, but doesn't always grasp their meaning. *Aboji ga* . . . your father? *Dachi shuh suh* . . . hurt me? Your father hurt me? The air catches in his lungs as the question forms a statement, and suddenly everything forgotten is familiar again. He turns Mae's face toward his, gently lifting her chin until he notices the bruises. Two in the center of her throat. Eight more fanning out on the sides of her neck. Fingerprints. When he backs away, the towel slides off her shoulders and falls to the ground, but Mae doesn't reach for it or even cover herself with her hands. She just stands there, trembling as he takes in everything that he missed before. The scratches on her arms and breasts. The bloody patches where her pubic hair has been ripped out. Bruises everywhere. Bruises again.

Behind him, the kitchen door squeaks open and bangs shut.

"Is she all right, Kyung? What's going on?"

As Gillian approaches, his mother buries herself in his arms and starts to cry, but it's like no cry he's ever heard before. She wails, long and low, like a wounded animal that any decent man would have the sense to kill.

One of the paramedics asks if Mae speaks English. Kyung insists that she does—she's fluent, he tells them—but she keeps scream-ing at all of them in Korean. Twice, she lurches up to a sitting position on the gurney and rips the oxygen mask off her face. When the paramedics try to strap her down, she fights them both, throwing punches as if she's gone wild. Kyung has never seen his mother act like this before. She's not the type to resist. He rests his hand on her shoulder, startled by the temperature of her skin, which is burning hot.

The female paramedic covers Mae with a thin, crackly sheet that looks like tinfoil. "Don't touch her," she warns. "She has frostbite."

"But it's June. And it was warm this morning."

"But it was raining last night," she snaps. "Those blisters forming around her ankles? That's trench foot. She was prob-ably out in the woods since yesterday."

The woman doesn't try to hide that she blames Kyung for what happened. He bristles at this, the idea that he's somehow responsible, or irresponsible.

"My father did this. She told me, right before I called you. She said, 'Your father hurt me.'"

The woman glances at her partner as he prepares an IV line. When he finishes inserting the needle into Mae's arm, he knocks on the sliding glass door that separates them from the driver.

"Ten-sixteen," he says. "Call it in."

The driver nods and picks up his radio.

Mae tries to say something, but it's muffled by the seal of her oxygen mask. Kyung leans down beside her ear. "Everything's going to be fine."

He's told this lie so many times in the past, but something about it feels different now. He's no longer a small child or a sullen teenager, lifting himself up to play a part. He's a thirty-six-year-old man with a promise to keep. Kyung was a freshman in college when he threatened to kill his father if he ever raised a hand to Mae again. Even though his voice cracked as he said the words out loud, even though he fully expected to become the object of the beating instead of the observer, the threat was surprisingly effective. Jin started going to counseling once a week. He became a regular at prayer group and Bible study. For eighteen years, he lived like a changed man—not a loving or caring man, but the absence of rage was change enough. Still, Kyung couldn't rule out the possibility that a day like this would come, and now, of course, it has. Why it started again, why it happened with such a different, demented kind of violence—he can't even begin to understand. His father was always a hitter. Open hand or closed fist. An occasional kick to the ribs or back. But the patches of pubic hair ripped out by their roots—this is something new. He shakes his head, trying to rid himself of the image. He can't imagine what his mother did to deserve such a beating, but that was always the point. She didn't deserve any of them.

Mae falls asleep during their last few minutes in the ambulance, despite a stretch of potholed road that jolts Kyung's spine. As he sees the hospital approaching in the window, he's tempted to ask the driver to circle the block. That's what he used to do with Ethan, who had colic as a baby. The car was one of the few places where he could sleep, so Kyung often drove around the neighborhood, over and over again, to soothe Ethan's frayed nerves and his. It always felt like a shame to wake him at the end of the ride. Despite everything that's happened, Mae appears peaceful for the first time since he saw her in the field, a peace that ends as soon as the ambulance stops and the paramedics fling open the doors.

Suddenly, people are coming at them like locusts. Everyone is talking over each other—the doctors, the nurses, the paramedics. Mae is screaming again, banging her head against the gurney with such force, a nurse has to hold her down. Kyung assumes he'll be allowed to go into the exam room with her, but a doctor waves him off.

"Check in over there," he says.

Kyung watches as they wheel Mae away, struggling against her restraints like a psych patient. He should be with her, he thinks. He feels terrible for being so impatient in the field, barking questions in her ear while she was asking for help.

At the front desk, a dough-faced woman hands him some forms to fill out and asks for Mae's insurance card.

"Insurance?"

"Yes, does she have any?"

He isn't sure what bothers him more—the fact that she's asking now, or the fact that he doesn't know.

"I think so."

"Any idea who she's covered by?"

"No."

"Fine," she sighs. "Just do the best you can."

Kyung fills out the top section of the cover sheet—Mae's name, address, telephone number, and birth date. He's not sure about the answers to anything else, so he slides the clipboard across the counter.

The woman scans the form and tries to slide it back. "You missed a bunch."

"I can't fill out the rest."

"You don't know if your mother has any preexisting conditions?"

"No . . . we're not really that close."

The woman lifts and lowers her eyebrows. "Okay, then. The police are waiting to talk to you. I think they're around the corner."

"They're here already?"

"The paramedics called ahead."

Of the three men standing beside the soda machine, Kyung recognizes two of them: Connie, Gillian's father. And Tim, her brother. Both appear to be off duty, dressed in T-shirts and jeans as if they were interrupted mid-barbecue. Their faces are angled toward a small television set hanging from the ceiling that's tuned to a Red Sox game. Kyung approaches slowly, then slower still until he comes to a stop and takes a deep breath. He didn't ask Gillian to call her family. He wishes she hadn't.

"Connie," he finally says.

His father-in-law turns around. "What's going on? Is she all right?"

Kyung nods, but he's not convinced.

"This is Officer Lentz. He's here to take your statement."

He looks at the third man's face, alarmed by the roundness of it, the absence of stubble or wear. "How old are you?" he asks. He blurts out the question before he realizes what an insult it levies.

"Twenty-nine."

Lentz emphasizes the word "nine," which Kyung assumes people mistake for "five."

"Matt's a good guy. He knows what he's doing." Tim rests a protective hand on Lentz's shoulder.

"So what happened?" Connie asks. "Gilly called in a fit about your mom getting beaten up."

Kyung nods again, staring at the checkered tile floor. This is too much to say in front of his in-laws, too much history that he's guarded from people like them.

Connie seems to sense this because he steps toward him, lowering his head to look Kyung in the eye. "She said you mentioned something about your father before the ambulance arrived? He's done this kind of thing before?"

Connie's eyes are blue, blue like Gillian's. For the first time, Kyung sees something resembling kindness in them. Not suspicion, like the day she brought him home to meet the family. Or apathy, like every other Christmas and Thanksgiving since. Being married to his daughter wasn't enough to earn this man's affection, but being a victim somehow is.

"It used to be pretty regular. A long time ago." Kyung pauses. "My mother told me he did this to her—when she came to the house today, she said so."

Lentz is taking notes with a small blue pencil, the stubby kind used by golfers. Kyung watches the lead leave a neat trail across the page. Every letter is perfectly slanted and looped; it looks like a woman's handwriting, or a young girl's. He wonders if Lentz has ever been assigned to anything more serious than a bike theft.

"That seems like enough to go talk to him, don't you think?" Connie asks. "Mind if we come along?"

Although he phrased it in the form of a question, it's obvious that Connie expects the younger man to defer to him, which he does.

"I want to go too."

The three men look at Kyung, then at each other.

"That's probably not such a good idea," Tim says. "Maybe you should wait—"

Connie swings his arm in front of Tim's chest like a barricade. "It's okay if he wants to come. Someone does this to a guy's mother, he has the right." He doesn't bother to consult Lentz about this. He simply starts walking toward the exit. "Just promise me you'll stay out of the way."

What he promises to do and what he thinks he'll do are two different things. Kyung is convinced that when he sees Jin, he'll go straight for the old man's throat, pressing his thumbs into the hollow until someone pries him off. Connie and Tim might respect him more for the effort, although the McFaddens are the kind of men who always seem ready to fight, which ensures that they never have to. Kyung doesn't feel comfortable around them, making their presence today even odder. He reminds himself that Gillian couldn't have known any of this was going to happen when she called. It's not her fault that he's sitting in the back of Connie's Suburban, following Lentz's squad car up the hill toward Marlboro Heights.

"I keep forgetting," Tim says. "What's your dad teach again?"

"Engineering. Mechanical engineering."

"College professor ought to know better than to hit a woman, don't you think?"

Tim turns around in the passenger seat, his expression a cross between menacing and sly. He's a hulk of a man, even taller and thicker than Connie. The question was probably his dumb idea of a trick. Kyung is a college professor too. Tim wants to hear him say the right thing.

"Everyone," he answers.

"Everyone what?"

"I think everyone should know better."

The main road into Marlboro Heights is a wide, neatly land-scaped street. The houses along this stretch are the cheapest in the neighborhood because of their proximity to traffic. Still, Tim whistles at the sprawling Victorians with their chemical-green lawns and tall, leafy shade trees. It occurs to Kyung that his in-laws have never visited his parents' house before. They were invited once, shortly after he and Gillian eloped, but they declined the invitation, which was never extended again. Under different circumstances, he would have been proud to bring them here. Mae and Jin live near the top of the hill in a stunning Queen Anne, built in the 1860s and restored to ornate, expensive perfection.

When they pull into the horseshoe driveway, Tim leans out his open window, taking it all in. "This doesn't look like a college professor's house."

"My father still earns money from his patents."

"His what?"

"He invents things."

"Never mind all that." Connie turns around in his seat. "Remember what you promised. You're going to keep your head in there, right?"

Kyung feels like a bullet sitting in a chamber. Compressed and powerful, ready to inflict damage. Sending his father to jail isn't the same thing as killing him, but it's close. Close enough.

"I'll be fine."

Lentz is waiting for them on the doorstep. As they walk up the flagstone path, Kyung notices that all the drapes have been pulled shut. Lentz picks up the brass knocker and raps the handle against the door. When no one answers, Connie pounds on it with his fist.

"I guess he took off," Lentz says. "No cars in the driveway."

Kyung lifts a flowerpot filled with marigolds and removes a spare key from the draining dish. His father is smart, smart enough to park the Lincoln a few blocks away to give the appearance that no one is home. That would explain the drapes. He tries to offer the key to Lentz, who steps away as if it's a grenade.

"We can't use that. We'll have to come back later."

"Hold on, hold on," Connie says. "You ever let yourself in with that key before?"

"A couple of times. Why?"

"And your parents didn't mind, did they? Didn't complain?"

"No. They told me where to find it."

Connie turns to Lentz. "It's not illegal entry if he had prior consent. I say we go in."

"Come on, Connie. That's a stretch. You know how much trouble we'd get into—how much trouble *I'd* get into if I had to explain this to someone?"

Their conversation is beginning to frustrate him. Kyung doesn't care about illegal entry or prior consent. All he knows is that his father is hiding somewhere inside, and he wants to see Jin's face when he realizes the police have come for him, that his own son brought them here for him. This is reason enough to go in. He turns the knob clockwise, surprised to find no resistance. Before Lentz can tell him not to, he pushes the door open, and the conversation behind him stops midsentence. In the entryway, the antique console that usually holds flowers and mail has been tipped over onto its side. One of its legs is broken, lying a few feet away like a junky dowel. There's paper everywhere, loose sheets that look like bills, and pages from books that have been torn out of their bindings.

"Je-sus," Tim says under his breath.

"Mr. Cho?" Connie shouts. "Police."

The three of them push past Kyung, their need for a reason to enter apparently satisfied by the damage now in plain sight. He follows them in, careful to walk around the broken house-plants and figurines in the entryway, if only to examine how methodically his father destroyed all of the things his mother loved. Above the staircase is a long stretch of wall where the family photographs used to hang. Most of the frames have been thrown to the floor and stepped on. There's glass everywhere; the photos have been torn into pieces like old receipts. Kyung stares at the ruined faces, the fragments of eyes and ears and lips pursed tight. The photos were originals, the only evidence left to document his childhood or birth. Gillian occasionally nagged him to get reprints, but he always assumed they'd be his to inherit one day. He can't imagine a more intentional insult from his father than the black-and-white scraps scattered across the stairs, tossed like makeshift confetti.

When he joins the others in the living room, the air smells thick with stale smoke. Connie is standing next to the book-cases, studying the damage as if searching for clues about the kind of family his daughter married into. A half-dozen empty liquor bottles are strewn around the room, and the paintings above the fireplace—paintings that Jin took such pride in collecting—are lying in the corner. The canvases have been kicked in, their peaceful seascapes damaged beyond repair.

"Classy," Tim says, picking up a crystal decanter filled with tobacco-colored liquid and floating stubs of cigars. "Your dad likes to drink, I'm guessing."

"No, not anymore. Not like he used to. The bar is just for guests."

"Looks to me like he went on a bender." He puts the decanter down and motions toward an empty bottle of cognac on the end table.

Tim's explanation should make sense, but it doesn't. Nothing in this room makes sense. The volume of chaos is too much for one person, especially a man pushing sixty.

"Does it always get this crazy?" Lentz asks.

"Never," Kyung says, and this is the part that's beginning to worry him. He knows his father is capable of hitting a woman. And taking a bat or a broom to his mother's antiques, he can imagine this too. But what bothers Kyung is that his father isn't the type of person to destroy his own things. The painting of Nauset Beach on Cape Cod—the one torn out of its frame and lying on the floor—it was one of Jin's most prized possessions. He shakes his head, unable to sort through the mismatch between what he knows and what he sees.

"I don't think my father could have done all this," he says quietly. "I think, maybe—they were robbed."

Connie is the first to pick up on the panic in Kyung's voice, the first to understand they might not be alone. He lifts the back of his shirt and removes a gun from his waistband while Tim quickly does the same. For a moment, Lentz seems as startled as Kyung is to realize they've been wearing holsters under their clothes, but he follows their lead and draws his weapon. Connie puts a finger to his mouth and points three times—at the staircase, the hallway, and the front door. Suddenly, Kyung feels someone grabbing his shirt and pushing him toward the entryway against his will. With one quick shove, he lands against the porch rail, flung out into the daylight like a drunk at a bar. He turns to see Tim running up the stairs as the front door clicks shut.

He wonders if he's supposed to do something—use the radio in Lentz's car to call for backup, or ask the neighbors to call 911. His only point of reference is movies, bad ones that frighten him nonetheless. He expects to hear gunfire or see a chase across the lawn, but minutes pass, and nothing happens. The neighborhood is the same rich kind of quiet it always is, punctuated by birdsong and little else. A woman jogs by with two children in a running stroller, the littler of whom offers Kyung a wave that he doesn't return. Occasionally, a car drives by at a respectful, residential speed. The longer nothing happens, the more he begins to accept the possibility that everything is fine, or will be soon enough. The people responsible for the robbery are probably long gone by now, and his father probably went to the police station to report what they'd lost. He's comforted by this theory, the safety of it, even though it doesn't begin to explain what happened to his mother.

Kyung circles the porch, looking into windows that offer no view of the rooms inside. He should have known something was wrong when he saw the drapes. Mae's only hobby is making the house look nice. Her philosophy is to let the neighbors see. All her work over the years—the antiques and art and books arranged just so—he can't believe how much of it has been destroyed. Something about the damage almost seems personal, as if the people who robbed them knew exactly what his mother valued most.

As he walks around to the front of the house, the door opens and Tim appears with Marina, his parents' housekeeper. She's the last person he expected to see, wrapped from head to toe in a bedsheet, clutching the ends together with her fists. The flowery green print is thin, thin enough to notice that she's naked underneath. Kyung understands what this means. Two naked women, both brutalized. Marina's left eye is swollen shut and the bridge of her nose is as thick as a pipe. Her long brown hair is ratty, electrified. He's about to say something to her—what, he doesn't know—but Tim locks his jaw and shakes his head violently. *Not now.* Marina passes Kyung without saying a word, her expression glassy, stunned by the light. Jin follows a few steps behind, supported by Lentz, who struggles to stay upright under his weight.

Kyung isn't prepared for the sight of his father so bloodied. He's imagined it a thousand times—the twin black eyes, the split lip, the bruises turning an angry shade of purple—but not like this.

"What happened? How did this happen to you?"

"My glasses," Jin says, pulling on the hem of Kyung's shirt. "I can't see."

"Later. Tell me what happened."

"I can't see."

He wants his father to stop touching him and answer the question, but Jin keeps reaching for him in a panic. "All right. All right. I'll get them for you. Where are they?"

"In the bathroom upstairs. I have extras."

Kyung turns toward the door and runs into Connie, who sends him backwards with a shove to the chest.

"Where the hell are you going?"

"He said he left his glasses in the house."

"I'll send someone in to get them later."

"But he can't see."

Connie pushes him again, harder this time. "Forget the glasses. There's a body in there."

The name of the deceased is Lyndell Perry. "Dell" for short. Lentz removes two photographs of him from an envelope and hands them to Kyung. The first is a mug shot, faxed by the Georgia state correctional system. The second is a photo snapped in his parents' bathroom, where Lentz says he died of an overdose, probably heroin or meth. Kyung studies the pictures carefully, certain that he's never seen the man before, but not certain if he's looking at the same man. The Dell Perry pictured in the mug shot is young and vaguely handsome, with short black hair, pale eyes, and cheekbones that slice toward his temples. The hollowed-out man sitting on the toilet, leaning against the wall with a belt cinched around his arm—he looks like someone else.

"You sure?" Lentz asks. "You've never seen him before?"

Kyung shakes his head.

"Maybe he did odd jobs for your parents? Painting, maybe? Or moving some furniture around?"

"I don't think so. My mother uses a decorator for things like that."

"Then what about this guy?"

Lentz hands him another mug shot, this one taken by the

State of North Carolina. The man in the photo appears to be a relative of the first. He has the same face, but older and thicker, with less hair and more neck.

"I've never seen him either. Why are you asking?"

"They work together sometimes. They're brothers, actually, but this kind of robbery—it's more along the lines of the older brother's MO."

"What were they in prison for?"

Lentz doesn't respond.

"Come on. I've been here for hours and no one will tell me anything. I can't even get in to see my mother."

The population of the hospital's waiting room has tripled since Kyung returned from his parents' house. The police are everywhere. Some are in uniform, but most are off duty, wearing their shields around their necks like oversized pendants. The crime rate in Marlboro is low, almost nonexistent. Occasionally, a car goes missing or some college students throw a party that gets out of hand, but what happened to his parents is different, a fact that everyone in the room seems to understand. Kyung wouldn't mind being surrounded by the police if they were actually being helpful, but none of them appear to be doing anything, not even Connie, who keeps moving around from person to person, talking to everyone but clearly avoiding him.

Lentz leans in and motions toward the picture of the first man. He lowers his voice to a whisper. "This one's been in and out for drug possession, breaking and entering, and robbery. His older brother here, Nathan, his sheet is about twice as long. Assault with a deadly weapon, robbery, armed robbery . . . He was in Walpole for six years and then jumped parole back in

February. We were lucky the state police had an APB out for him."

Kyung studies the photos again. Dell and Nathan Perry. White trash names if he ever heard them, probably from some country backwater down South. He doesn't understand how they ended up in Marlboro, in a neighborhood so wealthy that driving an older-model car feels like a crime.

"What was this one on parole for?"

Lentz pretends not to hear the question.

"What was he on parole for?" Kyung repeats, loud enough to turn heads this time.

"It was rape, okay? Jesus, be quiet." Lentz collects his photos and walks away, disappearing down the corridor.

Kyung knew the answer before he heard it. He knew the minute he saw Marina leaving the house. As she walked down the front steps, the wind lifted a corner of the bedsheet and he caught a glimpse of her bare skin. There were rope burns around her ankles. He could guess what the ropes were for. Marina is young and pretty—a nice Bosnian girl with a figure that's hard not to notice. Usually, she cleans for his parents on Tuesdays and Fridays. It's Saturday now. He wonders how long they were trapped in that house together, and his chest begins to tighten. He wants to know what they did to his mother. He does, but he doesn't.

Across the room, Gillian appears, her long red hair looking even wilder than usual. She seems harried, as if she sped the entire way and left the headlights on in the parking lot. She tries to squeeze into the waiting area, but three officers form a wall to block her from entering. Before Kyung can get up, his father-in-law pushes the men aside and leads her through the crowd, depositing her in the empty seat next to Kyung.

"Where's the kid?" Connie asks.

"I finally got a neighbor to watch him." She takes Kyung's hand, squeezing it tightly. "Tim told me everything on the phone. I'm so sorry," she says. "I'm so, so sorry."

"You shouldn't be here right now, Gilly. Neither of you, really. Maybe you should both head home for the night."

"*Dad,*" Gillian snaps. "We'll decide whether to stay or go."

Kyung has seen this a thousand times. Connie pushing, Gillian pushing back. Tim could never get away with it, but Gillian always does, probably because she's a girl, the baby of the family. Connie returns to a huddle of older officers, most of whom are standing with their arms crossed or their hands in their pockets as if they're waiting for something. Waiting for what? he wonders.

"Who's looking after Ethan?"

"Marianne."

He pictures all the women in their neighborhood, unable to match the name with a face. "Which one is she?"

"Don't worry. He'll be fine. What do you need right now?"

A gun comes to mind, not that he'd know what to do with it. "I couldn't even tell you."

"I'm so sorry," she repeats, rubbing circles into his back.

She wasn't supposed to be here. He told her to stay home with Ethan, but now that she's sitting beside him, Kyung doesn't mind. Gillian knows he's not a talker; he never has been. She doesn't press him for details or ask any unnecessary questions. She just reaches into her book bag and hands him a bottle of water. Then she opens one for herself. He wonders if she'll offer him a cookie or granola bar next because this is who she is now, the type of woman who carries snacks in her bag. They sit like this for several minutes, looking around the room but not speaking to each other. Kyung studies the elderly couple wedged in the corner, shaded by the canopy of a potted palm. The husband is dressed in pajamas and a robe, sucking oxygen from a portable tank while his wife flips through a *Reader's Digest*. No one has spoken to them since they checked in. The construction worker too. He's been waiting even longer, holding a melting bag of ice against his bloody thumb.

In high school, Kyung spent most of his spare time in hospitals, doing internships or community service. He liked watching the doctors race through the halls, so competent and professional, motivated by purpose. It never occurred to him that he'd be anything other than a doctor when he grew up, an idea he was quickly disabused of after dropping out of med school. Now hospitals make him nervous. He dislikes their antiseptic smell and sickly desert color palettes. And the whispering—so much whispering—like the walls will collapse if the sound level rises above a murmur. Occasionally, Kyung overhears something about the mayor or next year's union contract. But mostly, the conversation is about his parents—what happened, what the cops think happened, what will probably happen next. He learns that Jin has multiple broken ribs, a dislocated shoulder, and a concussion. Marina is in surgery—for what, he doesn't know. The cops refer to the men who did this as animals and degenerates. They say the dead guy is lucky that he's dead. Only once does he hear any mention of his mother.

JUNG YUN

That poor fucking woman, someone says, which sends Kyung's eyes straight to the ceiling, to an old water stain blooming on the paint. It feels like the roof is about to fall on top of him.

When Gillian finishes her water, she removes a textbook from her bag, a huge brick of a book called *Educational Psychology*. A fringe of Post-its lines the pages she marked—so thick and colorful, it seems like she marked everything. He's surprised that she brought it, but she brings it everywhere these days, squeezing in a few pages of reading whenever she can. Gillian is studying for her master's degree in school counseling, usually a class or two every semester. The plan is for her to go back to work when Ethan starts kindergarten, to finally start making some money like she used to. Kyung covers his eyes, overwhelmed by the thought of ever having a plan again. It feels like they'll never leave this waiting room. For the rest of their lives, they'll always be here.

"What's the matter? Do you not want me to read right now?"

"I'm sorry."

"Sorry for what?"

"I never told you." He wonders if this will be enough, if the nature of his sin is so obvious that she won't need more than this to understand.

"We don't have to talk about that right now." She closes her book anyway. "It makes sense, though."

"What does?"

Gillian shrugs. "I thought it was kind of strange—how you never wanted to spend time with your parents. And then when we had to, you'd get so stressed out." She stares at her book, running her hand over the shiny cover. "Some school counselor I'm going to be. I had no idea your dad used to hit you."

Kyung jerks his head at her. "I didn't say he hit me."

"Honey, it's okay. You don't have to—"

"No. Listen. He never hit me, not even once. He only hit my mother."

"But that's not common. You know that, right?" Gillian shakes her head. "I'm sorry. Let's, let's just talk about this when you're ready."

Kyung doesn't know if he'll ever be ready. He wants to discuss it now, and then never again. "My father didn't hit me. It probably would have been better if he did."

"That's awful. Why would you even say that?"

Because it's worse to listen to someone in pain, he thinks. Because hearing a beating and not being able to do anything about it are their own form of punishment. This is the truthful answer, the one Kyung knows he should give, but he doesn't like the damage it implies.

"I always thought that if my mother didn't do certain things, if she behaved better, like me, then he wouldn't have a reason to." He glances at Gillian, at the perfect O her mouth makes when she doesn't know what to say. "I don't think that *now*. I used to, though."

Gillian sits back in her seat, leaning her head against the wall. He can see the wheels spinning, the way she's reconciling everything she knew about him with what she knows now. There was a reason why he didn't want a big wedding, why he hates family gatherings, why he threatened to move when his parents bought a house so close to their own. He's tempted to tell her not to apply her little textbook lessons to him, but her arguments would probably make more sense than his denials. He waits for her to continue where they left off. Instead, she places her hand on top of his, not quite holding it, just resting it there as she would on a table or chair.

"What?" he asks. "I know you want to say something, so just say it."

"I guess I don't understand, then. Your mom—the way you're kind of mean to her sometimes."

Kyung pulls his hand away. "Just shut up, Gillian."

He's never dismissed her like this before, not even as a joke. She isn't the kind of woman to take that from anyone, which is what he liked about her in the beginning, what he likes about her still. He waits for a response, but the longer nothing happens, the more he begins to accept the fact that she's given him a bye. When she opens her book again, he sits back in his seat, not certain if he feels terrible or relieved.

At half past six, a doctor appears in the waiting room. He's an Indian man with dark skin and a full head of shock-white hair. Something about him is different from the others, the ones who wandered in to see what the commotion was about and then left. This one is searching. His eyes sweep the crowd slowly, stopping when they land on Kyung.

"Will you please come with me, Mr. Cho?"

The police back up to clear an aisle, their bodies parting like some strange, biblical sea. Kyung tries not to look at their faces as he and Gillian pass. All he feels in this gauntlet of men is pity. He realizes this is what everyone has been waiting for, the moment in which he learns how bad is bad. Near the end of the row, Connie takes a step forward, volunteering to join them, as if he'd ever thought twice about Mae or Jin in the past. Kyung squeezes Gillian's hand, hopeful she knows him well enough to understand the message he's trying to send. *Keep him away from me.*

"Should I come with?" he hears Connie ask.

"No. Not right now, Dad." Gillian pats him gently on the chest, her voice lowered to minimize his embarrassment. "I'll let you know."

The doctor leads them into a break room and shuts the door behind him. Despite the tables and chairs, no one bothers to sit—Kyung has been sitting long enough. He and Gillian stand next to the window, which overlooks the hospital parking lot below, and just beyond it, the back end of a car dealership. The doctor leans awkwardly on the corner of the table, resting an expensive brown loafer on one of the chairs while he pages through his records. His name is long and unpronounceable, both first and last. Kyung studies the tag clipped to his white coat, trying to parse out the syllables. *Ra-jen-dra-ku-mar Ba-nu-su-bra-man-i-am.* He should know the name of the man who's treating his parents, but as he listens to the doctor introduce himself, he still can't make sense of what to call him.

"Your father's in stable condition now. His CAT scans and vitals are all good, and we've injected an anesthetic into the area around his ribs, which seems to be making him more comfortable."

"What about my mother?"

"She's resting now. I suspect she'll sleep through the night. Normally, I would have let the police talk to her before using that much sedative, but the physical exam was—challenging."

"She'll be all right though, won't she?" Gillian asks.

The doctor nods, but Kyung doesn't like the way his expression changes. People who work in emergency rooms are supposed to have a high tolerance for the worst kinds of injuries. The discomfort on the doctor's face suggests that he's still struggling with Mae's.

"Physically, her injuries weren't very severe. Mostly lacerations and bruises. A sprained ankle. All the same, I'd like to keep her here a few days for observation."

There's a clock above the water cooler, an old-fashioned one with black hands and a red line that sweeps through the seconds. Kyung has been at the hospital all afternoon. It was light when he arrived, and now the sky outside is turning a deep, ink-washed blue. The streetlights are all lit, their halos swimming with mosquitoes. Six hours, he thinks. Six hours and no one will confirm what he already knows.

"They raped her, didn't they?"

The doctor lowers himself into a chair, settling into the molded plastic as if preparing for a longer conversation. "There's evidence of that, yes." He doesn't look at Kyung as he says this. Instead, he stares at a scuff mark on the floor. "I've taken all the necessary precautions against STDs and HIV—antibiotics and antiretrovirals—but I opted against the morning-after pill since she's postmenopausal. Like I said, she'll recover from the cuts and bruises soon enough, but everything else . . . I think she'll need quite a lot of counseling to work through."

Kyung rests his forehead on the window, gently tapping his head against the glass. Postmenopausal, STDs, HIV, morning-after pill. These are words that don't belong together in any sentence. He doesn't understand what kind of people would rape a fifty-six-year-old woman. Even the word: "rape." It rings and rings in his ears, and he can't make it stop.

"Enough, Kyung. That's enough."

Gillian is digging her fingernails into his skin. The doctor is trying to pin back his arms.

"Do you hear me?" she shouts. "That's enough."

Kyung staggers back a step. There are prints all over the window, greasy prints from his fists and forehead that he doesn't remember making. He has no idea how long he's been banging on the glass, but the pain catches up with him quickly. He puts his hands out for balance, struggling to stay upright as pinpricks of light float through the room. The doctor eases him into a chair while Gillian slides a cup of water in front of him.

"You need to calm down, Kyung. That's not helping anyone."

He brings his fist down on the cup, smashing the paper flat and spraying water across the table. Gillian and the doctor jump back. She looks at him disapprovingly, straight down her nose, and wipes a stray drop from her cheek. Then she turns to the doctor as if Kyung is no longer there.

"What about Marina?" she asks. "The housekeeper?"

"She's stable now too. I meant to ask, does Miss Jancic have any family in the area? Anyone we can contact?"

"I don't think so. I've never heard her talk about having relatives in the States. Why?"

"Well, she's uninsured," he says lightly. "Eventually, this will become a problem—not for me, but for the hospital. In the short term, my biggest concern is releasing her into someone's care. She'll need a fair amount of help while she's recuperating." The doctor runs his fingers through his hair. He looks exhausted, worn out behind the eyes. "In any event, why don't you both go home for the evening? Everyone's resting now. We'll have more news tomorrow."

"We can't see his parents?" Gillian asks.

"No, not now. Mrs. Cho is heavily sedated, and Mr. Cho requested no visitors this evening. You understand."

Kyung understands that his father doesn't want to explain what happened, how he let it all happen. And for the first time, he realizes that he made a mistake when he found Mae in the field. She didn't say, "Your father hurt me." She said, "Your father is hurt." Her loyalty to this man is insane. Even in that state, beaten and brutalized and reduced to nothing, she was trying to protect him, to save him. It should have been the other way around.

TWO

The Presbyterians first came to visit when Kyung was fifteen. It was a common interruption in their old neighborhood—zealots of every denomination ringing the bell at odd hours, selling their magazines or peddling salvation. His father would usually bark something unkind and slam the door in their faces, but not so with the Presbyterians. With them, it was different. Maybe it was because they were Korean. Or maybe it was because they were poor. Whatever the reason, Jin invited the ragged-looking couple inside to join him for coffee. A week later, two more couples followed. And four more after that. Within a month, the parlor was teeming with Koreans, who eventually convinced Jin to worship at their church. Kyung didn't understand what his father saw in them, why the sudden change of heart, but he knew what they saw in him. His big house, his generous checks, his willingness to sponsor anything they asked.

When Kyung returns to the hospital in the morning, it feels like he's gone back in time. The waiting room is no longer crowded with policemen. Instead, it's filled with Koreans.

The irritable woman at the front desk, the same one from the day before, stands up and snaps at him as he walks in. "Can you *do* something about them? Visiting hours just started, but they've all been sitting here since seven."

Kyung shakes his head and continues down the hall. There's nothing he can do about these people. He has no rank with them, although they all seem to know who he is. He can feel the weight of their judgment as he walks toward his mother's room. *Doesn't go to church. Not dutiful to his parents. Took a white girl for a wife.* He has no idea how the news spread so fast, but as he enters Mae's room, an even more confusing sight awaits him. Standing at his mother's bedside are five men: his father, Connie, Tim, Lentz, and the Reverend Sung. All of them have their eyes closed and their heads bowed in prayer. They're holding hands limply, not quite committed to the act.

"What are you doing here?" he asks, not certain who deserves the question most.

Everyone looks up. Reverend Sung opens one eye and quickly closes it. "We ask you to guide our beloved brother and sister in the days and weeks ahead. Heal their hearts and bodies and minds, dear Lord, and grace them with the absolute power of your love. In your name, we pray. Amen."

Connie and Tim make the sign of the cross and mutter "amen," something that Kyung has never witnessed before. The McFaddens aren't a religious family. Their faith—ceremonial as it was—seemed to die with Gillian's mother, who dressed everyone up for Mass and confession because that's what families in their neighborhood did. Gillian talks about this part of her childhood like she talks about her mother, with more fondness than either probably deserves. Occasionally, she mentions the idea of going back to church like it's a long-lost hobby, something she'd pick up again if she had more time.

"Come join us," Reverend Sung says.

Mae turns and angles her face toward the window as Kyung approaches the bed. Now that she's clean and dressed, she doesn't seem as injured as his father, who has his arm in a sling and an alarming array of bruises. Still, Kyung understands the difference between them. What happened to Mae was worse. He places his hand over hers, rubbing the soft, papery skin with his thumb. Everything he wants to say escapes him, so he just stands there, dumb for words, while the others try not to watch.

"Well, I should get back to the station now," Lentz says. "Thank you for your statement, Mrs. Cho. I'll be in touch."

Kyung wanted to be with Mae when she spoke to them. He assumed the police would take her statement when visiting hours started, not before.

"None of you thought to call me for this?"

Again, he isn't sure who should answer the question, who among this odd group of men he holds most accountable. He settles on Connie. "Why are you even here? This isn't your case."

Connie shrugs. "I was just trying to be helpful, seeing you're family and all."

Kyung is tempted to ask since when. Since when have Connie and Tim ever treated him like family? "Please leave now. Both of you. I didn't ask you to come."

"You don't have to talk to them like that," Jin says. "At least they were here. They showed up early—not like you."

The earth feels like it's spun off its axis. His father often refers to Gillian's family as bigots—poor working-class white people, jealous of anyone with a little money to their name. Now he's defending them as if they're old friends.

"I *did* come early. I just don't understand why none of you told me to come earlier." He glances at Mae, who has yet to look at him.

"Your mom was ready to talk," Tim says, "so we let her. There wasn't time to send you an invitation and then wait around until you got here."

"Don't be such a dick, Tim." Connie's face reddens. "Sorry, Reverend. And sorry for intruding. You folks need anything from us, just give me a call. Kyung knows how to reach me."

They leave the room, Tim trailing behind his father and Lentz, his shoulders still sagging with reproach. The earth is now in free fall. Connie has never taken his side over Tim's before, never bothered to apologize for anything, no matter how big or small the offense. Kyung is so stunned, he almost doesn't notice the reverend patting him on the shoulder.

"It was nice of your father-in-law to offer to help. An event like this brings out the best in most people."

The phrase "most people" stings Kyung's cheeks. It feels like a reprimand, even if it wasn't.

"I need a few minutes with my mother now." He glances at Jin. "I'd like to talk to her in private."

Mae grabs the sleeve of the reverend's jacket. She shakes her head no.

"What's wrong? Why don't you want to talk to me?" Kyung's voice rises, injured like a child's. "Why won't you even look at me?"

Reverend Sung pries loose her fingers, knitting them neatly between his. "As you can imagine—actually, as none of us could ever really imagine—this was a very traumatic experience for your mother, for both of your parents. You have to understand how upsetting it might be, talking about the details of what happened with you. These aren't the kinds of things you'd ever want to say in front of your own child."

Kyung looks to Mae for some confirmation of this, but sees nothing. No sadness, no anger, no pain. All of those emotions have come and gone already. What's left is a pale shell, ready to crack with the slightest hint of pressure. It's strange—the sight of another man holding his mother's hand, speaking on her behalf. But the reverend's interpretation makes sense. If someone had done this to Gillian, Kyung can't imagine trying to explain the details to Ethan, whether he was four years old or forty.

"Your father has some things that he'd like to discuss with you. Maybe the three of us should go outside and let Mae rest?"

Jin drops his eyes to the floor. Kyung wonders what he has to say for himself, what sorry excuses he'll come up with.

He leans over to kiss his mother's forehead. "You'll let me know if you need anything?"

She shrinks into her bed, stiff to his touch, and it occurs to Kyung that maybe she's not over it, the way he spoke to her in the field. He wants to apologize for his reaction, to explain why he didn't understand, but not in front of the reverend or Jin.

The three of them walk into the corridor, waiting for Mae's door to float closed on its hinges. Kyung stares at the shiny bald patch on his father's head. There's a cut running diagonally across it, and a thick wad of gauze taped over another cut on his brow line. He's wearing his glasses now, unaware of how crookedly they rest on his nose, which is swollen and bookended by black eyes.

"Don't bother her about what happened," Jin says. "She's not right in the mind."

"I'm not going to bother her. I just want to talk."

"No." Jin grabs his forearm, his grip still firm. "Never. Never talk to her about what happened. She won't survive that. It's better if we all let her forget."

Kyung pulls his arm away. "How could she possibly forget? She's going to need months—years of counseling to deal with this."

"I've offered to counsel Mae, every week if she'd like," Reverend Sung says. "For as long as she'd like."

"No, not your kind of counseling. The kind with a doctor, a therapist. God isn't what she needs right now."

The reverend and his father glance at each other uncomfortably, but the truth seems obvious to Kyung.

"God didn't help her when those men broke into the house and did what they did to her. God didn't help you either when they were beating you up. What do you think he's going to do now?"

"It's only natural . . . ," the reverend begins.

"No," Kyung snaps. "Nothing about this is natural. You can hold hands and pray and do whatever it is that you people do, but don't tell me that forgetting is what's best for her, that God is going to help her forget. She will *never* forget—do you understand that? She needs a doctor, a psychiatrist." And then, because Jin looks so stricken by his outburst, he throws him a jagged bone. "You too. You need to see a psychiatrist. Again."

An orderly passes, studying the three of them carefully. Kyung realizes he's been talking much louder than he should. He turns around and sees everyone in the waiting room staring at him. The woman at the front desk is craning over it, frowning at the commotion.

"I'm sorry for upsetting you," the reverend says. "I know how stressful this must be."

The fact that he's apologizing only upsets Kyung more. He's the one causing a scene; he's the one who should be sorry. Now he's just embarrassed. He came here to be helpful, which is hardly what he's done.

"It's almost a quarter after nine." Reverend Sung taps the face of his watch. "I have to go lead services now. We'll all say a special prayer for you and Mae." He shakes hands with Jin and glances at Kyung, the expression on his face still quiet and kind. When he heads toward the exit, the entire population of the waiting room files out behind him, the sheep following their shepherd.

"You should have been more polite to him," Jin says. "His family's done a lot for us."

"All he ever does is ask for money."

"You know what I mean."

The reverend inherited the congregation of First Presbyterian from his father, who'd recently moved back to Korea after his retirement. Kyung preferred the elder Reverend Sung, a serious, bookish man who could silence any room by simply entering it. He was the only person Kyung could think to call after he'd threatened to kill Jin. When the reverend arrived at the house, he took Jin by the arm and made him kneel on the floor beside him. They stayed that way for over an hour—eyes closed, hands clasped together, praying in Korean while Mae and Kyung looked on. Jin cried the entire time, but Kyung wondered if it was all just for show, if he'd later be punished for bringing an outsider in. He stood off to the side, studying the candelabra on the mantel, the statues on the ledge, wondering which would make for a heavier weapon, which would crack open a human skull when he finally had to make good on his promise. No one was more surprised than he was when the hitting actually stopped, a change that Kyung always attributed to the elder Sung's intervention.

"How did all those people in the waiting room find out what happened?"

"I called the reverend last night."

"But if you're so worried about putting this behind her, then why did you tell anyone? Now everybody at your church is going to know."

Jin shakes his head. "There are different kinds of forgetting."

Kyung wonders if his father still has a concussion, if he thinks he's making sense when he really isn't. He looks him over, stopping when he notices a small gold crucifix that someone—the reverend, probably—pinned to his sling.

"Stop staring at me," Jin says.

"I'm not staring."

But he is. Kyung turns and scans a nearby bulletin board. The only poster he can see clearly is for a needle-exchange program. IF YOU SHARE YOUR DRUGS, DON'T SHARE YOUR BLOOD, it warns in bright gold letters. The other posters are too small or far away to read, so he watches a pair of nurses walk through the corridor, wheeling equipment that rattles and scrapes across the floor.

"I'm fine, by the way. Thank you for asking." Sarcasm doesn't sound right coming from Jin's mouth. When his words hit the air, they turn into acid.

"I can see that already."

What Kyung actually sees is his father looking old for the first time in his life. Gone are the expensive clothes—the precisely ironed dress shirts and hundred-dollar ties—against the backdrop of his enormous house and office. With the fluorescent lights bearing down on him, turning his skin a bluish shade of gray, Jin appears to have aged a decade overnight. Looking at him now, no one would ever guess what he used to be capable of.

"Not once," Jin says, shaking his head.

"What are you talking about?"

"Not once did I think you'd save us."

"Save you? How could I save you when I didn't even know what was happening?"

"That's the point."

There's a familiar thread of insult woven into all of this, but Kyung refuses to have the same argument again. He's not a good son; he knows this already. But he's the best possible version of the son they raised him to be. Present, but not adoring. Helpful, but not generous. Obligated and nothing more.

"Where's your doctor? The Indian one? I want to talk to him."

"He came by earlier this morning before his shift ended."

Kyung is upset with himself for arriving late and frustrated that everyone else forgot him. He lowers his voice to a sharp whisper. "The next time Mom talks to a doctor or a policeman or anyone else, I want to be here. Do you understand? I want you to call me immediately."

"So now you actually want me to call."

"I should be here when they question her."

"You never wanted to be around us before."

"Things are different now."

"This," Jin almost shouts, "this is not the reason why things should be different."

The sudden change in volume sends Kyung back a step. Before he has a chance to respond, a young, ponytailed doctor approaches them, tilting her head to the side like a little girl. She seems tentative, as if she overheard their argument and doesn't know if she should interrupt.

"Excuse me, Mr. Cho? I'm Dr. Keller. Could I talk to you for a few minutes about Miss Jancic?"

It takes Kyung a moment to realize that he's not the Mr. Cho she's addressing. "Why? He's not family."

"We couldn't track down any relatives, so we requested her records from school. She listed Mr. Cho as her emergency contact. And you are?"

"His son."

"Pleased to meet you," she says, although she's already looking away by the time she says it. "Would you mind coming with me, sir? I have a room around the corner where we can talk."

Dr. Keller rests her hand in the hollow of Jin's back, gently steering him down the hall. Jin doesn't bother to say good-bye or even cast a passing glance in Kyung's direction. He just leaves him there, frozen like a pedestrian in the middle of the street while everyone else speeds past.

"What am I supposed to do now?" Kyung calls out.

But Jin is already rounding the corner, playing deaf or dumb to the question.

Gillian and Ethan are doing a puzzle on the kitchen floor when he returns home from the hospital. It's not where he expected to find them, still dressed in their pajamas with mugs of orange juice at their feet. He was hoping to slip in the side door unnoticed, but the longer he watches them, the less he wants to hide. Seeing them like this reminds him of his mother, how they'd sit on the floor when he was little, coloring on the backs of paper bags. It was a rare activity, reserved for days when Kyung was too sick to go to school, but too bored to stay in bed. The cold ceramic tiles felt good against his feverish skin, so he and Mae would sit for hours, sharing fat, waxy crayons from a communal bucket placed between them. Sometimes, if the mood was just right, he'd ask her to draw an animal or insect so he could color it in. But trees, he learned, were her specialty. Tall oaks and pines and willows like the ones in their yard. All he had to do was point at one and watch as she sketched out a knotty trunk or feathered out some branches and filled them with leaves.

"So what are these called?" Gillian asks. In her hand is an oversized puzzle piece shaped like a bunch of grapes.

"Raisins," Ethan says.

"Almost. Do you remember what I told you about raisins? What were they *before* they sat in the sun?"

Ethan looks out the window, as if he might find the answer in space. "Grapes?"

"That's right. And which do you like better? Raisins or grapes?"

"Raisins are like grapes that died."

Kyung admires Gillian's way with Ethan. She's always sharing little facts with him, always ready with a smile or a laugh or a question. Her instincts with the boy are so much better than his own. Four years in, and parenthood still feels like a heavy new coat, one that he hoped to grow into but hasn't quite yet. Earlier that week, the three of them made pizza together, an activity she'd read about in a magazine article and taped to the fridge. BUDGET-FRIENDLY FAMILY NIGHTS. Every time Ethan did something—sprinkle a handful of cheese or make a face with slices of pepperoni—she complimented him. When they finished, the pizza looked awful. Lumpy and burnt and glistening with grease. Still, Gillian kept saying "good job" over and over again, elbowing Kyung in the ribs until he finally said it too. He finds himself doing this more often now—saying what he knows a good parent should—but he worries that it doesn't come more naturally.

"Okay, so what's next?" she asks.

He clears his throat so they'll notice him.

Gillian spins around, startled by the noise. "Oh. You're home already," she says cautiously. "You weren't gone very long."

Kyung pours himself a cup of coffee. "I know." He joins them on the floor, kicking off his shoes so he can sit cross-legged as they are, which seems to surprise her. He looks down at the half-assembled puzzle. It's the same one Ethan always plays with, the fruit bowl.

"So was everything—okay over there?" Gillian asks.

"What's this?" Kyung offers Ethan another piece.

"It's an apple."

"Do you like apples?"

Ethan nods. "And bananas too."

"Show me which one's the banana."

They go on like this for several minutes until all of the smiling pieces of fruit are in their proper places. Kyung can feel Gillian watching him the entire time, but she should be happy, he thinks. This is exactly the kind of thing she says he needs to do more often. Play more, discipline less.

When Ethan finishes reciting the names of every fruit, he turns the puzzle tray over, and the wooden pieces fall out, clattering against the tile. "Again?" he asks hopefully.

Children have a strange tolerance for repetition. Ethan has been playing with the same tool belt and puzzle since April. He's been demanding the same bedtime story since May. He doesn't lack for toys or books—Gillian's made sure of that— but he acts like the others don't exist. This is the pattern as Kyung has come to understand it: months of Ethan fixating on one thing until he moves on to something else, something equally mind numbing, and then the pattern begins again.

"Why don't you go watch TV now?" Gillian says. "You can take the puzzle with you if you want."

Ethan picks up the apple and walks into the living room, where the piece is sure to go missing.

"He watches too much TV," Kyung says.

"It's fine every once in a while. We grew up with TV, and there's nothing wrong with us."

Actually, Kyung grew up with tutors. Piano, French, swimming, golf. If he could afford it, Ethan would have tutors too.

"So what happened? Why are you home so early?"

"She'd already given her statement by the time I got there. Then she went to sleep, so I left."

"But what about your dad?"

"What about him?"

"Well, how is he? Did he tell you what happened?"

"Why don't you ask Connie or Tim?" His irritation spikes when he mentions his in-laws, who have no right knowing

53

more than he does, no right at all. "I got to the hospital five minutes before visiting hours started, and they were already there with the cop from yesterday. And that reverend from the church—he brought half the congregation with him."

Gillian slides across the floor until she's sitting behind him. "I'm sorry about my dad," she says, kneading the knots in his shoulders. "I'm sure he meant well. He probably thinks he can help. And you know Tim—wherever one goes, the other follows."

She's always making excuses for them, trying so hard to smooth things over. Connie irritates her from time to time, but she adores him like a daughter should, bouncing back from their disagreements as if they never happened.

"I snapped at them a little. You know, for being there."

The kneading stops. "What exactly did you say?"

"I told them to leave. Maybe I said get out. . . . I can't remember."

"Kyung! Why would you do that? They were only trying to help."

Of course, he thinks. She's always quick to take a side unless it's his. "Someone should have called me once she started giving her statement. It's not like I can ask her what happened. She's too embarrassed. The whole time I was there, she wouldn't even look at me."

"So why don't you just call my dad and ask him what she said?"

"Call?"

He can't remember having more than a handful of phone conversations with Connie in the past five years. Most of them started and ended the same way. *No, Gillian's not home. Yes, I'll tell her to call back.* There was never any middle to them.

"I can't call after telling him to leave like that."

"Then why don't you just ask Jin?"

Kyung shakes his head.

Gillian straddles him from behind, wrapping her arms around his shoulders as if she's expecting a piggyback ride. He's tempted to carry her up to their bed and close the door behind them, but to do that now would only invite a misunderstanding. She'll assume he wants sex, which is the furthest thing from his mind. The only thing he wants is to be quiet together, to feel the comfort of her presence, but not have to listen to her advice.

"So should we go to my dad's house, then? Maybe if Ethan and I are around, it won't be so awkward, and you're going to have to apologize eventually, right?"

Kyung doesn't think he owes Connie an apology. His father-in-law did something wrong—he even acknowledged it. They were intruding, he said. Intruders. He gets up from the floor, brushing off the flecks of dust and bread crumbs clinging to his pants.

"If you don't want to ask my dad, I still think you should try talking to yours. I mean, I know things have never been all that friendly between you two, but it's not like any of this was his fault. It might be nice for you to acknowledge that this happened to him too."

On some level, Kyung knows she's right. He just can't bring himself to that place yet. In college, whenever one of his roommates said his mother was on the phone, he picked up the receiver slowly, expecting to hear that Jin had hit her again. By the time he was in grad school, the years had stretched out long enough so he could take a call without having to brace for the worst. Until yesterday, the beatings seemed like another lifetime ago. Not forgiven, but in the past. How quick he was to assume that Jin had hurt her. And now here he is, feeling the same terror clutching at his throat as if eighteen years haven't gone by, and there's nothing he can do to make it go away.

"How long will it take you and Ethan to get ready?"

Gillian shrugs. "Ten minutes."

"Let's go to Connie's, then."

It takes her half an hour to change Ethan's clothes, pack his lunch and toys and books, and find a clean shirt and jeans for herself. By the time they're all seated and strapped in the car, Kyung is having second thoughts. He drives slowly—obeying the speed limit, coming to a complete stop at the lights—things he never does. At the fork in the road that leads to the Flats, he turns left instead of right.

"What are you doing? This isn't the way."

"I want to see something."

She doesn't bother asking what because two turns later, it's obvious. He's driving up the hill toward the Heights again. As they near his parents' house, he sees neighbors gathered on the sidewalk, small packs of them huddled in conversation. With every passing block, he sees more. More people, more cars, more congestion. A block away from the house, there's nowhere left to park on the street. Every space is occupied by vans with satellite dishes on their roofs and logos painted on their doors. Channels 6, 11, 22, and 64. Two local papers, three radio channels, seven police cruisers.

"Kyung . . . ," Gillian says quietly. "I don't think we should be here right now."

He looks in his rearview mirror. There's another van right behind him. "I can't back up."

"So keep going. Just get us out of here."

Kyung realizes that most of the people on the sidewalk aren't neighbors at all. They're reporters and cameramen. The slower he drives, the longer they look at him, their expressions curious, as if he's the quote or story they've been waiting for.

"This isn't right," he says.

The front door to his parents' house has a strip of yellow hazard tape stretched across it on the diagonal. The driveway is blocked off with orange and white police barricades.

"Is Grandpa here?"

"No, honey. Grandpa's not here. We're going to see Grandpa now." Gillian puts her hand on Kyung's leg. "Can we just go to my dad's now?"

"Aren't there supposed to be privacy laws for rape victims?"

"Please don't say that word. Not in the car."

"But how did they get this address?"

"Kyung, *I don't know.* Just keep going."

On the corner, his parents' next-door neighbors are talking to a reporter on camera. The elderly Steiners stand stoop-shouldered and frail, slight as scarecrows from a distance. Mr. Steiner has his arm wrapped around his wife. Both of them keep shaking their heads.

"Go faster," Gillian says. "Now."

He takes the long way back to where they started and hits traffic downtown. Three different churches are all letting out at the same time. Kyung rolls down his window as the parishioners cross the street, oblivious to the line of cars stuck at the intersection. The women are wearing summery dresses, some with hats and jewelry. All of the men are in suits. The children look like the adults who brought them, neat and shined up and glad to see the sun. Kyung taps his horn meekly. The sound is loud enough to turn people's heads, but not long enough to make them walk any faster.

"Now you're in a hurry?" Gillian asks.

"I just want to get there."

"Well, that's a first."

Connie and Tim live in the Flats, a neighborhood near the river that was developed in the '50s. The lots are small, divided and subdivided into narrow rectangles, built up with sad little ranches and Capes. After Tim's divorce, he moved in with Connie to save money for a place of his own. That was nearly ten years ago. No one ever talks about it—how the arrangement was supposed to be temporary, but now has the look and feel of something permanent. The two-bedroom bungalow they share is too small for them both. Everything is big inside. Big furniture, big appliances, big men squeezing around each other in the narrow spaces in between.

As they step into the house, Kyung can't help but notice the television set—a seventy-inch monster connected to every possible electronic device. In front of it are two overstuffed reclining chairs with a cup holder in each armrest. This is where they usually find Connie and Tim spending their off-hours, watching baseball or the History Channel, but strangely, the screen is black now, and the chairs are empty. Another first.

"Anyone home?" Gillian calls out.

The toilet in the bathroom flushes, and Connie appears, struggling with the zipper on his pants. "Oh, I didn't hear you come in."

Ethan runs straight for him, hugging his thick leg.

"You're like a boa constrictor, aren't you?"

"What's that?"

"It's a snake." Connie picks him up, pinning his arms to his sides. "It's one of those snakes that squeezes the air out of you. Like this, see?"

Ethan lets out a squeal, and the look on his face—a pure, unwitting look of joy—this is what Kyung realizes he has to preserve, what he wasn't mindful of in the car. Four is too young an age to learn what people can do to each other.

Tim joins them, dressed in uniform but holding a can of beer. Gillian gives him a peck on the cheek. "Would you mind taking Ethan outside while Kyung and I talk to Dad?"

"I go on duty at noon, but I've got a little time." He extends a gigantic hand, swallowing Ethan's small one in his. "You want to see the bird's nest in the backyard?"

"Are there eggs?"

Tim downs the rest of his can and crushes it as he leads Ethan away. "Maybe. Let's go see."

Kyung is aware that Connie and Gillian are waiting for him to say something, but he's too distracted by his surroundings. There's an empty bag of potato chips on the matted brown carpet, an uncapped jar of salsa on the table, and dozens of old magazines on the coffee table, all coming loose from their bindings. The messiness of the room reminds him where Gillian gets her housekeeping habits. The McFaddens aren't poor anymore, not like they used to be, but they live as if their situation hasn't changed. With their salaries, Connie and Tim could easily afford to tear down the wood paneling, repaint the walls, buy some new furniture that actually fits. They could even hire a cleaning lady to pick up after them once or twice a week, but that's not the kind of people they are.

"Kyung wants to apologize for this morning," Gillian finally says.

"Forget it." Connie sits in his chair, pushing on the armrests until it reclines. "You want a seat?" He looks at Kyung and motions to the other chair.

The recliner sinks like a sponge when he lowers himself into the well-worn groove formed by Tim's ass. He's never sat in his chair before, never been invited to, but he recognizes the offer as a gesture.

"I was hoping to be there when my mother gave her statement."

"You didn't miss much. Same story we heard from your dad last night, more or less."

"Oh." He glances at Gillian, not sure what to say or do next. He doesn't mind asking for her help, but it's still a stretch to ask for Connie's.

"Dad," Gillian says, resting her hand on his shoulder. "Would you mind telling us what you do know?"

Connie shifts uncomfortably in his seat. "None of it's good."

"We could have guessed that," she says.

This is the problem with being in the dark. All he does is guess. Kyung keeps seeing the Perrys hitting his mother, violating her over and over again like a film reel set to loop. The truth might be worse than his imagination, but knowing what happened has to be better than this.

"I'd appreciate it . . . ," he says. "I'd appreciate it if you could just tell me what you heard, from my parents or Lentz or who-ever. And don't leave out any details for my sake. Tell me like you'd tell someone you work with."

"It's on the news. Have you noticed?"

"We just drove by the house. Reporters everywhere."

"Any of them try calling you yet?"

Kyung shakes his head. "We're unlisted."

"It's a big deal, a home invasion in this area. Thirty-three years I've been on the force, and nothing like this has ever hap-pened before."

"But what happened, exactly?" Gillian asks. "How did those men even get in the house?"

Tim streaks past the living room window with Ethan on his shoulders. They're both carrying oversized wands that release giant bubbles into the air. Kyung jumps out of his seat and stands in front of the window, wondering if Tim notices the tree branches, how their sharp tips hang just inches above Ethan's face. Ethan, however, doesn't seem to mind. His head is tipped back, and he's laughing at the crowd of neighborhood kids now gathered on the lawn. They're all jumping up and down, beg-ging for a turn on Tim's shoulders, which makes Ethan laugh even harder. You can't catch us, he shouts. You can't catch us. Watching them, Kyung gets the sense that this scene has played out dozens, maybe even hundreds of times in the past. Connie carrying Tim as a boy, and now Tim carrying Ethan. It dis-turbs him, the fact that he has no memory of being the father or the son in such a happy moment.

"He's just having fun," Gillian says. "Why don't you come back and listen now?"

Kyung returns to his seat, grateful to reach out and feel her fingers lace with his.

"Thursday," Connie sighs. "It started on Thursday night. Your mom went for a walk a little after eight."

"But she never goes out after dark."

Connie shrugs. "Civil dusk."

"What does that mean?"

"You know, civil dusk. Right before the sun sets and there's still a little light out . . . Listen, are you sure you want to hear this?"

"Please," Kyung says. He hasn't said this word to his father-in-law in years, not since he asked for Gillian's hand in marriage and was refused. "Please," he repeats.

Connie takes a knuckle to each eye and rubs them in slow circles. "This is a bad idea," he says. "I don't know much, but I know that, at least."

Mae went out for a walk at eight. The doctor told her to, for her blood pressure. It was hot that day, so she waited until the sun had almost set. Then she walked down Crescent Hill, looped around the main road, and took Starling back to the house—a thirty-, thirty-five-minute trip at most. The men must have been following her—for how long, she didn't know—but as she unlocked the front door, one of the men put a gun in her back and shoved her inside. Her purse was on the table in the entryway, so she tried to give them the cash from her wallet, about fifty or sixty dollars. The younger one, Dell, took the money, but he laughed when he put it in his pocket, as if it was hardly enough. That was how they referred to each other from the start—Nat and Dell—which frightened her. They didn't seem to care that she'd seen their faces or knew their names.

Nat was the one who carried the gun. It seemed to come more naturally to him, even though the gun didn't look like it was his. It was the kind that you had to load bullets into—the old-fashioned kind—with a mother-of-pearl handle. It almost looked like a woman's, small enough to fit in a bag. Jin woke up staring into its barrel, listening to a voice he thought he'd imagined: You're coming with me. Before he knew what was happening, someone was dragging him out of bed, down the stairs, and into the kitchen, where Mae had been tied to a chair. They used duct tape on their wrists, ankles, and shoulders. A strip to cover their mouths. They left them like this for over an hour while they ransacked the house.

Jin thought they'd leave as soon as they'd taken what they could carry, but Mae knew they wouldn't. The liquor cabinet in the living room had a squeaky hinge. She heard them open and close it, open and close it again. The more they drank, the clumsier their footsteps became, the louder their voices. Dell kept insisting there was a safe somewhere. Big houses like theirs always had a safe. Look behind the paintings, he shouted. Take down those mirrors. When they'd looked long enough, he walked into the kitchen and ripped the tape off Jin's mouth. Where is it? he screamed. Where is it? The more Jin claimed not to have one, the angrier Dell became. That's when Mae thought something about him didn't look right. It wasn't that he was drunk. It was that being drunk wasn't enough. By the time Nat joined them, Mae was rocking back and forth in her chair, trying to get one of them to pull the tape from her mouth, which he did. Little lady, he said—that's what Nat kept calling her—Little lady, you've got one chance to tell us where that safe is, or your husband here loses an eye.

She told them there wasn't a safe, but they had jewelry, silverware, and some gold coins in the house. There were furs and computers too. Dell said he didn't want their stuff—pawnshops were too risky—he wanted cash. Jin suggested taking them to an ATM. They could get all the cash they needed. Dell seemed to like this idea; Nat, less so. He looked at the gun, tossing it from one palm to the other as if he was thinking, and then *smash*. He hit Jin in the face with it, right above the eye. He seemed to know exactly where to hit to draw the most blood. Then he turned the gun over to Dell, told him to use it if he had any trouble.

Jin didn't want to be split up. He didn't want to leave Mae in the house with that man. Gun or no gun, Nat seemed like the more dangerous of the two, but he had no choice. He drove Dell to an ATM downtown, the one on the corner next to the clock tower. It was almost midnight when they arrived, and the streets were empty. He tried to take out a thousand dollars, but the machine wouldn't let him. Then he tried five hundred, and the machine spit out a stack of twenties. Dell told him to do it again, get another five hundred, but the message said he'd reached his daily withdrawal limit. They drove to another ATM down the block, next to the dry cleaners, but got the same message. Five-fucking-hundred? Dell kept shouting. That's all I get? Five-fucking-hundred?

Jin assumed they'd go back to the house after this, but Dell made him drive two towns over, to Westbury. He seemed to know the streets well, telling him to turn here, turn there, until they came to a corner next to some old row houses. A skinny teenager with a ring through his nose leaned into Dell's open window and sold him a handful of small envelopes and a marble-sized ball of something white. Then they had an argument about rigs. The kid said he wasn't in the business of selling rigs, there was a twenty-four-hour pharmacy the next town over, but Dell refused to go there. He said he needed one right away. They kept yelling about it, haggling back and forth over the price. Fifty dollars. Ten dollars. Forty, then twenty. Eventually, they settled on thirty. The kid ran into the first row house and came back a few minutes later with a single syringe in a plastic bag. It's clean, right? Dell asked. You're sure it's clean? But the kid had already taken his money and run off in the dark.

In a parking lot next to an empty dollar store, Dell searched the glove compartment and removed a small flashlight and the leather folder with the paperwork for the car. He tore open one of the envelopes and carefully emptied it onto the folder. The contents looked like little shards of glass, crystalline and white. Jin had never seen anyone do drugs before; he tried not to stare as Dell crushed the shards with the end of the flashlight, turning them into a fine powder. He wondered if Dell was going to inject himself with the needle he'd bought, but he snorted the powder up his nose instead, using one of the rolled-up twenties like a straw. Afterwards, Dell became animated, almost cheerful. He fiddled with the radio all the way back to Marlboro, stopping to comment on the songs he liked and stabbing his finger at the dashboard when he didn't.

When they returned to the house, Jin heard Mae crying upstairs. He knew what it meant; it was the reason he'd been so frightened to leave her. He tried to run toward the sound of her voice, but Dell tackled him from behind and dragged him into the kitchen. He tied him up again, pulling his arms back so tight, his shoulder popped out of its socket. Then Dell disappeared and all Jin could hear was the sound of footsteps overhead, the nauseating creak of the bed.

Mae tried to fight Nat off at first, but this only made him angry. He was drunk, and the more she fought, the more he hit. It happened three times—always with him, always with her hands and feet tied to the bed. Sometimes Dell sat on the other bed and watched, but he seemed more interested in his drugs. After Jin took him to the ATM, he walked into the room and gave Nat a small white ball. Cocaine, she guessed, because of the way Nat kept scratching at it, sniffing up the dust from the hand mirror on her bureau. The drugs made him meaner. He'd hit her for no reason—for crying, for not crying, for looking at him, for not looking at him. Nothing he said or did made sense. Twice, he picked a fight with Dell, who kept injecting himself every few hours. That stuff's going to wreck you, Nat said. My problem if it does, Dell snapped. Back and forth they went, shouting at each other about drugs, money, the bind they were in. Nat called his brother useless; he blamed him for their luck.

They left Mae tied up overnight, using her scarves and the sashes from her robes. The knots they made wouldn't loosen no matter how hard she tried. Mae didn't recall sleeping that night. She just listened to them wandering through the house, opening things, breaking things, wondering aloud if there was any way to pawn the jewelry and furs and not get caught like the last time. She learned they'd been planning the robbery for weeks, but everything was going wrong. Nat kept calling their house a bust. They needed cash, straight cash. They must have fallen asleep talking about it because she didn't hear anything for hours, not until the sun was coming through the window. At first, it sounded like a mouse in the walls, a scratching noise down below. Jin heard it too, from the kitchen. Someone was using the key in the back door, fumbling with the sticky lock. He held his breath, grateful that all of this might be over soon. And then he realized it was a Friday, a cleaning day.

Marina looked irritated when she walked into the kitchen, as if she thought they'd had a party the night before. When she saw Jin tied to the chair, she started shouting at him in Bosnian. He wanted her to take the tape off his mouth so he could warn her, but she went for his hands first, crowing like a rooster the entire time. It didn't take long for the men to come running, stumbling over themselves, hungover and strung out. Still, Marina was no match for them, not even the smaller of the two. Dell took her arms while Nat picked up her legs, and they started to carry her off this way until Marina managed to free one of her feet and kick Nat square in the jaw. The look in his eyes—Jin thought he might kill her right there in front of him. Instead, he reared his fist back and swung with the full force of himself, knocking her out cold. He chuckled afterwards, massaging his chin. He seemed amused with himself as he slapped her breasts from side to side.

Marina had loosened the tape around his wrists, enough to grab on to the end if he curled his fingers up at just the right angle. After they took her upstairs, he worked on the tape all morning, peeling it back, centimeter by centimeter. Only once did he stop, when Nat came down to look for food. He opened the refrigerator and rummaged inside, knocking over jars and containers until he found what he wanted. Then he just stood there, studying Jin while dipping rolled-up pieces of bread into a jar of mayonnaise. He ate three pieces this way while Jin sat perfectly still, the loose end of tape coiled up behind him in his fist. Playtime with the girls has been fun, Nat said, but I've got to figure out how to make some money out of you. The way he said it, Jin knew that once he got his money, he'd kill them all.

He continued working after Nat went back upstairs, undoing his hands first and then trying to loosen the tape around his ankles. They'd used so much of it. Every time he peeled some away, it made a snapping noise that he was certain they could hear. He was so close to freeing himself when Dell found him and started shouting. Jin wasn't sure who hit him first, but the force of the blow sent his chair sailing backwards, and Dell started kicking him as he lay on the floor. Not the face, Nat shouted. Not the face—I need him looking right. Jin didn't know what this meant. He just prayed for it to be over, prayed as he'd never prayed before. When Nat took a kitchen knife from the block, he closed his eyes and waited for the worst, but all he felt was a tug on his ankles as Nat sliced away his bindings. Then they marched him to the upstairs bathroom. Wash your face, Nat shouted. And put this on. He threw a clean white shirt at him, a pair of pants, and a pair of shoes. Jin did as he was told, trying to move as fast as he could. Comb your hair too, Nat said. We're going to the bank.

The cut above his eye had crusted over badly. The skin underneath was already purple and blue. Jin cleaned off the dried blood and put a bandage over the open wound, but there was no mistaking it was there, no mistaking the bruises forming around his nose. He couldn't hide the fact that something had happened to him, which wasn't entirely bad. Jin thought someone at the bank might notice and call the police. Just as he was beginning to feel optimistic about this, Nat opened the door to the master bedroom and shoved him inside. Mae was tied to her bed, splayed like an X, faceup. Marina was on the other bed, tied the same way but facedown. Both of them were naked. Nat tightened his grip on Jin's arm. I'm leaving the gun with my brother, he said. But if you pull anything at the bank, something bad's going to happen here.

Jin promised to cooperate. He'd do whatever they asked, give them anything they wanted. Dell kept pacing back and forth beside Mae's bed. He seemed twitchy, agitated. Come back quick, he said. Then he walked over to Mae and yanked out a patch of her pubic hair. The sound of her wailing, even with her mouth taped shut—it was the worst thing Jin had ever heard. You understand what I'm saying? Dell asked, pulling out another. Come back quick. Nat squeezed Jin's shoulder. That's what the tweaked-out fucker can do with his hands, he said. Imagine if I gave him a knife.

Dell continued pacing around the room after they left, muttering to himself like a homeless person on the street. Dummy, he kept saying. Big fucking dummy. Mae didn't know what he was talking about. She wondered how many of those little packets he'd gone through. There weren't any left on the end table; the torn envelopes were scattered across the floor. Dell kept studying what was left of Nat's drugs, walking back and forth to the bureau like a child who knew better. Mae didn't want him to use them, not if they made him act like his brother. The things Nat had done to Marina—Mae had to crane her head to the side to see if she was still breathing. For a long time, she thought she was dead. Dell left the room and returned several minutes later with something in his fist. She watched him in the mirror, holding a spoon over his lighter and drawing the melted drugs into his syringe. She didn't like how hesitant he was. She didn't understand it. Dell didn't seem like the kind of person who cared about risk. Her only guess was that he didn't want Nat to be angry with him for taking something that wasn't his. Dell took the syringe into the bathroom and closed the door behind him. She braced herself for when he came out, but almost an hour passed, and nothing happened.

Mae knew the men had no intention of letting them go, not that they'd ever humored her with the possibility. They'd been too careless from the start. She'd seen their faces, knew their names, carried the shame of them on her body. She wondered if Marina had a roommate or boyfriend who might notice she was missing, but she didn't want to waste what little time she had left wishing for something so unlikely. No one had called in days. No one was going to come looking for them until it was too late. She felt guilty for leading the men to the house. It was her fault that everything had happened as it did. She tried to say the Lord's Prayer, but she couldn't remember the words. All she could do was accept the death that she knew was coming. At the very least, she wanted the men to bury her or throw her body off a bridge so that strangers wouldn't have to find her naked and tied to her bed.

During the drive to the bank, Jin kept thinking about what they'd done to her, to Mae and Marina both. The trip downtown was his last chance to save them. He just didn't know how. He thought about slipping the teller a note, but Nat said he'd be standing behind him in line, watching everything he did. Then Jin mentioned the twenty thousand in his checking account. He knew a withdrawal that large would raise a flag, but when he suggested taking out the full amount, Nat just shook his head. Five thousand, he said. Five thousand won't make anyone blink, not with a rich guy like you. Nat's thoughts seemed to be in lockstep with his, canceling out every option for escape as soon as he came up with one. His last hope faded when they pulled into the parking lot and Nat handed him a pair of sunglasses from the glove compartment. Keep those on the entire time, he said. Don't want anyone to start asking about your shiners.

There were two tellers working at the window when Jin approached—one that he vaguely recognized, and another with the word TRAINEE printed on her name tag. They exchanged a short greeting as Jin slid his card across the counter and asked for five thousand dollars in cash. The older woman guided the younger one through the transaction, pointing at things on the computer. Jin wanted them to look at him and see the panic on his face, but neither of them did. All they cared about was the list of steps on the screen—do this, then that; check off this line and then the other. It took only a few minutes for the trainee to process his request, count out the money in neat stacks of hundred-dollar bills, and send him away with a thick envelope. Jin considered running for it—Nat didn't have the gun—but he worried what they would do to Mae if he didn't come back.

In the car, Nat counted out the money, smiling as he fanned the new bills against his thumb, admiring their crispness, their smell. It occurred to Jin that this was all their lives were worth. Five thousand dollars, money that would probably be gone in a few days, spent on drugs and alcohol and who knew what else. He didn't remember driving home or walking inside or sitting down in the kitchen so Nat could tie him up again. All of these things happened—they must have happened—but everything after the bank was a blur to him. The only thing Jin remembered for certain was the scream he heard when Nat went upstairs.

Mae's memory of the events began to break down at about the same time. She remembered Nat kicking open the bedroom door, smiling as he waved a thick envelope in the air. She remembered him going into the bathroom to look for Dell and screaming when he found him. And she remembered the look on his face when he climbed on top of her, all veins and rage and sweat as he wrapped his hands around her throat and squeezed until she could no longer see. Lentz kept asking questions about what happened afterward, trying to estimate how many hours Nathan Perry had been on the run, but she couldn't answer any of them. She had no idea how long she'd blacked out, or how she managed to free herself from her bindings, or what time it was when she left the house. The only thing she could add to her account was that she thought she was dead. All that time, wandering through the woods in the dark and the cold, she thought she was dead and God had finally sent her to hell.

THREE

Kyung spends all of Tuesday morning cleaning out the guest room. He washes the sheets and blankets, dusts the furniture, and empties the closets and drawers, which are filled with baby clothes and books. Afterward, he goes downstairs, polishing and vacuuming every surface, attacking one room before moving on to the next. By the time Gillian and Ethan return from the store, everything gleams and smells of soap and bleach. At first, she doesn't notice the difference. She's too busy unloading the groceries—twelve full bags that she piles on the countertop. The sight of so much food would usually worry him, but she did exactly what he'd asked—fill the refrigerator with things that his father might eat. Gillian removes the receipt from her purse and gently lays it on the table. When she leaves the room, he picks up the snakelike coil of paper and follows the trail of numbers all the way down to the end. The groceries cost $238, which she charged to one of their credit cards. Kyung tries not to think about it. This is something for another day.

His parents are tidy people, his father in particular, so Kyung wants everything—his house, his family, himself—to look just right. He shaves with a razor instead of his usual electric, and irons a clean button-down shirt and slacks. Gillian brings him two sundresses, holding them up on their hangers as if she wants him to vote. It's rare for her to do this—usually, she's the one who picks out their clothes—so he appreciates the gesture. She understands how important this is to him. He hesitates to tell her that neither outfit is quite correct. The white one is strapless; the red one, too red. Perhaps she could find something else, something more conservative? he asks. She nods and kisses him on the cheek, placing her hand on his chest. She seems sad for him when she feels his heartbeat, which is racing even though he's standing still.

They leave the house looking like they're headed to a photo studio—mother, father, and child all dressed up for their family portrait. Kyung suggests not wearing seat belts because they'll wrinkle their clothes. Gillian looks at him like he's crazy. Before she has a chance to tell him so, he says she's right, she's right. No need to get carried away. His cheeks burn as he reaches for his belt and inserts the clip into the buckle. Thirty-six years old, and he's still behaving like a child, trying so hard to please someone whose standards have always been too high. Kyung glances at the clock on the dashboard to confirm what he already knows. Since Ethan was born, they're never on time for anything. The doctor said he was planning to release Jin at three. It's almost three now. He passes two cars and runs a yellow light, gunning his engine, which sounds like a rocket hurtling into space.

Gillian braces herself against the armrest and door. "We can't pick him up from the hospital if we're dead," she says lightly.

This is her way of telling him she feels unsafe. She wants to nag without sounding like one.

"Should we review?" he asks.

"You think I won't remember?"

"I just want to make sure."

She looks out her window. "Go ahead, then."

Kyung runs through the list of things that Gillian should and shouldn't do in front of his father: Never interrupt. Serve the men first. Always place one hand under the other wrist when giving something to an elder. Don't talk about money. Discipline the boy in private. . . . He pauses, wondering if he left something out.

"Attend to him," she says. "Offer to refill his drink and clear his plate before he has to ask."

"Right."

The list is a strange combination of precaution and tradition, things that usually help a visit go well. He accepts it, begrudgingly, as a necessary form of insurance. Like most Koreans of a certain age, his father has no filter. When Jin sees something he doesn't like, something he doesn't consider respectful, he's quick to comment on it, which gets under Kyung's skin and stays there for days. It's better to be vigilant and give him nothing to criticize. Gillian is almost always good-natured about playing her part, despite the fact that the list dictates how a Korean wife is expected to behave. There aren't any rules or expectations for the Irish. His parents assume she knows nothing and seem pleasantly surprised when she does. Over time, she's earned their favor this way. Kyung would stop short of saying they like her, but they no longer actively dislike her, which is more than he could have hoped for in the beginning.

"I'm sorry if this is annoying you. I'm just nervous, that's all."

"But you're acting like I'm the only reason you and your parents get into it so often. You have your own list of things to worry about."

"You're right," he says. Right again.

At the hospital, the visitors' lot is full, so Kyung leaves the car in an emergency lane and runs inside, jangling all the coins and keys in his pockets. His father and Reverend Sung are sitting in the waiting room together. Of course, he thinks. The reverend is here again. The nurses probably assume he's a relative.

Jin is hunched over in a chair, wearing a thin white T-shirt, baggy drawstring pants, and a pair of slippers—all hospital issue. He seems tired and irritated. The bruises on his face look worse than they did the day before. They're Technicolor now. Purple and blue, yellow and red.

"Have you been waiting long?" Kyung asks.

"No," the reverend says. "He signed his discharge papers a few minutes ago. I've just been telling him about the arrangement we discussed last night."

Jin looks up, his expression curious. Kyung tries his best to smile. The reverend does too, although their conversation the night before was hardly cordial. The reverend called to tell him that Mae and Jin would be his guests at the parsonage after their release. Kyung said absolutely not. They belonged at home with him, with family. He was startled by the speed and force with which he responded, the lack of hesitation, but he meant what he said. He no longer trusted his parents' care to anyone but himself.

"Your house is too small," Jin says.

"We have the guest room all ready for you."

"Guest room," he mutters.

Kyung expected this reaction. In many ways, he deserves it. Brick by brick, he's built a wall around his life, trying to preserve his family and home as his alone. He helps out his parents when asked and visits when invited, but not too often, and never as much as he should. It's the most he's willing to do, the absolute minimum he can get away with and still be considered a son.

"If you don't have enough space, it really wouldn't be any trouble for Jin and Mae to stay with us."

Kyung ignores the reverend. They've settled this already. "Ethan and Gillian are in the car waiting." He mentions Ethan first, aware that time with his grandson motivates Jin in a way that other things don't.

"All right, then. Let's go." Jin gets up stiffly and shuffles toward the exit. Empty wheelchairs line both sides of the corridor, but Jin doesn't ask for help, and Kyung knows better than to offer.

Outside, a meter maid is walking away from his car, shaking her head at the audacity of his parking job, angled into a lane clearly marked for ambulances. Gillian lifts and lowers her shoulders as if to say she tried. Kyung pockets the ticket as he opens the passenger door. Something about the height or angle of the seat makes Jin flinch and cover his ribs with his free hand. Suddenly, Kyung sees his father curled up on the kitchen floor—knees up, head down—while Dell kicks him in the chest. He closes his eyes, trying to turn the image into something different, something blank.

Through the open window, Jin and the reverend say their good-byes.

"You can call me anytime, day or night," the reverend says.
"I will."

"And I'll see you on Sunday?"

Jin pauses. "Mae's being released later this week. We'll have to see how she's feeling."

There's something not quite honest about his answer. The reverend seems to understand this, but he lets it go with a smile and a wave. Kyung drives off and watches him in the rearview mirror until he disappears with a curve in the road. He wishes he could remember the name of the cartoon character he reminds him of, the one in the children's magazine he used to read in grade school. There were two of them, actually—twin brothers, he thinks—one who was polite and well behaved, and the other, who wasn't. Kyung always feels like the bad twin whenever he sees Reverend Sung around his parents, doting on them as a good son should. It's silly to resent someone for having a relationship that he never wanted, that he actively sought not to have. Still, he dislikes the way the reverend kept offering the parsonage to his parents as if Kyung weren't able to care for them. Unable and unwilling aren't the same thing.

Ethan leans forward, clutching the back of Jin's headrest. "I'm sorry you crashed your car, Grandpa."

This is how they've chosen to explain it to him. *Grandma and Grandpa had an accident.*

Jin seems confused for a moment. Then he looks at Ethan carefully. "You're so big now. You've gotten so big."

"My birthday was in April."

"I know. Have you been riding your bike?"

"What bike?"

Kyung refused to show Ethan the box that his parents had left on the front steps, wrapped in thick blue ribbon with a matching satin bow. He just covered it with a tarp and dragged it to the basement, where no one has touched it since. Gillian looked up the make and model online, and learned it was a six-hundred-dollar Italian tricycle, popular with the children of celebrities. She was excited about it until she noticed the look on Kyung's face, and then the obvious became obvious to her. They couldn't allow his parents to give Ethan a gift like that, not when their own gift consisted of a plastic tool belt and a puzzle.

"What bike?" Ethan repeats.

"Oh, never mind," Jin says, looking down at his lap. "I thought you had one."

The car settles into an uncomfortable, unnatural state of quiet. Minutes pass, and no one says a word, not even Ethan, who seems to understand that something isn't right. Kyung mentally cycles through a list of topics to fill the dead air—work, school, the weather—but it all seems too meaningless. He wishes he'd left Gillian and Ethan at home so he could say what's really on his mind: He's sorry for assuming the worst about his father. In the bank, when Jin had a chance to run, he didn't. He returned to the house, knowing he'd probably be beaten again, then killed. Kyung can't imagine doing this. He worries that he would have saved himself, that his instincts would have taken over, blurring the distinction between wrong and right. It pains him to know that his father was the better man in that moment, that perhaps he's been a better man all along.

"Pull into that lot over there," Jin says.

"What's the matter? Are you sick?"

"No. I need some clothes. Mine are at the other house."

"You want to buy them here?"

"Yes, here is fine."

He turns into the parking lot of a strip mall anchored in the middle by a giant Walmart. Kyung wonders if he should offer to drive somewhere else, somewhere more to his father's tastes, but Jin is already getting out of the car, wincing as he stretches his leg to meet the pavement. By the time Kyung jumps out and runs to the passenger side to help, Jin and Ethan are already walking toward the entrance. Kyung and Gillian follow as the doors slide open and an elderly greeter croaks an unfortunate hello.

"It's kind of cute, isn't it?" Gillian asks, pointing at the two of them holding hands. "Ethan seems to like spending time with him."

Kyung nods, but he's disoriented by the strangeness of it all. This isn't the kind of place he ever imagined visiting with his father. He considers Walmart a dirty little secret, a store he frequents more often than he'd like. It's cheap and depressing and sad, but cheap trumps everything these days. Kyung is no longer bothered by the poor people wandering through the aisles, the train wrecks from the Flats with their faded tattoos and unhappy, juice- and ketchup-stained children. He's more disturbed by the people who look like him—clean and well kempt, dressed in clothes that clearly weren't purchased here. He wonders if they shop at Walmart because they're cheap, or because they're struggling to make ends meet. He hates the fact that he and Gillian fall into the second category. Despite all appearances, they have more in common with the poor people than with the rich ones.

In the clothing section, Jin picks out two pairs of gray sweatpants, two short-sleeved shirts, a package of underwear, and a package of socks. He places these items in a little blue basket that Ethan carries for him. The clothes are so different from what he usually wears, but Kyung assumes these choices are about comfort, not style. It occurs to him that he'll have to help Jin change. With the sling, it won't be easy to do by himself. On their way to the checkout line, Gillian suggests picking up toiletries. A toothbrush, a razor, some deodorant and soap. The basket becomes too heavy for Ethan to carry, so Gillian takes it under her arm, plucking things from the shelves as Jin points to them. Jin buys more than he probably needs, but Kyung understands why. His parents' house is a crime scene. Eventually, the police will take the tape off the doors and allow them to return, but it doesn't mean they'll want to. He's discussed this with Gillian, who doesn't seem the least bit bothered by the possibility that his parents will be living with them for a while. She's remarkable sometimes. She never balks at doing the right thing when it comes to family, hers or his. If the situation had been reversed and it was Connie who needed their help, he doesn't think he'd give in so easily. The thought of this makes him feel grateful, but guilty, so he squeezes her hand.

"What was that for?"

He shakes his head and lets go.

At the checkout line, Jin pats down his pants. "I don't have my wallet," he says. "That's at the other house too."

"Oh. Well . . ." Kyung tries not to look panicked as he takes out his own. He fans through his credit cards, trying to remember which ones aren't maxed out or past due. He slides a Visa across the counter, but Gillian clears her throat loudly. Her eyebrows are arched high, frozen mid-forehead like a clown. He takes the card back, realizing that she probably charged the groceries on it.

"Airline miles," he says weakly. "Maybe I'll use one that gives me airline miles."

The cashier shrugs, dubious, as if she's heard it all before. Kyung hands her a card from the bottom of his stack, hopeful that it's on the bottom because he hasn't used it recently. Then he watches her scan the items, counting the number of beeps as he waits for the total.

"What's that thing?" he asks, pointing at the last item in the basket, a toy caterpillar with body parts that fit together like blocks.

"It's for the boy," Jin says. "For helping me."

Ethan doesn't need another toy. He doesn't even like blocks. Kyung wonders if he asked for it, although it hardly matters how the thing ended up in the basket. He can't refuse now. He nods and the cashier scans the caterpillar and swipes his card through the machine. His chest tightens at the thought of being declined while his father looks on—he'll never recover from the shame. He keeps his eyes glued to the box, the little white one next to the register that reads PROCESSING in red letters. *Processing, processing, processing.* It's taking longer than usual, which means something bad is about to happen. Kyung fans through his cards again, not certain which one to use when the first is declined. He doesn't think he has room left on any of them.

"Sign here," she says, tearing off the receipt and putting a copy in front of him.

Kyung stares at the slip of paper as if he doesn't believe her. Then he scribbles his name so no one will notice how badly his hand is shaking. His signature—a zigzagged line that looks like he was testing the pen for ink—doesn't even resemble the one on the back of his card.

"Thank you," he says. He knows the cashier had nothing to do with the purchase getting approved, but he thanks her as if she did.

As they walk back to the car, he and Gillian exchange a look, one that's becoming all too familiar lately. A ninety-dollar purchase at Walmart shouldn't terrorize them like this. Kyung makes a decent salary at the university. He has a goddamn Ph.D. But their mistakes are finally catching up with them. Their house payment is a nightmare. His student loans too. They've refinanced their mortgage, borrowed from their credit cards, and transferred their balances over and over again—all in the name of staying current on their bills, but they can't keep up with this shell game much longer.

"Can I have my bug now, please?" Ethan asks.

Kyung digs into one of the plastic bags and hands it to him. "Thank you."

Gillian smiles as she watches Ethan examine his new toy, confirming what he's always known about her. She's quicker to recover than he is; she's always been the more resilient of the two. Kyung's moist hand is still wrapped around his wallet like it's a brick he's about to throw. In a few years' time, Ethan will be old enough to understand their situation, to feel the same shame and worry and weight that he does. Kyung stops short in the middle of the parking lot and swoops the boy up in his arms, hugging him much harder than he should.

"Daaaaaaaad," Ethan protests.

Four is a kind age, he thinks. Four is wonderful and clueless. When they return home, Kyung leads his father upstairs to the guest room. The back of the house is in the shade now, and the space almost seems barren in the dim light. He's embarrassed by the stained blue carpet, the absence of anything resembling comfort or style. The only personal items on display are the alarm clock and two remote controls on the end table. It's a far cry from the antique-filled rooms in his parents' house, but it's clean. At the very least, it looks like they made an effort to receive him.

"Will you be comfortable here?"

Jin sits down on the edge of the bed, testing the springs. "I'd like to lie down now," he says, not answering the question.

"So do you want—do you want me to help you change clothes?"

They regard each other carefully, both seemingly aware of the problem. In order to help, Kyung would have to touch him, and Jin would have to let him, something they no longer do by choice.

"I'm fine in what I'm wearing. I just want to lie down."

"Well, let me help you unpack first." He puts Jin's new clothes in an empty drawer and places the toiletries on a shelf in the adjoining bathroom. The unpacking takes all of thirty seconds, hardly enough time to prepare for the apology he knows he should give.

Ethan runs into the room, picking up a remote control as he climbs into bed.

"Your grandfather needs to rest now," Kyung says. "Why don't you go play somewhere else?"

"It's fine. It's fine. Leave the boy here."

Ethan turns on the TV and leans against the headboard, stretching out his legs. Jin slowly does the same.

"Is there anything special you want for dinner?"

Jin shakes his head. "I'm not hungry."

"How about some juice or milk? Or maybe coffee?"

"Not now."

"A glass of water?"

"No, I just want to rest."

Kyung leans against the doorframe. It's obvious that his father wants him to leave, but there's still too much that he needs to say. If he doesn't say it now, he worries he never will. He glances at Ethan, wishing he'd go downstairs. It's hard enough to know where to begin.

"We have cable here. No premium channels, but . . ."

He pauses as Ethan curls up in the crook of Jin's good arm. The two of them look comfortable together, lost in their noisy cartoon while the television glows blue against their faces. This wasn't what Kyung's childhood was like at all. His father didn't have time for television. He didn't have the patience either, but it was better that way. He was always someone to be avoided. The sight of Jin and Ethan sitting together makes him both bitter and hopeful. It's too late for Kyung to have this kind of relationship with his father, but maybe his son will.

"That other remote control over there is for the air conditioner. Are you warm? Should I turn it on for you?"

"*No,*" Jin barks. "How many times do I have to say it? *No.* Just leave me alone."

Ethan sits up, startled by the change in volume. He looks like he's about to cry. Kyung wants to get him out of the room, but he can't. His arms and legs are locked, paralyzed by the sound of his father's raised voice. Whatever words of apology he intended to say recede inside him, canceled out by a swell of anger that he doesn't want his child to see. Jin pulls Ethan back by the shoulder and slowly, cautiously, the boy settles into his former position, his eyes darting from the screen to the door. Kyung and Jin exchange a look, the kind that men give each other when they expect the other to stand down, and *there,* right there—Kyung sees it. Something black and familiar that reminds him who his father really is.

The twenty-dollar bill is for emergencies. He keeps it in his wallet, folded tightly into a square, hidden behind a stack of old photographs and receipts. He can't remember how long it's been there, but he knows what it's for. Things of an urgent, unexpected nature—a category to which alcohol doesn't belong. Tonight, however, is an exception. Tonight, he considers it necessary. Urgent, even, in its own way. The question is: Where? Twenty dollars hardly buys anything these days. He needs to find a dive, a real one, the kind of place where a twenty can still get him good and drunk. Kyung makes one left turn after another, tracing the town's grid to its outermost edges. The cell phone on his dashboard keeps blinking, the red light angry and insistent. He's only been gone for an hour, but Gillian has already left five messages. When it rings again, he turns it off and decides to tell her he misplaced it. Kyung has a habit of forgetting where he left his phone, something they've argued about in the past. She says he should be more careful with it in case she needs to reach him, but he's willing to risk an argument later rather than explain why he had to leave now.

Just past the veterans' hospital, Kyung pulls over at an intersection where there's a bar on each corner. One is closed, the metal window gates shuttered for the night. Two others appear to be topless bars. The fourth, MacLarens, has a long green sign above the entrance with faded shamrocks that anchor each end like quotation marks. FINE IRISH PUB, the sign says, although the cracked front window appears to be held together by nothing more than duct tape and hope. When he opens the door, he's relieved to find it nearly deserted. The only other customers are two old men playing keno beside the jukebox, staring at numbers as they tumble across a screen. Their table is full of empty beer glasses and scraps of crumpled paper—litter from their previous games. Kyung sits down at the far end of the bar, keeping his head down as he orders a whiskey on the rocks.

"Kind?" a woman asks.

"Kind, what?"

"What kind of *whiskey*?"

Her tone is impatient; her accent, crude and South Boston. Kyung looks up, momentarily stunned silent by the woman's wrinkled appearance, badly camouflaged under layers of girlish frost. Frosted hair, frosted eyes, frosted lips.

"Cheapest you have." He tries to unfold the embarrassing origami of his money before she has a chance to see. "How much is that, by the way?"

"Four-fifty." She pours him the equivalent of a double from a plastic bottle of Black Velvet, forgetting the ice—a mistake he doesn't bother to correct.

"You all right?"

Kyung drinks slowly, not certain why a stranger would ask. What about him makes her think he's not?

"I'm just tired." He rubs his eyes as proof.

"That oughta help," she says, motioning toward the whiskey. She looks at him as if she expects their conversation to continue, but Kyung can't think of anything else to say. The standard questions—*How's business? How are you doing?*—seem useless. The bar is nearly empty and she works there for a living, so he already knows the answers. Besides, he doesn't have the energy for a stranger right now. He spent his entire day preparing for Jin's arrival, hoping that his efforts might be appreciated, or even just acknowledged. Instead, his father talked down to him in his own house, in front of his own child, when all he was trying to do was be kind. Kyung knows he was pushing too hard, asking one question after the next when Jin clearly wanted to be left alone. But the role of doting Korean son doesn't come naturally to him. He's still figuring out how to try. They'll never get through this if Jin doesn't try too.

The woman walks away, scattering coasters across the length of the scratched wood bar, occasionally shuffling them like a deck of cards. When she reaches the opposite side of the room, she stops in front of the television set. The Red Sox are on again. The Red Sox are always on in this town.

"Jesus. He's put on weight," she says, staring at the dreadlocked Puerto Rican at bat. "For nine million a year, you'd think he'd go on a diet." She turns around, seemingly eager for someone, anyone, to agree with her. Kyung looks down at his drink.

According to the coasters she left, MacLarens is Marlboro's favorite bar, an unlikely claim trapped in the speech balloon of a grinning leprechaun. It seems more like Marlboro's oldest bar. The place shows all the telltale signs of age: A wood floor that pitches and slopes as if the ground beneath it is sinking. A pair of rickety pool tables lined with threadbare green felt. On the wall nearest him, a dozen autographed photos of celebrities hang from a rail, but when Kyung scans their faces, he doesn't know who they are, or who they were supposed to be when their pictures were snapped. He takes another drink, a longer one this time, closing his eyes as the whiskey warms his throat.

It's been years since he went out to a bar like this. Although he likes alcohol, he's never really enjoyed bars, not even in grad school when his roommates made the rounds every weekend. Occasionally, they dragged him along, but Kyung hated all the noise and shouting, the absence of anything resembling personal space. It's strange that he and Gillian met at a bar, a detail about their past that still embarrasses him. She was working at a sports lounge back then, where her uniform was a tank top, jean shorts, and a push-up bra that squeezed everything north. Tits up to her neck, his roommates said, daring him to ask her out.

Gillian was supposed to be a fling, a pretty girl to help him get over a breakup, but Kyung didn't like playing the field that way. He preferred something steadier, something that required less work, and Gillian actually suited him better than anyone he'd ever dated before. She was twenty-nine and working two jobs to finish her bachelor's degree, so she wasn't always around. She accepted the fact that he didn't want to talk every hour of the day, and she never pressed him about the things he didn't want to talk about. "Needy" wasn't a word he'd ever use to describe her, which was exactly what he needed, someone who just let him be. He'd lost two girlfriends in a row because he refused to get married, as if he'd missed a deadline that no one ever bothered to tell him about. When Gillian started dropping hints after their first year together, he didn't refuse again.

"I got seven on this card," one of the old men shouts, holding up a slip of paper. He jumps out of his chair and brings his keno ticket to the bar. "What does seven pay out, Dee? That's like, what, fifty bucks?"

The woman slides the ticket through a machine, and the cash register beneath it opens with a ping. She counts out a thin stack of wrinkled bills onto the old man's eager palm. Kyung makes the mistake of watching this transaction, looking the man in the eye as he pockets his winnings.

"Hey, I know you," the man says.

"Me? No, we've never met."

"Sure we have. You came in here not even a week ago with your girlfriend."

Up close, Kyung notices that the man's eyes are bloodshot, his skin a bright, unhealthy shade of red. "You're thinking of someone else."

"No, don't you remember? Your girl and me, we're both from Rockport. You bought me a beer last time." The man tries to lean on the bar, but his elbow skids across the surface and he stumbles toward Kyung's chest.

"I told you"—he pushes him away, a little too roughly— "that wasn't me."

The man makes a whistling sound. "Sor-ry," he says, not sounding sorry at all. He shuffles back to his table, raising his voice as he tells his friend to avoid the asshole at the end of the bar.

Dee walks over and refills Kyung's glass. "Just ignore Arnie. He's a regular idiot. I'll have that fifty bucks back in the till in a couple of hours."

Kyung didn't ask for a second drink; he's not sure if he should have one. The first went down too quickly. He glances at his change on the bar, wondering if she'll charge him for it.

"Don't worry about that. This one's on the house."

"It is?" He doesn't understand why she's being nice to him; he's certain he's done nothing to deserve it. "Why?"

"Why? Hell, nobody ever asks that." She laughs. "I guess you just looked like you could use it."

"Yes, but *why*?"

Dee shrugs and starts wiping down the bar with a dirty rag. "You don't really seem like the type to drink on a Tuesday night without a reason." She pauses, then adds: "That's a compliment, by the way."

He looks himself over, realizing that he's still wearing his dress pants and button-down shirt, clothes that stand out in this part of town.

"So what do you do for a living?"

Kyung slowly turns his glass like a knob. It's another double; the whiskey is almost flush with the rim. "I'm a professor."

"That must be nice, getting your summers off and everything. What do you teach?"

"Biology."

"You mean like cutting up frogs?"

"Anatomy, yes."

Dee shudders. "So the kids who study that, they end up being doctors or something? Is that what you are?"

Kyung shifts in his seat, not certain how to explain that he's the wrong kind of doctor, that he dropped out of med school after his second year. His advisors said he was book smart, but too slow to think on his feet when real patients were involved. The chances of matching into his desired residency—into any residency, they said—weren't good. Kyung ended up transferring to a Ph.D. program in bio because he didn't know what else to do, where else to land. He suspects his colleagues don't think he belongs in academia, that he was only hired at the university because of his father's influence there, a possibility that feels true even if it isn't.

"Some of them become doctors, yes."

Dee pours herself a shot of Black Velvet and raises it to him, lifting her pinky up to the ceiling. "Come on, shoot one with me. You're killing me over there with your sad mug."

He wonders if this is Dee's idea of flirting with him. He raises his glass and downs the contents because drinking is easier than talking to her.

"You don't spend a lot of time in bars, do you?"

"No, not really."

"Well, here's how it works." She smiles, as if she's recited her next line a thousand times and still thinks it's clever. "I just stand here while you drink and tell me what's on your mind. You don't have to be shy either. I've heard it all before. Besides, the Sox are in the shitter, so you'd probably be doing me a favor."

Kyung studies the gouges in the bar, thick ones where people probably scratched off their lotto tickets with fingernails and coins. He's certain that Dee has never heard a story like his. Even if he wanted to tell her, he wouldn't know where to start, how far to go back, when it would ever end. He slides off his stool, surprised by the distance between the floor and his feet.

"Thanks," he says, taking his change from the bar. "I have to go now."

"Fifty cents?" Dee looks at the quarters still stacked on his coaster. "I buy you a drink and that's all the tip you're leaving? Fifty cents?"

"Oh, sorry."

From his original twenty, he now has a five- and ten-dollar bill—neither of which he wants to part with. He pats down his pockets, hoping he has more change.

"Forget it," she says, waving her dishrag at him like a fly. "You have a good night."

The street is empty when he opens the door to a rush of cool air. The only sound he can hear is the vague thump of music leaking from one of the bars nearby. He takes his keys out of his pocket, dropping them on the sidewalk, and then dropping them again not five seconds later. As he starts his car, the whiskey hits him all at once, two doubles drilling straight into his stomach. He can't remember what, if anything, he ate that day to absorb the blow. Kyung leans back on his headrest, trying not to think about his heart, the way it keeps pounding louder and faster than it should. It sounds like something out of a horror movie, ready to burst through his ribs. His chin bobs toward his chest, and his lids begin to blink, weighed down with lead. He can barely see, so he closes his eyes and tells himself to relax, don't panic, and don't throw up. When he opens them again—a minute, an hour later?—someone is shining a light into his car. Kyung swats at the armrest, locking the doors while the man outside raps on his window.

"License and registration."

Kyung's head is spinning; he thinks the man might be wearing a uniform, but the light is too bright. He rolls down his window an inch. "Officer?"

"License and registration, please."

"Why? I wasn't driving. I was just sitting here."

"I'm not going to ask you again."

Without the flashlight shining in his face, Kyung can clearly make out a uniform and badge, a gun in a holster. He slides his documents through the cracked window, being careful not to drop them.

The policeman examines the license, squinting at it as if it's a fake. "You know this is expired, right? It expired in December."

"No, that can't be right." As soon as Kyung says it, he remembers the notices that came in the mail. The first was printed on plain white paper, the second on urgent pink. He had a choice between paying the water bill that month or paying for his renewal. It wasn't hard to decide which one to ignore.

"I still don't understand what I did wrong. I wasn't driving. My car was in park."

"Step out of your vehicle, sir."

"For what?"

"If you haven't been drinking, then you won't mind taking a field test."

Kyung sits up straight, trying his best to look sober, although he knows his breath stinks of alcohol. His whole car does. This can't be happening, he thinks. This can't happen.

"Officer McFadden," he says. "Will you call Officer McFadden? I'm married to his daughter."

The policeman shines the light on Kyung's face again. "You're Connie's son-in-law? The one whose parents were involved in that thing up in the Heights?"

That thing. So this is what they're calling it now.

"Yes, that's me."

"Stay put," he says.

Ten minutes later, as a second cruiser pulls up behind the first, Kyung braces himself to say everything that he rehearsed during the wait. *I'm sorry for bothering you. I wasn't actually driv-*

ing. I know better than that. He repeats these words over and over again, reminding himself to speak slowly and clearly so he doesn't sound drunk. He looks in his side-view mirror as the car door opens and out steps Tim, not Connie. Somehow, things have just gone from bad to worse. His brother-in-law is an idiot, an asshole. He's always turning Kyung into the butt of a joke. His favorite is the one about teachers, how they teach because they can't do anything else, *harharhar.* Gillian tells Kyung to ignore him, to be the bigger man. She says her brother is insecure around educated people because the kids at school used to call him "retard" when he was little.

Tim circles around to the passenger side and stands with his hands on his hips, surveying the neighborhood. Kyung already knows what he's thinking. The topless bars are hard to miss—both of them have blinking neon silhouettes of women hanging in their windows. He unlocks the doors and waits for Tim to climb into the passenger seat.

"So who'd you manage to piss off tonight?"

It's not the first question he expected to hear. "No one. Why?"

"You must have. Someone called in a possible DUI. People don't normally do that in this neighborhood unless they're pissed about something."

Kyung thinks of Dee, having a laugh inside MacLarens at his expense. He wonders if this is what she meant when she told him to have a good night. "I wasn't driving—did the other guy tell you that? I was just sitting here, trying to sleep it off before I went home."

"You don't have to be driving. You started your car—that's all it takes to get a DUI in this state."

In his mirror, Kyung notices the first officer turn on his headlights and drive away. He's relieved—a little. At the very least, he won't be arrested. Now all he has to do is listen to his brother-in-law gloat.

"So which one did you go to?" Tim wags his finger from left to right, pointing at the topless bars.

"No, it's not like that. I went to the Irish one, the pub. You can ask the lady inside if you don't believe me."

"Oh, I don't care if you went to a titty bar. But if you want to see girls, you can find better places than these shitholes. Next time, you should hit up that big one on Route 5, next to the old airport."

Kyung's head is pounding. He needs a bathroom and a glass of water; he needs to stop thinking about Tim sitting in a strip club, slipping dollar bills into a woman's G-string. Drunk or not, he's still sober enough to understand that topics like this are off-limits with his brother-in-law. He and Tim aren't friends. They certainly aren't buddies. Even if Tim wanted that kind of relationship, Kyung isn't the type. Being an acquaintance, a roommate, a colleague—all of that was easy enough, but real friendships always seemed like too much work to him, too primed for disappointment.

"I don't go to strip clubs."

"Oh, sure."

"It's true. I'm married."

"I was married once too. I know how it is."

A car drives toward them, shining its headlights on their faces. Kyung crouches down in his seat to avoid being seen.

"I told the other officer to call Connie."

"He's not on duty tonight. He's on a date." Tim chuckles, as if the thought of his father taking a woman to dinner or a movie amuses him. It's odd, at the very least. Connie's been a widower for almost twenty years. This is the first Kyung has ever heard of his dating.

"So he doesn't know what happened yet?"

"Nope."

"And Gillian?"

"Nope."

Arnie staggers out of MacLarens, held upright by his friend. They weave along the sidewalk together, going who knows where. When they turn the corner and there's no more sideshow left to watch, Kyung realizes he has to do it. He has to ask, even though he already knows the answer.

"Are you planning to tell them?"

"What do you think?"

He thinks Tim is Connie's son, and Connie has never liked him, not even a little, so there's no use asking him to keep quiet. Everything about this experience has been humiliating enough. He doesn't need to add begging to the list.

"I'm fine to drive now, if you're willing to let me go."

Tim nods slowly, stretching out the moment for everything it's worth. "I'll follow you," he says. "Just to make sure you get home safe."

Gillian has a temper that flares from time to time, but rarely, and never without good reason. Since Kyung is almost always the reason, he's learned how to defuse an argument by simply apologizing before it starts. Because she doesn't like conflict any more than he does, this is usually enough to move on. Tonight, however, he thinks it might help to acknowledge that some of

his choices this evening—most of them, actually—were neither considerate nor smart. Never mind that his stomach was
empty when he started drinking or that he was sleeping it off
in the car when the cop woke him up. Never mind the circumstances of the past few days or anything else that might
sound like an excuse. Gillian is quick to confuse explanations
for defensiveness, which is the oxygen that keeps everything
burning.

He expects to find her waiting up for him, but when he turns
into his driveway, the house is completely dark. It's late, he
realizes—too late for a man with a wife and child to come home
like this, reeking of alcohol as if he's been dunked in a barrel.
Tim doesn't pull in behind him, but Kyung feels no sense of
reprieve as the cruiser disappears down the street. By morning, Gillian will know everything.

At the side door, he takes off his shoes and creeps through
the house, seeking out what he needs in the order he needs it
most: bathroom, water, aspirin, food. Every door and floor-
board seems to creak louder than usual. The flush of the toilet
sounds like a hurricane. In the kitchen, he finds a crusty pot
and some dirty bowls in the dishwasher. It looks like they had
spaghetti while he was out. He confirms that they left none for
him, so he raids the cabinets for his dinner, starting with an
expensive-looking box of crackers that he eats by the handful.
Then he moves on to the fridge, cutting off oversized chunks
of cheese and pâté with a knife. These pricey foods aren't meant
for him, and he knows it, but he continues eating to settle his
stomach.

Half a box of crackers and a block of cheese later, Kyung
hears footsteps on the staircase and a flick of a light switch down

the hall. Gillian walks into the kitchen, pulling on a furry yellow bathrobe over her nightgown. Her hair is lopsided, as if she's been sleeping—bees' nest on the right, flat and matted on the left—but she doesn't look surprised to see him hovering over the island, demolishing a sixteen-dollar wedge of pâté.

"I just got off the phone with Tim."

"He called you from his car?" Kyung should have known. Tim was probably excited to tell her, like it was the best thing to happen to him all year.

"So you ran off to drink tonight."

She says this in the form of a statement, not a question, so he doesn't respond. Instead, he leans against a cabinet—head down, eyes to the floor, ready. Gillian circles the island and brushes the crumbs off his shirt.

"Look at you. You're a mess."

Bits of cheese and pâté and crackers fall to the floor, snowing against the redbrick tile. He brings his fist to his mouth, trying to hold back a burp, but it's too late. The air smells like meat and milk, laced with something bitter.

"Damn it, Kyung." She covers her nose.

"Sorry . . ." He's about to continue so she understands the apology wasn't for the burp alone, but then he burps again.

She moves to the other side of the room, arms crossed, eyes hooded over with a frown. There are times when sorry alone won't save him, when his behavior has to be dissected and discussed before anything resembling forgiveness can occur. It's always the wait that he finds unsettling, that moment right before she opens her mouth when he can see it all building up inside. Gillian doesn't hide anything from him; she says she shouldn't have to.

"There are so many things I want to say to you right now—"

He raises his hand in the air to stop her. "Can I make a request?"

It was a bad impulse—they both know he's lost the right to ask for anything.

"What?"

"Can you please not yell? I don't want my father to wake up and hear us fighting." He doesn't bother to explain that his head feels like it's being crushed, trapped between the metal plates of a vise. This is probably the least of her concerns.

Gillian crosses her arms tighter, holding herself in. "You know what? I'm not going to say anything right now. I'm just going to let you do the talking."

He hates it when she does this. It's the same as asking, *What do you have to say for yourself?* but without the motherly tone. He thinks for a second, making a careful list of everything she might be upset about.

"I'm sorry for leaving without an explanation and not answering my phone. . . . I'm sorry for going out for a drink . . . and I'm sorry for getting pulled over by that cop and asking him to call your dad."

Her expression doesn't change after his string of apologies. It probably sounded too much like a recitation. Gillian believes that people can say sorry but not sound sorry. The difference matters to her.

"And?"

"And . . ." He realizes that Tim must have mentioned the topless bars. His brother-in-law is truly a shit. "And I swear I didn't go to a strip club tonight. I was at the pub across the street. I even told Tim to go over there and talk to the bartender if he didn't believe me."

Gillian looks confused. She didn't know about this part, and she clearly doesn't want to. "Listen, if this arrangement with your parents is going to work, you can't just leave me here anytime you feel like it. You can't make all of this my responsibility."

"Did my dad do something to upset you while I was gone?"

"No. All he did was watch TV with Ethan. That's not the point. The point is that you have to be here—I mean really be here. Your mother's coming home on Thursday and now we have to take in Marina too, and you can't just disappear like you did tonight. You're not the only one having a hard time dealing with all of this."

Her volume keeps rising, but Kyung doesn't try to stop her. He's still a few sentences behind. "What do you mean, take in Marina? Who said we have to do that?"

"Me."

He waits for something else, something more to follow, but this is all she's willing to give. "I don't understand—we barely have room for my parents. How do you suppose we're going to take in their maid?"

"We'll have to figure it out. And stop saying 'maid' like that. She's a person; she deserves our help as much as anyone."

Kyung burps again. His stomach feels worse now with all of the rich food floating inside. "I'm not suggesting that she doesn't need help or deserve it. I feel bad for her too, but there's no room here. . . . I bet if she asked my parents, they'd pay to send her back home to her family."

Suddenly, Gillian is almost on top of him, jabbing her finger at his face. "Do you hear yourself? Pay to send her back home? To *Bosnia*? Do you even understand why she left that country in the first place?"

He doesn't, not really. He's vaguely aware that the Bosnians and Serbians fought a war, but he can't remember who the aggressors were, which side won or lost. Either way, none of this makes Marina his responsibility. He has enough of his own without taking a refugee under his roof. He wraps up the rest of the pâté and puts it back in the fridge, trying to figure out how to say no without actually saying it.

"I'm sure there's another option we haven't—"

"Do you know what they operated on her for?"

"No. Why? Did my dad actually tell you?"

She flinches, as if the word she's about to say is a blade sitting on her tongue. "A perforated rectum. That's why she was bleeding internally. Can you imagine what kind of hell those men put her through? And now you want to send her back on the first flight to Bosnia with a colostomy bag and God knows what kind of nightmares for the rest of her life?" Her voice is getting louder again. She takes a breath, her pale skin flushed red. "This happened to Marina because she worked for your parents, because she was at the wrong place at the wrong time, just like they were, so now we have to help her. Do you understand that, Kyung? Do you understand why a good, decent person would want to step up like that?"

Kyung feels genuinely sorry for Marina, but she's a stranger to him, a girl who cleans his parents' house twice a week. The list of people who need him is long enough already, and he hardly knows what to do about the names that are already there. Marina's immediate problem—the fact that she has no one to care for her—seems like the easiest to solve. If she doesn't want to go back to her family in Bosnia, then why not let Jin hire a nurse to help her? Or put her up in one of those assisted-living facilities downtown? To suggest these things out loud would probably seem cruel, and of course, he has no money of his own to make this problem go away. If he did, he's certain that none of them would ever see Marina again.

"Well?"

Kyung leans forward and stretches his upper half over the countertop, resting his cheek on the cold Formica. He's exhausted—he wants to sleep. He wants his parents back in their house and Marina back in hers. He wants to rewind all of their lives to the point just before everything started to go wrong.

"Are you thinking or taking a nap over there?"

"Okay," he says. "She can stay with us. Are we done now?"

Although his eyes are closed, he doesn't have to see her reaction to realize he made a mistake. Suggesting they should be done already will only prolong the conversation.

"I'm going to ask you something, and I need you to be completely honest with me when you answer."

He opens his eyes, trying not to glare at Gillian, who doesn't seem to understand when enough is enough. She won the argument; she got what she wanted—now what?

"Will Ethan be safe here?"

"How should I know? You're the one who wants to invite a stranger to come live with us."

"No, it's not Marina I'm worried about. It's your mother. You said in the hospital that Jin never hit you when you were little, so I'll take your word for it, but you never said anything about Mae."

"What about her?"

"Don't pretend like you don't know what I'm asking."

Kyung switches cheeks. "Ethan will be fine."

"But that's not an answer. I need you to say it one way or the other. She either hit you or she didn't."

He's in no condition to explain that his childhood wasn't simple like this, with the fault lines so straight or clearly drawn. Mae was a teenager when she married Jin and barely in her twenties when they moved to the States. She had no friends, no job, no control over anything in her life except for Kyung. If Gillian took the time to think about it, she'd know the answer to her question already. His father hit Mae. Mae hit him. That was the order of succession in their family. He just can't bring himself to say so out loud.

"You're not talking anymore. Does that mean what I think it means?"

"My mother's not going to do anything to Ethan."

"But how can you be so sure?"

"I just am."

Gillian raises her empty palms to him as if to say, *That's all?*

He doesn't know how to convince her without steering the conversation to a bad place, but he owes her this much. She has the right to feel that Ethan is safe in their own home. "It stopped a long time ago, okay? I'm talking decades now."

"Yes, but *why* did it stop?"

"I was a kid, Gillian. I didn't bother to ask. What matters is that my mother had a miserable life back then. I understand why she took her frustrations out on me, but it didn't happen often, and you know how small she is—it's not like she could ever really hurt me."

Gillian doesn't look like she believes him. He hardly believes himself. Half of him still feels sorry for Mae. The other half only feels rage—not because she hit him, but because she stayed. Every time Jin beat her into a corner because of a lukewarm dinner or an innocent comment, Kyung wondered why she wasn't brave enough to run away, to take him with her and simply get out. She settled for a life of meaningless terror, dragging him alongside her when she should have wanted more for them both.

"My mother isn't that person anymore. You've seen her with Ethan, my father too. They're careful with him, happy with him in a way they weren't with me. I know you know this."

"But the sleepover invites, and all the offers to babysit—you always said no. It was like you were worried about them being alone with him."

"It wasn't like that. It was more about sending them a message . . . about punishing them." Kyung pauses, aware that he's a very small man, using his child to communicate all of the things he never could.

Gillian leans down on the countertop, stretching her arms out in front of her. She seems more relaxed now. Sad, but relaxed. From her posture, the way her elbow gently touches his, he knows the argument is almost over.

"You've been a good son," she says. "You figured out how to keep them in your life, even though you really didn't have to. It's not like you owed them anything."

"They're my parents, Gillian. What was I supposed to do?"

"What lots of people do—move to another city, get an unlisted number, avoid them. You had every right to cut them out of your life. Even a therapist would say so."

"That's an American idea. Koreans are different."

"But you grew up here. You're American too."

"It's not the same." He switches cheeks again, turning his face away from her. "Why are we talking about this anyway? A minute ago, you were giving me grief about being responsible and taking care of people. Did you change your mind already?"

"No, no. It's not that. I just want to make sure that if things get out of hand here, if it's not safe or healthy for us to be around them, you're going to take care of us, right? You're going to put me and Ethan first?"

What she's asking for is completely reasonable. His wife and child should come before everyone else. But this is an American idea too. On the other side of the world, the world he never fully left, it's parents first, children second, wife last. This is how Mae and Jin raised him, although he resents their claim as much as he struggles with Gillian's. Still, he's not about to explain something so incomprehensible to her, not when they're this close to the end.

"Of course you and Ethan come first."

Gillian brushes her thumb over his. He closes his eyes, trying not to think about the doubt implied in her questions. He could easily fall asleep folded over the countertop if she'd just let him.

"Kyung," she says quietly. "There's something else."

"What?"

"But now it's your turn not to yell."

"Why would I?"

She stands up and removes a piece of paper from a drawer. The font is so small—it takes a few blinks for his eyes to focus, to comprehend that what she's given him is an e-mail confirmation of a wire transfer. Three thousand dollars from Jin's bank account to theirs.

"He asked for our routing number so he could give me some money. He said I should buy all new clothes for Mae before she's released from the hospital. I tried to call you. . . . He was so insistent, but honestly, I thought he was talking about a couple hundred dollars or something. I had no idea he was planning to transfer this much."

Kyung scans the digits from left to right, counting and recounting the number of spaces they extend. "What else did he say this was for?"

"I don't know. I'm guessing it's for food, maybe."

"What else?"

"Nothing."

"This is important, Gillian. I need to know exactly what he said."

"Nothing, I swear. I told him it was too much and he said he wanted us to have it for our trouble. That's it. That was the whole conversation."

For our trouble. It's not worth it to explain that the money is Jin's penance for his outburst earlier, that three thousand dollars is now the going rate of an apology in his family. Kyung knows how desperate Gillian is to keep the money—he can see it on her face, the way it looks so old and lined with worry. She understands, just as he does, that pride won't fill their refrigerator next week. Pride won't get his license renewed or pay the water bill or keep the collection agencies at bay. It's a useless form of currency they can't afford to trade in anymore. Kyung folds the paper in half and returns it to her, reminded of the gifts that always appeared like clockwork after a beating, the art and jewelry and clothing with their price tags still attached. One of his clearest memories of Mae dates back to grade school, when she stood in the hallway outside his room for over an hour, staring at herself in a full-length mirror. She was wearing a new mink coat, a plush gray one streaked with black and white—the kind that actresses on television wore when their characters were supposed to be rich. Mae kept turning from side to side, swinging the coat to make the fur brush against her legs, which were purple with bruises. He hated her then— he hates her still—for teaching him that everyone had a price.

PART TWO

DUSK

FOUR

The man on the doorstep is dressed like a college student, with a T-shirt and jeans and a Red Sox cap pulled low over his eyes. Kyung doesn't recognize him; he doesn't recognize the car in his driveway either.

"No soliciting," he says, pointing at the sticker on the storm door that announces the same.

The man removes his cap and runs his fingers through his matted hair. "Oh, sorry, Mr. Cho. It's just me."

Kyung is startled to see Lentz again. He wonders if he came to tell him that Nat Perry is in custody, or maybe even dead like his brother, but the longer he examines him, the clearer it is. There's no good news on Lentz's dimpled face. It's a courtesy call, nothing more. He invites him in and leads him back to the kitchen, where Gillian is making lunch and Jin and Ethan are sitting on the floor, assembling his tricycle. The area around them is littered with parts, like a hardware store exploded and showered them in metal.

"That's a nice bike," Lentz says to Ethan. "You're going to have a lot of fun with that, aren't you?"

"It's from my grandma and grandpa. I named him Boomer."

Kyung dragged the tricycle upstairs earlier that morning, desperate for an activity that didn't involve sitting in front of the TV. Ethan shrieked when he saw the box, skipping around in circles and singing "bicycle" to the theme song of his favorite cartoon. Jin didn't seem to mind that his gift had sat in the basement for several months. The impromptu song and dance even made him smile. Kyung assumed the three of them would work on the bike together, but Jin was quick to deputize Ethan, assigning him to sort and organize the parts. Despite the occasional pang of guilt he felt for not helping, Kyung was actually relieved to sit on the sidelines. He'd always been terrible at following instructions; he could barely put a bookshelf together, much less a bike. From his seat at the kitchen table, he tried to read a book that Gillian had given him, but his attention kept drifting away from the pages. Assembling a bike required patience, especially with an excited child underfoot. He worried that Jin might lose his temper at any moment, but the moment never came.

"Do you have some news for us?" Gillian asks.

Lentz leans against the wall, glancing at the stacks of sandwiches that she's arranging on a platter. "We finished collecting evidence at Mr. and Mrs. Cho's house, so they're free to go back now."

Jin continues reading his instruction manual. He doesn't even bother to look up.

"Whenever you're ready, I mean. You're free to go back whenever you're ready. Also, we found your car in Newport."

Gillian frowns. "Newport, Rhode Island?"

"No, Vermont. Up near Canada." Lentz pauses, looking

aimlessly around the kitchen until he lands on Kyung. "How's your mother doing? The hospital released her, I hear."

The shower in the guest bathroom was running a few minutes ago. Now it's stopped. Beyond this, Kyung has no idea what she's doing up there, much less how. It's been three days since Mae returned from the hospital, and she hasn't left her room since. Every attempt to check on her has been met with silence and a locked door. Aside from the occasional flush of the toilet and the sound of her footsteps overhead, no one would even know that she's living among them again. She's the ghost in the house whose presence they all feel, but never see—not even Jin, who she exiled from the guest room within minutes of her arrival.

"My mother's resting. Is there anything else we should know?"

"About the house? Not really. You've got good insurance, I hope?"

The question was clearly directed at Jin, who makes no effort to respond. He just sits there with his chin tucked to his chest, staring at the manual, which appears to be upside down. Kyung isn't used to seeing him this way, so desperate to be ignored. At work, his father is always the center of attention, a position he says he earned over time. Back in the '70s, when Jin first started teaching, his research on renewable energy was easy to ignore, almost even laughable. Now he generates more grant money than anyone else on the faculty, and his patent revenues, a small fraction of which goes to the university, keeps the campus well fed. His success makes him popular in a way that his personality doesn't, and he abuses his colleagues freely, always talking more than he listens.

"Sorry," Lentz says. "I wasn't trying to pry. I just thought you might want to hire a cleaning crew before you go back."

There was no need to share this information in person. All of it could have been done on the phone. Kyung wonders if there's something else he came to say, but can't in front of a woman or a child.

"So that's it?" he asks. "Nothing else?"

"Well, there's a detective assigned to your case now. His name's John Smalley. He was the one who asked me to stop by today."

"Why didn't he come here himself?"

"His wife's been in and out of surgery this week. Blood clots or something. But don't worry. John's good—he's been around a long time. He already got a positive match on that guy I was telling you about. Fingerprints, hair . . ." He glances at Ethan. "You know, that kind of thing. He also sent a statewide bulletin out, so now we're just waiting for Perry to turn up somewhere."

Over a week has passed and this is all the progress he has to report. It hardly seems like enough. Kyung hasn't thought twice about the police—he's been too preoccupied with his parents to think of anyone else—but now it occurs to him that they aren't doing everything they should.

"Are you telling me you're just waiting around for this guy to make a mistake?"

"No, I didn't mean it like that."

"But that's what you said: Now we're waiting for him—"

"I didn't say we're not looking. We're *actively* looking."

"But how do you know he's not in Canada? What good is a statewide bulletin if he's not in the States?"

"Hey," Gillian says, pulling on his sleeve. "Calm down. He's just telling us what they've done so far."

She pulls again, harder this time, but Kyung doesn't care. He can't imagine a world in which Nat Perry is allowed to enjoy his freedom after taking so much of theirs. He wants this man in a prison or a grave. He expects the police to put him there.

"So what does 'actively looking' mean? Where are you actually looking? And how many of you are there?"

Lentz tosses his baseball cap back and forth from one hand to the other, looking nervous or confused—possibly both. He's just the messenger; Kyung understands that. But he has a message of his own that he wants Lentz to carry back.

"That day in the waiting room, when half the department turned up . . . I thought all of you were invested in this, but you're not really doing anything, are you?"

"Cut it out," Gillian says. "Now you're just being unfair."

"How is that unfair? You were standing right there—you heard him."

"There's a process, Kyung. I should know. I grew up with this. They're doing exactly what they're supposed to be doing."

His father is watching Gillian, studying her as she speaks. Her behavior is probably distasteful to him—a wife sharing an opinion that differs from her husband's, contradicting him in front of others. Mae would never dare, having learned long ago that dissent was the fastest route to grief. Neither of his parents really knows Gillian—how stubborn she is, how she doesn't hesitate to speak her mind. Over time, he's come to accept and sometimes even love this about her, but suddenly she's making him nervous. After a week of living together under the same roof, she's abandoned his careful list of dos and don'ts. With no advance warning, no discussion at all, she's letting his father see who she is, who they are as a couple. Kyung doesn't know how to interpret the expression on Jin's face, a queer mix of curiosity and embarrassment, maybe even anger.

"I'm sorry," Gillian says. "My husband's anxious—we all are."

"Why are you apologizing for me?"

"Everyone's a little on edge right now."

"But we're not the ones who should be apologizing. We're the victims." He stops and tries to glide over his mistake. "My parents are the victims. They shouldn't have to live like this, knowing he's still out there somewhere."

Lentz's cheeks flush pink, and he looks at the platter of sandwiches again. Something about this reminds Kyung of the kids he grew up with, the ones whose parents were too poor or neglectful to feed them properly. He was always grateful to Mae for offering them food, for encouraging them so kindly to take it. Kyung, however, regarded them differently afterward, saddened by the glimpse of something shameful about their lives. He realized how little it took to reveal a secret, and what a burden it was on people once they knew.

"If you want a sandwich, then just take one already."

He slides the platter across the island, pushing the slick plastic much harder than he means to. The platter veers off toward the edge of the countertop like a bowling ball headed for the gutter. Kyung sees it all happen in slow motion—the skid, the drop, the crash of the platter against the tile and the startled jump that Lentz takes to avoid the bread and cold cuts strewn at his feet.

"What is the *matter* with you?" Gillian shouts.

Kyung locks eyes with Ethan, whose face registers an early, confused stage of alarm. He can stop it, he thinks. He can stop it if everyone else plays along. He walks to the other side of the island and gets down on his knees, using his hand as a make-shift broom.

"Sorry about that," he says, not looking up.

Lentz gently kicks his foot to the side, discarding a piece of lettuce on his boot. "It's all right. Like your wife said, you're all on edge these days. You have every right to be."

This wasn't what Kyung intended, not at all. He wanted to be assertive in front of his father; he wanted to prove that it was possible to disagree with his wife without feeling the need to beat her into submission. Instead, he's crouching at another man's feet.

"I should probably get going now," Lentz says. "If you folks need anything, if you have any more questions . . ."

Kyung continues scooping handfuls of meat and cheese onto the platter until he realizes that no one is talking; no one is moving at all. He turns and finds Mae standing behind him with a towel draped over her shoulders and a head of dripping wet hair. She's dressed in the powder blue bathrobe that Gillian bought her, a cheap polyester one that zips all the way to the neck.

"What happened?" she asks.

Her face is even paler than usual. The skin hangs loosely from her chin. Mae has always been a petite woman—a hundred pounds wet, at best—but even the billowy, oversized robe can't disguise the fact that she looks thinner than before, almost skeletal.

"What happened?" she repeats.

"Nothing," Gillian says. "I knocked a plate off the counter-top. . . . I'm sorry if I disturbed you."

Kyung can feel Lentz staring at him, but he doesn't contradict what she said. No one does, not even his father. Everyone defaults to the illusion that everything is fine, everything is normal.

"I got out of the shower and heard voices—I thought that was you. Hasn't anyone offered you coffee yet?" She leads Lentz to the table, frowning over her shoulder at Gillian. "Can you get him a cup?"

Coffee was always his mother's way of making people feel welcome. Regardless of who the visitors were or how long they planned to stay, she tried to turn it into something special, breaking out her nice china and cloth napkins and tins of cookies that she stockpiled just for guests. Being a good hostess mattered to her—she said it was a skill that girls didn't learn anymore. Perhaps that's why she looks so upset when Gillian puts a manure-colored mug on the table, a gag gift from an old roommate with the words HOT AND STEAMY written on it.

"You know what, Mrs. Cho? I think I've had enough coffee for the day."

"So how do you take it? Milk or sugar? Or both?"

"Actually, ma'am, I was just leaving."

"No, you sit. Sit."

Lentz is one of them now—confused and bewildered by Mae's sudden appearance, her forceful hospitality. He lowers himself into a chair and nods.

"Just milk, please."

Everyone watches as Gillian adds a slow trickle of milk, clinking a spoon around until the coffee turns to a bland, watered-down shade of beige. Lentz brings the mug to his lips, blowing on it before taking his first sip. No one knows what to say or do next, so they watch this too.

Ethan walks up to Mae, shaking his tasseled handlebars in the air to get her attention. "Thank you for my bike, Grandma. I named him Boomer."

Mae stares at him blankly. Then she scans the parts scattered across the floor until she notices Jin sitting in the corner. She says you're welcome as she looks away, but the words sound more like a dismissal. Kyung spends so much time teaching Ethan his manners. *Please and thank you. May I and yes, ma'am.* Whenever Ethan remembers something without being reminded, Gillian lavishes him with praise. Clearly, he's grown accustomed to this reaction, because he waits for Mae to compliment him. When she doesn't, he lowers his handlebars and retreats to the corner with Jin. If Ethan is hurt by her lack of interest or affection, he doesn't show it, although Kyung feels the familiar sting for them both.

"It was nice of you to come over," she says, sitting down beside Lentz at the table. "Do you have any news about my house?"

"Yes, ma'am. You and your husband are free to go back whenever you're ready."

"Good, then. I want to go back today."

Everyone looks at her. Even Lentz seems surprised.

"But we have you all set up here," Gillian says.

"No, not to stay. I just want to start cleaning."

Jin clears his throat. "Maybe it's a little too soon for that."

"You don't have to come with me," she says. Her tone is sharp, sharper than she usually takes with him. "I'm tired of lying around."

"The department has a list of numbers, Mrs. Cho. Professional cleaners, I mean. It's going to be a lot of work for one person."

"No, that's fine. I'd rather do it myself."

Kyung thinks this is a terrible idea, possibly weeks or even months premature. Although he's relieved to see Mae out of bed and determined to do something—anything—he doesn't understand why she wants to clean her house. He worries that she hasn't thought through how it might feel to return, to revisit the rooms where things happened. He doesn't want her to go there alone.

"If you're sure you want to do this today, I'll drive you," he says. "I can help too."

Mae seems irritated by his offer, but they both know she has no choice. Her ankle is still too bruised to attempt the long walk again, and she never learned how to drive.

She turns to Lentz and smiles at him almost sweetly. "Why don't you let me make you some lunch before you go?"

"Lunch?" Lentz seems terrified by this. "Oh, no. You don't have to do that."

"But you must be hungry."

He's about to decline again, but Mae is already on her feet. She hobbles past Gillian and scans the ingredients spread out on the counter, frowning at the disarray. Then she takes over the kitchen like it's her own, opening drawers until she finds a knife to spread the mustard with, opening the refrigerator to search for another head of lettuce. Occasionally, she asks Lentz a question—Ham or turkey? Cheddar or Swiss?—but not once does she ask why he really came to visit, what news he has to report about the case. Kyung feels like he's watching her have a nervous breakdown. The others seem to think the same. Gillian nudges him in the ribs. He looks at her, not sure what she expects him to say.

"So maybe . . . ," he guesses, "maybe you should have something to eat too?"

"I'm not hungry."

Mae is searching through a tall cabinet. When she reaches up to grab a box of plastic wrap, the sleeve of her robe falls, revealing a forearm that looks like a branch, ready to snap in half. Gillian has been leaving trays of food outside her door—breakfast, lunch, and dinner—but all the plates keep coming back untouched. As he stares at Mae's wrist, it occurs to him that maybe she wasn't eating at the hospital either.

"There's a lot of work to do at the other house," he says gently. "It's probably a good idea if you eat something before we go, even something small."

"Listen to the boy," Jin says. "Eat something."

It's been years since his father referred to him as "boy." Instantly, he dislikes it, but his annoyance is quickly eclipsed by Mae's reply.

"Can't you hear?" she shouts. "I—don't—want—to." Her tone is so cold, the expression on her face so withering; every carefully enunciated word hangs in the air, suspended in ice. Kyung can't remember a time—not once in thirty-six years—when Mae talked back to Jin, much less raised her voice at him. The old Mae would never dare. His parents continue staring at each other, staring right through each other until their silence begins to feel dangerous. Kyung can't believe that his father is the first to look away.

Mae sets a plate down in front of Lentz. "Here you go," she says, her voice now quiet and composed.

The overstuffed sandwich has been hermetically sealed in plastic wrap. Beside it are a pickle, a handful of potato chips, and three miniature candy bars. On top of the plate is another tight layer of plastic, which keeps everything in place—the sandwich at noon, the pickle at three, the chips and candy at six and nine, a red plaid napkin underneath.

Lentz doesn't know what to make of this arrangement. It's probably more than he expected, and clearly more bizarre. Kyung is accustomed to Mae overdoing things—the plate resembles the lunches she used to pack for him in grade school until he begged her to stop—but seeing a stranger react to her domestic excess is embarrassing. It looks crazy because it is.

"Oh, well . . . Thank you. I didn't mean for you to go to so much trouble."

"It wasn't any trouble. I was happy to."

Mae volunteers to walk Lentz out. Kyung follows close behind, listening to their conversation. In the doorway, they shake hands, and Mae pats Lentz on the shoulder over and over again like a puppy or a child. Thank you, she says. Thank you, thank you, thank you. Lentz seems embarrassed by her gratitude, aware on some level that he hasn't done anything to earn it. As he walks to his car, he stares at his neatly arranged plate of food as if its contents might be tainted.

Kyung shuts the door as soon as he drives off. "What was all that about?" he asks.

"What do you mean?"

"Why were you thanking him like that?"

"I didn't think I'd be able to go back to my house for weeks."

"I'm talking about the"—he hesitates to use the word—"investigation," which might remind her of the events that need investigating. "I'm not talking about the house."

"Well, I like him."

"I can tell, but what does liking him have to do with anything?"

Mae turns toward the stairs, using the banister to pull herself up a step at a time. "He was nice to me that day . . ."

She leaves the sentence unfinished, but Kyung feels the unspoken like a blow to the chest. *He was nice to me that day—not like you.*

Kyung and his parents immigrated to the States when he was four. Jin had just finished his Ph.D., graduating with honors at the top of his class. His tenure-track job offer from an American research university made him the pride and envy of his classmates, who threw him a going-away party that seemed lavish for the times. Kyung still remembers the cake, a tall white one that tilted off to the side, and a gift of three new suitcases, all in matching green plaid. Life seemed very big to him back then. A big party, a big trip, a big plane taking them away, carrying their plaid suitcases in its underbelly.

Neither Kyung nor Mae spoke any English when they arrived in the States, so they relied on Jin to translate everything they didn't understand. One day, the elderly Russian woman in the apartment next door gave them a flyer for a free ESL class at the library. Good for wife and boy, she explained. At first, Kyung didn't mind being in the same class as his mother. They always went to the library early, weaving their serpentine trail through the shelves and imagining out loud what it would be like to read so many books. She was hopeful then; they both were, but their enthusiasm soon faded when it became obvious that Kyung was learning faster than she was. Jin berated her for this, shouting when she couldn't remember the words for things like "breakfast" or "laundry" and telling her he regretted marrying someone so dumb. Every night, Jin quizzed them at dinner, pounding his fist on the table if one of them—usually Mae—answered incorrectly. The look on her face when he screamed at her—such a helpless, terrified expression—this is what Kyung tries to remember whenever she needs a ride. He forces himself to, if only to stifle his annoyance that she never learned to drive, never learned how to do much of anything.

As he turns into the Heights, he glances at Mae, who's sitting quietly in the passenger seat with her hands folded in her lap. She didn't seem the least bit interested in conversation when they got in the car, but now he realizes she's been watching him, studying him the entire time.

"Is something wrong? Am I driving too fast?"

She shakes her head. "It's stupid."

"What is?"

"I can never go anywhere by myself."

Kyung understands that his mother wants to be alone, to lock herself inside her house just as she did in his. She has no idea how difficult it's going to be to return. Even he feels uneasy about crossing the threshold again.

"I'll stay out of your way. Just tell me what to do."

Mae looks out the window, leaning her head against the

glass, but barely a minute passes and he can feel her watching him again.

"Why do you keep doing that?" he asks.

"I'm just curious."

"About driving? I've offered to teach you. I still can, if you want."

"It's too late."

"No, it's not. I bet you'd learn really—"

She shoos him off, irritated.

It's sad that she thinks this way, but this has always been her problem. She never believed she was capable of anything. Jin made sure of that early on. Now isn't the time to convince her otherwise. She'll accuse him of not wanting to drive her around, which was always his motive for offering to teach her in the past.

Kyung slows down as he approaches the house, spooked by its eerie calm, even in broad daylight. The neighbors and reporters who filled the sidewalks the last time he drove by have all dispersed. But a scrap of forgotten yellow tape flutters from the front door, and the curtains are still drawn.

He parks in the driveway and turns to her, lowering his voice as if the house can overhear them. "You really don't have to do this right now. We can go back home if you've changed your mind."

Mae takes his cell phone from the dashboard and gets out of the car, slamming her door shut. He assumes she heard him, but she clearly doesn't care. She's too busy punching a number into his phone, squinting at the tiny buttons on the keypad. Kyung shakes his head, aware that they're falling back into the same old pattern again, the one in which he pities her and tries to help, and she treats him badly because she hates herself for needing him. It's impossible to be near someone like this, someone who brings out the best and worst in him, who punishes his attempts to be kind. Gillian says that rudeness is a weak person's idea of strength, a line she probably read on a bumper sticker or a box of tea. If she were here, she'd encourage him to try to be nice, even if Mae doesn't deserve it, even if trying makes him feel like the child he used to be, always pushed away for offering his mother a hug.

By the time he gets out of the car, Mae is talking to the landscaping company, asking someone to send a crew over to cut the grass and tend to the flower beds, which are lightly scattered with dead petals and leaves. There's also an issue with the trees, she says. One of the Japanese maples needs its branches trimmed. *Tomorrow?* he assumes the person on the phone asks, because Mae fires back: "No, it has to be done today." Then she adds, *"¿Rápido, comprende?"* and he's not sure what surprises him more—the fact that she knows some Spanish, or the sharpness of her replies. Not once during the conversation does Mae say the words "please" or "would you" or "could you." She just sounds curt and entitled, oblivious to the fact that it's a Sunday, a day when most people—even her gardeners—have other plans. Kyung doesn't see the problem as clearly as she does. The landscaping appears slightly less perfect than usual, but the Japanese maple that supposedly needs trimming looks no different from its twin on the left, and the grass is still short and even from the last time it was mowed. When Mae gets off the phone, she surveys the rest of the house, shading her eyes from the sun.

"Do you think it's necessary to have that work done now?" he asks.

"That's what I pay them for."

"But is it really necessary for them to come today—of all days?"

"This house is my business," she snaps. "You just mind your own."

Their arguments always begin like this. He gets angry with her for getting angry with him, and suddenly both of them are being equally awful to each other. This time, he resolves not to take the bait. The only way his brain can cope with what happened to Mae is to find a more peaceful way of being with her, to manufacture a silver lining even if he runs the risk of suffocating in it. He follows her up the lawn silently, trying not to notice the same things he saw the week before. Instead of the bank of drawn curtains, he stares at the pattern of the flagstone path. Instead of the flowerpot filled with marigolds, he studies the wrought-iron hummingbird feeder hanging from its post. When he unlocks the door and pushes it open, he braces himself for her reaction, but Mae doesn't even stop, much less react. She just speeds past the damage as if she doesn't notice it, stepping awkwardly over the broken furniture and toppled plants. There's something not quite right about this, something almost frightening about the way she disappears into the kitchen and returns with a fistful of garbage bags.

"Take these," she says. "You can start in here."

"Doing what?"

She waves her hand at the floor without looking at it. "Sweep up. But put any valuables you find on the dining table so I can go through them."

Kyung catches her wrist, holding the birdlike bones in his fingers. "You're sure about this? You don't want to—talk or something?"

Mae shakes herself free. "No, I just want to know what I lost."

She leaves him in the entryway, uncertain if he should follow or simply do as he was told. He's tempted to remind her that what she lost amounts to more than just things, but the longer he stands there, the more it makes sense. Her greatest source of pride, her greatest source of security in life was this house and all of its contents. Caring for them was the only thing she did that his father ever praised. Maybe putting it all back in order will help her feel normal again, whatever normal means now.

Kyung finds a broom in the hall closet and starts on the floor, sweeping potting soil and bits of broken glass into piles that look like glittering anthills. He takes several slow passes over the entryway, but despite emptying his dustpan twice, everything still seems dirty. Even the air feels thick with dust that makes it hard for him to breathe. He distracts himself by studying the debris collecting under the yellow bristles of his broom. In the entryway, it's mostly dirt and glass. In the living room, it's mostly paper—loose pages from *Treasure Island, Robinson Crusoe, The Call of the Wild,* all ripped from their spines. It bothers him to see so many books he loved as a child, plucked off the shelves and destroyed for no good reason. He always imagined giving them to Ethan one day. The books, the furniture, the valuables. Everything, actually.

At thirty-six, Kyung is beginning to accept the possibility that his fortunes will never change. It bewilders him, though, how he followed his father's example, but produced such different results. From an early age, he was led to believe that if he studied hard and worked even harder, he'd eventually be rewarded for his efforts. If an immigrant could come to this country and make something of himself, his son would surely continue that line of progress, multiplying the gains of one generation for the next. Kyung, however, hasn't moved the line forward so much as back. Other than his debts, he wonders what, if anything, he'll have in his own name to leave behind. The best he might be able to do for Ethan is pass on what he inherits from his parents, a thought that makes him feel oddly proprietary, as if the damage in the room were somehow done to him. It's only now that he realizes what good work Mae did, curating the house in such a way that nothing ever seemed out of place until it all suddenly was.

When he finishes sweeping the living room, he moves on to the hallway, which is littered with broken picture frames and glass, hundreds of splinters and shards scattered everywhere. In between, he finds knickknacks of the half-broken or lost variety. A porcelain bird's head, but no body. Jagged pieces of a china plate that appear to have no match. Torn photos too damaged to piece together again. He picks up a handful of scraps and examines them, but can't figure out who the disembodied eyes and ears and mouths belong to. The photos seem like junk now, things to be swept away with his broom, but he wonders if Mae would disagree. He imagines her spreading out the pieces, using tweezers and glue to reassemble them like some elaborate jigsaw puzzle. Such a waste of time, but what else does she have? He walks into the dining room and finds her sitting at the enormous twelve-person table, most of which is covered with collectibles and figurines. She's been making a list of everything on a legal pad, writing out what each item is, what it looks like, and who made it. He looks over her shoulder and follows her delicate, curlicued script down the left side of the page—*Limoges, Tiffany, Baccarat, Steuben*.

"What's all this for?"

"Insurance claim," she says, not looking up from her work.

He picks up a small crystal bowl that's much heavier than it appears and carefully sets it back down. "But don't they just need a list of everything that has to be replaced?"

"I can't tell them what's missing until I figure out what I still have."

"Oh."

Mae's tastes are expensive; they always have been. Perhaps the only good thing about being married to Jin all these years was that he could afford her. Their settlement is sure to be considerable. Between the art and everything else, Kyung would venture to guess a hundred, a hundred and fifty thousand at least. It's strange to think that the money his parents will recoup from their losses alone would change his life for the better—not fix it entirely, but enough.

"What about the photos and broken stuff? What should I do with all of it?"

"Put the valuables somewhere out of the way so I can look at them," she says. "The photos I don't need anymore."

He didn't expect her to dismiss the pictures so quickly. Many of them are sixty or seventy years old—vintage sepia-toned originals of relatives who passed away long before he was born. It's sensible of her to let them go. Sensible, but still surprising.

"I'm done with the living room now. Do you want me to start on the second floor?"

"No." She pauses. "That can wait until later."

He's grateful for this response. He isn't ready to see the master bedroom yet; he'd prefer never to set foot in that room again. He waits for Mae to give him another task. When she doesn't, he makes up his own, sweeping some broken glass beside the china cabinet.

"Can you not do that here?" she asks.

"What would you like me to do instead?"

"I don't care. Just do it somewhere else."

Kyung clenches the broom handle and walks away, digging his fingernails into his palm. When he returns to the living room, he stops in front of the window, startled by the sound of footsteps and a man's hushed whisper outside. He pushes back a corner of the curtain and sees two shadows cast long and diagonal against the porch. He runs to the entryway and lifts the broom like a bat, lowering his voice to a menacing baritone.

"Who is it?" he shouts. "What do you want?"

The person on the other side of the door knocks timidly— three quick raps followed by a meek "Hello?" He puts the broom down, embarrassed to realize that the landscapers have arrived, but when he opens the door to greet them, he finds his parents' elderly neighbors standing on the porch instead. Mrs. Steiner is holding a large glass tray covered with tinfoil.

"Lasagna," she says abruptly, thrusting the tray at Kyung's chest. "It needs an hour at 425."

"Oh . . . well, thank you." He doesn't know what to do next—leave it at that and send them away, or invite them in.

"How are your parents?" Mr. Steiner asks, peering inside.

Kyung remembers them from the news, shaking their heads and mumbling about what a good neighborhood they lived in, how people were supposed to be safe in the Heights. He wishes they hadn't spoken to a reporter, but he can't blame them for what they said. It was exactly what everyone else in town was already thinking. The Steiners own the biggest house on the street, a massive Victorian painted in various shades of purple, which would be hideous if not for the fact that it was done very well. He's not sure if Mr. Steiner is retired now or still runs his chain of sporting goods stores, but judging from the giant canary-colored diamond on his wife's finger, it hardly matters.

"My parents are doing better, thank you. They're staying with me for a while. My mother and I just dropped by to do a little cleaning. . . ."

The Steiners are no longer listening to him. Their attention has drifted over his shoulder to Mae, who's fixing her hair as she joins them in the entryway.

"Carol, Mort, hello. Why don't you come in?"

She sounds remarkably, unnaturally cheerful again, the same way she did with Lentz. He doesn't know why she feels the need to do this now. She can't possibly think anyone expects it of her.

The Steiners take a few steps inside, but both of them are tentative, as if the air just beyond the threshold is toxic. Carol's milky blue eyes wander over the broken pieces of furniture and trash bags propped up in the corner. She looks frightened. Kyung thinks it's lucky she didn't arrive a few hours earlier.

"We noticed a car in the driveway, so we thought we'd stop by," Mort says.

"And I made you a lasagna."

Mae takes Carol by the arm and leads her into the living room. "Thank you so much. Do you want to sit down and have some coffee? It's—it's messy in here. I'm sorry about that."

The difference in her tone is noticeable, so much kinder than the way she spoke to Kyung only minutes before.

"Here." She flips over a badly stained sofa cushion. "Why don't you sit down?"

"No, no. Don't go to any trouble, Mae. Carol and I just wanted to drop off some food. We'll let you get back to your work now."

"Oh, wait. Don't go just yet. I actually have something for you."

Mae disappears into the kitchen again, leaving the three of them looking at each other awkwardly. Kyung has no idea what to say. His parents and the Steiners have lived next door to each other for years, but he's never spoken to them before. What little he's seen or heard about them seems quaint and old-fashioned, as if they're stuck in a different era. Unlike his neighbors, who wave in passing and quickly move on, the Steiners drop by with flowers and vegetables from their garden. They stop to have long, extended conversations over the fence.

"So you and your family live down the hill?" Mort asks.

Kyung nods.

"There's some nice real estate down there these days."

He nods again. Normally, Mort's comment would bother him. People in the Heights never hesitate to point out the difference between living on the hill and below it. But he's too distracted by Carol to reply. She's wringing a pot holder, twisting the fabric tighter and tighter until her knuckles begin to turn white. She strikes him as a fragile sort of woman—rail thin and small, as pale as the double strand of pearls around her neck. He can't imagine what kind of bubble she lived in next door, or how it feels now that she's out.

"Here you go." Mae returns with an oversized silver fork. She hands it to Carol, who stares at it wide eyed, running her thin fingers over the elaborately forged handle.

"Where in the world did you find this?"

"I called about twenty different antique stores. I got this from a dealer in Springfield. It's the right pattern, isn't it? The Durgin Regent?"

"It is, it is. You remember this, Mortie? This is part of the serving set we got from your mother for our wedding. It's the fork we lost when we moved."

Mort puts on his glasses and studies the handle, which has an oval crest surrounded by an ornate floral trim. "That's it, best as I can tell." He seems vaguely interested, but uncomfortable focusing so much attention on a piece of silverware. "Thank you for finding it for us, Mae. That was very thoughtful of you." He rests his hand on his wife's shoulder, aware that she's starting to cry. "It's okay, Carol. Jesus, what are you doing that for? It's just a fork."

Carol hangs her head. Her shoulders begin to shake, small tremors that quickly turn into seismic ones. There's nothing worse than seeing a woman her age cry, Kyung thinks. He puts down the lasagna so he can get her a tissue, but she starts blotting her face with a pot holder instead.

"I'm sorry. You're just so nice. I can't stop thinking about what happened to you. Those men, they were monsters. . . . We keep hearing about them on TV."

She's crying too hard to notice Kyung clearing his throat, desperate to send her a signal to stop. The news never referred to his parents by name, but anyone who recognized the house filmed in the background knew what happened to the people who lived inside. Every time Kyung turns on the news or opens the paper, it's the same story, the same onslaught of reminders that he doesn't want his parents to hear or see. How mortified they'd be to realize their shame was so public.

"Our sons are always telling us not to keep so much cash in the house, but we just assumed we were safe here. Shows you what we know." Carol continues to weep. "Nobody's safe anywhere these days."

Mort flinches. "Okay, sweetheart. Time to go. We've bothered these folks long enough." He steers his wife toward the door. "I'm sorry about this," he says to Mae. "I'm so sorry about everything."

She smiles at him but says nothing as the Steiners walk down the steps and cut across the lawn toward their house. When they slip out of view, she shuts the door and sighs.

"Are you all right?" Kyung asks.

"I really thought Carol would be happier about that serving piece. It took me such a long time to find it."

"That's what you're upset about? A fork?"

She looks at him curiously. "I worked really hard to get that for her."

"But it's just a fork."

The expression on Mae's face could be the beginning of anything—anger, sadness, frustration. It has no shape yet, no hard edges or creased lines, as if she's still trying to decide what to be.

"I'm sorry. I didn't mean to say it that way. But you don't need to keep pretending like everything's the same as it was before. We all know it's going to be difficult for a while."

She continues staring at him, almost the same way she stared at Jin in the kitchen. Kyung understands now why his father was the first to blink. It's her eyes—the emptiness of them, like no light will ever break their surface again. As he turns away, Kyung feels the pain before he sees the source of it—Mae's hand, slapping him hard and fast across the cheek. The shock sends him back decades to his childhood home, to a room much like this one, with this miserable woman who was supposed to love him but barely even seemed to like him. He takes a step backward, supporting himself on the banister, waiting for the next hit to come. But Mae just stands there, her expression dissolving into something he doesn't understand.

"What do *you* know?" she shouts. "When have you ever wanted to know anything?"

She picks up the lasagna and walks away, kicking the kitchen door open. As soon as it swings shut, he hears a crash against the wall—not the accidental kind that would send him running to help—but something more intentional, something thrust or thrown with force. He imagines the lasagna pooling on the floor, covered with shards of broken glass, but he doesn't dare take a step in Mae's direction. His hands, he realizes, are balled into fists.

The car is silent during the ride home. Kyung replays the slap over and over again, his blood pressure spiking each time Mae's hand makes contact with his cheek. At first, his impulse is to shout at her, to make her regret what she did, but when he looks at Mae, the anger slowly begins to spiral down his throat. She's sitting in the passenger seat—forehead in her hands, elbows on her knees—gently rocking herself back and forth. She seems wounded, as if she feels more pain than she just inflicted.

"That can't happen again," he says, his voice quiet but firm.

Not once have they talked about the way she used to treat him. Avoidance was always the price of their détente. But now he worries that he dismissed Gillian's concerns too quickly, and whatever faith or confidence he had in Mae, she's just lost.

"If you ever put a hand on Ethan, if you ever scare him or hurt him in any way, I can't—I won't let you do that."

She rocks herself harder.

They drive through several lights without speaking, although Kyung keeps thinking that they should. If there was ever a time to have this conversation, to revisit the source of their resentments, now seems right. Now seems like their last best chance. He can't, however, bring himself to start. He knows why she stopped hitting him so many years ago, even though the subject has never been discussed. When he entered his teens, he was big enough to hit back. The thought of this makes his chest tighten, hardening the air in his lungs. He would never. But he allowed her to think so because the threat of violence was the only thing that protected him from harm.

As he turns onto his street, he swerves to avoid a car parked too close to the corner. Mae sits up, startled by the screech of his tires. Dozens of cars are parked along the curb, end to end down the length of the block. Kyung's neighborhood is full of families, young ones not much bigger than his own. Aside from the occasional garage sale or birthday party, crowds like this are rare. He wonders if a neighbor is hosting a barbecue that he and Gillian weren't invited to, but the slower he drives, the more he notices the bumper stickers with the telltale logo, and then there's the familiar red Buick in front of his house.

"No," Mae says, tapping her window. "No, no." She grabs

her door handle as if she wants to jump out. "I knew they'd do something like this."

"Why are they all here?"

"I think they came to see me."

He doesn't need to ask who she means by "they." It's Sunday, a day they own. When he woke up that morning, he assumed his father would ask for a ride to church, but the hours kept ticking away, and Jin never mentioned it.

"Should I keep going?"

"No," she sighs. "Just park."

Kyung pulls in behind the Buick, which has a shiny Jesus fish attached to its bumper. Beside it, there's a sticker that reads PEACE, scrawled in childlike cursive letters. He turns to Mae, who's examining herself in the mirror, pinching her cheeks to bring out their color. Her face is smooth but tense—the upper jaw locked tightly against the lower.

"Do you even want to see these people right now?"

"What does it matter? I'll have to see them eventually."

"But if you're not ready—"

Mae snaps the visor back into place. "Please," she says quietly. "Please don't make this any worse."

Reverend Sung is the first to greet them when they open the front door. A kiss on both cheeks for Mae and a stiff handshake for Kyung, followed by something he can't hear above the crowd.

"What did you say?" Kyung asks.

"Your parents couldn't join us at church today," he repeats. "So we brought church here."

The reverend makes it sound like he's doing them a favor, and Mae responds with a grateful nod of her head, but Kyung can't stand the sight of so many strangers milling through his house. It feels like they've been invaded.

"Where's my wife?"

The reverend cups his hand to his ear. "What?"

"My wife?"

"In the kitchen, I think."

He leaves Mae with the reverend and squeezes through the hallway, occasionally throwing his elbows to separate the bodies pressing in around him. He finds Gillian in the dining room, standing in a corner with her arms crossed over her chest. The room is overrun by women, all jabbering away at each other as they organize the meal. The table is covered with huge trays of Korean food, surrounded by neat little containers of paper plates and plastic utensils, bottles of soda, and stacks of napkins embossed with the church's logo. The women take no notice of Gillian as they go about their work, setting up a buffet line that would rival any restaurant's.

Kyung leans down to whisper in her ear. "Why didn't you call me?"

"I did. I've been calling for over an hour."

Kyung pats down his empty pockets. The last time he saw his phone, his mother was using it. "How long have they been here?"

"Since four, I guess. Did you know this was happening?"

"No, of course not." He looks around and lowers his voice. "I would have told them not to come."

"Actually, they've all been very nice. Did you see how much food they brought?"

"Who cares about the food? The point is, *that man*"—he's too frustrated to say the reverend's name out loud—"that man didn't even tell me they were planning this. He should have asked first."

Gillian just shrugs. She doesn't understand the way these people are—all smiles and politeness one minute, then vicious and judgmental the next. He's known this about them ever since they entered his parents' lives, felt it in their stares and questions and awkward attempts at conversation. They think he's a lesser person because he refuses to believe as they do. And Gillian—lapsed Catholic that she is—she matters even less, but she can't see through their act.

"Where's Ethan?"

"He's with your father in the living room."

"Doing what?"

"I think he's just playing—"

He leaves her midsentence, sidestepping past the women to rescue Ethan, certain that he's trapped by a gaggle of old ladies who keep asking if he accepts Christ as his savior. Kyung's first memory of them is exactly this. A crowd of pinched faces and perfumed hands, all pestering him about things he didn't understand, words he didn't even know. He's not about to let a stranger click her tongue at Ethan and tell him that hell is for bad children who don't believe.

The living room has been repurposed into a makeshift receiving area, with a long line that extends deep into the hallway. Jin is sitting in an armchair with Ethan on his knee, while Mae is sitting in the chair beside him. The small sofa and love seat are occupied by the very elderly, so the rest have taken to the floor, sitting compactly on their heels or with their legs tucked off to the side. His parents look like a king and queen, surrounded by their court, while a line of visitors slowly moves past to pay their respects. Jin greets them all with the same handshake and hello, but Mae does her best to make conversation, accepting their hugs and kisses with gratitude. Kyung wishes he could hear what people are saying to her and what she's saying so pleasantly in response, but it's too hard to make out anything above the din. Occasionally, someone passes through the line and pats Ethan on the head, but no one seems the least bit interested in him, and he only seems interested in his puzzle.

The reverend wades into the middle of the room and claps his hands in the air. "Attention, please. The ladies tell me they're almost ready, so it's time to give thanks."

Everyone reaches for the two people sitting nearest them. Ethan looks around; he seems confused by the sight of so many strangers holding hands. Kyung doesn't want him subjected to this, but one step forward, and he sees something that forces him to stop. At first, his parents take each other's hands like everyone else, but as soon as the congregation lowers their heads in prayer, Mae lets go with a violent flick of her wrist. She blames him, he thinks. That's why they've barely spoken ten words to each other since she came home, why she won't let him sleep in the same room with her. Kyung almost feels sorry for his father. Nat and Dell Perry were twice his size and half his age. There was nothing Jin could have done to prevent what happened to her. He assumes Mae will understand this eventually, but he doesn't want to rush her to that conclusion. She needs to get there on her own.

After the prayer, the reverend's wife, Molly, walks into the room and asks everyone to form a line for dinner. The crowd surges toward the buffet as she presents two full plates to Jin and Mae and bows deeply from the waist. Kyung looks for Gillian, who's nowhere to be found. This is why he always has to remind her how to behave around his parents. She says she knows what to do, and can recite the list as proof, but deference doesn't come naturally to her. Molly removes two napkins from the pocket of her skirt and spreads them across Mae's and Jin's laps. Then she bows again and backs away.

Kyung always feels nervous when he runs into Molly, whom he's known since junior high. She went by Mi Young back then, and he remembers her as not terribly pretty or smart, but loud and destructive and loose. Among certain types of boys, this latter quality seemed to make up for most of her failings. By the time they started high school, she'd earned an unfortunate nickname for herself. "The Car Wash." Whenever fifth period approached, Kyung could overhear boys clad in letterman jackets discuss the impending lunch hour: "So who's going through the Car Wash today?" During their senior year, Molly's parents caught her in bed with a boy and shipped her off to a private Christian college after graduation. Through friends of friends, Kyung heard that she tried to run away on more than one occasion, so it surprised him when she returned home four years later, born-again and perfect wife material for a young reverend. All of this happened so long ago, but Kyung can't help comparing the awkward, trampy-looking girl he remembers with the plain but pretty woman she is now.

"Hello, Kyung." Molly takes both of his hands in hers. "How are you?"

He wonders if she noticed him staring, although it wouldn't be the first time if she did. Molly, he assumes, is well aware that he admires her, and some part of her secretly enjoys it.

"All right, I guess."

"I hope you don't mind that I organized this."

"You?"

"Yes, my husband said it might be too soon, but I thought your wife—I thought she might enjoy a night off from cooking."

She glances at Jin, who's leaning over his plate, shoveling food into his mouth without coming up for air. Kyung assumed he'd been picking at his meals all week because he wasn't hungry, but he realizes that Jin probably didn't like Gillian's cooking. The blood rushes to his cheeks as he watches his father eat like some kind of wild animal. Slow down, he thinks. People will wonder if he and Gillian have been feeding him at all.

"I haven't seen your son in a while. He's getting so big," Molly says. "I bet he'll want a little brother or sister soon."

She adds this wistfully, making no attempt to conceal what his parents have speculated about for years—that Molly and the reverend can't have children of their own. Kyung assumes they're right. People like the Sungs are all about God and family. They don't wait to get pregnant. For them, there's no good or bad time. He wonders what Molly would say if he told her he doesn't want a second child, that there are days when having one seems like the hardest thing he'll ever do.

"Ethan hasn't said anything about siblings yet. A dog, maybe."

Molly begins to laugh, but quickly cups a hand over her mouth. "I'm so sorry."

"For laughing?"

"Now's not the time for it."

"Better to laugh than cry, right?"

He's playing a part for her, badly, and the awkwardness of

his attempt makes him overheat. He can feel the beads of sweat collecting above his lip, suspended in stubble that he wishes he'd shaved.

"Some of the ladies have offered to stop by and bring you food, or help around the house. Your wife shouldn't have to take care of so many people on her own."

She doesn't, he thinks. That's what's so odd about the people from his parents' church, especially the ones his own age. Most of them grew up in the States or came here from Korea when they were young. But the way they behave around each other— it's as if they never left. The women are all subservient to their husbands and fathers and in-laws, which always seems so sad to him. Everywhere he looks, a woman is serving a plate of food to someone else. The daughters-in-law are the easiest to spot, the way they seem so eager to please. Kyung has been attracted to Korean girls before, but he never wanted to marry one, not even Molly. He didn't want to subject someone he loved, or even vaguely liked, to the life of a foot servant like his mother. A few times a year, Gillian plays the part to keep his parents content, but a Korean wife would never be able to pick and choose when to be Korean.

The reverend returns from the kitchen and threads his arm around Molly's thin waist. "Would you like my wife to make you a plate?"

He shakes his head. The reverend seems to understand, just as Molly does, that Kyung finds her attractive. On the rare occasions when they see each other, the reverend always inserts himself into their conversations, laying his hands on her in a gentle, chaste way that signals his ownership. Molly appears unfazed by it, but Kyung can't stand to look at the mismatch of them. Despite the plainness of their clothes and the diamond-crusted crucifixes they wear—a pendant for her and a lapel pin for him—he still remembers the person she used to be. Sometimes he daydreams about converting her back to her former state, if only for an afternoon.

"I promise we won't stay long," the reverend says. "We just wanted to give everyone a chance to see your parents and get something to eat. Then we'll be out of the way."

"And the ladies and I will leave your house exactly as we found it."

Every female in the church, young and old alike, is referred to as one of "the ladies." Mae talks about them often, how the ladies are hosting a flower show, or the ladies are having a prayer meeting. Kyung has never seen a group of women spend so much time together and yet know so little about each other. He doesn't like the idea of the ladies cleaning up his house, but there's no use trying to resist.

"Excuse me." He glances over at Ethan, who seems perfectly happy where he is. "I need to get some air."

"Are you sure I can't make you a plate?" Molly asks.

The reverend is about to encourage Kyung to stay and eat, but he seems to think better of it. "Let him go, Molly. We've bothered him long enough."

In the backyard, Kyung drags a folding lawn chair under a tall window, hopeful that no one will notice him sitting outside. He leans his head against the hot metal frame and looks for the sun, which is almost hidden behind the house. The angle of it in the sky suggests that it's only five or six, leaving so many hours before he can climb into bed and not be obligated to anyone. A gust of wind sweeps through the trees, scattering dead leaves and dried-out blossoms through the grass. He can't remember the last time he raked or weeded, and it shows. The layer of mulch covering the flower beds is thin in some places and completely bare in others. Weeds are sprouting their green and yellow heads through every crevice, choking out the perennials that should be blooming by now.

Gillian rounds the corner, carrying a plate piled high with food. "I've been looking for you. I figured you were hiding somewhere." She sits cross-legged on a shady patch of grass and kicks off her sandals, revealing the undersides of her feet, which are gray with dirt. "You ran away before I could ask how it went at the house. Was your mom okay there?"

He doesn't consider telling her about the slap, not for a second. She'd never let Mae near Ethan again. "She was all business, actually. She just wanted to clean up and figure out what to send the insurance company."

"If that's what she wants to do right now, I guess you should probably let her." She offers him a dumpling from her plate, which he declines.

"The hospital called while you were gone. They're releasing Marina this week. You remember what we agreed to, right?" She leans her face toward his, searching for a reaction, but he's too tired to have the same argument twice.

"Yes, I remember."

The wind picks up again, pushing the clothesline around in a creaky circle. Two car doors slam shut in front of the house, one after another, but Kyung can't tell if the occupants are coming or going.

"You want to sit in this chair?" he asks.

"No, I'm fine here."

She stretches her legs out on the dandelion-covered grass, a shady patch where they once planned to build a deck. Gillian had never lived anywhere with a deck before, and he liked the thought of sitting outside with her after dinner, staring at the sun disappearing just beyond the green wall of trees. It was the ideal, idyllic image of what their marriage was going to be, but that image seems so dusty now, like an old photograph that neither of them has looked at in a while.

"So, Kyung"—she hesitates—"that thing with Lentz and the sandwiches today—that was really disturbing."

"I'm sorry. I wasn't trying to—"

"There's a lot we haven't been talking about. We probably should at some point."

"Like what?"

"Like how you're feeling about all of this."

Kyung shrugs, staring at the field of wildflowers and grass. He hasn't set foot in the backyard since the day Mae turned up, which seems like another lifetime ago.

"I'm fine."

"You know that's not really an answer, don't you? 'Good,' 'fine,' 'okay'—they're just words, not feelings. I'm asking you how you *feel*."

Gillian's response seems practiced, as if she's been waiting to have this conversation for a while. This isn't the way they usually talk to each other, and he resents the expectation of change at a time when everything has already changed enough. Kyung has no idea what he's feeling because it's never the same from one minute to the next. He's angry with his parents and sad for them. He hopes they'll get through this for their sake and worries for himself that they won't. He knows Mae deserves his pity now more than ever, but he's tired of handicapping her, giving her so many excuses for being a bad mother. Everything he feels seems so contrary or conflicting, it all cancels each other out.

"You're not licensed yet, Gillian."

"What's that supposed to mean?"

"It means I don't want to be treated like your patient."

Another set of car doors slams shut, but this time, Kyung distinctly hears voices approaching his house, not leaving it.

"That's not what I'm trying to do. I'm just worried. And I'm sorry to say this, but I think I have a right to wonder what you're not telling me." She shoos a mosquito hovering too close to her face. "Besides, it's not such a hard question."

"If it's so easy, then you answer it. How do *you* feel right now?"

Gillian puts her plate on the ground, pausing as she hugs her knees to her chest. "I feel guilty, Kyung."

"What do you have to feel guilty about?"

"It's actually been kind of nice having your dad around. It's almost as if we have a nanny now, the way he's always looking out for Ethan. You know they finished the bike this afternoon while you and your mom were cleaning? And I've gotten so much reading done since he's been here." She stretches out her hand, showing off freshly polished nails, done up in a glittery shade of peach. "This probably sounds stupid, but how long has it been since I had time to give myself a manicure? Or didn't have to worry about bouncing a check?" She shakes her head. "I don't know. All this time we've been together, you had me thinking your dad was such a terrible person, and I'm not saying he wasn't when you were little, but I wonder if he's trying to make up for it in some way."

He's glad, for her sake, that Jin's presence hasn't been the nightmare he assumed it would be. But he bristles at the thought of what Gillian might be saying, that Jin is a better father and provider than he is.

"You have no idea how we used to live. There's nothing he can do to make up for that."

Gillian picks up a dumpling, pinching the greasy ball between her fingertips. He watches it slide down the curve of her throat in two labored swallows. She's deciding whether or not to continue the conversation. He can tell by the way she chews much longer and slower than she needs to.

"I think you have to let people change, Kyung. I think your father probably regrets the way he was with you. Maybe that's why he's being so sweet to Ethan now."

"People can't change that much."

"Some people can."

He rips out a clump of grass and chucks it toward the field. "You're only saying that because you didn't know what he was like before. All you see is this nice old man who wants to spend time with his grandson, but he's still the same person he used to be. Both of them are."

"You don't necessarily know that."

"They're my parents. I know them better than anyone. Haven't you even noticed the way they're just sitting in there, shaking hands and making conversation as if nothing happened to them?"

"Maybe being around their friends makes them feel better."

He rips out another clump and aims for the clothesline, but

comes up short. "This is what they do, Gillian. What they've always done. They're good at putting on a show for people, but it doesn't mean they're different inside."

"Your dad, though, he's been so helpful these past few days. Isn't it possible that this experience changed him? I mean, it's not unusual for victims of trauma to—"

"Stop saying things like that," he shouts. "Stop talking like you know anything about them."

A car pulls up to the house with its radio blaring. Gillian turns toward the noise, keeping her face angled away from him after the song ends. He worries that he's ruining her, ruining the part of her that wants so badly to have faith in people, but this isn't a subject they can afford to disagree about. He needs her on his side.

"When I was six, my parents got into an argument about something. I'm not sure how it started anymore—it never took much back then—but he went after her with a belt right before we had to leave for an open house at school. So there I was, sitting between them while they're talking to my teachers, and my dad's asking all these questions about my grades, while my mom's sitting perfectly straight, her hair and makeup just right even though her back was covered with gashes. And I remember thinking, even before I really knew the meaning of the word, that my family was just so fucked, and I'd never be able to explain that, because who would believe me? We were all too good at pretending to be normal, like the world would end if anyone realized who we actually were inside—"

He stops when he notices the look on Gillian's face. She's devastated—by him, or for him, or maybe both. He can't remember where he left off, or what more he planned to say.

All he knows is that he made a mistake. The story implicates him too.

"Is that what you do with Ethan and me?" she asks.

Gillian knows him better than anyone; she's loved him better than anyone. But even she can't see who he really is. Kyung's face reddens; his palms and armpits go damp. Every part of his body begins to betray him, sending signals he can't hide. The only answer that she wants and deserves to hear is no. The word is right there, a single syllable on the tip of his tongue. All he has to do is say it, but the coupling between his mouth and brain suddenly seems disconnected. He pries his legs off the plastic straps of the chair, crossing and uncrossing them again as time slowly runs out. The longer he doesn't respond, the less truthful he'll sound when he does, but something inside him feels broken now, worn out with overuse. Gillian waits for him to deny it until she can't wait anymore. Then she dusts herself off and walks toward the house, taking in the silence like the reply that it is.

FIVE

Marina's release from the hospital brings the math into sharp focus. Kyung's three-bedroom house is too small to accommodate five adults and one child. There's nowhere to put her except on the living room couch, where she sits and sleeps in plain, uncomfortable sight. Although Gillian won't admit it, he thinks she regrets taking her in. Marina's presence isn't good for the boy; it isn't good for anyone. One look at her is an instant, unwanted reminder of the attack, so they all scramble to leave the house in the morning, to be somewhere she isn't. Jin takes Ethan to the park or zoo, while Kyung and Mae return to her house to clean. Gillian offers to divide her time between them, but neither pair is eager for her company, so she goes to the library or coffee shop, unaware of the slight and grateful for the time to read.

Mae is furious that Marina is staying with them. Like a scratched record that skips in the same predictable place, she suggests that Kyung send her somewhere. A home, she says vaguely. Although she never explains whose home or where this home might be, it's obvious that if Mae could snap her fingers and make Marina disappear, she'd do so without thinking twice.

Kyung assumed that his mother would have more sympathy for the girl, but no such bond or loyalty exists. If anything, they seem to operate in sharp contrast to each other. Marina's pain medications leave her in a stupor, a state she lingers in throughout the day, while Mae is a blur of activity, focused only on returning things to right.

"A maid," she sneers. "Who in the world would take in a maid?" Mae is standing in her living room, placing figurines on the bookshelves as Kyung looks on. "And you didn't even ask if I'd mind."

By now, their argument is so familiar, Kyung knows his lines by heart. "Where do you expect her to go?"

"It's not like she's homeless. She has an apartment of her own."

"In a building with no elevator and six flights of stairs. Imagine Marina trying to live there without any family around to help her."

"But why is that your problem? You barely even know her."

"It's not my problem—it's Dad's. Remember? Marina listed him on her college forms as her emergency contact."

"So tell your father to give her some money so she can go to a hotel."

"Why don't *you* tell him?"

Mae runs her fingertip across the length of a shelf, inspecting it for dust—something she's already done twice. She ignores his suggestion, just as he ignored hers. Kyung would like nothing more than to get Marina out of his house, but he's never talked to Jin about money. He's not about to raise the subject now.

"Marina needs people," he says. "People who can check on her, make sure she's okay."

"Your father can buy people too."

She makes a point of turning to look at him as she says this. Kyung isn't sure what he sees in her eyes. Not judgment. Complicity, maybe. She goes back to her work, exchanging a small glass vase on one shelf with a set of candleholders from another.

"I don't like coming downstairs and seeing her on the couch . . . the way she's always sitting there, just staring at me."

Earlier that morning, Kyung heard voices drifting up from the living room while he was getting dressed. He cracked his door an inch and heard his mother and Marina speaking in angry, muted whispers, the kind that people reserve for arguments they don't want others to hear.

"What were you two talking about today? Before I came downstairs?"

Mae moves the vase an inch to the left, and then a fraction of that to the right. She crosses her arms and steps back, cocking her head as she examines her work. "I don't know."

"It sounded like an argument."

"I'd remember if we had an argument."

She didn't answer his question, but he can tell that she doesn't intend to. Mae walks to the center of the room and turns around in a slow circle, taking it all in. Aside from a few pale stains on the upholstery and some empty spaces on the walls and shelves, the house now resembles its former self, tidy and grand. She hasn't thanked him for helping her all week, carting out the garbage and hefting the things she couldn't carry. But it's thanks enough to see things as they were, to pretend—if only for a moment—that the attack never happened because there's no evidence that it did. Now that they're finished with their work, he's tempted to ask if Mae plans to move back in soon, a thought that prompts both relief and worry. It's obvious that things still aren't right with his parents, who continue to keep a noticeable distance from each other. He's certain they haven't exchanged more than a handful of sentences in days, and Jin is still sleeping on a cot in Ethan's room every night.

"I think it's ready," she says.

"Ready for what?"

Mae collects her notepad from the end table, tucking her careful inventory into her bag as she sets off toward the door. She does this more often now—drift in and out of conversations, as if she's having others that only she can hear. Kyung follows her outside and joins her in the car. The clock on the dashboard reads half past noon.

"So"—he hesitates—"should we go home now?"

She purses her lips at him, as if to hold something back. They both know what the problem is—Marina, sacked out in his living room, staring at the walls as they try to maneuver around her.

"Or maybe you're hungry. Should I take you out to lunch?"

Mae shakes her head. Lately, she's been eating. Not full meals yet, but small bites of things, which is better than nothing at all. For this, he has Molly and the ladies to thank. Ever since the impromptu Sunday potluck, they've been dropping by his house with deliveries. They're surprisingly unobtrusive about it; they don't even knock on the door to say hello. A cooler just appears on his steps every day. He's not sure what to be more grateful for, the Korean food that his parents clearly prefer over Gillian's cooking, or the lack of conversation as it's handed off. He glances at the clock again. Only a minute has passed since he and Mae got in the car. They have hours to kill before

Marina takes her midafternoon nap, when she pulls the blanket over her face and drifts off to sleep.

"Maybe you can teach me how to drive now," Mae says.

Kyung has been waiting for this for years, but had given up hope that she'd ever want to learn. "Are you serious?"

"It's something to do."

"Okay, then. Let's go." He throws the car into reverse and backs out too fast, scraping the undercarriage against the pavement.

There's too much traffic in the Heights to let Mae take the wheel, so he heads to the university's athletic stadium, where the parking lot is bigger than the field. As he follows the main road around campus, ringed by classroom buildings covered in unkempt ivy, he drives past his office. The lot in front of the weathered brick building is almost half-full. His heart skips as he recognizes his colleagues' cars. Technically, none of them are required to report to work in the summer. The break is paid time off to do their research, although Kyung hasn't given his a moment's thought. It's now mid-June, nearly a month since classes ended, and it's his first time back on campus. In another field, maybe something in the humanities, an absence like this might go unnoticed, but scientists are different. He should be here, he thinks, working in his office a few days a week, making sure everyone sees his face. Two years from now, he's scheduled to go up for tenure, something he tries not to think about because he knows what to expect. The personnel committee will tell him that his teaching scores are just average. He hasn't published or presented enough of his own research. And his success rate with grants is abysmal—he neither submits many proposals nor wins the few that he does. In an entirely fair world, where the process worked as it should, Kyung would be denied tenure. He hasn't earned it, and two years is hardly enough time to catch up with his colleagues, who seem to do everything right and on schedule. The only advantage he has is his connection to Jin, who funnels millions into the campus through his grants and patent revenues. Despite the state of his finances, Kyung doesn't worry about losing his job; he worries about what it would mean to keep it.

"What's wrong with you?" Mae asks.

"Nothing, why?"

"You're driving so slow."

He looks at the speedometer. He's going twelve miles an hour.

"If you don't want to teach me—"

"No, no," he says, stepping on the gas. "I just got distracted."

Kyung drives to the center of an empty lot and turns off the engine. The stadium casts a long shadow over the asphalt, hiding the sun somewhere behind its walls. He switches places with Mae and shows her how to adjust her seat.

"Accelerator and brake," he says, leaning over and tapping each pedal with his hand.

"Accelerator and brake," she repeats, moving her seat so close to the steering wheel, only a few inches of space separate her forehead from the windshield.

He wants to tell her to back up; there's no need to sit that close, but Mae gets easily discouraged. One wrong word from him could cut their lesson short. He tries to channel the instructor who taught him how to drive when he was sixteen, going so far as to emulate the man's calm, even tone. *Seat belts first, hands at ten and two, foot on the brake when shifting out of park, mirror check before pulling out.*

Mae drives much like Kyung did when he first learned, accelerating with unnecessary bursts of speed and braking as if to avoid wildlife. After her first few attempts, she begins to smooth out, driving in huge loops around the parking lot at a steady, consistent speed. Kyung rolls down his window to let some air in. When he looks over at Mae, she's smiling as the wind blows her hair back; her eyes are clear and bright. He should be relieved to see her this way, but instead, it feels like someone has taken a lead pipe to his knees. Such a simple thing they're doing, and she's never looked happier, as if she never had reason to be happy before.

Mae reaches over and turns on the radio, which is tuned to an oldies station that Gillian likes. Kyung doesn't care much for music, but even he recognizes the song that's playing a few seconds into the chorus.

". . . watching the tide roll away . . . ," Mae sings quietly.

"You've heard this before?"

"Just sittin' on the dock of the bay . . ."

"I didn't think you liked this kind of music."

"I like music."

"No, I meant—I thought you mostly listened to church music."

"That's your father. Not me." She turns to him, taking her eyes off the road in a way that makes him nervous. "You know I have a record collection now? I've been buying a lot of old records—"

"That's nice," he says, grabbing hold of the wheel to correct the car's drifting path. "Hey, maybe"—he pauses, trying to choose his words carefully—"maybe it'd be a good idea if you watched the road instead of me."

She looks straight ahead and starts singing again. "Two thousand miles I roamed . . . just to make this dock my home . . ."

At the edge of the parking lot, Mae loops around a light post, her arms and shoulders more relaxed than when she began, and it all seems like some strange, wishful dream, listening to Otis Redding with his mother while she learns to drive. He should sit back and just let the moment be what it is—he knows that—but he can't help himself. He has to ask.

"So you and dad—what's going on with you two?"

"What do you mean?"

"I don't know. . . . You're not really talking to each other. Eventually, you're going to have to, right? When you move back into your house?"

"Why? Do you want us out already?"

"No. That's not what I said. I just, I just want to know what your plan is, when you're going to start seeing a therapist, maybe work some things out."

"I'm not doing that again."

"Why not?"

"Because I don't want to sit there while some stranger tells me I should change things about my life. That was insulting the last time."

"I don't think the doctor was trying to insult you."

"Why should I pay someone to tell me things I already know? I *know*. I'm not as dumb as you think I am."

Kyung never thought of his mother as dumb, not in the way she means it. Her disinterest in books, her lack of a college degree—he doesn't judge her for these things. What matters is that she wasn't brave enough to leave, and neither was he. He understands this more clearly now, sees it as the weight and counterweight that he balances across his shoulders. He made a choice to live his life in careful proximity to hers, and not once did she ever acknowledge what he lost, what they both lost because they were afraid to go. Where he would have ended up, what kind of person he'd be right now—he tries not to wonder. All he knows is that his life could have been different; it could have been better in ways that he can't even imagine anymore.

Mae continues driving, but the expression on her face—he's ruined it. Gone are the lines on her cheeks, bookending her smile like apostrophes. Everything has smoothed out, the skin perfect and creaseless, but cold. Kyung sits back and counts the light posts as she drives around in silent loops. After half a dozen passes, he tells her to switch directions. Mae looks anxious. She hits the brake too hard and the car lurches to a stop before she takes an agonizingly slow and wide turn in the other direction.

"Your father wants to sell the house," she says.

He turns down the acid twang of a Jimi Hendrix song, not certain if he heard her correctly. "Sell your house?"

"He told me yesterday."

She hardly seems bothered by this, but Kyung is quick to feel the outrage she doesn't. "You can't just let him decide things like that. You love that house; you've spent years—"

"I don't care what he does with it."

"But all the work you've done—"

"I can't live in that place again."

It never occurred to Kyung that his parents wouldn't eventually return to their home, and he still hasn't forgotten the proposition that Gertie mentioned not long ago, when his greatest fear was renting out his house and moving into theirs. What are they supposed to do now? Where will they all go?

"You might regret it, though—later, I mean."

"No, I won't."

"But the market—it's not a good time to sell right now." He hears himself saying these words out loud, which hardly matter. Mae doesn't want to live in the place where she was attacked. It makes perfect sense, but he's not prepared for the ways in which it throws his own life out of balance.

"Well, I guess you can put it up for sale and see what happens." He inhales slowly, bracing himself for what he has to offer next. "You and Dad are obviously welcome to stay with us as long as you need to."

Mae doesn't acknowledge his invitation. The importance of it seems to sail right over her head. "He wants you to call a realtor for him. Get the house listed as soon as you can. He said he doesn't care how much he loses."

It's a terrible idea—the kind so reckless, it can only be the product of someone who knows how to spend other people's money, but has never earned her own. "Dad didn't really agree to this, did he?"

"Ask him if you don't believe me. Also, we want to move to the beach house for the rest of the summer."

"The two of you—together?"

"No. All of us. There's more space there. And he said to invite your father-in-law this weekend, to thank him for being so helpful lately."

The ground beneath him feels like quicksand, sinking each time Mae opens her mouth. There are too many things he doesn't understand, too many scenarios he can't begin to imagine. When did the word "we" suddenly reenter her vocabulary? And when did his parents even have this conversation? It would take weeks, maybe even months for him and Gillian to make these kinds of decisions.

"I don't know," he says, referring to nothing in particular and everything at once.

"It'd be good for us."

"But I thought you didn't like the Cape."

"I like it enough."

This is news to Kyung. His father bought the house in Orleans years ago. He seemed to enjoy telling people that he owned a second home, but after Mae finished updating every square inch with her decorator, she quickly lost interest. It was too far away, she said. Too isolated from everything. At best, she and Jin spent only a few days a year there, sometimes skipping years altogether.

"The Cape is hours from here." He struggles to think of another reason not to go. "And my work—I have to go back soon. Maybe Dad does too."

"It's summer. You don't have to be on campus every day. You can drive back once or twice a week if you need to. We have six bedrooms at the beach house. Everyone can have their own."

Kyung mentally assigns the rooms. One for him and Gillian. Another for Mae, Jin, Ethan, and Connie. There's still space for one more. "What about Marina?"

"What about her?"

"Would she come with us?"

"No, of course not," she snaps. "She'll just stay at your house while we're gone. Then she can sit around all day and no one has to see her do it."

"But how's she supposed to eat? Or get to her doctor's appointments?"

"Let her figure it out. Maybe she'll finally realize she's not welcome and just leave."

The hostility in Mae's voice is impossible to miss, but Kyung doesn't understand its source. What was Mae doing during her first few days back from the hospital, if not staring at the walls? Where's her sense of empathy for this girl who suffered as much as she did? Although he'd never dare say this out loud, he thinks his parents are partly to blame for what happened to Marina. None of this would have happened to her if she didn't clean their house.

"Listen, I don't like having her around any more than you do, but what you're suggesting—it's not right. Marina needs some time to get over this, so if that means we let her sit around for a while and—"

"No!" Mae stabs her finger at the steering wheel, thrusting it with such force that she accidentally honks the horn. "You have to get up. You have to keep going. If you just think about it and think about it, it won't ever go away. You have to have a plan."

The "it" she's referring to requires no explanation. It's the thing they haven't been able to talk about, the absence and the everything all at once. For the first time, Kyung sees how much pain she's holding on to, the way it affects everything she's doing, whether he understands it or not. He reaches out and gently lowers her finger, pressing it against the steering wheel until she grips it safely again.

"All right," he says, not quite agreeing with her, but knowing he'll have to. "All right. Why don't we practice parking now?"

Mae turns around a light post and overcorrects as she straightens out. "I don't need to know that."

"Well . . . eventually, you'll have to park somewhere, right?"

"Later," she says. "I'll learn that later. This is all I want to do right now."

She turns up the radio again, as if to drown out the sound of anything else he might say, and Kyung is content to let her, to give her this moment in which the road ahead is all that's on her mind.

The neighbor's new dog is at it again. MILO is the name freshly painted on his house, but Kyung usually refers to him as "the werewolf" because of his appearance—a hairy mottled brown that reminds him of a German Shepherd, with legs as long as a Great Dane's. Until recently, the werewolf used to bark at all hours of the night and howl at the moon when it was full. Then Gillian went next door and complained. Kyung doesn't know what she said or how she said it; all he knows is that it worked, sort of. The werewolf doesn't bark or howl anymore, but something in between, tortured by the expensive new collar around his neck that shocks him when he tries to do either. The result is a low, painful whimper that sounds neither animal nor human. Usually, Kyung is tired enough to sleep through the noise, but the day's events have drugged him awake, leaving him staring at the ceiling tiles above his bed. Not only did Jin support Mae's desire to sell their house and go to the Cape, but Gillian thought it was a good idea too. "A vacation," she called it, and nothing he said afterwards could dissuade her. Even Connie seemed uncharacteristically open to the offer, going so far as to ask— if it wasn't any trouble, if it wasn't too impolite—would there be enough room for his new lady friend to come too?

He turns and looks at Gillian, who's asleep with a pillow clutched to her chest. She was visibly excited when he mentioned the beach house, cutting him off before he had a chance to tell her they shouldn't go. Vacations always appealed to her sense of being a grown-up, of being cosmopolitan enough to own a passport and actually use it. Her first trip outside the United States was their honeymoon, a seven-day cruise to Bermuda that he paid for with student loans. They've been returning to a different island in the Caribbean every year since, charging one trip after another but never paying any of them off. It was a luxury they allowed themselves despite knowing they shouldn't. The indulgence of living outside the hole they'd created, if only for a week at a time, somehow made the rest of the year more bearable. Kyung understands why Gillian was so excited about the beach house, even if she couldn't bring herself to say it out loud. The Cape is their only chance to pretend like they can afford to get away. Still, the thought of the upcoming weekend, surrounded by their parents in an unfamiliar place, sends all the acid in his stomach straight to his throat.

Kyung sits up and rubs his chest in circles when he hears the noise clearly for the first time. Not the dog outside, but something much closer. What he previously dismissed as the house settling isn't that at all. It sounds like cans rattling around in a container. The rattling starts, then stops, then starts again, not following any pattern. Had he been more tired or less alert, he might have missed it entirely. Kyung slides out of bed and goes downstairs, pausing every few seconds to confirm that the noise is getting louder. As he inches toward the kitchen, he tries to translate what he hears, to turn it into something ordinary and reasonable instead of frightening. His mother is making herself a cup of tea. Or his father came down for a glass of water. But as he approaches the door, the more he can identify the sound behind it and the less it makes sense. It's not tin cans after all, but the metal clank of pots and pans, as if a family of raccoons is ransacking the house. The blood pulses in his ears as he opens the door a crack, gently pushing it wider and wider until he sees Marina kneeling on the floor, surrounded by Gillian's cookware.

"What are you doing?"

"Oh, Mr. Kyung." Marina stands up, using the countertop for balance. Her dark brown hair hangs in her face, unwashed and unkempt. She's wearing a nightgown that belongs to Gillian, an ugly oversized T-shirt with a picture of Bugs Bunny on the front.

"I'm sorry I wake you." Marina hooks a piece of hair over her ear. "I get up early to clean."

"*Clean?* Right now?" He rests his hand on a chair to steady himself as he glances at the clock. "But it's two in the morning."

"Oh. I'm sorry. I didn't know."

"Why are you doing this, anyway? You don't have to clean my house."

Marina goes to the sink and returns with a plastic hand broom and dustpan. Inside the pan are furry clumps of lint and stray pieces of rice, cereal, and hair. "But your cabinets need good clean, see? Once a year, I wash inside of all cabinets for your parents. I do for you too."

No one has seen Marina leave the sofa since she returned from the hospital. She still has bruises and cuts that haven't healed, a slight limp in her step when she walks. Kyung wonders if her process is similar to Mae's. Nothing for days, and then a sudden, uncontrolled burst of housekeeping.

"Marina, you're a guest here. You don't have to clean anything. Now, why don't you go back to sleep?"

"But I make myself useful, Mr. Kyung. I help you and Miss Gillian."

He's always found Marina's accent charming, but now her sweet trill and broken, insistent English are starting to grate his nerves. He scans the floor, which is covered with pots and pans, a bucket of water and sponges, and rolls of paper towels. He takes the dust broom away and leads her to the table. When he turns around, Marina is standing perfectly straight, staring at his thumb resting over her wrist. He quickly releases it and pulls out a chair, offering her a chance to sit. Marina remains where she is.

"I clean more quiet," she says. "You don't notice me anymore."

"It's nice that you want to help—it really is—but you don't have to. You're a *guest*. Do you understand that?"

Marina stares at the floor, nodding as if she does, but clearly, it makes her uncomfortable. He wonders if the idea of being in someone else's home and not having a job to do is simply too strange for her to comprehend. When she looks up at him again, her huge brown eyes are filled with tears.

"What's the matter? What did I say?"

The tears stream down her cheeks as she shakes her head. "I cannot go home again, Mr. Kyung. I cannot see my family, not like this."

"Who said anything about you going home?" He asks even though he already knows the answer. He just wants to hear it from her. He pulls out the chair a few inches more. "Come sit," he says, not offering so much as ordering.

Marina does as she's told and knits her fingers together on the table. Up close, her hands don't look like they belong to a twenty-four-year-old girl. The nails have been bitten down to the quick, and her skin is dry and cracked, aged by a lifetime of work. On her right pinky, just below the knuckle, there's a tattoo of a faded black cross, which he's never noticed before. The proportions are uneven; the placement, slightly crooked. It looks like she did it herself. He wonders how long it took to carve the lines into her flesh until they could never go away.

"When did you get that?" he asks.

She looks at the tattoo as if she'd forgotten it was there. "I was teenager. Maybe thirteen or fourteen. Why?"

"It's a cross?"

"Yes?"

"A crucifix?"

"Yes."

"But—you're from Bosnia. I thought Bosnians were Muslim." Instantly, he can tell by the look on her face that they're not. "Sorry. I don't know a lot about that part of the world."

"Orthodox Christian," she says quietly. And then, in a noticeably sharper tone, she adds: "Not Muslim."

The tears on her face have dried, but she still seems upset, and Kyung recognizes the same distant expression he sees in his mother, as if her body is here but her mind is somewhere else.

"Does it help you?" he asks. "To believe in something?"

"You mean God?"

He nods.

She reaches for the saltshaker, moving it from one side of the pepper mill to the other and then back again. "The men in my country—they did bad things to people because they believe in something. The Muslims too. They all think God give them the right."

He was hoping she'd just say yes, hoping for her sake that she still had faith, if nothing else. But it's obvious that Marina is no more of a believer than he is. She's completely on her own.

"So why do you think we're going to send you home?"

"I don't know."

"I'm just trying to help."

Marina circles the room with her eyes, trying not to look at him. Then she takes a napkin from the stack on the table and blows her nose.

"It was my mother, wasn't it? She said we didn't want you here anymore?"

"Mrs. Cho," she says slowly, "she tell me you all go to the Cape on Friday and I leave here before you return. She offer me ticket home, and money, but I cannot see my family like this, Mr. Kyung. My father . . ." Her eyes well up again and spill over, but she doesn't look sad so much as terrified.

"What about him?"

"He tell me not to come here. He think something bad happen. My father is—coward, afraid of everything since the war. He always talk about girls who go to America, to Europe, how men trick them into being prostitute. But I said no, I go to work, to study. Maybe I come back as lawyer or doctor one day, but he warn me over and over. Something bad happen if I leave." She blows her nose again, crumpling the wet napkin in her fist. "I have sisters, Mr. Kyung. Four sisters, all younger than me. If I come home like this, my father will never let them leave, not even to study. He will say he was right."

Kyung can't remember the number of times he's passed

Marina on the couch and wished her gone, blinked somewhere far away. But sitting across from her now, he sees how young she is, how permanent the damage of her life back home and her life here. There's a point, he thinks, when no amount of psychiatry or pharmacology can help a person lead a normal life. He passed his long ago. There's no helping her either, but he still feels the need to try, to extend the hand that was never offered to him.

"I won't let anyone send you away." Before he has a chance to second-guess himself, he adds: "This is my house, and you can stay here as long as you need to."

Marina brightens immediately. She doesn't understand the dynamics of his family or the hell he'll take to defend this decision, and for the time being, he doesn't want to think about it either.

"Thank you, Mr. Kyung. I be helpful here, I promise. I make things easy for you and Miss Gillian."

She gets up from her seat and tiptoes through the maze of cookware, resuming her place beside an empty cabinet. He's about to tell her no—just leave it—but she's already kneeling on the floor and leaning into the cabinet, scrubbing the far reaches with a sponge. In this position, the back of Marina's petite figure resembles a violin. Wide at the shoulders and hips, cinched narrow in the middle. The further she reaches, the higher her nightgown climbs, revealing faded pink underwear with blue and yellow stripes. Nothing about what he sees—the Bugs Bunny shirt, the thick woolen socks, the baggy, stretched-out underwear—should appeal to him, but the longer he stands there, the more turned on he feels. It's disgusting, he thinks. *He's* disgusting. He backs out of the room, his face lit with shame, and walks stiffly up the stairs. For a moment, he considers waking Gillian, but he knows better than that by now, and just the thought of her irritated, exhausted rejection begins to deaden what Marina awoke.

Upstairs, he opens Ethan's door to check on him and finds the boy asleep next to Jin. The two of them are curled up together on the cot. Ethan's little bed is empty; the race car–patterned covers are still made up, as if he didn't spend a minute there before crawling in beside his grandfather. Kyung wonders how many nights they've been sleeping like this, and who suggested it first. It's jarring, such an outward display of tenderness from someone who never seemed the least bit tender. Kyung tiptoes to Ethan's side of the bed and tries to lift him up. He whines and turns toward Jin, stretching himself out long. The boy is taller now, even taller than when the summer began. It's hard to believe that anything could grow so fast. Kyung was terrified when Gillian gave birth, watching the doctor raise their tiny baby into the air, so slick and fragile and noisy from his first breath. He didn't feel any of the joy he expected at the sight of his son, only worry. He worried when Ethan cried and cried for no apparent reason; he worried when he wouldn't walk like other babies his age and then worried he'd crack his skull open when he did. He worried that Ethan was slow to learn his letters and numbers. He worried that television would make him sullen and rude like the neighborhood kids. Parenthood felt like nothing but a lifetime of worry, which made Kyung worry even more.

He tries to pick him up again, but Jin startles awake, clutching Ethan with one hand and the bedsheets with the other.

"It's me," Kyung whispers. "It's just me."

Jin adjusts his glasses, which are still perched on his nose. He keeps blinking at Kyung, as if he doesn't trust that he's awake. "What are you doing?" he whispers back.

"Nothing. I just came to check on him." He motions toward Ethan, who's still asleep, his mouth open and whistling.

Jin adjusts himself, pulling the sheets higher and the boy closer.

"You should let him sleep in his own bed."

"He's fine here." Jin looks down and brushes a sweaty wisp of hair from Ethan's forehead. "Just let him be."

His father and son look like they belong together, like they've always been this close. But it bothers Kyung to see them this way. It feels like Jin is slowly taking over everything that matters.

"We have a system now, and you're ruining it. It took us months to train him to sleep alone."

"He can sleep in his own bed tomorrow. He'll wake up if you move him now."

Jin is right, but Kyung doesn't know how he can stand it. When Ethan was younger and prone to nightmares, he often crawled into the space between him and Gillian, who continued to sleep through the night. But Kyung could never get comfortable. He'd feel his arm tingling under the weight of Ethan's head, and then a deadness as his blood began to slow. It usually took him hours to drift off again, and even then, he slept lightly, frightened that he'd crush the boy simply by turning the wrong way.

"How's your mother?" Jin asks.

The question irritates him, not because it's meant to change the subject, but because his father shouldn't have to ask.

"Why don't you"—he lowers his voice again as Ethan stirs in his sleep—"why don't you try talking to her?"

"I have."

Kyung is about to tell him to try harder, but he remembers the cruel flick of Mae's wrist as she let go of his hand during the prayer. It's not Jin's fault that she's mad at him.

"She's all right, I guess." No sooner has he said it than Kyung quickly reconsiders. "I mean, not really. Now that she's done with the house—I'm not sure. I don't know what she'll do next."

"Whatever she wants."

"What does that mean?"

"Let her do whatever she wants, whatever she needs to do."

This has never been the dynamic of his parents' marriage. Everything was always about making Jin happy, or at the very least, not making him unhappy. Sleep, food, silence, absence—whatever he wanted, Mae tried to give it to him. And she always managed to get it wrong. Years ago, she had to throw a dinner party together with less than an hour's notice. A visiting professor had come to campus for a lecture and Jin invited him and his colleagues to the house afterward. Kyung had never seen his mother run so much or so fast in his entire life, cooking and cleaning and making herself presentable, sometimes all at once. When the guests finally arrived, he still remembers the expression on her face when one of them asked for a glass of white wine. She didn't have any—only red. The woman didn't seem to mind, but from then on, his mother looked different to him. Uneasy. It didn't matter how many compliments she received about the house or the dinner or her hospitality. The wine was the only thing she could think about. The irony of it was, when the guests left and Jin flew into his usual rage, he said he was hitting her because she'd looked so unhappy all night.

"Don't," Jin says.

"Don't what?"

"Don't raise your voice."

Kyung doesn't understand at first, but he realizes he's been frowning. He softens a bit, aware that his son's presence provides a barrier of safety he's never felt around his father. Jin doesn't want to scare the boy again.

"Why did you two even get married in the first place?"

"What kind of question is that? You shouldn't ask—"

"But I'm asking."

The mirror of his father's face startles him. Kyung feels like he's seeing himself aged by thirty years. The eyes are droopier, the skin redder and more wrinkled, but the outline is still the same.

"We weren't even supposed to. I wanted to marry her cousin."

"So why didn't you?"

"Because she was poor."

"But your family was poor too."

"My parents thought I could do better. I was almost finished with my degree—that was a big deal back then." Jin scowls, but now that he's started, he can't seem to stop. "If I couldn't marry a rich girl, they said, I should at least marry someone middle class. Your mother's parents—they owned a store. Not a big one, but respectable. They offered mine a dowry."

"You mean like money?"

"Yes, money."

Somehow, it seems only fitting that what brought his parents together, what's kept them together all these years is the same thing that Kyung worries about every waking minute of his life. It's like a disease they passed on through their bloodlines, mutated into a new form for his generation.

"I still don't understand why you're selling the house."

"Because she likes to decorate. If we start somewhere new, it'll keep her busy."

"But busy isn't the same thing as happy."

"People your age," Jin says, not making any effort to hide his disdain. "All you do is think about happiness. You think I was happy when I first came to this country? When I was trying to get tenure and no one said I could?"

"There's nothing wrong with—"

"If you think too much, you won't ever accomplish anything."

Had the words been phrased differently—a little kinder, a little earlier in life—they could have formed the basis for something meaningful passed down from father to son. But said in this moment, they don't resemble advice so much as judgment.

"It's crazy to sell your house so she can decorate a new one. The market—you're going to get killed." Kyung regrets his choice of words, but his other option—*you're going to take a beating*—is no better than the first. "You're not going to get what that place is worth, not even close."

"I don't have to worry about things like that anymore."

It's hard to tell whether Jin is bragging or simply being objective about his wealth. But either way, he's earned the right not to worry, to do something foolish because he wants to and can.

"It's your decision, I guess." Kyung pulls the covers over Ethan. "You should take those off now."

"Take what off?"

He motions toward Jin's glasses. "You'll break them."

"I can't sleep without them anymore."

Kyung nods, aware on some level that sharing a bed with Ethan, feeling the boy's warm breath and small hands against his skin, probably helps his father feel safe. But their closeness has the opposite effect on him. "Tomorrow," he says.

"You'll call the realtor for me tomorrow?"

"Yes, but that's not what I meant. Tomorrow, you have to let him sleep in his own bed."

Gertie is clearly pleased with the house when she pulls into the driveway. She bounds out of her car like a Labrador and starts taking pictures of the exterior, something she never bothered to do at Kyung and Gillian's. Instead of the conservative black pantsuit he saw her wearing last, she's dressed in a T-shirt and shorts with a sweater wrapped around her waist, and her hair is tied back into a stubby ponytail that looks like a paintbrush.

"Morning," she calls out. "What a gorgeous home your parents have. Absolutely beautiful."

He's standing on the front steps waiting for her, but she continues to click away with her camera, assuming what hasn't been agreed to yet—that the listing is hers to sell. Kyung is content to wait and stare at the sky, which is cloudless and blue, still like water. He doesn't remember when the seasons changed and spring finally turned into summer.

"Sorry about the workout clothes," she says sheepishly. "I'd just finished with my trainer when you called."

"Thank you for coming so quickly," he says, bracing himself for her furious handshake as she joins him on the steps.

He didn't expect her to be available the same day he called, but he could sense something change in her voice as he gave her the details. A property in the Heights seemed to interest her. The address did too. Is it one of those houses at the very top of the hill? she asked. And as soon as he confirmed it: yes, of course, she said. How soon could he meet her there?

Gertie snaps a photo of the garage and two more of the lawn. "Nice landscaping," she says. "But I can see why your parents want to sell, given their situation."

He glances at her, confused by her cheerful tone.

"It's a lot of upkeep," she continues. "Way too much for an older couple."

Gertie doesn't seem to understand what happened here, but Kyung isn't sure if he's obligated to tell her, if a crime is something he has to disclose, like a leaky roof or a bad furnace. He holds the front door open and follows her into the entryway, which has been cleared of its rubble, leaving only a tall bronze coatrack and a matching umbrella stand.

Gertie runs her hand along the polished wood banister. "Stunning," she says. "The details are in pristine condition."

Her enthusiasm for his parents' house is so different from her reaction to his own, which in retrospect was largely disinterested and diagnostic. Having never seen this house before, Gertie doesn't understand all of the things that are wrong with it. And she misses the clues—the stains on the drapes that the dry cleaner couldn't remove, the faint discolorations on the walls where so many paintings used to hang, but no longer do.

"Did your parents restore everything themselves, or was the work already done when they got here?"

The house had been built in the 1800s. The previous owners

bought it as a wreck and spent nearly ten years on renovations, only to run out of money as the end was in sight. Jin quickly stepped in and bought the house, the furniture, and anything else the couple was willing to sell—even their massive boat, which had only touched water twice since changing hands. He was pleased with himself for finding such a bargain, which never sat right with Kyung. He often wondered what had happened to the couple and where they ended up.

"All the big projects were done before my parents bought it," he says. "Mostly, my mother just focused on the decorating."

They move into the living room, where Gertie examines a lamp with a base made of dark blue crystal. It was once part of a set, but its broken twin had to be swept out with the trash, lampshade and all.

"She has an amazing eye for period pieces. Nothing in this room seems out of place."

Kyung feels like a goldfish in a pot, slowly being boiled to death as the water temperature rises. His palms are sweaty; the collar of his shirt is too tight. Gertie keeps walking past the vague outlines on the walls where things used to hang. She notices only the ornate built-in bookshelves, not the gaps left behind by the books that were destroyed. She admires the high-back sofas upholstered in pale beige silk, but has no idea about the stains and tears on the undersides of their cushions.

"Forced-air heat?" she asks, studying the antlerlike shadow of a chandelier.

He'd forgotten about the list in his pocket that his father wrote out for him. He unfolds the sheet of paper and scans Jin's shaky penmanship. "Yes. Forced air," he says, and because the information is right there in front of him, he adds: "Three zones. And central air too."

"My goodness."

Gertie has wandered into the dining room, where she's opened the built-in china cabinet in the corner. He doesn't know whether her remark was about the heating system, or the number of place settings behind the door—enough to feed twenty-four. Each plate and bowl, saucer and cup is rimmed in gold. Real gold, Kyung recalls Mae once saying. Not the cheap plated kind.

"So if your parents are selling, I assume you're not planning to rent out your house anymore?"

"No, they'll be staying with us for a while until they find something else."

She looks at him over her shoulder, radiating her best attempt at warmth. "I hope you'll pass on my name if they need a realtor."

Kyung isn't sure if he's impressed by her frankness, or repulsed by it. "Do you sell a lot of houses in this price range?"

"What was that?" Gertie leans toward him.

It's an odd reaction, he thinks. They're standing less than three feet away from each other. He didn't whisper the question; she could hear him just fine.

"How many houses have you sold in this price range?"

Gertie smiles and shakes her finger, pretending to admonish him. "I haven't even told you how I'd price this house yet," she says in a grating singsong.

"I know, but—"

"I've been the top seller in the area for the past eight years, and I've already cleared three million in sales since January."

"Yes, but that's not really what I'm asking." He doesn't understand why she's avoiding his question, but it's obvious that she is. "If we can agree that this place is worth at least a million—"

Gertie looks down at her hands as if she's counting on them. "Two."

"Two what? This house is worth two?"

"No, I've sold *two* houses in this price range," she says briskly. "But you have to understand, property in the upper Heights rarely comes up for sale, especially in this economy. You won't find anyone in the area who sells more than I do."

Something in her voice crosses the line between eager and desperate, a lapse she seems to regret. She's flustered all of a sudden, fiddling with the settings on the camera hanging from her neck. Until now, Kyung didn't understand what Gertie, with her barrage of colorful billboards and bus ads, probably knew the second she pulled into the driveway—this house is out of her league. She's like the Costco of realtors. She makes her money by selling in volume.

"I'm still not sure my parents are actually going to sell. I feel like this is something they could change their minds about at any time."

She lowers her camera, drawing her lips into a thin smile. "Of course. It's a very big decision. But we might as well finish looking around since I'm here. Can I see the upstairs now?"

Kyung leads her through the kitchen and up the old servants' staircase, ducking to avoid the low, angled ceiling as they wind their way to the second floor. He opens the doors for Gertie in the order they pass them—study, guest room, guest room, bathroom—unintentionally saving the master bedroom for the end of their tour. Mae cleaned this room herself, rejecting his repeated offers to help. Although he didn't understand her insistence, he was almost grateful for it. He'd never seen where his parents slept before the attack, and he had no desire to see it afterward. He pushes the door open and stands by to let Gertie pass. The bedroom is large and square, sparsely decorated compared to the rest of the house. The air is musty, but light streams in through the lace-covered windows, brightening the pale green walls, which makes the room seem less forbidding than he imagined it. He steps inside, relieved to find everything neat and clean, absent of any reminders of what happened here.

"This is a big master bedroom," Gertie says. "It's not common for a house this age."

"I think it used to be two rooms once."

"But your parents sleep in twin beds. If they do decide to sell, you might want to consider moving these out and getting a cheap king-size one instead."

"Why?"

"It's just a generational thing. Younger buyers have to imagine themselves actually living here. They're not going to be able to with these."

The matching twin beds are made of dark black wood, each with a four-poster frame. Gertie runs her hand down the length of a post, leading Kyung's eyes to a cluster of scratches near the mattress before she moves on to the adjoining bathroom.

"Any idea when the plumbing was last updated?" Her voice echoes off the cavernous tile walls.

The information is right there on his sheet of paper, but Kyung can't read it out loud. He's petrified, shaking as if the temperature has just plummeted. He sees the room as it was that day, with Marina tied to one bed and Mae on the other. He sees their hands gripping the posts, their fingernails turning white and digging into the wood, clawing at it like animals when Nat Perry climbs on top of them. He flinches at the thought of each slap and punch, at the look on Mae's face as Perry presses his thumbs into her throat. His piece of paper drops to the floor, but he leaves his empty hand extended.

"Plumbing updates?" Gertie asks, popping her head out the bathroom door.

Kyung sits down on the rug and covers his eyes.

"What's wrong? Did you hurt yourself?"

He shakes his head.

"Are you sick?" She kneels down beside him. "Do you need a doctor?"

When he doesn't respond, Gertie opens her purse and rummages through the compartments. "I'm calling 911."

"No, don't."

"Then tell me what's going on."

He needs to pull himself together. He has to. But when his eyes are open, blurry with tears, he sees the room. And when his eyes are closed, he sees what happened here. All he wants to do is cut them out.

"Please say something. Tell me what's happening."

"Jesus," he shouts. "Don't you ever read the papers?"

"What?"

"My parents were attacked here. My mother was—raped here."

Gertie blinks as she looks around the room. Then she folds her arms over her chest as if she feels the same sudden cold that he does. "Didn't someone die in this house?"

He nods.

"I heard about a home invasion in this area. I had no idea—"

"It was here." He punches the bed frame. "Right here."

He punches it again, harder this time, hearing the strong, sturdy sound of bone against wood. The pain travels up his arm, spreading deep into his shoulder, and he welcomes it, the complete inability to feel anything else. Gertie tries to pull him back, but not before he lands three more blows that crack the thick black veneer.

"Let's go," Gertie pleads. "Let's go now."

She helps him up and leads him to the kitchen, where he collapses in a chair, too stunned to speak or move. Kyung has never hit anything before—not an object, not a person—and he's horrified for acting this way, for giving in to the impulse and liking the result. He wishes that Gertie would leave now, but it's obvious she doesn't intend to just yet. Although his back is to her, he can tell what she's doing. Running the faucet, opening the cabinets, cracking ice from a tray into the sink.

She returns with a plastic bag wrapped in a towel. "Here. This might help."

Two of Kyung's knuckles are dark red. The one in the middle has already started to swell, rising high above the skin like a knot in a tree. The ice pack stings when she lays it over his hand, but he leaves it there, the pulsing blood fighting the numbing cold.

"Thank you," he says hoarsely.

He looks up at her, and she does her best to smile, but her face is the color of chalk.

"I'm so sorry," he says, and suddenly he's crying again.

"Why? What do you have to be sorry about?"

"For scaring you."

He's never cared much for Gertie, but he realizes he should be grateful for her presence now. If not for her, he'd still be sitting on the floor, punching the bed frame until his bones turned to dust.

"Oh, you can't scare me," she says unconvincingly. "I was just worried. Now, why don't we have some tea? That always helps me relax."

Gertie puts a kettle of water on the stove. She comes back with two cups and saucers and a sampler basket still wrapped in cellophane and Christmas-colored ribbon. She slices through the packaging with her nails and rifles through the contents.

"Calming Chamomile," she reads aloud. "Revitalizing Ginger . . ." She lists off the names on every envelope, as if she doesn't know what else to say. "Maybe we need something stronger. How about Earl Grey?"

He doesn't like tea, but he nods anyway, wiping his face on his sleeve.

"So that day when I met you and Gillian at your house, when your mother was walking around without any clothes on—that was the day, wasn't it?"

"Yes."

"I see." She scratches at a small chip on the edge of her saucer. "I was so booked up with appointments that week. I heard about what happened on the radio, but I didn't really pay attention, I guess."

"Why would you? Who wants to think about something like that?"

"I know, but a woman walking around naked in broad daylight . . . I should have made the connection."

"It's better you didn't."

The teakettle sings its alarm, and Gertie gets up to retrieve it. When she returns to the table, she opens two envelopes and dunks the bags with her fingertips until the water turns almost black. As he reaches for his cup, she waves him off.

"Not yet." She digs through her purse and removes a silver flask, shaking it gently to confirm that there's something left inside.

Gertie didn't strike him as the type of person who carried alcohol in her bag, but upon closer inspection, it starts to make sense. No one who looks so pulled together ever really is. She empties the flask into their tea, turning it upside down to shake out the last few drops.

"Times like these . . . ," she says, then looks away, embarrassed. "I actually don't know what I was going to say there."

The bourbon and Earl Grey don't mix well together, but he drinks the acrid concoction anyway. Gertie adds two sugar cubes to her cup, dissolving them slowly with her spoon.

"So . . . how are they now?" she asks. "Your parents?"

Something about his expression must answer the question for him because she doesn't bother to wait for a response.

"It was good that your mother came to you that day. That must give you some relief, at least."

"Why would it?"

"Well, she trusts you. She came to you for help."

He doubts that Mae trusts anyone. Not him, not his father, not even the people from her church. It was proximity that led her stumbling into his backyard that day, nothing more.

"I'll give you the listing," he says. "How soon can you get it on the market?"

Gertie hesitates. "I don't think I can sell this house, Kyung.

I'm sorry. . . . I really wish I could, but no one's going to be able to sell it, not for a while."

"Because of what happened here?"

She nods. "Maybe if you waited a year. People might start to forget, and the market could be in recovery by then," she adds optimistically. "For now, though, there's no way. Someone just died here. Your mother was . . . assaulted here. Even if you slashed the price, I can't see buyers getting past that kind of history. Not yet, at least. It'd be easier to get rid of this place by burning it down."

Kyung would like nothing more than to take a match to the drapes and watch the flames engulf them, erecting violent walls of amber where real ones once stood. Everything in the house is so old; every piece of its ancient frame is wood. It wouldn't take long for a fire to reduce it all to an expensive pile of ashes.

"So my father and I are the same, I guess."

"I don't follow."

"We both own houses that you can't sell."

At first, Gertie appears hurt by his comment, ready to object. But she takes a long sip of tea instead.

"I'm sorry. I didn't mean to criticize. I understand that my family's situation is—complicated."

"Well, at least you have each other, right? You're all in this together."

"Yes," he says, having resolved not to cry in front of Gertie again. "We all have each other."

SIX

Kyung unlocks the door to his office and turns on the lights, bracing himself for the noise and flicker of the fluorescent tubes hanging overhead. One by one, they buzz to life, rendering the walls an unpleasant, tobacco-stained shade of yellow. He assumed things would look different when he returned to work, but his books and papers are exactly where he left them, scattered in their usual disarray across the length of his desk. The only thing that's changed in his absence is the smell—a musty shut-in odor that reminds him of a warm attic. Kyung opens his window, which overlooks a tree-lined quad of office buildings. The campus below is barely awake. A handful of maintenance men and early-bird secretaries travel the sidewalks, their pace leisurely, not yet hurried by the start of the day.

He deposits his mail on the ledge and turns on his computer, knocking over a row of picture frames like dominoes. The cluttered display of family photographs is Gillian's doing. When he was first hired at the university, she decided they should decorate his office, insisting in a way that she'd rarely done before. She said she wanted him to feel at home there, and he understood the source of her excitement even though he didn't feel it himself. None of the men in her family were the office type. He wasn't about to take that from her, so he let her do what she wanted, organizing the bookshelves and hanging his diplomas with care.

The computer takes longer than usual to boot up, but Kyung doesn't mind the wait. He's afraid to see how much got away from him during his absence, the missed meetings and dead-lines and requests for recommendation letters from anxious students. Classes ended in mid-May. He'd intended to take a week or two off after commencement, but over a month has passed, and he forgot to set up an auto-reply while he was gone. Now every e-mail will demand an apology or explanation, de-pending on how serious the delay. Despite not looking forward to this, Kyung dreads the thought of something else even more. He sits down at his desk and rolls his chair toward the aquar-ium in the corner. The lights in the tank are off, the water black and still. He stares inside, searching for the school of zebra fish. The fish are purely decorative—they have nothing to do with his research—but they're living, breathing creatures nonethe-less. At least they used to be. He expects to find them floating at the top, cocooned in several weeks' worth of mold, but all twelve are alive and well, zipping from left to right and back again. He gives them a liberal pinch of food, surprised that they managed to survive for so long without it.

"Marcy took the liberty of feeding them while you were away."

Kyung recognizes the voice before he turns to see his de-partment chair standing in the open doorway.

"Oh. I'll have to thank her for doing that."

Although he doesn't like the idea of Craig's secretary letting herself into his office, he's not in a position to complain. His absence has been noted—that much is clear—and he struggles to come up with a reason for it.

"It's early," Kyung observes. "You're here early, I mean."

Craig walks in and puts his gym bag on the floor. Tucked in the outer pocket is a tennis racket. "My rec league gets together before work. I just played two sets."

"Did you win?"

He runs his fingers through his damp hair and smiles weakly. "Yes, but not by much."

At six feet six, Craig is all arms and legs. It's hard to imagine him playing a sport like tennis, with a racket that extends his reach even farther, but the man is constantly in motion. He walks to work every day, swims laps in the pool during lunch, does hundred-mile bike races on the weekends. At fifty, he probably does more exercise in a week than Kyung does all year.

"It's getting harder and harder to beat him, though." Craig opens his bag and takes out a bottle of ibuprofen, swallowing a pair of pills dry. "Don't tell Steve you saw me taking these. I'll never hear the end of it."

Kyung doesn't know which of the many Steves in their acquaintance he's referring to, but right now he doesn't care. He just wants a chance to think. In retrospect, he knows he should have handled things differently from the start. He should have called or e-mailed to say he was taking time off to handle something personal. Had he made an effort to do this, his reentry would be so much easier now, but after disappearing for nearly five weeks without so much as a word, he knows he doesn't deserve easy.

"I honestly didn't expect to see you here, Kyung."

"Yes, well . . ."

He doesn't know what he's doing here either. He couldn't work even if he wanted to. His family left for the Cape earlier this morning. Kyung dreaded the idea of going with them, so much so that he lied—to his parents, to Connie, even to Gillian. He said his department chair called, upset that he hadn't spent any time in the office all summer. He said he needed to show his face at work and he'd join them on the Cape the following day. What he couldn't say was the truth—that he didn't want to sit in a car with all of them, trapped on a drive that might take two hours or six, depending on traffic.

"I'm sorry I haven't been around for so long. I've had some personal things going on?" The end of his sentence lifts into a question, as if to test whether such a vague explanation will suffice.

"Kyung, I know what happened. I'm not even sure what to say about it. It's just . . . horrible. Unbelievable."

He blinks for a second. "How?"

The only other chair in his office is covered with books, so Craig takes a seat on the edge of the desk. "You know how this place is." He looks down at his wrist, at the pale white strip of skin where his watch should be. "Faculty are nothing more than a bunch of gossips. It doesn't take long for news to travel from the engineering building to this one."

"I see."

Jin never mentioned telling anyone in his department. Kyung is surprised that he did. His father should have known how quickly the word would spread, but maybe he didn't care. Maybe he knew there was no point trying to hide what had happened to him, that some secrets would be too hard to keep.

"So how are your parents doing? How are you?"

"We're all right, considering."

"Is there anything you need?"

What he needs is for Craig to leave. The area around his desk is tight enough without someone sitting on top of him like this. He turns on his monitor, hopeful that Craig will take the hint and go away.

"Thanks for asking, but I'm fine. I think I just need to—refocus."

Craig reaches over and turns off the monitor just as the desktop pattern begins to appear. "Shouldn't you be with your family right now? Whatever you're working on can wait."

Kyung blinks again, staring at the black screen. He can't even remember what he was working on before all of this happened. "I probably have a thousand e-mails to catch up on."

"Given the circumstances, I'm sure people will understand if they don't hear from you for a while."

"So everyone in the department knows?"

Craig nods. "I think so. But I haven't made any announcements about it, if that's what you're asking. Obviously, I wouldn't do that."

As far as department chairs go, Craig is actually a good one. He's honest and organized. He knows the names of everyone's spouses and kids by heart. At five o'clock, he always encourages the workaholics to go home, have a life. If Gillian or his parents knew Craig better, they never would have left for the Cape without him. They would have realized that Craig Tunney doesn't make irate phone calls demanding that his faculty do this or that.

Kyung reaches for his monitor again. "I've been gone too long. I can't just leave."

"Yes, you can. I'm telling you to. Think about it, Kyung. In five years, it's not going to matter if you finish an article now or a month from now. But your family, the time you spend together this summer—that's going to make a difference."

Suddenly, the dread that Kyung felt while driving to campus, parking in front of the building, taking the elevator up to his office—all of it dissipates, replaced by an unfamiliar resolve to stay where he is. He understands what Craig is saying—agrees with it, even—but the weight of his responsibility keeps him anchored to his seat.

"What's the matter? You don't look well."

"I don't?"

"No, you're really pale. Have you eaten?"

"Not yet. But I will, though."

Craig taps him on the shoulder. "Come on. Get up."

Kyung remains seated, not certain what would be worse—to refuse or to do as he's told.

"Let's go get some breakfast."

"But—"

"If you come to the cafeteria and have breakfast with me, I'll stop pestering you. I promise."

It's hard to be annoyed with Craig, who's always been kind to him, perhaps even kinder than he should be. But as they walk across the quad, Kyung feels something bubbling up to the surface, prickly and hot under his skin. All he wants to do is be alone. He wishes everyone would let him.

"You didn't miss anything while you were gone," Craig says. He looks at Kyung sideways, as if to examine him without being noticed.

"I appreciate what you're trying to—"

"I'm serious. You know how dead this place is during the summer. I mean, look at it."

The steps to the Campus Center, which are usually teeming with students during the school year, are empty except for a pair of giant stone planters. Even the cafeteria is quiet enough to hear the clink of glasses and plates. Craig hands him a green plastic tray as they enter, and heads off toward the omelet line. Kyung looks around, worried that he might run into someone he knows, but the only other people in the cafeteria are wearing name tags. They look like conference attendees, not colleagues.

Kyung pays for his breakfast and finds a table in the corner, far from where anyone will hear them.

When Craig joins him, he looks down at Kyung's tray, seemingly crestfallen. "That's all you're having?"

There's a dried-out blueberry muffin, flecked with too much sugar, sitting on a square of wax paper. He doesn't have any appetite for more. "I have coffee too." He lifts his mug as if to prove it.

Craig's tray is crowded with plates. An egg-white omelet, made to order. A side of fruit. Toast and yogurt and a carton of grapefruit juice with a red straw poking out of it. Kyung is equally disappointed by the size of Craig's breakfast. They'll be here all morning. Although small talk has always felt unnatural to him, he's desperate to avoid where their conversation is headed next, so he picks a subject that Craig can discuss at length.

"How's your wife? And the kids?"

"Oh, they're all doing great."

The Tunneys have twin girls—one now at Wesleyan, the other at Brown. Kyung met them years ago when they came to the office to borrow Craig's car. Even as high school students, they struck him as exceptionally poised and polite. They shook hands and spoke with confidence and seemed to regard their father as a friend. If Craig had one bad habit, it was the way he wandered the halls, talking about his daughters' accomplishments with anyone willing to listen. Whenever Kyung found himself on the receiving end of these conversations, he wondered what Craig and his wife had done to ensure that their children turned out so well. There were times when he wanted to ask, but he couldn't figure out how to phrase the question. It felt like something he already should have known.

"Lydia's interning at the Federal Reserve in D.C. this summer, and Elizabeth is in Panama building ecohousing with a nonprofit."

"Panama," he repeats thoughtfully, for no other reason except to buy time. "Does she speak Spanish?"

"A couple of semesters' worth. But she's quick with languages. We sent her off to France a few summers ago, and she came back jabbering away like she was fluent." Craig stops suddenly, as if he realizes what Kyung is trying to do. "But enough about the girls. Is there anything I can help you with, Kyung? Do you want to talk about taking a leave of absence next semester?"

The thought of a leave never occurred to him.

"It would have to be unpaid, unfortunately. A situation like this—it doesn't really fit the university's requirements for paid medical leave. But I'd be happy to arrange it if you'd like some more time at home."

The idea floats past him like a balloon. Bright and buoyant for a moment, then gone with a prick of a pin. He couldn't afford to take a leave even if he wanted to.

"Actually, I'm looking forward to teaching again. It'll be good for me, I think."

He pulls his muffin apart to avoid looking Craig in the eye. It crumbles into a pile of dry, dusty pieces that he pinches into his mouth. It alarms him that he can't remember what classes he's supposed to teach in the fall—Anatomy, Physiology, Cell Biology? Every semester just feels like a variation of the one that came before.

"Well, I'm here," Craig says.

"Sorry?"

"I'm here if you need anything. Even if you change your mind and we have to make some last-minute adjustments, it'll be fine. You just have to tell me what's on your mind."

Lately, Kyung has been thinking about Nat Perry, wondering where he is, what his life is like. He imagines him in some barren northern stretch of Canada, trying to reinvent himself. That's what Kyung would do if he suddenly found himself on the run. Pick a place where no one would ever look for him. Start over. Do everything differently. The idea of California still tugs at him from time to time. During his senior year in college, he applied to the medical school at Irvine, which his advisors warned was a stretch. None of them knew what to say when he was accepted but chose not to go. Kyung couldn't tell them why he needed to stay in Marlboro, the things that might happen if he went away. He convinced himself there would always be other opportunities to leave. At twenty-two, he didn't have the foresight to understand how one decision could affect so many others. Now that he's older and everything has settled into a just-tolerable state of atrophy, the options he once had—options that his young students still have—feel like they've passed him by.

"Are your parents back home, or are they staying with you?"

"With me and Gillian. Actually, they all left for the Cape today. It was getting a little crowded at home."

"And you're still here? Because of work?"

He's about to nod until he notices Craig shaking his head.

"Give me your keys," he says, holding out his hand.

Kyung removes the ring from his pocket and sets it on the table. He knows what Craig is about to do before he does it.

"There." He slides off the oversized key to Kyung's office and slips it into his bag. "I don't want to see you here for the rest of the summer. There's nothing that can't wait for you until August."

Kyung has a spare key at home, not that it really matters. He doesn't want to be here either. He eats another pinch of muffin, washing down the stale crumbs with the last of his coffee. He can feel Craig watching him, waiting for a thank-you, perhaps—and on some level, he knows he deserves it. This is his idea of being kind.

"Thank you."

"It's the least I can do, Kyung. I'm sure it can't be easy for you right now, but trust me. Work can wait. You won't regret the time that you spend with your family, later on."

Behind him, Kyung hears the metal scrape of a chair against

the floor. He turns to find the cafeteria nearly twice as full as it was before. On the other side of the room, Marcy is standing in the cashier's line. He'd prefer to avoid running into anyone else from his department today, and Craig has all but ordered him to leave. Leave and do what, though? He doesn't think the time he's been spending with his family has helped them in any way.

"What would you do if you were me?" he asks.

"If I were in your situation?" Craig stares at his breakfast; he seems terrified to imagine the possibility. "I guess I'd just try to be there for everyone."

"Yes, but beyond just being there."

"I don't know. I mean, what your family's been through—the only word that can really describe it is 'evil.' Just the worst kind of human evil. I'm not sure there's anything you can do about that other than love each other and trust that things will eventually go back to the way they were." He pauses. "I'm sorry, Kyung. Maybe I misunderstood your question? I don't think I'm answering it the way you want me to."

"No, no. That's fine." He pushes his chair back from the table. "I was curious, that's all. I should probably get going now."

Craig has hardly touched his breakfast, but he moves his tray off to the side. "You'll make decent time if you head to the Cape now. Reverse traffic." He stands up and shakes Kyung's hand, resting his other on Kyung's shoulder. "You'll get in touch if you need anything? Anything at all? You just have to let me know."

From another man's mouth, the offer might sound hollow and perfunctory, but Craig isn't the type to say less than what he means.

"Thank you."

As he feels Craig's grip loosen, he squeezes harder, realizing that the answer was right there in front of him the entire time. The twins turned out well, not because of anything that Craig or his wife did but because of the kind of people they are. Good, decent people who always put the needs of their children ahead of their own. It was never more complicated than love, one generation raising a better version of the next.

"I never really had a chance, did I?"

Craig squints at him. "A chance at what?"

"Nothing," he says. "I was just thinking out loud."

He can count the number of times he let his anger get away from him. What he lost track of years ago is how often he had to walk himself back from that cliff. Control is the only thing that separates his anger from his father's; he's known this for years. But as he stares at the red Buick parked in his driveway again, his insides blister with rage, and there's nothing he can do to stop it, nothing he wants to do anymore. Kyung slams his palm against the horn and leaves it there, drawing neighbors out of their homes as the seconds multiply into minutes. They stare at him, confused and startled by the unbroken sound, wondering why he won't make it stop. He throws his head back, hitting it against the headrest until everything around him becomes a blur. In the corner of his eye, there's a flash of pink, and then a loud click as the door flings open and a hand reaches over to grab his.

"What are you *doing*?" a woman shouts.

His eyes slowly focus on Molly, not the reverend as he assumed.

"Why are you here?" he shouts back.

"I, I came to pick up yesterday's containers. And I brought you more food."

"I don't need it." He gets out of his car and walks toward the house, ignoring the neighbors still gathered outside. "Everyone's gone."

"Gone where?"

He hears Molly's voice trailing after him. Don't follow me, he thinks. Don't.

"Well, where did they all go?"

The key to the side door sticks. He shakes it harder than he should, not caring if the thin glass window crashes to the ground.

"Here, here. Let me." She takes the key from him and unlocks the door.

Kyung brushes past her, through the hall and into the kitchen, which still smells like bacon. The sink is filled with dirty dishes smeared with egg yolks and bluish streaks of jam. Perched on top is an oily frying pan, slick with grease. He doesn't know whether Gillian forgot to clean up her mess or if she was just in a hurry to leave. Both explanations are equally plausible. Neither does anything to improve his mood.

"So where did everyone go?" she repeats.

"Could you please just leave me alone?"

"But there's no one here to help you."

He can't explain the relief he felt as he watched his family pile into Connie's car and drive away. It was like a gift, especially his mother's last-minute decision to take Marina along with them. The house was quiet for once, quiet until now.

"Help me do what? What exactly do you think I need help with?"

"I don't know. It just doesn't seem like you should be on your own."

He turns his back to her, staring at his reflection in the window. His face is strangely bloated; the bags under his eyes are more swollen than usual. He looks old all of a sudden, like the bell curve of his life is in permanent decline. To admit this to Molly would only invite her cheerful, biblical brand of consolation, and he's not in the mood to hear it right now.

"I'm worried about you, Kyung. I've never seen you like this."

"I asked you to leave."

"But maybe—maybe you need someone to talk to?"

He doesn't know why she thinks this is her responsibility. They've never been anything more than casual acquaintances, distantly positioned on each other's periphery. He hooks his fingers through a handle, opening and closing a drawer because it's there. The inside is stuffed full with windowed envelopes—bills, he assumes, that Gillian wanted somewhere out of sight. The thick, haphazard stack makes him nervous. He wonders how long they've been there and how many of them have actually been paid.

"Penny for your thoughts?" she offers brightly.

"God, you're awful."

He says these words with none of the anxious planning that usually precedes his attempts to talk to her. And although her face registers a sort of wounded surprise, he recognizes something familiar just below the surface. He looks her up and down, not making any effort to be discreet this time. The flash of pink he saw in the car was her dress, a bright pink sundress with a sweater tied around her shoulders. For modesty, he assumes.

The neckline is lower than usual, inches below the pendant that he rarely sees her without. He reaches for the flash of diamonds, brushing her bare skin as he lifts the crucifix to examine it.

"What happened to you?" he asks.

She swats him away and the pendant falls to her chest. "What happened to *me*? What happened to *you*? Why are you acting like this?"

There, he thinks. There's the girl he remembers from so long ago. Insolent, angry. Not afraid to raise her voice. This is the girl who threw a chalkboard eraser at their English teacher for picking on her, the one who always smelled like smoke and patchouli and sex.

"I liked you better in high school," he says. "You were more honest back then."

"Honest? What am I not being honest about?"

"About who you really are."

She shakes her head. "I don't know what that's supposed to mean."

"It means I think you're a fake. You and everyone else from that church, but you in particular."

Molly's mouth is open, but she doesn't make a sound. She just backs away and braces herself against the edge of the sink. She looks like she's about to cry, which would disappoint him. The old Molly would never cry.

"Maybe that's your opinion," she says. "But you haven't spent enough time with us to really know."

He opens the refrigerator and rummages through its contents until he finds a six-pack of beer, hidden behind the gallon jugs of milk and juice.

"You're having beer now? It's not even ten o'clock yet."

He stares at her over the rim as he downs half a can. "It's been a long day."

Molly looks away, embarrassed or uncomfortable—probably both. "So where did everyone go?"

"To the Cape."

"And they just left you here?"

"Maybe I wanted to be left."

She nods. "I'll get going too, then. There's food in the cooler if you want it, but it has to be refrigerated soon."

"You still haven't answered my question."

She blinks at him. "What are you talking about?"

"What happened to you? What brought on your . . . conversion?" He makes no effort to soften his ridicule as the word slides from his tongue. He wants to see the old Molly, the real one. He wants the truth that only she can tell.

"You're too closed off to God to hear anything I say."

"Try me."

He stares at Molly in profile, at the way her long black hair falls over her shoulders, appearing almost red in the sun. He's tempted to push a strand away from her face, but her expression is too pretty to disturb. She's looking out the window into the backyard, her eyes framed by a thick sweep of lashes. There's a pale brown mole on her cheek—he's never stood close enough to notice it before—and another at the base of her collarbone.

"I wasn't a good person when I was younger. I think everyone in school probably knew that. I had problems, lots of them, and after a certain point, it was hard to forgive myself for some of the things I'd done. But I was lucky—the people I met at college, my friends, they helped me realize that it wasn't my forgiveness I needed to seek."

"That sounds like your husband talking, not you."

"It's the truth."

"But what good is that? It's not like you had a conversation with God. It's not like you said 'I'm sorry' and heard him accept."

"No, but I have faith that he heard me."

"That kind of forgiveness is all up in here." He taps the side of his head too hard. "It's what my son does with stuffed animals. It's make-believe."

Molly takes a sponge from the sink and wipes a puddle of juice off the counter. She goes over the area again and again, long after it's dry. "Maybe it'd be better if you talked with my husband about this. I don't think I'm expressing myself very clearly."

"It's not about being clear or unclear. I just don't buy this devout little wife act. You're either fooling yourself or the rest of us—I can never tell."

Molly throws the sponge down and squares her shoulders, appearing much taller than she did before. "You don't have the right to talk about me like that, like you actually know me. You never tried to befriend me—not back in school and not as adults either. You have no idea who I am."

Her tone is barely civil now, and he likes the unguarded spike of hostility, returning like a memory she long ago blocked out. All these years, he had it wrong. Being kind to Molly, being a gentleman—that wasn't what she wanted. Some part of her still responds to being abused.

"I didn't try to befriend you because I felt sorry for you. Everyone knew how easy you were, how you'd go off during lunch with anyone who asked. I didn't want to be one of those guys who just used you in the back of his car and then never gave you the time of day."

"Ha," she shouts, thrusting her face just inches in front of his. "I saw the way you always looked at me. You still do it now. You were just too shy to do anything about it when you had the chance."

Her expression is angry and defiant, a break in her carefully composed veneer. Kyung sees the victory in this, the dare. One second, his arms are crossed over his chest. The next, he's clutching the back of Molly's head, pushing his tongue into her mouth. The effect is ugly and sloppy, more probing than kissing until a switch goes off somewhere, wired deep in the back channels of her brain. Gone is the woman so prim and eager to please. In her purest state, Molly is all instinct and aggression. She wraps her arms around his neck, snakes her leg around his leg, kissing him so furiously that her teeth knock and scrape against his. They stumble against the sink, and a pitcher falls off the counter and shatters on the floor. He can feel bits of glass crunching under his shoes, but the strangeness of this sensation quickly gives way to another—her hand on his pants, tracing and retracing him through the fabric.

This is what being with a woman is supposed to feel like. Dangerous and unfamiliar, on the edge of something because it's both. By now, he knows every pale curve and freckled hollow of his wife's body. He knows exactly how Gillian will respond if he touches her in one place versus another, if she wants him to be gentle or rough. The sex is never bad so much as predictable—rushed, usually—as if both of them would rather be doing something else. With Molly, it's different. He's not accustomed to her reactions, to the sounds she makes as he lowers a strap of her dress to kiss her bare breast. Her back arches as if it might break; her hips press tightly against his. He wants to take his time, to enjoy her while he can, but nothing about this feels patient. Kyung lifts her onto the countertop, centering himself between her legs. He yanks her underwear to her knees and slips his fingers inside her, higher and higher until she almost loses breath.

"Wait," she says.

Kyung reaches for his belt, but the metal buckle won't release. He fumbles with it, trying not to let his clumsiness become a distraction. He closes his eyes and kisses her again, imagining Molly on all fours while he takes her from behind. She wouldn't mind this position, he thinks. But by the time he undoes his belt, something has started to change. Her body goes limp. Her right hand leaves his neck, and then the other soon follows. Kyung opens his eyes, startled to see that Molly's are open too, but not open as they should be. Up close, they're wide open, unblinking, the whites latticed with red. Her pupils are dilated; the blacks are all he can see. He backs away slowly, still joined by a long string of saliva connecting her mouth to his. It stretches and stretches, thinning to a hairlike strand that finally breaks.

Molly slides off the counter, hugging the cabinets as she slowly moves to the other side of the room. She looks disoriented, or maybe even sick.

"Are you all right?"

She stares at him, her lower lip in full tremor.

"Molly? What's going on?"

"Why did we do that?" she asks. "Why?"

He doesn't know what she expects him to say. He can't

answer for her; he can hardly answer for himself. "Because we wanted to, I guess."

She continues staring at him, clutching the ends of the sweater still tied around her neck. Whatever confusion she may have felt is gone now, replaced by something that begins to resemble fear.

"Maybe you should sit."

When he takes a step toward her, she jumps away, nearly tripping on the underwear around her ankles. He reaches out to break her fall, but this only seems to frighten her more. She picks up the frying pan in the sink, raising it at him like a weapon.

"Why are you acting like this?"

"Don't touch me," she says. She takes a small step to her left, then another, and another, still holding the pan as she nears the door.

"What do you mean, 'Don't touch me'? What were we just doing?"

The trembling in her lower lip returns, and suddenly, she's sliding down the wall, knees splayed as she falls to the floor, all limbs and noise and tears. The thick, perfect lashes he admired only minutes ago streak down her face in watery black stripes. A bubble of mucus expands and contracts from her nostril with each breath. Kyung stands perfectly still, too stunned by her reaction to respond, but the sound of her voice—that awful, hiccupped wail—he can't listen to it much longer.

"Molly," he says quietly. "What happened? What just changed?"

She shakes her head.

"Did I hurt you somehow?" He reaches for her again, but

she leans away to avoid being touched. "Look, I don't under-stand what's going on right now, but I'm not sorry we did that."

The statement doesn't quiet her, but it reassures him to hear the words out loud. He has nothing to apologize for. He didn't do anything that Molly didn't want, that she didn't respond to eagerly. Regret is the only reason she's sitting on the floor.

"Could you please—please stop crying?"

This only makes her cry louder, so much so that he begins to worry the neighbors will overhear. He shuts an open window and fills a glass with water from the sink. When he offers it to her, she knocks it away, sending the plastic cup spinning like a top. It skitters across the tile, spraying water on the cabinets and floor. When the cup stops moving, he sits down beside it, fold-ing his hands in his lap where she can see them. He tells himself to be patient; eventually, she'll wear herself out. But minutes pass, and she continues to wail.

"Do you remember when you lived in that house on Larkin Street?" he asks.

She stops crying just long enough to gasp for air.

"That big one with the white fence?"

"Why—why are you asking me that now?"

Kyung still sees the house clearly, with its brick face and or-ange shutters and matching orange mailbox. In junior high, he walked past it every day after school, slowing down as he neared the fence to listen and wait. Sometimes he heard nothing. Sometimes he heard Molly's parents fighting inside. He knew what a punch and a slap sounded like. He was all too familiar with the sound of a woman crying. He listened as long as he could, stopping to tie his shoe or search his book bag for some-thing he didn't need. The next day, he'd watch Molly in the cafeteria or in the halls, acting out as if the world owed her something. Secretly, he admired her for this. She'd earned the chip on her shoulder and she wasn't afraid to show people it was there. She did what she wanted, got in trouble, and made her parents as miserable as they made her, which was exactly what they deserved. He looked up to her for this until she decided not to be that person anymore, which always felt like a betrayal.

"I wish we could have been friends back then," he says. "I think we would have understood each other. Helped each other, maybe."

She's no longer crying so much as fighting the urge to cry, choking off the sound as it reaches her throat. "It's too late."

"I know." He stands up and offers his hand, trying to get Molly on her feet. "Come on."

She looks at him, her face still smeared and striped with black, her hair as disheveled as he's ever seen it. He smiles at her anyway, wondering how she'll explain her appearance when she gets home. The thought is nothing more than that at first. A thought, a flicker. But suddenly, it combusts.

"You're not—we're not going to tell anyone about this, are we?"

Molly closes her eyes and wipes her face with her dress, leaving a stain on the fabric that looks like an inkblot. Then she exhales and slowly reaches for his hand, staring at him until her fingertips are almost touching his. Kyung is so relieved to see her accepting his help, he doesn't notice the flash at first, another bright blur of pink as something sharp and painful rips across his cheek.

"Molly!" he shouts. But she's already running for it, her sweater flapping behind her like a cape.

Kyung stands in the open doorway, watching the Buick back out and tear down the street. Half a block away, and she's still gunning the engine, as if she expects him to follow. Molly doesn't yield, much less stop at the intersection before turning, causing another driver to slam on his brakes. When her car disappears, he reaches up to touch his stinging cheek. There's blood on his fingertips. There's blood everywhere, actually. Fresh red drops of it on his hands and shirt and pants. He walks back inside and closes the door, scanning the kitchen, which is even messier than it was before. The pitcher that fell off the counter is lying in big, jagged shards beneath the sink. A fine powder of crushed glass dusts the area where they were standing. He looks himself over again, hopeful that the blood is all his, when he notices his feet, clad in thin, flimsy sandals. His bare skin is cut in so many places, it looks like he kicked in a window.

Kyung cleans up the glass and carefully deposits the broken pieces into an empty plastic bag. Then he ties the handles and pushes the bag deep into the trash where Gillian won't find it. But covering his tracks is useless, he thinks. Molly is going to tell everyone. Her husband, his wife, maybe even his parents. Isn't that what devout people do? Sin and repent; sin and repent again. He returns to his beer on the counter, emptying the rest of the can and immediately opening another before he can convince himself not to. Drinking is a choice, he thinks. His choice. Molly was too, and now he has to live with the consequences, however bad they might be. He's fucked—he knows that—but for the first time, he's fucked by something he chose to do, not something that was done to him, or something he had to do out of guilt or obligation or fear. He laughs even though his heart is pounding. This one belongs entirely to him.

Every summer, Kyung's parents invited him to visit the beach house with Ethan and Gillian. And every summer, he declined, unwilling to spend an entire weekend in their company. His only glimpse of the property was the painting on his parents' mantel in Marlboro, an abstract piece commissioned by his mother's decorator as a gift. On canvas, the house seemed large, but unexceptional—a tall white block with a red front door. In person, it's something else entirely. When the GPS tells him to turn onto a private road, Kyung hesitates, not quite believing what he sees. At the far end of the road, a single house sits high on a bluff, surrounded by a spectacular, expensive kind of nothing—no neighbors, no trees—just the sky above and a steep drop to the bay below. The three-story colonial looks like something out of a postcard, lit brightly from within as the last sliver of sun descends into the horizon.

He imagines Gillian's reaction as she drove up the same road earlier that day. Mouth open, fingertips pressed against the window, looking like the girl from the Flats that she really is. He knows what she's probably thinking now; he knows the inconsistency of her mind. Pride is her Achilles, but she wouldn't hesitate to accept Jin's help if he offered. With a few keystrokes or a checkbook and pen, his parents could erase all their debts and give them a fresh start. But their help would come with a price far worse than what they live with now. Every invitation his parents extended, every request for help or company or time—they wouldn't be able to refuse if they took their money. Kyung isn't about to indenture himself to them now, not after so many years of trying to avoid it. The minute he moved out for college, he juggled part-time jobs, shared apartments with too many people, took out loans to pay tuition, and took out more loans when he was short on cash—all because he didn't want to owe his parents anything. Still, he feels a flare of resentment as he surveys the enormous property. He never asked for their help, but not once did they offer.

The long, unpaved road curves toward the water, rattling the car and everything inside it. In the passenger seat, eight empty beer cans clank against each other, accompanied by the noisy ping of loose gravel churning in the tire wells. Kyung switches off his headlights, trying to make his approach less noticeable. He wasn't entirely committed to coming to Orleans when he started driving, and despite all the beer he drank along the way, he can't resummon the courage he felt back at the house. By now, he assumes that Molly has confessed everything to her husband, begging for his forgiveness, and God's too. It's only a matter of time before he'll have to tell Gillian, a conversation so daunting, it feels like a wall of stone—something so tall, he has to crane his neck up to see where it might end. His only choice is to climb over it or wait to be crushed if it falls. There's no other way around this time, and maybe this is what he wanted all along, to force his own hand.

Kyung pulls into a parking space, hidden from view by the shadow of Connie's huge Suburban. He gets out and closes his door, pushing it into place with a click instead of a slam. As he walks up the front steps, he considers turning back. No one saw or heard him arrive. No one is expecting him until tomorrow.

But his desire to flee gives way to the blurriness of his eyesight, the spinning sensation in his head. To attempt driving back now would land him in jail or a ditch or the ocean, so he knocks and holds his breath, waiting for the door to open. When it doesn't, he tries the knob, which should be locked but isn't. He steps into the entryway, relieved to find it empty. To his left, there's a living room with a long wall of windows that overlook the bay. To his right is a study filled with books and a soft, pillowlike couch that screams his name. Nearly everything in the house is white. White walls, white ceilings, white furniture. Like the house in Marlboro, Mae clearly spared no expense on the renovations. The place looks exactly the way a beach house should. Open and airy, like something out of a magazine where no children or pets or people actually live.

He takes a few more steps inside, following the muffled sound of voices toward the back of the house. The farther he tiptoes, the more the air begins to smell like butter and brine. At the end of a long hallway, Kyung stops before an open door and presses his back against the wall, listening to the conversation in the adjoining room. Jin tells Connie that the fishing is terrible in Nauset Bay, but offers the use of his boat to visit Salt Pond Bay instead. A woman whose voice he doesn't recognize exclaims that she loves boats; she has ever since she was a child. Gillian encourages Ethan to climb into his chair by himself. You're big enough now, she says. You can do it. The conversation is much easier and lighter than he imagined, moving amiably from one topic to the next without so much as a pause. He doesn't know where his mother and Marina are—in the kitchen, probably—but so far, everything seems to be going well, better than he would have expected.

He smooths out his shirt and hair and walks into the dining room. "Hi," he says casually, stopping to kiss Ethan on the forehead.

"Well, look who's here," Connie says. "I thought you weren't coming until tomorrow."

"I finished early."

Jin seems disappointed to see him. He nods in Kyung's direction, but the gesture conveys nothing. It's barely a greeting. It's certainly not a welcome.

Gillian gets up to give him a hug. She sniffs his breath suspiciously and then forces herself to smile. "What happened to your face?"

Kyung touches the bandage he slapped on his cheek before he left home. He wonders if she can make out the fingernail marks through the thin layer of gauze. "Books," he says, glancing at the wall of books behind her shoulder.

"Books?"

"I was reaching for something—at the office. They fell off the shelf and hit me in the face."

"Oh."

Everyone is seated around a long planked table that looks like it was salvaged from an expensive Italian farm. Kyung takes the empty chair next to Gillian. Across from him is a middle-aged blonde.

"Hi, I'm Vivian." She reaches over the flower arrangement to shake his hand, clinking all the shiny bracelets on her wrist. "But you can call me Vivi."

"Nice to meet you."

Connie's new girlfriend is prettier and more cheerful than Kyung would have expected. Such a difference from his first wife, who never appeared happy in any of their pictures. Until now, he always assumed that Connie liked his women short and thick, but Vivi is exceptionally fit for her age, which he'd put at mid- to late fifties. She's tan too, in a carrotlike way that suggests fake sun out of a bottle, not vacations at the beach.

"We've been having such a wonderful time here," Vivi says. "Thank you so much for inviting us. I was just telling Connie how I was hoping to get to the Cape this summer, and not two days later, you called."

She has a pretty laugh. Feminine and natural, with a flash of straight white teeth. Connie is clearly enamored of her, which is strange. He looks like he's on his best behavior, dressed in a shirt that actually has buttons. The fact that he's here with his in-laws suggests that he's serious about making this woman happy. Serious, or simply too cheap to take Vivi on a getaway of their own.

"Grandpa and I found shells today," Ethan says from the other end of the table. He lifts a hermit crab shell in the air so that Kyung can see.

"Did you have fun?"

Ethan looks at Jin, giggling in a way that seems almost secretive. Such an innocent gesture, but it confirms what he's suspected for weeks. There's a transfer of affection happening, a slow siphoning off from Kyung to Jin. He doesn't know how to make it stop, much less reverse it. If he tells Ethan to stay away from his grandfather, he'll demand to know why. Kyung would never be able to answer his son's questions truthfully, not without changing him.

"I'm glad you had a good time." He takes a bottle of wine from the table and fills his glass just shy of the rim.

His excess apparently amuses Connie, whose laugh sounds like a donkey's bray. "That must have been one heck of a drive."

"Save some for the rest of us," Gillian suggests gently.

"But you were the one who said we're on vacation." Kyung takes a long drink, surprised by the pleasant, unfamiliar taste in his mouth. He picks up the bottle and examines the label. It's a 1989 white Burgundy. There are two more bottles just like it on the table.

"You had the same reaction I did," Connie says, his mood as jovial as Kyung has ever seen it. "I guess we were just drinking the cheap stuff all these years, right?"

From the kitchen, Mae and Marina file out, carrying plates of bright red lobsters sitting on beds of lettuce.

Mae takes one look at Kyung and frowns. "I thought you weren't coming until tomorrow."

"I finished early," he repeats, hopeful that no one will ask what he actually finished.

"But I didn't buy enough lobsters."

"It's fine, Mae," Gillian says. "These are big. We can share."

Mae looks put out by the offer. She doesn't like running out of food, which she says is a sign of a bad hostess. "I need another place setting," she tells Marina.

"Yes, Mrs. Cho."

Vivi studies Marina as she leaves the room. There's something about Vivi's expression—curious, but pleased—that suggests she's never been attended to like this. It's obvious now why Mae did such an about-face and decided to bring Marina to the Cape. She wanted her around to help serve the guests. She probably assumed that people like Connie and Vivi would be impressed.

When Marina returns, she sets a plate of lobster in front of Kyung.

"Where did this come from?" he asks.

"I don't like lobster, Mr. Kyung."

"But it's yours. You should have it."

He tries to return the plate to her, but Marina is already heading back to the kitchen, turning only to exchange a glance with Mae to see if she approves. Mae ignores her as she takes her place at the end of the table, whipping a cloth napkin open and spreading it across her lap. She's dressed more elegantly than she has been for weeks, with an emerald green blouse that ties at the neck and a thin gray skirt. Everyone, it seems, has dressed for dinner. Even Ethan, who's sporting a miniature blue bow tie. Kyung glances at his shirt, which is spattered with flecks of dried blood. He realizes that he forgot to bring the suitcase that Gillian packed for him, a lapse he hardly knows how to explain.

"So Gillian tells me you're a biology professor," Vivi says.

Kyung accidentally glances at her cleavage. He can't help himself. There's so much of it, and so clearly arranged for display. He turns his attention to the vase of tulips on the table, but the blurry yellow buds appear to be moving in circles, orbiting and reorbiting each other.

"Do you enjoy teaching?" she asks.

"Ha!" he laughs too loudly. Such a stupid, predictable question. "You don't really want to know the answer to that, do you?"

Vivi seems charmed by this. "I guess I feel the same way. I mean, I love teaching, but seventh graders aren't exactly what they used to be." She gives Connie a knowing look. "I can't wait to retire in a few years. There are so many places I've put off visiting, and now I finally have someone to travel with."

The polite response would be to ask Vivi where they're planning to go, but the room is incredibly bright. The chandelier reflects light everywhere. Even the silverware is too shiny. Kyung lowers his head and studies a spot of blood on his pants. Like the tulips, the spot won't stay in one place. It resembles a heart at first, then an ace, then a leaf. When he looks up again, the conversation has come to an awkward pause. Everyone is trying not to stare. Kyung empties his wineglass and leans over Gillian for an open bottle that's too far to reach. She nudges him away with her elbow and fills his glass for him, pouring a stingy half inch that he finishes in one gulp.

"So . . . these are darling." Vivi picks up one of the porcelain seashells scattered across the table. "I didn't even notice them before."

The shells have a thick gold band in the middle, separating them into two halves held together by a button. When Vivi presses hers, the shell pops open like a box.

"What's it supposed to do?" she asks.

"Sometimes I lean place cards on them," Mae says. "Mostly, they're for decoration."

"How sweet. They remind me of something my grandmother would have collected. She loved anything porcelain."

"You should take them, then. The whole set. I think I have twelve."

"What?" Vivi looks to Connie for help. "Oh, no. I couldn't."

"They're not valuable, if that's what you're thinking. And I almost never get to use them. It would make me so happy if someone did. Besides, it's my way of thanking you for your help today."

Kyung glances at Mae. "Help with what?"

Gillian clears her throat. "Vivi helped your mom with that inventory she's been working on. They were at it all afternoon." Something in her voice suggests that she doesn't think much of her father's new girlfriend, but no one else seems to notice. Her disapproval registers just below the surface, like a frequency only audible between husband and wife.

"I thought that list was just for the other house," Kyung says.

"It's important to have a record of things." Mae leans toward Vivi again. "If there's something else you saw today that you liked more, please—"

"The shells are perfect, really. Thank you so much." She turns hers over, squinting to read the underside. "Lime . . . Lime-oh-jess? Huh."

Kyung frowns at the badly mangled French. It's Limoges, and it's expensive—hardly the insignificant little trinket that Mae made it out to be. He sits back and examines Vivi, wondering if Gillian's assessment of her is the same as his own. She's a gold digger of some sort, accustomed to being taken care of, which would explain the perfect hair and tan and body. The nails and jewelry too. Connie isn't a wealthy man, but he earns a good salary and has a house, a car, and a pension. Maybe that makes him wealthy to her.

"Kyung." Connie snaps his fingers. "Earth to Kyung."

He realizes he's been staring at Vivi again because she turns away, flustered, straining to hear the conversation at the other end of the table.

"It has bug eyes," Ethan whines, cocking his head at the lobster on his plate.

"Here." Gillian picks up a silver cracker. "Let me get you some of the meat from the claw. That's the best part."

"You mean the hand?"

"It's not a hand, honey. It's a claw."

"But I don't want any."

"Just try it. Your grandma worked hard to make this for you."

"No."

Kyung dislikes how everything has come to a standstill because of the boy. He never would have dared to act out in public as a child. "Don't talk back to your mother," he says. "Just eat your dinner like she asked."

Ethan looks at Jin, who doesn't respond, but something about this exchange bothers Kyung. What was his son hoping for when he turned his head? For his grandfather to overrule him?

"Eat your dinner," Kyung repeats.

"But I don't want any."

"Eat—your—dinner." The words come out slowly, but there's no mistaking his menace as he brings his hand down on the table, causing everything—the china, the crystal, the silverware—to rattle. Gillian, Connie, and Jin are all quick to interject: "Take it easy." "What are you doing?" "Stop." The voice he hears last and loudest is his father's, and this, he won't abide.

"*You* don't have the right to tell me to stop. You, of all people. Where do you think I learned this from?"

Vivi coughs into her napkin. "My goodness," she says to no one in particular. "I've never tasted lobster this fresh before. I guess all those others I ate were frozen."

Mae glares at Kyung as perfect circles of pink bloom on her cheeks. Then she turns back to her guests. "We get them right off the boat at the dock. I like how easy they are to prepare. . . . Would you like some more butter?"

"No," Kyung shouts. Everyone at the table jumps, their shoulders stiff, their spines perfectly straight. He's not about to let them sit there and act like this is a normal meal, a normal family, a normal life. "Stop with the fucking butter. We're not going to do this anymore."

"I'm sorry," Mae says, looking at Connie and Vivi. "My son—I think he's had too much to drink tonight. It's not like him—"

"No. No. No," he repeats. "No more excuses for each other. No more pretending everything's fine. No fucking more."

Vivi narrows her eyes at Connie, mouthing the words, *Should we go?* Poor woman, Kyung thinks. Gold digger or not, he almost feels sorry for her, walking into this sideshow when all she wanted was a free weekend at the beach. He stands up, raising his glass to her as if to give a toast.

"See, Vivi? What you need to know about my parents is that this one"—he points to Jin with his glass, spilling an arc of wine across the tablecloth—"this one used to hit my mother. And this one"—he flicks his finger at Mae—"this one used to hit me. So don't be fooled by all their nice things and nice manners. They're not good people."

Gillian buries her face in her hands, mortified. Jin lifts Ethan out of his chair and whisks him out of the room. Mae throws her knife down so violently, it cracks her plate in two as she runs into the kitchen. Kyung remains standing, teetering from side to side like a tree caught in the wind.

"Why would you do that?" Gillian asks, still holding her face in her hands. "Why, Kyung? What good did that just do?"

"I—have—been—waiting—" He enunciates his words slowly, aware that he's starting to slur. "—I have been waiting my *entire* life to say that, Gillian. They needed to know."

"Know what?" she snaps. "They *know*."

"Do they?" He raises his voice, shouting at the ceiling so his parents will hear. "Those people ruined me. Why don't they understand—why don't they act like they understand that?"

"Kyung . . . you have to let them be sorry. You have to let them make it up to you. They're trying. Can't you see how they're trying?"

"Oh, right." He sits down, nearly missing the edge of his chair. "Of course that's what you'd say. You just want my dad to keep writing us checks. That's how you want them to make it up to me, don't you? So we can go on vacations again and drink nice wine every night?"

Gillian leans forward, propping her elbows on her knees and clutching the back of her hair. He can't tell if she's crying, or simply trying not to look at him. Either way, it doesn't matter. She's crossed over to their side, and now he doesn't want her back.

"Why don't you tell me what I'm worth, Gillian? Give me a number."

"What are you talking about?"

"The number. The amount." He slams his hands on the table, upturning glasses and bottles and shells. "Tell me what my life is worth. Tell me how much they should write the check out for so everything they did to me, everything they did in front of me—how much will it take to make that go away?"

Gillian sits up and looks at her father. Her eyes are completely dry. "I can't talk to him when he's screaming at me like this. I'm going to bed."

Before Kyung has a chance to respond, she walks out of the room, leaving him with Connie and Vivi, who both seem desperate to be somewhere else. Vivi won't look up from her shell, which she keeps turning over and over again in her hands like a giant worry bead. Kyung waits, expecting Connie to light into him for yelling at Gillian, but no such lecture comes. Instead, his father-in-law just shakes his head and speaks to him quietly, almost tenderly, in a tone that breaks him almost as much as the actual words.

"You poor son of a bitch."

PART THREE

NIGHT

SEVEN

The car is missing. These are the first words he can make out. The car—his car—is missing. Kyung sits up slowly, shielding his eyes from the light that slices through the open blinds. His head is trapped in a vise again. The pristine white couch he slept on is filthy, trampled with footprints. He should have taken his shoes off before lying down, but this is the least of his worries.

Upstairs, footsteps thunder over his head. People are yelling at each other. "Not in this room." Doors open and close, then open and close again. "Not in this room either."

I'm right here, he wants to shout, but his mouth feels dry and sandy, stuffed full of cotton. On the floor, next to his feet, there's an empty bottle of wine. He doesn't remember drinking it, or moving his car, or falling asleep in the study, and his lack of recall bothers him. The things he said and did last night—he doesn't want them diminished by how much he drank. He said exactly what he meant, what he always wanted everyone to know. The alcohol simply made him brave.

In the bathroom, Kyung examines himself in the mirror. His eyes are bloodshot, and a pebbly pink rash is spreading across his unshaven skin. He doesn't have any clean clothes to change into, not that it really matters. He's leaving the Cape today; he's sure of it. As soon as his parents see him, one or both of them will tell him to get out, but the likelihood of this doesn't concern him. The worst that can happen is another argument, which they'll want to avoid more than he does.

Kyung washes his face in the sink, feeling the pinch and pull of muscles stretched unnaturally in his sleep. Everything aches, but despite the condition of his body, his mind has never felt more liberated. All the weight he's been carrying around for years—it's as if he threw it into the bay last night, and now here he is, blinking at his newer, lighter self in the mirror. He peels the wet bandage from his cheek, revealing three long burrows of red. It's obvious they weren't caused by books falling off a shelf. He reaches for the medicine cabinet, tempted to open the door and search for another bandage, but he steels himself with a reminder: No falling back into old habits. No more avoiding what simply is. Kyung hears people coming downstairs, and his natural inclination is to creep away, to delay the confrontation that he knows is coming. Instead, he takes a deep breath and follows the voices into the living room. Connie is there, talking on his cell phone while Gillian looks on.

"I'm calling about a missing person," Connie says. "It hasn't been twenty-four hours yet, but there's a missing vehicle too."

"I slept in the study," Kyung says. "I didn't go anywhere."

Gillian jerks her head at him. She has bags under her eyes, and her skin looks gray and bloodless, even in the light. "We're not looking for *you*," she says. The sharp spike of her voice tacks on the words "you idiot," even though she didn't say them out loud.

Connie moves toward the window, plugging his ear as he continues his conversation in the corner.

"What's going on?" Kyung asks.

"Do you have any idea what you've done?"

He thought he did, but the more Gillian narrows her eyes at him, the more confused he feels. Dinner is the dividing line of his memory. Everything before and during, he remembers clearly, proudly even. Everything afterward is a blank.

"When?"

Her expression is unlike anything he's ever seen before. She's more than just annoyed. She's searching, as if she asked a question and the answer is imprinted somewhere under his skin. Five years they've been together, and she's staring at him like a stranger, like someone she doesn't know or wishes she'd never met.

"Excuse me. Could I get by, please?" Vivi brushes past, carrying a large silver tray. She sets it on the end table and pours three cups of coffee, careful to avoid any eye contact with Kyung. Like Gillian, she has no makeup on, and she's still wearing pajamas. Her hair, which was so perfectly coiffed last night, has deflated like a balloon. Everyone looks ugly this morning.

"Will one of you tell me what's going on?"

Gillian and Vivi both turn to Connie, who now has his back to them. He keeps saying, "I see, I see," and then occasionally, "I understand."

"Who's he talking to? Where's everyone else?"

As soon as Kyung mentions the others, he realizes who's present and who's not. And despite the lightness of his mood only minutes earlier, something wraps him tight in its grip, stopping the blood to his heart.

"Where's Ethan? What happened to Ethan?"

"Lower your voice," Gillian hisses. "He's right outside."

Kyung runs to the window, searching for proof that Ethan is where she says. He spots him near the steps to the beach, crouched on all fours while examining something in the sand. Kyung has no regrets about last night except for one. He wishes he hadn't snapped at Ethan about the lobster; he wishes he'd had the sense to send him to his room. He's relieved to see him no worse for the wear, dressed in swim trunks and chatting happily about the animal or insect he's just discovered. Jin is standing beside him, his attention clearly divided between his grandson and the house, which he keeps looking up at. When he notices Kyung in the window, the distance between them fails to soften the expression on Jin's face. It's the same look that Gillian gave him, the one that says everything is different now, that there's no going back to what was before.

Connie motions for a pen, which Vivi springs from her seat to give him. He writes something on his hand and thanks the person on the other end.

"Come on," he says to Kyung. "We have to go."

Gillian and Vivi crowd around him for an explanation, but Connie waves them away. "Later," he says, grabbing his keys and heading toward the door. "I'll know more later."

Kyung follows him outside, not certain where they're about to go, or why Connie is calling Jin over. "Will you tell me what's going on?"

"Mae and Marina were in an accident."

"When? Where?"

"This morning. Not far from here, I think."

Jin sends Ethan into the house and joins them in the drive-way.

"The police found them," Connie says. "They were in an accident off Route 28. You know where that is?"

Jin is sweaty from standing in the sun for too long. When he nods, his glasses almost fall off his nose. "Are they hurt?"

"I'm sure it was nothing. They just can't release any details on the phone."

The three of them climb into the Suburban—Connie and Jin in front, Kyung in back. As soon as Kyung puts on his seat belt, he feels an uncomfortable pressure against his bladder, but it's too late to stop for the bathroom now.

"How did this happen?" he asks.

"They must have taken your car this morning before every-one got up."

The Suburban bounces along the gravel, shaking Kyung like a loose marble in the backseat. He clutches the door handle to steady himself, trying to make sense of what he just heard.

"I don't understand," Jin says. "Marina doesn't drive."

"Apparently, Mae was the one driving."

"But she can't drive either. There must be some mistake."

"I taught her," Kyung says quietly, not certain if he's admit-ting or explaining.

"You did what?"

"She asked me to. She wanted to learn, so I taught her."

"So she can handle a car, then?" Connie asks. "She knows what she's doing?"

Kyung isn't sure how to respond. "We only practiced that one time."

Jin glares at him in the rearview mirror. "You did this," he says. "You and your drunk ranting last night . . . in front of your own child, in front of our guests. You have no respect for anyone. That's why your mother and Marina left this morning. You think those two haven't been through enough without you making more trouble?"

"You've done a thousand times worse in front of me."

"Children are supposed to honor their parents."

"And parents are supposed to take care of their children."

"You ungrateful little—"

"Grateful for *what*? What exactly should I be grateful for?"

"Enough," Connie says. "I can't think with the two of you shouting in my ear."

Kyung is about to continue when Jin leans forward in his seat and points at a small marker approaching on the side of the road. "There," he says. "That's where you want to turn. Right there."

The change in direction takes the air out of their argument. The three of them sit silently as they join a narrow two-lane highway that winds through a residential area, a homelier part of Orleans that reminds Kyung of the Flats. The houses they pass are modest. Small and untended and built up right along the side of the road, with no view of anything worth seeing. He assumes this is where the real people live, the ones who work the cash registers and wait on tables and bag groceries for the vacationers who invade every summer. He watches their rusty cars and yards filled with garage-sale junk pass through his window, wondering where Mae and Marina thought they were going. There aren't any stores in this area, and if they needed a pretty drive to clear their heads, this wasn't the right place to do it.

"Dickinson Farm Road," Connie says. "That's the cross street they gave me. How far is that from here?"

"Not far. But why would they be in this part of town?" Jin asks.

Kyung assumes that Mae got lost and flustered. He taught her to drive in circles, not to find her way home. "She was a fast learner," he says, if only to reassure himself.

They follow the highway for a few miles until traffic begins to slow, then crawl, then simply stop. The car in front of them is a pickup truck with a noisy exhaust and too many bumper stickers. The driver is hanging his sunburned arm out the window, drumming his fingers impatiently on the door. In front of him are at least two dozen cars, and possibly dozens more after the wooded curve they can't see around. They sit in traffic for several minutes, not moving an inch until Connie suddenly cranks his wheel and pulls over onto someone's yellow scrap of lawn.

"We should get out and walk," he says. "We're not going to get any closer driving."

Everyone they pass seems angry and annoyed, which worries Kyung. When Connie said there was an accident, he assumed it was a fender bender, something inconvenient but insignificant. He imagined cuts and stitches, a cast or concussion at worst. But the farther they walk, the clearer it is that the accident was something more. A woman in the passenger seat of a vintage Beetle is smoking a skinny brown cigarette. The ground beneath her open window is littered with butts.

Most of the drivers have their engines turned off to conserve gas, as if they lost hope of moving a long time ago. When they round the curve, Kyung sees the flashing red, white, and blue of emergency vehicles in the distance—too many for just a minor accident. It looks like the Fourth of July. He breaks into a sprint, kicking up a cloud of dust while the others trail behind him.

There's a crowd gathered in front of a faded gray house, packed tightly with neighbors and kids, all standing on tiptoes to catch a glimpse. Kyung is so winded by the time he reaches them, he has to rest his hands on his knees until Connie and Jin catch up. He hears someone breathing heavily alongside him, and then feels a tap on his shoulder as Connie begins to trudge through the crowd, waving his badge at people too distracted to care. The flash of silver and gold is enough to clear a path for them toward an area cordoned off by hazard cones and tape. Kyung's stomach sinks when he sees his car being towed away from a huge tree, the entire front end crushed like an accordion. Both air bags have deflated. Jagged outlines of glass are all that remain of the windshield and windows. There's no sign of his mother or Marina. No ambulances on the scene. Only a swarm of police cars and the tow truck driver. Connie tells him to stay put and climbs over the tape, lifting his badge to approach two officers standing near the tree.

"You did this," Jin repeats.

And because he believes this too, Kyung can't summon a response. All he can do is stare at Connie, studying his reactions from a distance—nodding, nodding, nodding, and then a surge of air that expands his chest, followed by a slow shake of his head. One of the officers leans over and whispers in his ear. Not a sentence or two, but something that takes much longer. When he finishes, Connie nods again and starts walking back, keeping his eyes on the road. By the time he returns, his lips pursed and skin ashen, Kyung already knows what's coming. His mother and Marina are gone. As he hears the words out loud, he pushes Connie away, harder and harder until Connie has no choice but to wrap him in his arms and hold him still. Kyung's legs go out from underneath him and he falls on the hot asphalt, screaming as the crowd of strangers looks on. Women begin to corral their kids, leading them away from the spectacle, while the men turn their heads, unable to watch.

The things he said at dinner were meant to hurt Mae, to hurt both of his parents as much as they'd hurt him. But not once did he imagine that something like this would happen. All he wanted was for them to know. He was tired of pretending. Why did saying so make her react when so many things never did? It makes no sense to him—the fact that she wouldn't leave a man who beat her, but this was the moment she chose to flee, that *he* was the person she finally chose to flee from. Kyung can't stop crying. He's desperate to tell Mae he's sorry, to hear the same words from her. However much he denied it, he always hoped they'd be kinder to each other one day, like people who were grateful to survive something instead of people still fighting to survive. Wherever that small seed of hope resided, it no longer exists, and what they were to each other is what they'll always be. Tethered, somehow. Drawn together by a force that should have kept them close but repelled them instead.

"Worthless," Jin shouts.

Kyung feels a hard slap to the head.

"You worthless, no-good waste of life."

He lifts his arms to shield himself, but the blows keep coming at him from above.

"You did this, you selfish, no-good son of a bitch. You were never any goddamn good. Never—do you hear me?"

Kyung rolls over onto his side, bringing his knees to his chest to make himself small. The blows are coming faster now, the open hands turning into hard, tight fists.

"Easy," Connie says. "Easy."

He remains on his side, waiting for his father to continue. When he doesn't, Kyung looks up and sees Jin standing over him with his arms pinned back by Connie. His glasses are bent and crooked. What little hair he has left is wild. Even now, with a bigger, stronger man holding him back, he's still as frightening as ever.

"Jesus," Connie says, staring at Kyung's pants.

A warm sensation spreads below him, lasting only a few seconds before it turns cold and damp. Kyung covers himself, not so much ashamed of what he did, but confused that he didn't notice it before.

"You pathetic, worthless—"

Jin is about to kick him, but Connie quickly blocks his path. The shuffling of their feet raises a cloud of dust in Kyung's face that invades his eyes and mouth. He gets on all fours, trying to cough out the dirt and grit.

"Take it easy now. Leave him be. It wasn't entirely his fault."

Jin shakes free. "You heard what he said last night. The only reason she got in that car was to get away from him. She had no business driving—she barely knew how."

"She knew what she was doing," Connie says.

"What does that mean?"

"The officers will come talk to you when they're done."

"Talk to me about what?"

Connie offers his hand to Kyung, getting him on his feet. He tries to avoid looking at the wet spot on his pants, or the puddle of piss he left on the road.

"Nothing," Connie says. "You just have to be prepared, is all."

Jin marches in front of him, pushing his face directly beneath his. "What are you saying? What did they tell you?"

"They'll come over and explain in a second."

"*No.* I want you to explain it to me now."

Connie takes a step backward. "I'm sorry, Jin." He hesitates, scanning the crowd for the officers, both of whom are guiding the tow truck as it backs out into traffic. "They don't think it was an accident."

"Of course it was an accident. She didn't know how to drive."

"But the road"—Connie points at the asphalt, drawing a straight line from where they're standing to the tree in front of the house—"there aren't any skid marks. That means she didn't hit the brakes."

"Maybe she got confused about the pedals."

"Some of the neighbors said she sped up on purpose. Right before the tree, they heard her gun it."

Jin doesn't blink as he examines the unmarked stretch of asphalt, slowly tracing the car's path from the road to the lawn to the tree. "She was confused, that's all. She thought the gas was the brake." He studies it again, as if to convince himself that what he said was true. Then he turns to Connie, stabbing his finger at him. "We're Christian—do you understand what that means? She wouldn't have done this to herself on purpose; she can't. It's not allowed."

Connie looks pained, as if he regrets opening his mouth, but now he has to finish what he started. "She left a note, Jin. It was on the floor, next to her seat. I'm sorry, I should have let them tell you."

The tow truck drives off, dragging the carcass of the Jeep behind it. Kyung follows the swirling lights until they disappear into the distance. The lanes open up from one to two and traffic begins to move again, filling the air with a dense cloud of exhaust. Behind him, Jin is still arguing with Connie, but their voices fade out, replaced by a memory of something his mother said not long ago. It never made sense to him as completely as it does now. *You have to have a plan.* Kyung repeats these words to himself as he looks at his shadow stretched diagonally across the pavement. The longer he studies the rough black surface, the more clearly he sees it, the moment of impact. Marina's face has sunk into itself—eyes closed, mouth open, screaming. But his mother is staring right at it, at the death she knows is coming, and for once, she's not afraid.

The note she left behind isn't a note at all. It's an inventory, the same one she was compiling for the insurance company. The handwritten list is twenty-eight pages long, documenting every item she ever bought for the houses in Marlboro and Orleans. Kyung spends the first two days after the accident sitting on the beach, studying the list through a haze of Valium. On the far right, Mae had added a column indicating who should receive what upon her death. Molly's name is there, beside a bowl described as *Regency, glass, 8 inches wide, living room.* He also recognizes the names of her decorator and several women from church. Gillian is nothing more than a footnote at the end, one that makes it entirely clear how Mae felt about her. *Anything my friends don't want can go to my daughter-in-law.*

The inventory seems like proof of the obvious. Mae was planning to end her life long before they arrived in Orleans. That's why she wanted to learn how to drive, why she was willing to go to the Cape, why she chose to bring Marina with them. She had a plan all along. Knowing this should provide some thin sliver of comfort, but Kyung is crippled with doubt, unsure if the things he said hastened the plan's timeline or confirmed the need for it to exist. As the haze begins to lift and he sees the signs he missed, Kyung considers walking into the ocean, walking and walking until the water's pressure crushes the guilt building up inside him. He doesn't know how else to make it go away.

Gillian and his father refuse to speak to him. Not on the ride home to Marlboro, not in the days after they return. Kyung is relegated to the guest room of his own house, sleeping in the same bed his mother occupied only a few nights before. Vivi comes by daily to help with the funeral arrangements, having recently planned services for her father. He listens in on their conversations, sitting at the top of the staircase as they select flowers and music and menu items for the reception. Not once does anyone mention Kyung or ask for his opinion. His only notice of the funeral date is the sudden appearance of his suit on the bathroom door, wrapped in dry-cleaning plastic with a note skewered through the hanger: *Be dressed at ten.*

With one car gone and only Gillian's battered hatchback as a spare, Connie has to pick them up for the service. Kyung would rather walk across town than spend time with his father-in-law again, but he accepts the favor for what it is. When Connie and Vivi arrive, he climbs into the far backseat of the Suburban, where he sits by himself like the family dog, hot and sticky and ignored as he stares at the backs of everyone's heads. No one says a word during the drive except for Ethan, who complains bitterly about his itchy new suit, which looks like a miniature version of Kyung's. He wonders if Gillian explained to him what a funeral is, and whether four is too young to attend one. The fact that she didn't consult him before letting Ethan come says everything about the state of their marriage now. She's no longer interested in being partners in their child's upbringing, or any of the things she used to aspire to before Ethan was born. Their relationship is beyond aspiration, and if he allows himself to see things from her point of view, he understands why she would think so.

First Presbyterian is on the outskirts of town, on a fading commercial strip lined with stores that are either vacant or closed. Although the neighborhood looks different now—poorer and a little dirtier—the building itself has hardly changed since he last attended services there as a teenager. The tall brick church sits on a corner lot, elevated from street level and flanked by beds of bright orange daylilies that provide the neighborhood's only color. The matching brick sign in front offers a Bible quote to random passersby. PRECIOUS IN THE SIGHT OF THE LORD IS THE DEATH OF HIS SAINTS, PSALMS 116:15. Kyung doesn't know if the quote is a coincidence, or if it was changed for their benefit, but it makes him uncomfortable to think of his mother as a saint. It doesn't seem right to embellish her memory, to turn her into the person she thought she had to be for everyone else. He wants to remember Mae as she really was, flawed and fragile and the product of a life that never gave her a chance to do or be anything more.

Connie pulls into the fire lane in front of the church and turns around. The starched collar of his shirt appears to cut off the circulation to his neck. "I'll let you out here and find a place to park."

"I'll stay with Connie," Vivi adds. "You all should go in."

People are streaming into the building, so many that Kyung keeps losing count. He'd rather use a side door and slip in unnoticed, but he knows what's expected of him today. He gets out of the car, trailing behind his father and Gillian, each of whom is holding on to one of Ethan's hands. As they make their way up the path to the front steps, people he doesn't recognize stop to pay their respects. All of them, even the children, are dressed in black and gray—colors that seem at odds with the fierce blue sky and the heat of summer, which is stifling even though it's barely midday. As he listens in on their conversations, he hears the word "accident" over and over again: "What a terrible accident." "Such a tragic accident." "I'm so sorry about the accident." His father doesn't correct this interpretation of events; he simply thanks everyone for coming and moves on.

As they step into the sanctuary, Kyung is immediately overwhelmed by the smell of flowers. Bright white gardenias, displayed to excess everywhere—not a cheap carnation in sight. They were Mae's favorite flower, but it almost seems grotesque, spending so lavishly on decorations for a funeral. The gardenias are arranged in gilded planters, ascending along the steps to the altar. They're bunched together in clusters, tied with white ribbon and clipped to the pews. The most elaborate display is the twin wreaths—huge, tire-sized wreaths, one on each side of a black-and-white photograph of Mae. Kyung doesn't recognize where or when the photo was taken, but he thinks it captures her well. Straight spined and imperial, with the slightest lift of the corners of her mouth instead of a smile. Tucked behind the photo is a silver urn on a pedestal, a detail he hadn't considered before. He's grateful for the absence of a coffin, open or closed, but he worries where the ashes will go after the funeral. He doesn't understand the idea of keeping the dead.

Kyung follows Jin and Gillian to the first pew, struggling with the heat and perfume of flowers as he scans the crowd of people already seated. He notices Tim immediately, sitting a full head and shoulders taller than everyone else. He also notices the Steiners, Craig, and some familiar faces from campus. Strangely, the faces he's least prepared to see are the ones he should have expected the most. When Reverend Sung and Molly appear, hands outstretched, he feels a spike of panic. His body goes rigid, ready to be hit, but he quickly finds himself wrapped in the reverend's arms, bear-hugged in a way that seems wrong among men.

"I'm so sorry for your loss," he says.

Kyung blinks as the reverend sweeps down the pew in his shiny black vestments, greeting everyone with the same octopus embrace, even Connie and Vivi, who managed to slide into the seats next to Jin unnoticed. Molly follows close behind, bowing and shaking hands. He expects her face to reflect some memory of the last time they were together, but she keeps her eyes fixed to the floor. It's obvious she didn't tell her husband what happened, which is both a relief and a disappointment. Even the devout have their secrets.

"We have a nice gathering of people here today," the reverend says, staring out into the pews.

The sanctuary is almost two-thirds full. Most of the mourners are members of the church—Koreans with lined faces and dark clothes, blotting their sweaty foreheads with handkerchiefs. Over a hundred, maybe even 150 have turned out, which is more than he would have expected. He wonders who, if anyone, will show up for Marina's services, if she had any friends to remember her at all.

"When is Marina's funeral?" he whispers to Gillian.

"Why are you asking that now?" she snaps, barely attempting to conceal her irritation at being spoken to.

"Because I want to be there."

"We're sending her body back to Bosnia. Now stop talking."

The reverend climbs the steps to the altar and asks everyone to be seated. The low murmur of conversation comes to a halt as he thanks people for coming to celebrate Mae's life. Kyung thinks of Marina's parents, standing on an airstrip in some wretched little town, waiting for men to unload their daughter's coffin. He's certain there won't be any gardenias at her funeral. No gardenias or carnations, probably no flowers of any kind. Just a modest grave that people will visit for a while until they eventually don't. The memory of his first and last real conversation with Marina still haunts him, the way she kept insisting she couldn't go home. Death made it easier, strangely. Everything she didn't want her family to know will remain secret now. He assumes that Mae understood this, and the bond he couldn't see was actually there all along. She thought she was doing right by Marina, ending their suffering together, the same way it began.

"Our sister, Mae, is no longer with us . . . ," the reverend says. "I know that her loss may seem like too much to bear, and you're tempted to ask yourselves, Why? Why did the Lord have to take her?"

In the corner of his eye, Kyung sees several people nodding, but it's not the right question, he thinks. God didn't take her. She took herself. And the guilt he feels is multiplied by the fact that he prayed for this as a child, back when he thought his prayers might still be answered. He wanted his mother to run. He wanted her to be brave. But he knows it wasn't bravery that made her get in that car. It was him.

"Some of you may even find yourselves blaming the Lord for her absence." The reverend lowers his head, shuffling through pages and pages of notes that everyone can hear through the microphone. When he looks up again, he pauses much longer than he should, flustered in a way that Kyung has never seen before.

"We'll now have a reading from Sister Han."

A small Korean woman stands up across the aisle. She watches the reverend for a signal, confused perhaps by the brevity of his remarks. When he doesn't give one, she approaches the altar, nervously folding and unfolding a slip of paper. Kyung thinks he recognizes her. She and her husband used to run a copy shop somewhere. Her round face is more withered now, and her hair has turned gray, but her footsteps sound the same, the way they clunk in thick black orthopedic shoes that correct the uneven lengths of her legs. Despite the shoes, Mrs. Han's face barely clears the podium.

"From Thessalonians . . ." She adjusts the microphone, cranking it down near her mouth with a screech that rings through the sanctuary. "'For since we believe that Jesus died and rose again, even so, through Jesus, God will bring with him those who have fallen asleep. For this we declare to you by a word from the Lord, that we who are alive, who are left until the coming of the Lord, will not precede those who have fallen asleep. . . .'"

Kyung turns to look down the pew at his family. Everyone is listening intently to Mrs. Han as she struggles through the reading, her accent too thick to fully enunciate the words. No one is crying except for Vivi, who dabs at her face with a handkerchief, consumed by a fit of grief that seems out of place beside the others. Gillian squeezes his leg—not affectionately, but forcefully, as if to snap him back to attention. He scans through his program, a long list of readings and remembrances by people he barely knows. When he looks through the names more closely, he notices that Jin isn't scheduled to speak on Mae's behalf, and of course, no one trusted Kyung enough to ask. He's never attended a funeral in which a family member didn't say at least a few words about the deceased, but their omission seems entirely appropriate. He and his father lost their rights to Mae long before the Perrys entered their lives. It's better that people who treated her kindly have a chance to say their good-byes.

"'. . . And the dead in Christ will rise first. Then we who are alive, who are left, will be caught up together with them in the clouds to meet the Lord in the air, and so we will always be with the Lord.'"

The reverend thanks Mrs. Han for her reading and assumes his place behind the podium again. Kyung expects him to begin his eulogy in earnest, but he introduces the chorus and retreats to a corner as an army of people take to the stage. They arrange themselves in two long rows, dressed in royal blue robes with their hands clasped in front of their chests, the same way Kyung was taught to sing in public as a child. Behind them, a man begins to play the pipe organ, which lights up the sanctuary with noise—too much noise, almost. It drowns out the solo of the woman in the center, whose reedlike voice drifts aimlessly toward the ceiling. The rest of the choir eventually joins in, singing something about Jesus being a redeemer, but what the actual lyrics are, Kyung can't hazard a guess. There's a muddy quality to their performance. The song feels unpracticed or unplanned. He looks at his program again, confirming that what they meant to sing was "Amazing Grace," which this certainly isn't.

After the music concludes, an older woman approaches the podium with a stack of index cards. She raises the mike, filling the sanctuary with the same unfortunate screech as Mrs. Han. The woman's face glows white and oily under the spotlights as she introduces herself as Elinor Hamel, Mae's decorator. Kyung has never seen her before. For years, Elinor was nothing more than a voice on the phone or a name in a story. She was the person Mae spent the most time with, and probably spent the most money on as well. At first, Elinor doesn't seem like much of a speaker. She clears her throat too much and fumbles through her prepared remarks until she eventually puts her note cards down.

"I wasn't sure if I should bring this up today, but it's difficult to talk about Mae's life without at least referencing the things that happened to her recently."

All the ambient noise in the room—the coughing, the fanning, the shifting in pews—suddenly stops and the sanctuary is quiet. Kyung sits up straight, wondering if he'll finally hear something uncomfortable and true.

"I'm sure there are people out there, people who didn't know Mae like we did, who thought of her as nothing more than a victim. But Mae was just the opposite. She was strong and smart. She survived something terrible, something that would have broken an ordinary soul. And I have to believe that God had his reasons for testing her as he did and then taking her away so soon afterwards. Maybe he had a special place for her. . . ."

Several people raise their Bibles. A ripple of amens makes its way to the back of the room. Kyung feels like he's sitting on the bottom of a swimming pool, looking up at a distorted view of a world in which no one understands what really happened. And his father and Gillian, people who should understand, refuse to believe.

Elinor concludes with a passage from John 14. " 'Do not let your hearts be troubled. Trust in God; trust also in me. In my Father's house are many rooms; if it were not so, I would have told you. I am going there to prepare a place for you. And if I go and prepare a place for you, I will come back and take you to be with me so that you also may be where I am. You know the way to the place where I am going.' " She pauses and puts her note cards down again. "Mae is with our Father now, making his home more beautiful for him and for us, which was always her way. I'm grateful that I had the opportunity to be her friend in this lifetime, and I know we'll meet again in the next."

There are other remembrances and readings after Elinor's, brief ones that are hard to listen to nonetheless. Everyone talks about Mae in generalities, confirming his fear that she never let anyone truly see her, not once in fifty-six years. Kyung tips his head back and stares at the huge stained-glass panels in the ceiling—bright red, blue, and gold crosses surrounded by bursts of color as if he's viewing them through a kaleidoscope.

"Pay attention," Gillian whispers.

Kyung looks at her, not certain if she's speaking to him or to Ethan. Then he feels the sharp point of her elbow in his ribs.

Ethan leans forward in his seat as an elderly woman climbs the steps to the altar. She's dressed in a traditional Korean gown, floor length and white, with a long-sleeved jacket that ties in the front with a bow.

"Is she a bride?" he asks Gillian, who responds with a gentle "shhh."

Kyung studies Ethan's profile, quiet and focused as he tries to make sense of what the woman is wearing. It's embarrassing to see his four-year-old behaving better than he is, so he defaults to an old trick, counting everything in his line of sight. There are 73 gardenias in the planter in front of him, 214 words in the program, 48 fake bulbs in the candelabra on the altar. As a child, he often counted to pass the time, distracting himself until the beatings ended and the house was quiet again. Whatever comfort he took from this activity—it fails to soothe him anymore.

By the time the service concludes, the heat outside is brutal. Kyung and his family form a receiving line on the front steps of the church. The reverend is noticeably absent. Embarrassed, probably, by his strange showing inside. An hour-long service and he barely managed to utter five complete sentences in a row. As the guests file out of the church, Kyung feels moist, rough hands press against his, one after another. Women he doesn't know embrace him, pushing their warm breasts against his body. Several have helped themselves to the floral arrangements, toting them out like gift bags, which strikes him as rude.

Before he has a chance to fully form this thought, Lentz appears with his hand outstretched. "I'm so sorry for your loss, Mr. Cho."

Beside him is another man dressed in a cheap brown suit with the disposition of an old marine.

"This is Detective—"

Kyung cuts him off. If this is the detective he never heard from, he doesn't want to meet him now. "Thank you both for joining us," he says.

He turns to face the onslaught of mourners coming at him, squeezing through the doors of the church. Lentz and the detective take their cue and move on, replaced by more people, more handshakes, more sweaty hugs and stolen flowers. Kyung hears himself saying what he knows he should—"Hello." "Thank you." "I appreciate that you came."—and the irony of this isn't lost on him. He told everyone at the Cape that he didn't want to pretend anymore, and now here he is, just getting through the script, waiting for the line to thin. When it finally does and the last of the elderly stragglers have left the building, he walks to a small patch of shade near the side of the church. His father is still standing by the door, trying to remove the boutonniere from his lapel. Jin frees the gardenia and spins it by the stem, clockwise and counterclockwise, over and over again. He seems hypnotized by it, staring at the pinwheel of white until he's the last person left on the steps. Suddenly, he rears his arm back and hurls the flower into the bushes, startling a pair of birds that flap and flutter their way to the roof. It happens so quickly, no one notices except for Kyung.

The reception is at the parsonage, a detail he didn't overhear until it was too late. He assumed everyone would come to his house to pay their respects, but the actual location is much worse. He has no desire to enter the reverend's home, to be anywhere near Molly again. During the two-block walk from the church to the parsonage, Kyung brings up the rear, cycling through every possible reason to leave. Illness, anxiety, fatigue. Nothing seems important enough to excuse himself from his parents' friends, a fact that Gillian confirms as they near the front door.

"Don't go disappearing on us," she whispers. "Everyone will want to see you."

Kyung reaches for her hand, a nervous instinct that she mistakes for affection. She pulls away before he can touch her.

"When is this going to end?" he asks.

The question could refer to so many things. Even he's not entirely sure what he meant.

"You're incredible," she says.

This is the longest she's ever been angry with him, the longest she's ever gone without wanting to talk things through. Whenever he tries to start a conversation, she's quick to interrupt, filtering everything he says through the worst possible lens. It's not like her to be so closed off to him, but there's nothing he can do to fix this right now. His only goal is to get through the day.

Despite the church's carefully maintained appearance, the parsonage hasn't received the same kind of attention over the years. The crooked little house looks the same as it did when the elder Reverend Sung lived there. Although everything is immaculate, scrubbed clean and pine fresh, there's no hiding the peeling linoleum in the entryway or the trampled shag carpet in the living room—carpet that Kyung still remembers staring at whenever his parents dragged him to Bible study. Even the furniture looks the same, just older and more abused. The sofa cushions sag. The tables and bookcases are all marred and mismatched. Kyung can't imagine living in the house he grew up in, much less leaving everything as it was before. The thought of this is so strange to him, but he reminds himself that not everyone had a childhood like his. Maybe the memories here are happier; the sameness, a source of comfort.

Without any prior discussion, Kyung and his family branch off into different areas of the house. Gillian and Ethan gather with the women and children in the kitchen. Jin deposits himself on the living room sofa while Connie and Vivi head toward the buffet line in the dining room. Kyung continues down the hall, looking for a place where they're not. He shakes hands and says hello to people as he passes by, but never stops long enough to exchange more than a polite sentence or two. At the end of the hall, he finds a bathroom behind one door and a study directly across from it behind another. He doesn't think Gillian can accuse him of disappearing if he leaves the door open, so he slips into the cramped study, surprised by the volume of furniture and clutter inside. The reverend's desk is the length of a dining table, with loose sheets of paper covering every square inch. Stacked on top is an oversized hutch lined with boxes of ancient software and seemingly broken printers. Kyung sits down in the chair, studying the books on the shelves.

About half of them are religious, with titles that seem like self-help: *Your Relationship with God. Spirituality in Troubled Times. Lifting Your Soul with Prayer.* Curiously, the other half is science fiction, the cheap paperback kind with aliens and spaceships landing on their covers. Kyung picks one up at random and flips through the yellowed pages. The writing is neither terrible nor inspired—just pulp that he wouldn't think to associate with the reverend.

Across the hall, someone closes the bathroom door, scraping a metal chain to lock it from inside. Kyung puts the book back on the shelf and turns to the desk, scanning the papers in front of him. He notices his mother's name on one page, and then another. The closer he looks, the more he sees Mae's name scattered everywhere. The reverend must have been working on his eulogy here, printing and reprinting the text at least a dozen times. He reads a random paragraph about Mae's devotion to God, and then another about her generosity toward the less fortunate. Like the sci-fi book, the writing isn't terrible. But it's not special either. The eulogy reminds him of a horoscope, something so general that it could apply to almost anyone, which he doesn't necessarily fault the reverend for. What else is a minister supposed to do at a funeral besides say comforting things about the dead? What he doesn't understand is why the reverend never said any of it at all.

When the bathroom door opens, an elderly man appears, catching himself midstride as he notices Kyung in the study. He walks in and bows, taking Kyung's hands as he attempts to offer his condolences in Korean. When Kyung explains that he doesn't speak Korean, the man starts over again in quiet, stilted English. After he leaves, he's replaced by another old man, then a pair of young women, then a couple with a baby in a sling and a boy about Ethan's age. The study turns out to be the worst possible place to hide. People stop to pay their respects on their way to or from the bathroom. They form a line down the hall, waiting until their turn finally arrives. Kyung remains standing the entire time, nodding through one conversation after the next with no break in between. Everyone seems genuinely sad and sympathetic, but it's hard not to notice how they all say a variation of the same thing. They tell him his mother was wonderful and generous. They tell him she was helpful and special and kind. He tries to listen attentively to everyone who walks through the door, but it's painful. He and Mae were nicer to strangers than they were to each other.

After an awkward attempt at conversation with a woman who doesn't speak English, he notices Elinor poking her head inside the door. She enters the room and introduces herself, crossing her hands limply over her chest. Up close, Elinor is one severe swipe of color after another. Her hair is an unnatural shade of red that reminds him of an old penny. And her lips are red too—a bright, thickly applied shade of fire engine.

"Thank you for coming," he says. "And for reading at the service."

He shakes her warm, perfumed hand, trying not to stare at her unusual outfit—a shapeless blue jacket that hangs from her shoulders like a cape, and white pants so billowy, they look like a skirt.

"It's nice to finally meet you, Kyung. How are you holding up?"

"I'm all right, thanks."

She looks at him skeptically, but doesn't try to press the

matter. "I was devastated when I heard about what happened. I mean, no one can be more devastated than you and your father, but—"

"It's not really something we have to compare like that."

"Yes, of course. I just meant . . . it was such an exciting time in her life. Before I went on vacation, we were on the phone almost every day making plans."

"Well, she loved to redecorate."

"Oh, we weren't redecorating anything. She was going to come work for me."

"Work? You mean like volunteer?"

"No. It was a full-time position, with benefits and everything."

Kyung shakes his head. The idea of Mae having a job, a real job, doesn't compute. "You mean you were going to hire her in exchange for an investment? My father was going to give you a loan or something?"

Elinor stiffens. Suddenly, the nervous, tongue-tied woman is gone, replaced by a visibly piqued businesswoman. "I've never needed a loan from anyone, not even when I first started out. I have three employees and more work than I know what to do with." She pauses, softening a bit. "I wanted Mae to join us because she had an exceptionally good eye. You knew that about her, didn't you? How she could track down almost anything she put her mind to? I mean, really obscure pieces that other decorators would usually give up on."

He didn't mean to insult Elinor, to insinuate that her intentions weren't good when she offered Mae a job, but this is the only way he knows how to make sense of it. His mother had never worked before. She'd never expressed any interest in it either.

"I'm not sure why she didn't tell you about this. She beat out two other women who had much more formal training. One of them even had a master's degree in design. Every time I talked to her, it seemed like she was so excited to get started."

"Wait . . ." Kyung still can't imagine his mother going into an office every day or bringing home a check at the end of the week. He also can't imagine his father being amenable to it. "When was this supposed to happen?"

"She was planning to start after I got back from vacation, but the day came and went, and she didn't show up, so I kept calling and calling. It wasn't like her to not call me back, so I drove up to the house and there were all these news crews there. Of course, it made sense after that. It was so awful, what they did to her. . . . I'm sorry. I don't know what's wrong with me. I shouldn't be talking about this now." She rummages through her bag and removes a key attached to a small plastic disk. "I'm guessing you'll probably want to get her things at some point? I wrote the address on the key chain for you."

"What things?"

"In the apartment . . ." She frowns, studying his face as if she might be speaking to the wrong person. "The apartment above my studio? She asked if she could rent it. She'd been having some things moved up there." She looks flustered again. "Is there someone else I should be talking to about this? Your father, maybe?"

"No, no." He takes the key from her. "I just don't understand why she needed an apartment."

"The drive, I suppose. I got the sense she wasn't comfortable asking you or your father for a ride every day."

It feels like Elinor just shoved him into a wall. His reaction must register on his face because she quickly tries to smooth things over.

"I mean, she never said that directly. But it's a long drive from here to Connecticut. Two hours, round-trip. Four, if you had to drop her off in the morning and come back for her at the end of the day. It would have been completely impractical."

Kyung stares at the key, trying to understand why Mae never mentioned any of this before. He remembers her talking about Elinor—endlessly, in fact. Whenever he had to drive her somewhere or drop by the house because she'd complained so bitterly that he hadn't, Mae would go on and on about a project they were working on together. Rather than fight to change the subject, he'd simply tune her out. He wonders if Mae told him about the job while he wasn't listening. Or maybe she didn't bother to tell him because she knew he wouldn't listen at all.

"It's not like it's a big apartment or anything," Elinor continues. "It was just a place to stay during the workweek." She turns at the sound of someone clearing his throat and sees the reverend standing outside the door. She seems relieved to have a reason to end their conversation. "She paid the rent through the end of the year, so there's absolutely no hurry. You should feel free to come and go as you please. I just thought you'd want to have the key for whenever you're ready."

"Thank you. I appreciate it. . . . I appreciate you being so nice to her all these years."

"It was mutual." Elinor's eyes begin to well up. She searches through her bag and removes a small package of tissues. "I never expected we'd become such good friends when we first met, but she was such an amazing woman." She dabs at her eyes as they begin to spill over, leaving watery brown smudges on the tissue. "Look at me. I'm a mess. I should really get going now. Please, take all the time you need with the apartment."

He has more questions he wants to ask, more things he wants to know, but Elinor leaves before he has a chance to tell her not to. The reverend is quick to enter as she exits, stopping when he notices the papers on his desk.

"I'm sorry. I didn't realize I left such a mess in here." He collects his eulogy and deposits the sheets of paper into the trash. "Gillian asked me to check on you. You know there's plenty of space in the living room, right? You don't have to sit here by yourself."

"I'd prefer it, if you don't mind."

"I understand. You've always been a little shy."

"Shy" is a generous assessment of his personality, and a completely incorrect one, but Kyung lets the comment pass.

The reverend gently kicks the trash can. "So, did you read any of this?"

"I didn't mean to, but yes, I got a sense of what it was."

"And you're upset with me, I assume."

Kyung shrugs. It's not the right word, "upset." He can't bring himself to feel that much about an event he didn't plan, a rite of passage he doesn't fully believe in. The service wasn't perfect, but his mother wasn't there to see it. And the longer he drifts through the day, the more he realizes that everyone is pretending in some way. They have to. The truth has no place in the etiquette of mourning.

"I don't have anything to be upset about." He turns around

and scans one of the bookshelves. "Have you always read so much science fiction?"

"I used to, but not anymore. This was actually my bedroom when I was little. I just have a hard time throwing out books."

"It's not strange, living in your father's house?"

"It's a parsonage. It was no more my father's house than it is mine."

Something about Reverend Sung strikes him as more human today, more benign. From a distance, he always seemed several ranks above everyone else, beyond reproach in a way that made Kyung feel distrustful and judged. But the reverend looks so stricken now, almost childlike in his remorse.

"It was fine, you know. The service. I'm sure it's a lot of pressure to deliver a eulogy."

There's a couple standing in the hallway, but the reverend politely waves them off and closes the door, trapping Kyung in the study with him.

"My father was planning to come—did you know that? He was looking for a plane ticket from Seoul up until the very last minute, but I'm glad he couldn't find one now. He would have been so embarrassed."

"It was nice of him to try. That's a long trip for a funeral."

"He was very fond of you and your parents."

Kyung pauses. "I always liked him. He did a good thing for me once."

"I know," he says, looking over his shoulder, confirming Kyung's suspicion that his family's history had been passed down from one reverend to the next. "And I like your father too, despite some of his past behavior."

The fear of being known like this, it was always the thing

that governed him. He didn't want to be the subject of other people's pity, but the reverend's tone is so matter-of-fact, with no judgment or condescension at all. He looks at Kyung calmly, waiting for him to continue, as if nothing between them has changed.

"I was terrible to my mother the night before she died. I said things to her, things I can't take back."

"We all say or do things we regret from time to time. God made us imperfect so that he could—"

"Please," Kyung says, raising his hand in the air. "Can you please not talk to me like that right now? I can't—I just can't listen to that."

The reverend nods. "I think I understand. You've always had a difficult relationship with your parents, and now that Mae's gone, things will never improve with her. Is that what's bothering you?"

Kyung doesn't think it boils down to something so simple. The "it," in fact, feels like an ever-thickening mass, the threads too twisted and tangled to find their beginnings or ends. The reverend isn't entirely wrong, but he's not completely right.

"I was the reason she drove off that morning."

"But it's not your fault she gave up, Kyung. Mae chose to take her own life. And what she did to herself and that girl—I know you don't want to hear it in these terms, but it was a sin. It was as much a sin as what those men did to them, hard as that might be to hear."

The awkwardness of the service—the things that were said and the things that weren't—begins to makes sense to him now. The reverend wasn't nervous. He simply wouldn't lie.

"Who told you?"

"Your father called me this morning, right before I left for church." The reverend kicks the trash can again. "I accept the fact you don't have faith at this particular moment in your life, so the idea of sin probably doesn't mean anything to you, but I just couldn't stand there and read what I'd written about her, not after I knew."

The inventory should have left no doubt that the accident was intentional. But for days, Jin refused to look at it, refused to accept the truth of what Mae had done. Kyung understands this impulse more clearly now. To hear the reverend describe her death as a sin is terrifying, not because of his own beliefs, but because of his parents'. Mae knew what she was doing when she got in that car and asked Marina to join her. How miserable her life must have been to choose hell instead.

"I know you and your father have never been close, but if you could have heard his voice this morning, you might think differently of him. He was distraught, Kyung. He *is* distraught."

"He hasn't spoken to me for days. Neither has Gillian."

"So I'll tell you the same thing I told him. They're wrong to blame you. It doesn't matter what you said to Mae or how you said it. You can't be held responsible for her actions. Are you listening, Kyung? You're not to blame for what happened."

Of all the people in the world, he never expected Reverend Sung to be a source of comfort, the first real sense of comfort he's felt in so long. He's thrown by it, stunned silent by the possibility that he isn't so undeserving of kindness as he believes himself to be. Kyung sits down and takes the reverend's hand, squeezing it to convey the volume of things he can't, and the reverend, in another act of kindness, simply stands there and lets him, saying nothing in return.

EIGHT

Gillian sends Ethan and Jin away the next morning. She suggests a trip to the zoo, the park, the library, anywhere. Kyung is standing in front of the window, watching dark gray clouds streak across the sky as the wind bends thin treetops like bows. He thinks of the roof in Gillian's car, how it leaks on the driver's side when it rains, but he keeps this to himself. He wants them out of the house as much as she does. Kyung can't remember the last time he and Gillian were alone together, when they could say what needed to be said without worrying who would overhear. As soon as the car pulls out of the garage, he braces himself for an argument, but Gillian goes upstairs to their bedroom and shuts the door behind her. She's trained him over the years—a closed door means *don't bother me*—but an hour passes and nothing happens. Then another hour passes and nothing still. He wonders if the rules are different now, if the very thing she's told him not to do is the thing she actually wants.

Kyung continues to wait, circling the living room and kitchen in long, idle loops. He doesn't know how to start the conversation they need to have. All his previous attempts have ended badly. No amount of apologizing has been able to soften Gillian. Apologies, in fact, only seem to upset her more. He's not sure how many times he can say it, or how to say it differently. He's sorry for what he did at the Cape; he'll always be sorry. The fact that she doesn't believe him feels like another kind of loss.

He lifts the edge of a curtain and looks at the rain, which is coming down in sheets now. It cascades from the gutters and pelts the windows with pea-sized hail. There was no mention of a storm in the forecast today. If it keeps up, Jin and Ethan will probably come back from their outing soon, and nothing with Gillian will have changed. Kyung doesn't know how much longer he can live like this, exiled and ignored in his own home. He goes upstairs and presses his ear against the door, listening to her walk back and forth in the bedroom.

"Can I talk to you?" he asks.

The door doesn't open, not that he expected it to. He leans against the wall and glances at one of the night-lights in the hallway, a fluorescent green palm tree they bought in South Carolina. Five feet away, there's a seahorse-shaped night-light from Florida. And down the stairs are two more from Bermuda and Saint Croix. Night-lights were the only things they allowed themselves to buy when they went on vacation. Whatever guilt they felt about maxing out another credit card was mitigated by coming home with light bags.

"Remember when we drove down to Charleston after I defended my dissertation?"

This isn't what he intended to say when he went upstairs, but it feels better than offering another apology that she won't accept.

"Maybe we should go back there again and spend a little time by ourselves, stay at a bed-and-breakfast or something. . . ."

He has no idea why he's saying this, or how to pay for such a trip, although money—or the lack thereof—never stopped them before. Their sense of want was always more powerful than their sense of reason. Gillian was the first to pull back when they couldn't keep up with their bills. She drew up a budget and limited their purchases to the basics. She devised a plan to sell their house. "Retrenching," she called it, a term that made him think of men digging holes in the dirt. Because his idea of being a husband meant giving her the things that made her happy, it was harder for Kyung to adapt. Even now, in the midst of so much chaos, getting away with Gillian feels like a necessity to him, as important as food or water or shelter.

"It wouldn't have to be a very long trip, and I bet your dad would be willing to look after Ethan while we're gone. What do you think? We can go to the beach for a few days, get some sun. . . ."

He realizes that mentioning the beach was a bad idea. He doesn't want to remind her about the time they spent on the Cape.

"What was the name of that area you liked? The one with the big historic mansions? The Batten?" He pauses, studying a knot in the door. "No, the Battery. The Battery, right? We can go there again if you want."

The trip to Charleston still stands out as a happier and more hopeful time in their lives. It was Gillian's first trip south of D.C., and he enjoyed showing her around the city, introducing her to new architecture, new restaurants, new experiences that she'd never imagined before. She looked at him with admiration then, as if her life were opening up because he was in it, but he understands how differently he must appear to her now.

"Gillian? Are you listening to me?"

He lifts his hand to knock, but quickly decides against it. If she doesn't tell him to come in, he'll be no better off than he was before. He takes a deep breath and turns the knob, opening the swollen wood door with a shove. The first thing he notices is the suitcase on the bed. Gillian is standing beside it with a shirt tucked under her chin, holding the hem in place as she folds in the sleeves.

"I should have suggested a trip sooner," he says. "You deserve something nice."

Instead of acknowledging his presence, she folds another shirt, which doesn't feel right to him. Also not right is the suitcase. It's too big.

"You're not packing for Charleston, are you?"

He asks even though the answer is obvious. But when he looks in the suitcase, he realizes that the clothes arranged so neatly inside are his, not hers. The left half of the closet has been emptied of his things, and the floor is littered with a sad array of mismatched hangers—wire and plastic and wood.

"Could we talk about this, please?"

Gillian walks to the other side of the bed, turning her back to him. He walks to the same side to face her, but then she moves again. It's not like her to be the quiet one during an argument; it's usually the other way around. The role reversal disorients him, shifting what little ground he thought he stood on.

"Don't you think you're taking this too far?"

She places the shirt in the suitcase and starts on his dresser drawers.

Years ago, Kyung learned that when he asked a question in class and his students didn't respond, he had to resist the urge to answer for them or fill the dead air with more questions. If the wait became unbearable enough, someone would eventually blink. Gillian, however, isn't one of his students. She seems to tolerate the silence, to prefer it over the sound of his voice.

"Could you please stop what you're doing for a minute?"

She empties one of his drawers on the comforter, wincing at the pile of loose socks that tumbles out. Kyung doesn't know what to do except sit on the edge of the bed and watch as she sorts, matching black with black, brown with brown.

"I really wish you'd say something."

She glares at him as she twists a pair of socks into a ball, her expression similar to the one he saw on the Cape. But her frustration has evolved into something different now. It looks and feels like loathing. He glances at the door, tempted to walk out, but he doesn't dare take a step. Absence was always his best weapon against Gillian. Whenever he left in the middle of an argument, he usually returned to find her in a more reasonable state than she was before. His absence, however, is exactly what she wants now, and he worries that if he leaves, she won't let him come back.

"One day after my mother's funeral and you're throwing me out? Where do you expect me to go? Under a bridge somewhere?"

She continues putting his things into the suitcase, not bothering to ball or fold anything now.

"I'm not kidding, Gillian. Tell me—where do you want me to go?"

"Away."

Her voice isn't as sharp as it was at the funeral. It's quiet and tired, the same way she used to sound when Ethan was a baby. The lack of volume surprises him. He sees it as an opening.

"I'm asking you to just listen now, to really listen, okay?" He waits for her to turn around, but she keeps her back to him. "I'm sorry for what I did at the Cape. I had no business yelling in front of everyone like that. There were other ways I could have handled myself, but I was drunk and stupid—not that I'm using that as an excuse. I just couldn't take it anymore. I'd kept too many things bottled up inside and they came out badly, but it's not like I don't know that. I'll be thinking about what I said and how I said it for the rest—"

He's not even finished when he hears the metallic sound of the zipper making its way around the edge of the suitcase. When it's closed, Gillian drags it off the bed and pulls the handle out.

"Were you not listening to any of that?"

"You have a strange way of making peace with people."

He reminds himself not to shout, which won't get him anywhere. Shouting is how she thinks all of this began. "Please, I'm asking you to believe me. What my mother did . . . I feel bad enough without—"

"That's not what this is about."

His mother, his father, Marina—that's all they've been about for weeks. He doesn't know what else there is to them anymore.

"I don't understand what's happening, then."

She flips the suitcase around, turning the handle toward him as if she expects him to take it. When he doesn't, she walks to her dresser and opens the top drawer, rummaging through layers of nightgowns and T-shirts.

"Who do these belong to?" she asks.

She throws something at him. A handkerchief? Another sock? It hits him in the chest and falls on the floor next to his feet. When he looks down, he sees a pair of underwear. Pale beige satin with white ribbon trim.

"Who do they belong to?"

He didn't notice that Molly's underwear was beige that day in the kitchen. He also didn't notice that she left them on the floor when she ran out. Kyung remains seated, staring at the shiny fabric, a small island of color against the blue carpet.

"Who was it?"

He doesn't know if it's wise or even safe to say what he really thinks. The "who" isn't the point. It's the "what" she won't forgive. His relationship with Gillian was never based on a romantic or even demonstrative form of love. Neither of them was built for that kind of outpouring. At its best, their marriage was practical and utilitarian—the sort of thing that people of a certain age entered into with a vague notion of improving their lives. Although Gillian asked very little of him from the start, fidelity was a basic assumption. Fidelity, security, honesty, decency—all the things he's proved himself incapable of over time.

Kyung knows why he did it, why he married her despite believing that he probably shouldn't marry anyone. On some level, he was grateful that a woman like Gillian would choose to be with him. Her goodness was redeeming; it made him want to be worthy of her. But whatever impulse he has to fight for them is checked by the knowledge that this person he loves—and he does love her, more than he ever imagined possible—would be better off without him, a thought he's had so many times before. Kyung looks up at Gillian, at the way she's standing with her arms crossed loosely over her chest. She seems resigned, as resigned as he is to let this be how it ends.

"I can't keep asking you the same question, Kyung. Who was it?"

"You don't know her," he says. "She was just some girl."

Gillian nods slowly, struggling to take it all in. "You can't get out of your own way," she says. "Do you even understand that about yourself? No one's holding you back. No one's trying to make you unhappy—not me or Ethan or even your parents. You can blame us as much as you want, but at a certain point, maybe you just have to accept the fact that it's you. It's all the things you can't let go of."

"But how can I—?"

"No, Kyung. Just stop. I know you had a hard life before we met. I understand that now, I really do. But your parents were responsible for that. Not me or Ethan. All we did was love you, so you owed it to us to be a better man. I can't just stand here and watch you disappoint us anymore."

She hasn't raised her voice at him, not once, which is actually worse than being yelled at. It's taken him five years to realize that Gillian only shouts when she's invested in what happens afterwards. What happens to him from this point on, she clearly doesn't care.

"Use your credit card," she says. "For the hotel, or wherever you decide to go."

"Which credit card?"

"It doesn't matter. Your father paid them all off."

He pauses. He knows he didn't mishear her, but he still doesn't understand. "What do you mean, 'paid them all off'? How could he do that?"

"I asked him to. Begged him, actually."

"Gillian!"

She startles at the sound of his voice, biting her lip as she lifts and lowers the handle of the suitcase. "He was happy to do it," she continues. "A little shocked that I asked, maybe. But it wasn't like we hid things all that well. He could tell we were in trouble."

"Of course he was happy to do it. Don't you realize that he just bought you? That he bought me too?"

"He's not like that."

Kyung never understood how his father could hit his mother, how he justified his actions as reasonable or right. Even now, his mind doesn't get it, but his body is starting to rebel. He looks at himself, at the way he's choking the sheets and blankets in his fists, holding himself down on the bed.

"How could you do this to us?" he asks.

"I didn't do it *to* us. I did it because I had to. I was tired, Kyung. Tired of waking up in the middle of the night, feeling like something was sitting on my chest. It was getting too hard to breathe."

She looks at him as if she expects him to agree, but Kyung is still holding himself down, fighting the urge to scream at her.

"I think you felt the same way, but you could never bring yourself to admit it, to do anything about it. All those books I gave you, the Web sites and articles . . . I couldn't just wait for you to fix it anymore. And your father was actually so understanding. He kept saying I shouldn't be embarrassed. The amount didn't even seem to faze him."

Kyung has no idea what the amount even is. Forty? Fifty thousand? Probably more. He lost track of the total years ago, ignoring the telltale envelopes and phone calls at all hours of the night. Occasionally, he allowed himself to imagine what it would feel like to pay off their debts in one fell swoop, but his father never entered into any of these daydreams.

"Tell him to cancel the check, or however he paid it."

"No. It's already done."

"Then tell him to call someone and get the money back."

"I just said no."

"Fine, then. I'll tell him."

"It won't matter. He's not doing this for you. He's probably not even doing it for me. This is for Ethan."

"I take care of you and Ethan just fine."

He has to look away as he finishes the sentence. His voice, his expression—he can feel how ugly they are—and he doesn't need her to confirm what he already knows. He hasn't been taking care of either of them, not for a long time, not in any of the ways that matter. Gillian chooses to let this go, and it occurs to him, as it's occurred to him in the past—she deserved much better than he gave her. She'd always been a good wife; she wasn't capable of being anything less. Even now, as she's casting him out of her life, she's packed his things for him, making sure he has what he needs.

"You should probably leave now, Kyung."

"How? We don't even have a car here."

"I can call you a cab, or there's the bus stop over by the middle school. The 38 drops off near those hotels downtown." Gillian lifts a corner of the blinds. The rain is letting up, but the clouds still look bruised and gray, ready to open again. "It's getting late. They'll be home soon."

She has it all worked out for him, as if she's been planning this for days. They just needed to get past the funeral so she could send him away. If this is going to be their memory of the end, Kyung wants to leave the house like a man, a decent man, but the fact that she went to his father behind his back, that both of them have been keeping a secret from him—it's a greater betrayal than he ever thought Gillian capable of.

"I still don't understand how you could do this."

"I did exactly what you did," she says, lowering the blinds.

"What does that mean?"

"I asked your father for help because I knew it was the one thing you'd never be able to forgive. But unlike you, at least I got something out of it. Ethan and I might have a chance of making it now."

She doesn't sound entirely convinced of this, but she's right about everything else. He can't forgive her, no more than she can forgive him, and he understands that she probably planned this too. It eliminated the possibility that either of them would circle back in a moment of weakness, asking for another chance. It made the break clean.

"And my father—he's, what? He's just going to live here with the two of you? Pay the mortgage? Babysit my son?"

"I haven't discussed any of that with him, but he's welcome to stay as long as he wants."

"You mean as long as he's willing to pay the bills."

Gillian looks out the window again. "I really need you to go before they get here. I'm asking you nicely. If you care about

Ethan at all, please don't let him see you angry again. He's a little boy, Kyung. Just let him be a little boy."

It's ten past four in the morning when he pulls off the highway into a brightly lit service area. The lot is half-full of trucks and semis, with only a few passenger cars scattered in between. He parks his rental and gets out to stretch his legs, looking up at the open dome of sky. There aren't any stars in western Pennsylvania. He assumed there would be, but the haze makes it hard to see anything other than a pair of commuter planes blinking red in the distance. Kyung buys a map, a bottle of water, and a pack of cigarettes from a bored-looking girl at the gas station and then walks next door to the diner. The people inside—all truckers, he assumes—look up from their plates when he enters. He hesitates for a moment, sensing that the crowd is rougher than he's used to. The men are uniformly big and white and burly. They have bags under their eyes and constipated expressions that flicker with curiosity at the sight of Kyung. He's not in a college town anymore, a difference he can feel as he slides into a seat at the counter and lifts an oversized menu in front of his face. He quickly orders a sandwich to go from another bored-looking girl who might be the sister of the one working next door.

"Coffee while you wait?" she asks.

He's had nothing but coffee for nearly ten straight hours. Another cup would kill him. "No, thanks."

The girl seems confused by someone declining coffee at this hour, but she takes her carafe and moves on. Kyung spreads his map over the counter and stares at it, not looking for something so much as trying to avoid being looked at. He traces his route from Massachusetts to Pennsylvania, disappointed that the distance he drove barely amounts to the width of his pinky.

"Waste of time," he hears someone mumble.

On the other side of the counter, a middle-aged couple sits side by side, stirring their coffee in slow, sleepy unison. Husband and wife, he assumes, because of the matching gold bands on their fingers. They're also dressed in matching plaid shirts—blue for him and green for her—that appear soft and broken in from years of wear. Both of them are heavyset and unhealthy looking, with oily pink complexions that remind Kyung of lunch meat.

"If all you wanted was coffee, then why'd we even stop?" the man asks.

The woman rolls her eyes and runs a hand through her hair, which looks fried from too many dye jobs and home permanents.

"So?" the man says.

"So, what?"

"So *drink it already.* Let's go."

The woman downs several gulps of coffee and slams her cup on the saucer. She wipes the drops that spilled on her shirt with the back of her hand, camouflaging them into the plaid. "You happy now?"

"No, I'm not happy. We just lost half an hour. I thought you wanted to eat."

"Oh, quit your bitching." She peels off some bills from a small wad of money held together by a rubber band and throws them next to their check. "I told you I'd take the next leg."

They collect their things and head for the door, lumbering single file because they're too wide to walk next to each other.

As they reach Kyung's end of the counter, the woman looks

at him in passing. "Are we so damn interesting?" she snaps, not stopping or slowing down to wait for his response.

The bell on the door rings as it opens and closes, but Kyung doesn't turn to watch them leave. He didn't mean to stare at the couple, but it was hard not to. The farther he drives, the stranger people seem to him, and the smaller the town, the more everyone treats him like some kind of alien, as if they've never encountered an Asian person before.

"Husband-and-wife driving teams," mumbles another man sitting a few stools away. "Now, that's my idea of hell."

One of the cooks passes the galley window that opens onto the kitchen. He's talking to someone Kyung can't see, laughing as he waves a spatula in the air. How long does it take to make a sandwich? he wonders. He looks around the diner for the waitress, who's standing outside smoking a cigarette and staring vacantly at her cell phone. He wants to get her attention and ask her to rush his order, but he worries it won't help. The girl doesn't appear capable of rushing. Everything she does seems lethargic and slow. She even smokes slowly, blowing misshapen attempts at rings into the air.

"She's pretty, isn't she?"

Kyung doesn't think so, but he nods as if he does.

"Kind of a space case, though." The man picks at the oozing yellow egg yolks on his plate with a fork. "I asked her for scrambled."

He glances at the man, alarmed by his overgrown mustache and beard. The cap on his head can't contain his long hair, which spills out the sides and back in ragged salt-and-pepper strands. Kyung isn't sure if he's trying to make conversation, or simply observing out loud. He hopes it's the latter and returns to his map. He finds Massachusetts again, a small patch of green no bigger than a postage stamp, crisscrossed by red and blue strands of interstate.

"You need directions somewhere?"

Kyung doesn't need directions so much as a destination. "Maybe," he says, following a long red line farther and farther west.

"Where you headed?"

"California," he says, trying it on for size. It's strange to hear the word out loud, which makes the idea feel more real than it did in the car.

"Oh, that's easy." The man doesn't bother to look at the map. "You're on 90 now, which'll turn into 80 soon. You just stay on 80 all the way through Nebraska, and then right before you hit Colorado, it'll turn into 76."

"How long will it take to get there?"

"Depends. Which half you headed to? North or south?"

Kyung names the first city that comes to mind. "Los Angeles."

The man shrugs. "I've made it from Erie to L.A. in about thirty-three hours, but I was drinking coffee and pissing in a jug pretty much the entire way. What kind of car you driving?"

He points out the window at the bright yellow Mustang he rented. From a distance, the car looks even more ridiculous than it did on the lot, like a midlife crisis on wheels. The only reason he picked it was the price. As long as he was using a credit card that his father had just paid off, he decided he might as well do some damage, which has been his motto for the entire trip. Kyung intends to charge every tank of gas, every pack of cigarettes, every meal, every last everything on his cards. It feels like free money. Fuck-you money.

"A good V-8 like that should probably get you there by Wednesday if you're in a hurry, but you're going to be in rough shape for a while. Don't plan on doing anything for a couple of days besides taking baths and getting back rubs."

Kyung has no idea what he's doing, no plan at all. When he left the house, he took a bus downtown and checked into the first hotel he saw. He couldn't bring himself to unpack his things, so he sat on the bed, staring at the walls, the carpet, the pattern of the bedspread. There wasn't anything wrong with his surroundings. The room was no different from others he'd stayed in before. He just couldn't accept that this was where he'd landed, and suddenly, after hours of sitting and staring without purpose, he felt a desperate need to get out. One minute, he was signing the paperwork for his rental car. The next, he was on the highway passing signs for Albany, then Syracuse, then Buffalo. There was something comforting about the drive and being on the open road, which made him feel like he had a place to be, even though he didn't. He blasted the radio for hours, polluting the car with noise to avoid thinking about his conversation with Gillian. When his head began to ache, he turned off the music and chain-smoked through his open window, littering the black interior with dusty gray ash. The thought of California came to him not long after he spotted the signs for Lake Ontario. It was nothing at first. Just a random idea among many that he initially dismissed, but the farther he drove, the more he began to think: Why not? Why not California? Why not now?

"You headed out there for a visit?" the man asks. He dabs his lips delicately with a napkin, littering his beard with toast crumbs.

"No." He pauses. "I'm moving there."

"You're lucky you're not towing all your stuff. Might not be easy to do in that car once you hit the Rockies."

All Kyung has is a suitcase full of clothes. He has no job lined up, no place to live, no other belongings, and once again, he's living on credit—a thought that begins to weigh on him now. Gillian knows their account numbers and passwords by heart. She could easily cancel every last card in his name when she realizes he's racking up charges again. Where will he be when that happens? Sitting in this sad little diner? Or stranded somewhere on the side of the road? Kyung shuts his eyes, aware that he's ruining the idea before it's even real.

"You okay, buddy?" the man asks.

"Where's the bathroom?"

"Well—"

Kyung spots the sign on the wall and jumps out of his seat without waiting for an answer. When he opens the door to the men's room, he's almost knocked over by the smell of piss, bleach, and urinal cakes. He enters tentatively, scanning the bathroom from floor to ceiling, certain he'll find something filthy to account for the stench. The room, however, actually seems clean. His only real complaint is the long, shatterproof mirror hanging over the bank of sinks. It's almost like a circus mirror, the kind that stretches out people's reflections when viewed from a distance. Kyung takes a few steps toward it, waiting for his appearance to become less distorted. His nose is barely inches from the glass when he can finally see himself clearly. His eyes are bloodshot and he desperately needs a shave, a toothbrush, and a comb. But above all, he looks worried. The wrinkle between his brows where the skin usually creases into

a frown—it seems permanent now, as if every fear he's ever ex-
perienced has burrowed into that space. How does he make it
stop? All this worrying about other people, worrying about
himself, worrying about things that might happen before they
even do—what did any of that get him except a life he wants
to leave? He washes his face, scrubbing off the grime with flowery pink hand soap. Then he dunks his head under the tap,
letting the cold water run over him. He tries not to think about
baptisms and the new beginnings they promise, but maybe
that's just what he needs. A baptism in a truck stop bathroom.

When Kyung returns to his seat, his foil-wrapped sandwich
is sitting on the counter beside his check, and the man is gone.
He isn't sure why he expected a formal good-bye—they didn't
even exchange names—but he's sorry that he didn't get a chance
to thank him for the directions. Not hearing another person's
voice would have felt like a gift to him a few weeks ago, but
now it seems like all he has. He pays for his food and goes outside, looking up at the sky, which is lighter than it was before.
There's a moody sliver of purple inching up along the horizon,
promising sun or rain—he's not sure. As he walks to his car,
he hears someone call out, "Hey, buddy. Buddy." He turns and
sees the man jogging toward him from behind the gas station,
zipping up his pants while his unbuckled belt dangles noisily
from his waist.

Kyung backs up several steps, not certain where this is headed
anymore. "What were you just doing?"

"I tried to warn you, but you got out of your seat so fast.
None of us regulars use that bathroom. It smells like a goddamn litter box. We just piss in that field over there."

"Oh." He watches the man buckle his belt again, relieved

that he isn't coming on to him. Kyung actually enjoyed their conversation, the relative ease of it. It would have disappointed him if it ended with some sort of awkward proposition in the parking lot.

"Any chance you'd let me bum one of those?" the man asks, pointing at the cigarettes in Kyung's shirt pocket.

"Okay, sure." He unwraps the pack and hands him one, not certain if he should stay and smoke with him. He never quite learned the etiquette of smokers, having picked up the habit for a brief period in med school and only starting back up today. Despite smoking a full pack in the car, Kyung still doesn't know how to hold the cigarette correctly; it feels like an awkward sixth finger that gets in the way. He studies the man for a second as he takes a drag, and then lights one for himself.

"Jesus, these are awful."

"You mean the brand?"

"No. Cigarettes in general," the man says, even though he's smiling. "I quit buying them years ago. Doctor's orders. Only time I have one now is if I meet a friendly stranger on the road. It's kind of a love–hate thing."

Kyung has never heard anyone describe him as "friendly" before. What little effort he made to meet new friends or keep up with his old ones ended when he began dating Gillian. He was content to live in their little cocoon, and after the baby, she was too. From time to time, they went to a party hosted by one of his colleagues from school, but they usually arrived late and left early, citing Ethan as the excuse on both ends. Marriage made them both lazy this way. It was easier to be with someone predictable than to invest the time in figuring out someone new.

"So what's in L.A.?" the man asks. "You got a job there or something?"

"Yes," he says. "I'm a doctor."

"A doctor who smokes—I've never seen that before. What kind of medicine you practice?"

"Radiology."

The fictions keep spilling from his mouth, an alternate reality in which he undoes the choices of his past and imagines what might have been. It doesn't feel like lying so much as wishing.

"Do you go to L.A. a lot?" Kyung asks.

"I usually head out there about two or three times a year. Seems like a pretty nice city if you don't mind the traffic."

"Any place you'd recommend for a newcomer?"

"Well"—the man takes a thoughtful drag on his cigarette— "the Getty, if you've never been there before. I'm not much for the art, but the building's something worth seeing. They have these big plazas and gardens, and you can stand outside as long as you want and look out over the whole city." He takes another drag, blowing plumes of smoke through his nose. "I've only been there that one time, but if you catch it on the right day when the smog isn't too thick, you don't need to see it twice."

Kyung never would have guessed that this man, who looks like such a particular type, would recommend a museum. "You don't go to bars when you're on the road?"

The man's laugh turns into a phlegmy cough. "That's a young man's game, prowling around town. I'm long past those years now. Me, I'm just happy to get a clean room and a hot breakfast the next morning."

At thirty-six, Kyung wonders if he's even a young man anymore, if he has the energy or will to do what it takes to live differently. Moving somewhere, finding a job, making some friends—all of it would require him to try. It's been so long since he tried to do anything, but it doesn't make sense to change his geography and not change everything else.

"I know you're probably in a hurry to get going," the man says, "but you're barely fifteen minutes away from a real good view of Lake Erie." He crushes what's left of his cigarette under his shoe. "You should head out there and take a drive on the shoreline before leaving town. The sun's coming up soon. It'll probably be the prettiest thing you see from here to California."

"Thank you," Kyung says. He means these words sincerely, almost with regret. He's embarrassed by how quickly he formed his first impression, and how wrong he was from the start.

By the time he pulls over at an empty lakeside picnic area, the sun appears whole just above the horizon. Bright pink, purple, and orange swaths of color surround it, the entire scene mirrored in Lake Erie below. The man, whose name Kyung wishes he'd learned, was wrong about the view. It's not the most beautiful thing he'll see on his drive. It's probably the most beautiful thing he's seen, ever. Unlike the pale blue Caribbean beaches he once admired, nothing about this landscape is calm or serene. It looks like the sky is on fire, setting the lake and all the trees ablaze with it. Kyung gets out of his car and sits on top of a splintered wood picnic table, lighting a cigarette as he stares at the violent display of color. The haze he couldn't see through earlier has settled into a whispery fog, floating above the lake like a legion of ghosts. He takes a photo, moving his phone up and down to change the angle and light. The tiny lens doesn't do the scene much justice, but the last of his twenty-odd shots turns out to be decent. Not quite vivid or true, but clear enough to help him remember that he was here one day.

The clock on his phone reads 5:05, which hardly seems right to him. He doesn't know how many hours he's been awake. Twenty-two? Twenty-three? He can barely summon the math to do a simple calculation anymore. It occurs to him that Ethan is probably waking up right now, ready for his breakfast and morning dose of TV. When he opens the bedroom door, only Gillian will be there, and Kyung wonders if he'll understand what this means. He drops his lit cigarette on the grass, sick with the thought of his son. He tried so hard not to think about him during the drive, but the exhaustion is finally chipping away at his resolve. The only thing Ethan had ever done was arrive in this world needing him, and the greatest failure of Kyung's life, the one he felt daily, was not knowing how to respond. The part of him that wanted to be a good father was constantly at odds with the part that didn't have one, leaving him with only two defaults as a parent—correcting Ethan or keeping him at a careful distance. Although his methods often changed from one minute to the next, his intentions were always the same. He wanted his son to turn out so much better than he did.

This person Kyung imagines running off to be—this more open, more willing, more expansive version of himself—this is who he should have been for Ethan all along. Not the stern disciplinarian too quick to correct every perceived step in the wrong direction, or the absentee father so convinced that mere proximity would damage him for good. He gravitated toward one extreme or the other, never finding that comfortable place in between.

Kyung removes the cigarettes from his pocket, throwing the pack in a nearby trash can. Whatever California is to him, whatever promise he thought it held, he knows it's over now. It was over before it even began. He takes one last look at the lake and stretches his arms in the air, preparing himself for the long ride home.

Elinor doesn't recognize him when he pulls into the parking lot. She shields her eyes from his headlights and squints, her expression confused and maybe even a bit frightened. Kyung realizes that his timing couldn't have been worse. It looks like she was locking up for the night. Had he arrived a few minutes later, he could have avoided her altogether. He gets out of his car and shakes his legs, which are tight and stiff from the drive. Elinor picks up her bags as he walks toward her, hooking the handles over her arms protectively.

"Hello," he calls out.

"Hello?"

"It's me, Mae's son. Kyung."

She looks visibly relieved to hear his name. "Oh. I'm sorry. I couldn't see who pulled in. For a second there, I thought I'd forgotten a meeting or something. . . ." The closer he gets, the more the pleasant chattiness in her voice begins to fade. "Kyung, are you all right?"

He knows he looks awful. He doesn't even need a mirror to confirm it. He made it back from Erie in just under ten hours, waylaid by a flat on his return. He should have slept while waiting for the auto club to arrive, but all he wanted to do was get home. It's a miracle he's still upright now. He scratches his itchy, oily head, catching a whiff of his body odor as he lifts his arm. He stops a safe distance away, hoping she won't notice the smell.

"I just drove back from Pennsylvania. I was there—for work." He feels the need to mention work, if only to assure her there's a reason for his appearance, but the lie doesn't sound convincing enough. "So, is this your studio?"

"Yes, this is it."

The building is a two-story brick box with a shiny black door and a sign beside it that reads HAMEL INTERIOR DESIGN. It's not quite the successful-looking business that Elinor made it out to be at the reception, but it's clearly a real business—not something she's running out of an extra bedroom in her spare time.

"May I?" He gestures at the bags in her arms, aware that it might help to act like a gentleman since he doesn't look like one.

"Yes, thank you. I'd appreciate that."

She hands him the bags, which are achingly heavy. All three contain thick plastic binders and fabric samples held together by metal rings. He looks at her uncertainly, his shoulders curling forward with the weight.

"They're design folios," she explains. "Homework for a meeting tomorrow. My car's just over here."

He deposits the bags in her backseat, catching a glimpse of himself in the passenger window as he shuts the door. The skin under his eyes is discolored and inflamed. It looks like he recently lost a fight.

"I didn't expect to see you here so soon, Kyung. I thought

you might need more time." She smiles at him hesitantly. "It's kind of late to start packing, don't you think?"

He's not sure how to tell her that he has no intention of packing at all.

"And you do know you're eventually going to need a truck, right? You won't make much of a dent taking things in that—that car."

There's a vaguely distasteful sound in her voice, and he thinks he understands why. The flashy yellow Mustang that looked so slick in the rental lot just looks sad and abused now, streaked with dirt and dead bugs.

"Actually, I wasn't planning to move out today so much as move in."

"Move in—here?"

"Yes, if you wouldn't mind."

Elinor seems confused again. Kyung has been alone with his thoughts for too long. It takes him a few moments to realize that she needs more explanation to understand the things he decided in the car.

"You said my mother paid the rent through the end of the year, so I thought I'd make use of the place. I shouldn't be here for more than a month or two."

"But why? What are you going to *use* it for?"

Her suspiciousness doesn't offend him; he'd distrust someone in his condition too. She probably thinks he'll wreck the apartment and maybe even the studio beneath it.

"My wife and I, we've been having some problems because of all the things that happened this summer, so I need a place to stay until I find one of my own. I thought, maybe since my mother paid through December, I could just crash here." He immediately regrets his use of the word "crash," which he worries implies destruction. "I'd like to be close enough to see my son while I look for an apartment in Marlboro. . . ."

Elinor seems embarrassed for him. "I'm sorry to hear you've been having troubles lately. Your mother wouldn't have wanted that for you. Of course you're welcome to stay for a while. Actually, why don't you come inside for a few minutes? Let me show you around."

Kyung thinks he might pass out right there in the parking lot. He'd prefer to forgo the escorted tour, but it doesn't feel safe to decline. Marital difficulty seems to be a topic that inspires some sympathy in Elinor, who isn't wearing a wedding ring on her finger. He assumes she'll lead him up the metal staircase to the apartment on the second floor, but she unlocks the door to her studio instead.

"This is where your mother would have worked," she says, flicking on the lights.

He braces himself for the cold shock of fluorescents, but instead, the room is awash with the amber glow of oversized light bulbs. Dozens of them dangle from simple black cords across the length of the room, their thin orange filaments suspended in midair. Kyung has never been in a design studio before. He doesn't know if they're all supposed to look this way, or if the arrangement is unique to Elinor's. There are four distinct areas that resemble small living rooms, each with a sofa, two armchairs, a coffee table, and stacks of binders similar to the ones he carried to her car. The color schemes are all in the same family of off-white or beige, but subtle differences set one area apart from the next—the pattern of a rug, the style of furniture, the lamps and decorations.

"This would have been Mae's area for meeting clients."

She sweeps her hand over the space with a flourish, seemingly happy to show it off. He tries to imagine his mother sitting there among the throw pillows, talking with people she didn't know, selling them things they probably didn't need.

"So . . . what do you think?"

Elinor leans against a sofa, which looks like the one he slept on at the beach house. He takes in his surroundings as appreciatively as he can, trying not to think about the last time he slept.

"You don't have desks?"

"No, not anymore. Actually, most of this setup is new. It was your mother's idea. She said she always liked sitting with me in her house, looking at things together instead of sitting across from each other at a table. It's much more personal and relaxed this way, don't you think? Like chatting about design with a friend instead of someone you're doing business with."

"She thought of this arrangement?"

Elinor hesitates. "Thought of it . . . no. But inspired it, certainly. Your mother had strong opinions about what made her comfortable, and she definitely had a sense for making others feel comfortable too. Just wait until you see the apartment."

As they walk back outside and up the metal staircase, Elinor tells him there's no direct entrance from the apartment to the studio—a warning to keep out, he thinks. She also asks him to take off his shoes during business hours so her clients can't hear him walking around. And no loud music or television either, she adds gently. He mumbles in agreement, trying to keep track of her sudden list of rules.

"I hope you don't mind me saying all of this, but I'm not used to having anyone living up here. This space used to be a storage area. I was only willing to rent it to your mother because she needed a place to stay during the week. . . . Oh, and before I forget . . . Indian food."

"What?"

"The ventilation in this building isn't terribly efficient, so I'd appreciate it if you didn't cook Indian food, or anything with a strong odor. I can't have my customers walking in and smelling curry."

Kyung watches her unlock the door to the apartment. He'd gladly agree to almost anything if she'd just let him sleep. When they enter, his eyes go straight to the high ceiling, which is painted a stark shade of white. The storeroom is much bigger than he expected, and more finished too. All traces of its former use are gone now. Although there aren't any walls separating one room from another, each space is carefully contained by a large Oriental rug. There's a long, plush sofa in the living area, upholstered in a deep red shade of velvet, with careful rows of matching velvet-covered buttons lining the cushions. Kyung gently touches the chocolate-colored throw blanket draped over one of the arms, and the excess of it surprises him. Not only is the material cashmere; it's a quality of cashmere ten times thicker and softer than any sweater or scarf he's ever owned. He sits down on the end of the sofa, sinking into the perfect balance of feathers and foam, and takes in the rest of the room. Along the wall, two tall bookshelves have been meticulously arranged with books and antiques. The upper shelves feature old brass and copper trinkets, while the lower shelves house coffee table–sized books on architecture and design. Kyung gets up to examine the art hanging from the walls, all of which is framed in a similar style of ornate carved wood covered in gold leaf. He realizes that the choices his mother made for the houses in Marlboro and Orleans must have been a concession to Jin, who always preferred landscapes. Clearly, his mother preferred objects. Each framed piece is done in a different style but features a single image. A watercolor of a Victorian teacup. A charcoal rendering of a feather pen. An oil painting of a birdcage.

"Beautiful, isn't it?"

"How long did it take you to decorate this place?"

"I didn't do any of it. This was all Mae." She looks at him with a curious tilt of her head. "If you don't mind me saying, you seem to have a hard time believing how talented she was."

He knows his mother had a good eye for things. But he didn't see this as a talent so much as a hobby. He never understood that she wanted a livelihood or was capable enough to have one.

"I know she was talented," he says, because it kills him that he didn't.

Kyung moves into the bedroom area along the opposite wall. There's a sleigh bed with a pale gold duvet, which he assumes is real silk even before running his hand over the smooth, unwrinkled surface. The right corner has been turned over like a hotel maid's handiwork, and he's tempted to crawl under the inviting fold and pass out. Elinor joins him, drawing his attention to tall stacks of design magazines on the twin end tables, arranged according to the color of their spines. She straightens one, adjusting it no more than a few millimeters, and he recognizes the gesture, sees who his mother learned it from.

"You taught her a lot," he says. "I can tell."

"She taught me a lot too. I was so excited for her to get started here. She would have been a wonderful addition." She clutches his shoulder, studying his face carefully. "I'm so sorry. I feel like I'm always saying the wrong thing in front of you."

"No, no. It's not that. It's just kind of odd to imagine my mother—I don't know—working."

"She was a very hard worker, Kyung. She ordered every piece of furniture in here. All the paint and lighting too. She also sourced the decorations and artwork, managed the crew. She did everything. And the fact that she did most of it over the phone—that was always the thing I found so impressive about her. She could be very commanding when she needed to be." Elinor smiles. "Actually, you might think this is funny. The men we usually hire to paint, they were always talking about how Mrs. Cho wanted this and Mrs. Cho wanted that and Mrs. Cho wouldn't like it that way. . . . Oh, she used to get them so worked up! They were all completely terrified of her."

Kyung is examining an old upright turntable in the corner. On the floor beside it is an antique leather suitcase filled with records by Johnny Mathis, Simon & Garfunkel, and the Platters. He shakes his head, wondering why he didn't hear her that day in the car, why he never truly listened when she spoke. All she wanted to do was tell him about her records.

"I hope you know—I wasn't suggesting that the painters didn't like your mother. It was just the opposite, really. They didn't want to disappoint her because they respected her so much."

He understands that Elinor is gently trying to improve his

memory of Mae, to convince him that she deserved more credit than he was ever willing to give. But the thought of grown men being terrified of her isn't funny. And although he's impressed by her work, he's also saddened by it. The apartment was clearly designed as a refuge, a place for Mae to stay during the week and be the person she wanted to be, a person he didn't know or pay any attention to. He imagines her walking upstairs after a long day's work, opening a bottle of wine, playing a record, and reading one of her books or magazines. She was planning a life for herself here, a small and quiet life, and Kyung wishes she'd had the chance to live it. He thinks she would have been happy for once.

"Did I say something to upset you?" Elinor asks.

"No, I think the drive just caught up with me."

"Well, let me get out of your way, then." She walks to the door and turns to say good-bye. "You're sure I haven't upset you?"

"No, not at all. It's nice to be here, to see what she could do."

"All right, then. You get a good night's sleep. You look like you need it."

Kyung crawls into bed as soon as Elinor closes the door. It's a luxurious combination—the clean silky sheets, soft down pillows, and firm king-sized mattress. It's a far better setup than he's used to, better than a five-star hotel, he suspects. He turns over onto his back and notices the painting attached to the ceiling, directly over his head. There's a woman sitting on the grass, staring at some hills in the distance. The style of it doesn't quite fit with anything else in the apartment, but it's peaceful, the mix of blues and greens and grays, the content expression on the woman's face. He can see why Mae chose it as the last thing she wanted to look at before closing her eyes.

His own eyes begin to blink, heavy and sore, so he sits up, not wanting to fall asleep before calling Gillian. Being in the apartment inspires him, energizing him in a way that California didn't. If a person like Mae could finally change her life, he has no excuse not to do something about his own. The cell phone in his pocket is dead, so he reaches over and picks up the cordless on the nightstand. The line rings much longer than it usually does. He realizes he's not entirely sure what time it is, other than night.

"Hello?"

"Hi. It's me."

"What number are you calling from?" Gillian sounds irritated to hear from him.

"I'm staying at a place in Connecticut. It doesn't matter. . . . Anyway, would it be okay if I stopped by in the morning? I didn't get a chance to talk to Ethan before I left."

She pauses much longer than she should. "I'm not sure that's such a good idea."

"Why? Is he sick?"

"No."

"Is he upset I'm not there?"

"No, he's fine with it."

Kyung's hurt, but not surprised by this, which Gillian seems to understand.

"I didn't mean it like that. He just thinks you're off somewhere for work. I haven't really explained everything yet."

"Would it be all right if I came by, then? I think there are certain things he should probably hear from me."

He can almost picture her right now, cradling the phone under her ear and biting her lower lip.

"If you're worried about what I'm going to say to him, you're welcome to join us. I figure we're going to have to work out some sort of—accommodation, right? Maybe it'd be nice for Ethan to hear what's going on from both of us."

It bothers him to think that Gillian might not trust him to be alone with their son, but his invitation is sincere. He wouldn't mind if she was there. She deserved to see him try for a change.

"So . . . ?"

"Kyung, it's really not the best time. . . ."

Again with the long pause, he thinks. She's not making this easy for him, but he reminds himself that people don't switch on and off like machines. He's given her no reason to respond differently.

"Well, how about in the afternoon, then? Would that be better than the morning? Maybe we can take Ethan to the park for a while. He likes it there—"

"No, Kyung. Stop talking about the park. It's not that. It's . . . They asked me not to tell you yet."

"Who asked you? Tell me what?"

She covers the receiver with her hand, but he can still hear her moving around in the kitchen. There's a clank of something that sounds like a pot, and then the hollow thud of a cabinet door. "Shit," he thinks she says.

"Hello?" he calls out. "Are you there, Gillian? Tell me what?"

She clears her throat as she uncovers the phone. "I think you have a right to know, Kyung. They found him today."

"Who? What are you talking about?"

"That man—Perry? Nat Perry? The police brought him in a few hours ago. He's at the station in Marlboro."

NINE

He doesn't stop to think who "they" are until a few hours later. *They* asked her not to tell him yet. But when he pulls up in front of the station, he knows immediately. The three of them are waiting outside the main entrance. He sees Connie first, and then the huge outline of Tim. The third man is the detective from the funeral. Smiley, Smalley—he can't remember and doesn't care. Kyung walks toward them, not certain how to get past a barricade of men who clearly want to keep him out. He's no match for any of them, not on a good day and definitely not now.

"Jesus. You look like hell," Tim says.

"When's the last time you slept?" Connie asks.

"I'm not sure."

He wonders if his in-laws know they're not going to be in-laws anymore. The relief, the satisfaction they must feel. It's what they wanted all along. He expects to be told to leave, but no one says a word. They just keep staring at him, as if their silence alone will turn him back. Kyung looks at the cigarette butts on the sidewalk and grass. He tries to count them but keeps losing track. The spike of adrenaline that got him here is down to almost nothing now, and his mind is too scattered to connect one thought with the next. How does he get past them? How does he make them understand how much he needs to?

"I'm not sure if you remember me, sir. I'm Detective Smalley. We met a few days ago?"

The detective's breath stinks of rotten eggs, but Kyung shakes his outstretched hand anyway. "Where did you find him?"

"He was holed up with a girl the entire time. Never even left town."

"But the car—Lentz said you found it near Canada."

"Why don't we go upstairs and talk? You look like you could use a cup of coffee or something."

Kyung glances at Connie and Tim, but neither of them do anything to prevent him from entering. Connie even opens the door and waves them all inside. They walk past the front desk, where the receptionist is sitting behind a wall of glass, yawning as she flips through a magazine. When she notices Connie and the detective, she pushes the magazine off to the side and covers it with an envelope. The four of them stop in front of the elevators where a large white plaque announces that visitors to the upper floors are required to sign in. Tim presses the UP button impatiently.

"Sir, do you know where your father is?" the detective asks.

"He's not here already?"

"No. I called him after the arrest and he agreed to come by to make the ID, but he never showed up."

Kyung responds without thinking. "He's afraid, probably."

"Afraid?"

"To see him again. I think most people would be."

Detective Smalley doesn't look like the type to be afraid of anything, actually. He's old, but fit, with thick forearms and shoulders so broad, they almost look padded. Kyung notices a scratch above his left eye, bandaged but still bleeding through the gauze.

"Did he put up a fight?"

"They always put up a fight," Tim says.

The elevator door opens onto a vestibule painted in a strange, medicinal shade of pink. Kyung grips the handrail as the car jerks its way up to the third floor, spitting them out into a narrow corridor. The station feels like a rabbit warren—big, but more broken up than he ever would have guessed from the street. The building is on his route to the grocery store. He never thought he'd have a reason to go inside, and a part of him still can't believe that he is.

"Why didn't you want Gillian to tell me you found him?" he asks Connie.

"Because it wasn't worth bringing you in yet. The guy was out of his mind."

"On drugs?"

"At some point, probably. But we were more worried about the booze. He said he'd been drinking for two days straight. We've had him in a cell sobering up ever since he came in."

Something about this explanation doesn't sit right with him. "So you didn't want me to know he was here because . . . ?"

Connie shrugs. "I thought you'd probably want to see the interview, but no one was going to get a word of sense out of him, not in the state he was in. I figured we'd spare you the wait."

Kyung searches Connie's face, then the detective's and Tim's. It doesn't seem possible that they did this to be kind, but nothing in their expressions contradicts what he just heard.

"Meet me in number three," Detective Smalley says. "I'll bring him over."

Connie, Tim, and Kyung walk single file to the end of the hall and squeeze into a small room with an oversized window. On the other side of the glass, there's a table and chairs. On their side, there's nothing.

"You reek," Tim says, covering his nose. "How long's it been since you had a shower?"

"Give him a break. You want a coffee or something?"

Kyung shakes his head. The space they're standing in is no bigger than a closet. It's warm—there aren't any vents or air ducts anywhere—and Tim is actually right for a change. Kyung smells awful; the room smells awful too, like food left out in the sun to spoil. He leans against the far wall, trying to put as much distance between himself and the others.

"What kind of place is this?" he asks. "It's like an alley in here."

"We use it for lineups, mostly," Connie says. "The regular interview room's got mold in the ceiling, so we're stuck with this. You understand how it works, right? They can't see us through the glass, but we can see them."

"I don't care if he sees me."

"Don't be stupid, Kyung. John's doing me a favor. I thought it might give you some peace to see this guy locked up, but you can't go crazy in here."

If there was ever a time for crazy, Kyung thinks it's now. He has nothing to lose anymore. His mother is gone. His wife no longer wants him around. His child, he'll probably only be allowed to see on weekends and holidays. His attempt to start over in California has been exposed as the fantasy it is. Before the attack, Kyung's life was far from perfect, but now he has even less than what he started with, and that hardly seems fair. Without the Perrys, the stasis he lived in could have continued indefinitely, and he would have been glad to accept that safe place in the middle where nothing moved him too greatly or hurt him too much.

The door in the other room opens and a uniformed officer places a paper bag and a soda on the table.

"McDonald's?" Kyung asks, realizing that he hasn't eaten anything since Erie. "You're giving him food?"

"We have to," Connie says. "He's been in custody too long. Besides, it'll help sober him up."

Another officer leads Perry in, handcuffed from behind and shackled around the ankles. He doesn't appear drunk so much as tired. Kyung always assumed he was a physically intimidating man, but Perry isn't much taller than he is, only wider. His stomach is distended like a cannonball, and the ridge of his chest sags like old breasts through his T-shirt, which is stained at the neck and underarms, the fabric more yellow than white. The thought of such a filthy, disgusting man even looking at his mother, much less touching her, makes him want to hurl something through the glass and grab Perry by the throat.

"Knock it off," Tim says.

"What?"

"The tapping. Stop it already."

Kyung looks down. He didn't notice he was tapping his foot on the floor. He has energy all of a sudden, too much to know what to do with. He crosses his arms and watches as the officer frees one of Perry's wrists and cuffs it to the back of a chair. Perry sits down and opens the bag on the table. He unwraps a cheeseburger one-handed and scrapes the onions and ketchup off with a pickle, leaving them in a bloody-looking pile on a napkin. Then he leans over like a pig to a trough and alternates between his burger and fries, shoving them into his mouth in huge bites that Kyung wishes he'd choke on. The detective enters and sits down at the table to read him his rights, but Perry doesn't seem to be listening. He eats his second burger exactly like the first, his eyes glassy, his hunger primal.

"I need a verbal response that you understand what I just told you and you've waived your rights to an attorney."

Perry nods dumbly, his mouth still full.

"A *verbal* response." Detective Smalley pushes the microphone and tape recorder toward him. "Do you hear what I'm saying?"

"Yes, sir. I understand."

His accent is unexpected, as is his use of the word "sir," but Kyung remembers the mug shots that Lentz showed him. Perry's a Southerner, at least he used to be.

"You put up quite a fight today."

He shrugs. "I get that way when I drink."

"But you did more than just drink, didn't you? There must have been a couple dozen bindles in that apartment. It looked like you had a party or something."

"What's a bindle?"

"The little envelopes you buy meth in."

"I wouldn't know anything about those. I was just staying there—with the girl. It's her place . . . her stuff."

"Right. The girl." Detective Smalley removes the rubber band wrapped around his folder and pulls out a sheet of paper. "Sharon Julie Andrews." He chuckles. "Her parents had a weird sense of humor, didn't they? Julie Andrews?"

"Who?"

"The actress? The little blond one? You know—*The Sound of Music*?"

The reference doesn't seem to register. "I'm not sure I follow."

There's a slow, syrupy quality to Perry's responses that almost makes him seem harmless, but Kyung isn't fooled. He knows what this man is capable of. The last time his mother saw him, he looked like a monster.

"So is Sharon your girlfriend?"

"No, not really. She's just a friend."

"She must be a pretty good friend to drive the car you stole all the way up to Vermont. You know that's how we found you, right? She just left a brand-new Lincoln on the side of a road and hopped the bus back home. Didn't even stop to think that maybe she should have found a better hiding place for it. I bet you told her to wipe the prints, right?"

He waits for an answer, but doesn't get one.

"Lucky for us, meth heads aren't too thorough. Sharon left a couple on the armrest." He laughs again. "It took us a while, but we finally caught up with her this morning while she was out trolling the park with the other junkies. Didn't have her in a holding cell for more than a few hours before she started telling us all about you. It doesn't really look like you're going to be friends anymore."

Perry balls up the wrappers from his food and puts them in the bag. He doesn't appear fazed by what he just heard, not at all. "Can you tell me where my brother's buried?"

Detective Smalley seems thrown by the question. "How do you know he's dead?"

"Because I saw him. In the bathroom of that couple's house. He was dead when I left."

"You're admitting you were there?"

Perry looks at him, exhausted and unwilling to play. Then he turns to the window, as if to address everyone standing on the other side of it. "I think you all know I was there. I'm willing to cooperate. I'd just really like to know where my brother's buried."

Tim nudges Kyung in the ribs. "This one's finished," he says, smiling. "He's not even smart enough to lie."

The detective thumbs through the contents of his file until he finds what he's looking for. "It says here that your brother's in a potter's field out in Westhaven."

"Five generations of us, all buried in potter's fields." Perry shakes his head. "Seems like a fitting end, I guess."

Kyung should be relieved—relieved to be spared a trial, to know that Perry will spend the rest of his days in prison and then be buried in an unmarked grave like his brother—but he can't summon anything resembling relief. A prison cell is hardly enough punishment for all the lives this man ruined. He wants Perry to suffer. He wants him to feel more pain, more regret, more loss, more everything. Multiply it tenfold and it still wouldn't be enough.

"So tell me what happened." The detective moves the paper bag off to the side and centers the microphone on the table. "Start from the beginning."

Perry takes a long drink of soda and clears his throat. "My brother, Dell, and I—we'd been watching the neighborhood for about a week. We decided to hit the big blue house on the corner."

"What blue house?"

"Maybe it was purple? I've been told I have trouble with colors."

"You mean the house next door to Mr. and Mrs. Cho?"

He nods. "We'd been watching the old couple. Three nights in a row, the husband closed up his store downtown, but he never went to the bank afterward. Never went the next morning either, so we figured he kept his money at home."

"Okay . . ."

"So that night—I don't know, Wednesday or Thursday or whenever it was—we headed over there around dark. The plan was to say our car broke down, ask to use their phone or something, but just as we were about to go up the front steps, this little Oriental lady came flying out of the house next door saying 'Oh, help me, help me.' So we figured, why not? Anybody living in that neighborhood had to be rich."

Detective Smalley scribbles a note on the outside of his folder. "So you're telling me that a complete stranger just invited you into her house?"

"Her husband was beating the crap out of her." Perry motions toward his face. "She was all banged up, her lip was bleeding everywhere. She needed help, I guess. Didn't really seem to care who she got it from."

The detective turns around and looks at the window, visibly startled. Even though he can't see through the glass, he seems to know exactly where Connie is standing. He lifts his hand as if to scratch his cheek and discreetly points toward the exit.

Kyung immediately feels a tap, followed by a firm grip on his shoulder. The sensation snaps him back, back from a dreamlike state in which nothing he just heard seems right or real. What Perry is describing—it can't be the way all of this started. It can't be the cause of everything that happened afterward.

"I made a mistake," Connie says. "You shouldn't be here for this."

"Get your hand off me."

"Kyung, you don't need to hear—"

"Get—your—hand—off—me." He stares at Connie, suddenly feeling much bigger than he is, bloated with adrenaline and anger. *"Off,"* he repeats, not blinking or breaking until Connie removes his hand.

"So what happened after that?" the detective asks.

"We followed her next door and she let us inside. And there was furniture and stuff in pieces everywhere, like they'd been at it for a while. So for a second I thought we should just leave, but my brother jumped in and told her he wanted the money. There wasn't much I could do after that but go along with it." Perry seems almost irritated by this. "My brother was hard up for crystal those last few months. I kept telling him"—he raises his voice, thrusting his finger at the empty chair next to the detective—"'You got to get off that junk. It does something different to your brain, but no. You can't be fucking bothered to listen, can you? Always thinking about yourself.'"

Perry appears almost mentally ill, talking to the chair as if his brother were in it. He lingers there for a moment, finger outstretched, and then quickly turns back to his soda, emptying the cup in several large gulps. "So what else?"

"Go back to the beginning. . . . You're saying all that damage in the Chos' house—you didn't do any of it? It was already there when you walked in?"

"I don't know. Maybe we did a little of it. I honestly can't remember. I was pretty far gone the entire time." He shrugs. "Jesus. Leave it to us to walk in on the middle of something like that. We should have just taken off when we saw her coming."

In the corner of his eye, Kyung notices Tim shaking his head.

"That piece of shit," he mutters.

Connie elbows him. "Quiet, Tim."

"Why? He *is* a fucking piece of shit."

Kyung doesn't know whether he's talking about his father or Nat Perry, but from the look on Tim's face, and Connie's too, it no longer matters.

"Can I get another one of these?" Perry shakes his cup of ice.

"Hold on." The detective finishes writing something on his folder. "So what exactly did Mrs. Cho say when she saw you outside?"

"What I told you before. She asked us for help." He scratches himself under the arm. "I think she also said something like 'Make him stop.'"

"Then what did you say?"

"I'm not sure. It was probably something like, 'Don't worry, little lady.' You know, because she was small and pretty. . . ."

Kyung throws himself against the window, causing Tim and Connie to jump, but the sound of his fists pounding on the glass doesn't register on the other side. The detective and Perry continue talking as Kyung tries to push his way out of the room.

"Where do you think you're going?" Connie asks.

"You know exactly where I'm going."

"No, you aren't."

"I'm going to kill him, Connie. I told him—I told him I would if he ever did this again."

"You're not going to kill anyone."

Connie opens the door and lets him out into the hallway. Kyung bolts toward the elevator, only to be pushed aside as Connie jumps in front of him with his arms out, blocking his path. When he turns around, Tim is standing the same way, blocking the door to the stairs. He's not sure which of the two he has a better chance with, so he takes a running start at Connie, who sends him stumbling backward with barely a shove.

"I know you're angry right now."

"You don't know what I am."

"I do. I understand, Kyung. I'd feel exactly the same way if it were me. But let us handle Jin from now on. You're not the one who has to deal with this."

But he is, he thinks. He always has been, and he failed at it, miserably. And just as the full force of this thought is about to crush him, another bears down with all of its weight.

"The apartment," he says, leaning against the wall. "That goddamn apartment."

"What apartment?"

"She was going to leave him."

"How do you know?"

"She had a place to live, a job lined up. She was finally going to leave and he wouldn't let her."

Connie shakes his head. "Don't assume things like that, Kyung. You can't see what goes on behind closed doors."

What he wants to say, but doesn't, is that he does see. He sees everything so clearly now. Mae turned on his father for a reason. She exiled him from the guest room, refused to touch him or speak to him for a reason. It was always his father. It all started with him.

They drive Kyung to a convenience store for food and a gas station for beer. They circle the park and the school and the campus. They go all the way to the town's northernmost border and all the way back south. Up, down, left, right, over and over again, sometimes retracing the same routes they were on only minutes before. The clock on the dashboard says it's twenty after midnight, but they continue driving with no particular destination—Connie and Kyung in the Suburban, Tim following close behind in the rental. Kyung knows why they're doing this; he doesn't even need to ask. The beer and the drive have a sedative effect. Occasionally, a long, smooth stretch of road almost puts him to sleep, but when he closes his eyes, the images begin to appear on the blacks of his lids. He sees Mae tearing out of her house, so frightened and desperate that she begs the Perrys to help her, and just like that, he's awake again, unwilling to watch the things that happen next.

Connie hasn't spoken to him since the gas station. He sits with his arm out the open window, a can of nuclear-green energy drink in his hand. Every few minutes, he takes a sip and glances in the rearview mirror to check if Tim is still behind them. He seems worried and tired, almost as tired as Kyung is, but Connie will do this all night if he has to. Kyung alternates between studying the lock on his door and the speedometer on the dash, which hovers near thirty-five. At this point, his best chance of ditching his in-laws is to jump out of the car, but the risk of hurting himself is too high. He needs to be able-bodied when he sees his father, capable of doing harm. He chucks his empty beer can into the backseat, frustrated by how much time they've wasted.

"I have to piss."

Connie turns onto a state road, a large artery that will eventually leave Marlboro and connect with the highway.

"Did you hear what I said? I have to piss."

"I'll stop at the next gas station."

They follow the road toward the old airstrip, an area that's been under development for years. The two-mile stretch is now home to several new bars and restaurants, all vying for business with wattage. Huge neon signs flash and flicker, blinding passersby with their offerings. LADIES' NIGHT. HALF-PRICED PITCHERS. ALL-YOU-CAN-EAT SHRIMP.

"Why can't we just stop at one of these places?"

"I'm a cop, Kyung. Not an idiot."

"What does that mean?"

"It means I know you're planning to bolt if we go somewhere crowded, and I don't really feel like chasing you right now."

Kyung's bladder is swimming with cheap lawn-mower beer. He actually does need to piss, but it never occurred to him that he could turn a basic human need into a chance to run. Connie is too many steps ahead, too practiced in the ways of desperate men. Kyung worries that he's never going to get rid of him.

"I'm exhausted," he says. When this fails to elicit a response, he says it even louder. "I'm *exhausted*."

"Then go to sleep already."

"I can't, not in a car. That's what I've been trying to tell you. I've never been able to sleep in a car."

"So what do you want me to do about it? Sleeping and pissing are your only options right now."

"But couldn't we just go to your house for a while?" Kyung looks out his window. They're driving farther and farther away from town. "We're still close, and maybe if I get some rest, it'll help me clear my head."

Connie considers this for a moment, rubbing his bloodshot eyes.

"I haven't slept in almost two days. I couldn't even run if I wanted to. I just need a place to lie down."

A few minutes later, Connie swings a wide U-turn, doubling back along the same neon strip. Eventually, Kyung begins to recognize the modest housing stock that makes up the northern end of the Flats. He sinks into his seat, trying not to let on that he's hopeful about where they're headed. He didn't think Connie would be willing to take him back to his place. He can't remember if he's ever been there without Gillian or Ethan before, but he's relieved by the sudden change in course. Now all he has to do is outlast his in-laws.

When they walk through the front door, Vivi is asleep on the couch with a magazine open on her chest.

She jumps up at the sound of their footsteps, wrapping her shiny green robe over her nightgown. "It's so late," she says. "I was worried. Is everything all right?"

"We're fine." Connie gives her a kiss on the forehead. "Why don't you go to bed now, Vivi?"

She looks at the three of them uncertainly. "Have you eaten?"

Tim takes off his jacket and throws it over the arm of a chair. "You need me anymore?" he asks Connie.

"No, it's fine. I've got this."

"I'm going to bed, then."

Tim stalks off down the hall and closes his door, not bothering to answer Vivi's question or even acknowledge her presence. He treated her the way a little boy might, sullen and rude to his father's new girlfriend despite her attempts to be kind.

Vivi seems slightly hurt by his reaction, but she quickly turns her attention back to Connie and Kyung. "What about you two? Are you hungry? I can heat up some leftovers."

"No, honey. We're fine. Just go to bed."

She looks the two of them over, waiting for an explanation.

When Connie doesn't offer one, she hangs Tim's jacket on the coatrack behind the front door, frowning as she smooths out the wrinkled sleeves. "Aren't you coming too?" she asks.

"No, not just yet."

Kyung can almost see the questions forming on Vivi's tongue: *Why did you bring him here? Why does he look like that? What's wrong with him now?* But she's too polite to ask and slowly retreats to their room.

Kyung didn't expect to see her here either. He didn't think things had progressed this far yet, but it's obvious that Vivi is making her presence felt in this house. The living room is much tidier than it was the last time he visited. Homey, almost. There are pictures on the walls now—small prints of fruit and trees and fishermen, similar to the kind hanging in his dentist's office. The magazines have been neatly arranged on the coffee table in the shape of a fan, and there are candles everywhere. Big red ones in glass jars that make the place smell like cinnamon, an improvement from the stale smell of chips and popcorn that was always here before. He wonders if Vivi's interest in decorating has anything to do with his mother's influence, and the thought of this is so sad, he has to shut it out.

"Didn't you need to use the can?" Connie asks.

There's a window in the bathroom, right above the tub. Kyung can see it from where he's standing. The streetlights outside cast shadows of tree branches on the glass. It's half the size of a normal window, but still big enough to crawl through. He looks at Connie, not certain how he could overlook something so obvious.

"Well, what are you waiting for? Go ahead."

Kyung walks into the dimly lit bathroom, locking the door

behind him. He turns on the fan and relieves himself, staring at the trees outside. The bathroom is on the first floor, so it worries him to see treetops instead of bushes. He wonders how many feet he'll fall when he climbs out. Quietly, he steps into the tub and pulls on the window, but the frame won't budge. He flips the latch in the opposite direction and tries again, but still nothing, not even an inch. On the other side of the door, he hears Connie open and close the hall closet. When he walks away, Kyung reaches up and feels around the inner edge of the frame for a stopper, kicking up the ancient layer of dust on the sash. His heart sinks when he realizes the entire window has been caulked and painted shut. He assumes Connie already thought of this—he wasn't worried for a reason—and for a moment, Kyung doesn't know what to do but just stand there, staring at the moon rising high and bright above the trees.

Connie is shoving a pillow into a case when Kyung returns from the bathroom. "The sofa's not the most comfortable thing in the world," he says. "But these chairs recline pretty far back. I fall asleep here half the time anyways."

There's an army green blanket on Tim's chair that wasn't there before. Kyung sits down and spreads the itchy wool across his legs, putting his feet up to appear ready for a nap. He's disappointed when Connie throws him the pillow and sits down in the chair beside him.

"You don't have to stay here with me. I don't need to be watched."

"Actually, I think you do."

They sit silently, both of them with their arms crossed, studying the black television screen in front of them. Minutes pass, and he doesn't know how much longer he can take it—the nervous, uncomfortable energy, the sense of being trapped. His car keys are in Tim's left pocket. He noticed their faint outline when Vivi hung up his coat. All he needs are the keys and a few seconds to get away. He wonders if he should pretend to fall asleep or ask for a glass of water from the kitchen, but he knows Connie would see right through him.

"Should we turn on the TV?"

"The noise won't help you sleep."

"So we're just going to sit here all night?"

"As long as we have to." Connie knits his fingers over his stomach.

The silence doesn't make Kyung tired. It simply feeds his frustration, expanding it like a balloon that can't hold all the air being forced inside.

Connie must sense this because he turns to him a few minutes later, his expression softer than it was before. "Hey," he says, seemingly hesitant about what he wants to say next. "It's going to be all right, you know. It might not feel that way right now, but trust me, it will be."

"*How?*" Kyung asks. "You were standing right there—you heard the whole thing."

"You just have to give yourself some time—"

"Time for what? Time won't change the fact that my father was hitting my mother again. That's how all of this started, Connie. That's why she and Marina aren't here anymore. So what am I supposed to do? Just pretend like he's not responsible for what happened?"

"I'm not saying you have to pretend anything. But you can't run off half-cocked like you did earlier. Tomorrow, I want you to call Jin and tell him to pack up his stuff and move back to his place. And then you're going to stay as far away from him as possible, understand? Let the police handle him from now on. You have a wife and child waiting at home, a life to get back to, so take my advice and don't go looking for trouble, Kyung. You've had more than your fair share lately."

Optimism isn't a quality he associates with Connie. But it makes more sense to him now. Connie doesn't know that Gillian threw him out. Part of him feels like this is her news to share, and she didn't for a reason, but he's also curious. Everything that Connie's doing, everything he's saying—would it change if he knew?

"Gillian and I aren't together anymore. She asked me to leave yesterday, or maybe it was the day before." He can't remember when it actually happened. The days, the hours—they've all bled together.

"So why'd she finally do it?"

Finally, Kyung thinks. The word says it all. For five years, Connie has been waiting, quietly wishing their marriage would end, and now he doesn't have to hide it anymore, not that he ever hid it well.

"What do you care? It's not like you actually wanted us to stay together."

Connie considers this for a moment. "Okay, I deserved that. I'll admit it. Maybe at first I wasn't so happy about you two getting together, but after the kid . . . I rooted for you."

Kyung can't think of a single time when anything like this occurred. His relationship with his in-laws had always been tepidly acknowledged, as if his connection to them were something to be tolerated or waited out.

"When did you ever *root* for me, Connie? You and Tim, you never liked me, never liked me for Gillian. You probably wanted her to marry some nice white guy, someone you could sit around and watch baseball and cop shows with. And don't even bother trying to deny it—I saw the look on your face the first time she brought me here. It was so obvious. You were like, 'Who the hell is this Asian guy?'"

Connie lowers his head, covering his eyes. "You think that's why I didn't like you for Gilly? Because you're not white?" It almost sounds like he's laughing, but when he looks up, his skin is furious and red. "Jesus, you're the dumbest smart person I've ever met. I don't care what color you are. You could have been black, for all it mattered. I didn't want you dating my daughter, because of that goddamn chip on your shoulder. You think a father can't see that kind of thing from a mile away? I knew— not even five minutes after meeting you—that nothing was ever going to make you happy. Not a nice girl on your arm, not a kid or a house or a fancy job. All the things that other people want in life, they were never going to be good enough. That's why I didn't want Gilly getting involved with you."

Connie has never spoken to Kyung in so many consecutive sentences before. Each one indicts him more harshly than the sentence that preceded it, but he can tell there's more to come, years' worth of more.

"I saw how Gilly sidled up to you so fast. She probably figured, here's a nice-looking guy, something different to bring home to Dad. He's smart; he'll probably make a decent living when he's done with school. That's good enough. And nothing I said would talk her out of it. She never thought she'd do any better than you, and you know how bad it felt to know what I passed on to her, to both my kids?"

"What are you talking about? What did you pass on?"

"There's a saying for it. It was like"—Connie circles his hands, as if to grab the words he's searching for from the air—"like low expectations or something. Gilly's mom and me, we didn't yell or scream at each other, but we didn't enjoy each other either. Eighteen years Marlene and I were married, and I don't ever remember feeling happy with her, or excited to be around her or hear what she had to say. We were just *there*. And that's exactly where I saw Gilly headed with you."

Kyung knows what this is all about. Connie's newfound romance suddenly has him talking like a philosopher, like someone who thinks he knows about love. If he weren't so tired, it might almost seem funny, but he doesn't see the humor in it now.

"I'm not trying to criticize," Connie continues. "I understand a lot more about you because of everything that's happened, and I get why you're like this now. My dad was a son of a bitch too. It's hard to be happy when you don't know what it's supposed to look like. But I'm telling you, things can change. That woman in there"—he points to his bedroom door—"that woman makes me happy. She makes me want to be a different person. Maybe if you tried to convince Gilly that you can change too—"

"I cheated on her," Kyung says. "I cheated and she caught me. That's why she asked me to leave."

The position they're both sitting in—backs reclined, legs stretched out—is at odds with the sudden tension in the room. Kyung realizes he made a mistake. He wanted Connie to stop babbling like some love-struck teenager, but he didn't think about the consequences before opening his mouth. Now he's staring at a man twice his size who looks like he's about to beat him senseless. Kyung tips his head back and stares at the ceiling, at a small spiderweb fluttering from the vent. He listens to

Connie breathing—in, out, in, out—relieved to hear that he still sounds calm. He's not huffing and puffing like someone getting ready to throw a punch.

"I don't know why she didn't tell you herself. Maybe she was just waiting for the right time or something. Anyway, I'm sorry you had to hear it from me."

Connie doesn't respond. He just sits there with his hands folded over his stomach. Kyung wishes he'd say something. Despite all appearances, he's always respected his father-in-law, always wished for a scrap of that respect in return. Over the past few weeks, Connie has been the steady one, the one who tried to help everyone else, even though he never heard a word of thanks for his efforts. Kyung feels terrible for disappointing him. Or at the very least, he feels terrible for confirming what Connie always knew.

"Gillian deserves better than me. I think we all understand that. So I'm going to let her get on with her life, and you're going to let me get on with mine." Kyung slowly tilts his seat back up and begins to stand. "I'm sorry, Connie. I appreciate what you're trying to do, but there's no fixing what happened with Gillian. I made sure of that. Maybe—" He stops, realizing there is no maybe. "You were right about me from the start."

He takes a step toward the door, then another and another, but as he lifts his hand to reach for Tim's jacket, Connie brings his chair upright.

"Sit down," he says.

Kyung doesn't move.

"Sit your ass down."

"You're not my father-in-law anymore. You don't need to be responsible for me."

"You and my daughter have a kid together, so even though you're a miserable little shit, I'm not going to let you run off and do something you can't take back. My grandson's not going to spend his weekends visiting you in prison. Now sit down."

"But he needs to pay for what he did, Connie."

"Sit down and shut the fuck up. You don't want to know what's going to happen if I have to get out of this chair."

Kyung waits, listening for Vivi or Tim to stumble out of their beds. Connie spared no volume, which was meant to intimidate him, to make him behave. He realizes how different he must have sounded when he told Jin not to hit Mae again. He can almost hear his weak, frightened voice, just trying to spit out the words. Connie spoke with the kind of force that Kyung didn't possess as a teenager, leaving no room for doubt about the consequences of his decision. If he doesn't sit down again, he's going to suffer. Kyung is terrified now, terrified and desperate and filled with an overwhelming desire to make his father feel exactly as he does, if only Connie would let him. He rests his hand on a table, and the idea comes to him quickly, so quickly that he doesn't stop to think before he acts. He picks up a candle and swings, hearing the hard strike of bone against glass. Connie slumps forward in his chair, dropping his arms to the floor.

The room is suddenly quiet. Nothing, no one—not even Kyung—moves. He holds the jar in his outstretched hand, counting the seconds as they pass. *Five, ten* . . . He's never hit a man before; he thinks he hit him much harder than he meant to. Connie remains folded over his lap, his back rising and falling with each breath. *Fifteen, twenty* . . . As Kyung returns the candle to the table, a single word begins to beat through his head like a drum. *Run.* The longer he waits, the louder he hears it, but he inches toward Connie's chair instead.

"Are you . . . are you okay?" he whispers, pushing him upright.

Connie slowly opens his eyes at the sound of Kyung's voice, blinking like someone waking from a heavy sleep.

"What"—he reaches up, wincing as he touches the back of his head—"what happened?"

He stares at Kyung, his expression confused. Dazed, almost. And then there's a flicker—a bright, angry flicker in which Connie appears to remember exactly what happened. "Idiot," he says hoarsely. "You stupid . . . stupid . . ." He shifts in his seat, about to get up, but standing seems to require more strength than he has. He winces again as he leans against the headrest. Then his chin rolls forward and he passes out.

The word continues to beat, even louder and faster than it did before. *Run.* And this time, Kyung has to listen. Every muscle in his body is awake now, vibrating with the horror of what he's done and what he knows he has to do next.

There's a single lamp glowing in the living room window, a single figure sitting on the sofa inside. The front door is unlocked, as if Jin is expecting him. There's no use trying to deny it now. He and his father share the same mind. Jin knew what Kyung would learn at the police station, so he returned to his house in the Heights to spare Ethan, to prevent him from witnessing what Kyung had so many times as a child. His choice to come here is the closest thing to an acknowledgment of his wrongdoing, an invitation to end this where it all began.

Kyung makes no effort to enter the house quietly. He announces himself by throwing his keys on the floor. It's not the element of surprise that he's after. What he wants to incite most is dread. He remembers it so clearly from his childhood—hearing something as innocent as a plate or glass break and then the awful wait, wondering when the screaming would start, wondering how long he'd have to count before it stopped. No wall was thick enough, no door closed tightly enough to keep the words from reaching him. *Ha ji mah! Ah pa.* "Don't! It hurts." There was no such thing as mercy then. No mercy, no pity, no god, no grace. Only open palms and closed fists and the seed of this moment planting somewhere deep inside him.

Jin remains seated on the sofa when Kyung enters the living room. He doesn't seem alarmed, or even worried to see him. He just sits there with his elbow propped up on a pillow, drinking a bourbon or Scotch. He empties what's left of his glass and refills it, three fingers high, from a bottle on the end table. Kyung walks past the sofa, saying nothing as he pours himself a whiskey from the bar.

"You saw him at the police station?" Jin asks.

"Yes."

"And?"

"And what?"

"Was he sorry?" He clears his throat. "About what he did to us?"

Kyung thinks for a moment as he settles into the armchair across from Jin. The word "sorry" never crossed Nat Perry's lips. "No, he wasn't. Not at all. Are you sorry?"

"Would it matter to you if I was?"

Kyung thinks about this too. "No."

"Then there's no reason to say that I am."

They sip their drinks, and it all seems strangely civilized. A father and son, sharing a round of cocktails as the night ticks slowly toward dawn. Kyung was hoping for this, this last window of quiet when he could ask the things he's always wanted to know.

"You got mad at Mom for something when I was ten. Something that happened at a party, I think. You ended up knocking out one of her teeth." He pauses, trying to erase the image of the bloody, broken tooth, an incisor that he later found under the edge of a rug. "What made you mad enough to do that?"

"Is this really what you want to talk about right now?"

Mae was more traumatized by the loss of her tooth than by any bruise or black eye she'd ever received. She cried about it for days, probably because it was something she couldn't hide under her makeup or clothes. Kyung remembers trying to comfort her when they were alone, wrapping his arms around her shoulders as she sat on the bathroom floor. For his efforts, he limped away with a backhand to the face.

"Yes, this is exactly what I want to talk about."

"It was the price tag," Jin says, staring into his drink. "My department, they had a reception for everyone who got tenure that year. All the wives were invited. I didn't want your mother to come—the men and women used to socialize separately in those days—but it would have been strange for her not to be there." He crosses his legs, frowning as he flicks a stray piece of grass from his shoe. "I told her to buy a new outfit, an expensive one. I even gave her a list of things the other wives would be interested in, so it'd be easier for her to make conversation. But during the reception, I noticed some of the women laughing at her, talking about her behind her back, and then some of the husbands too. It kept getting worse and worse. So there I was, trying to feel proud of what I'd done. I'd finally gotten tenure after six years of people whispering about whether I was good enough, whether my research even mattered. I'd put up with my idiot students trying to correct my English and having colleagues pick me apart in meetings because they knew I wouldn't challenge them. I'd survived all these things, and it was like none of it even mattered that night because of her."

The thought of people talking down to his father or complaining about his work is completely at odds with Kyung's understanding of him. In Korea, everyone openly admired Jin. Their neighbors and relatives called him "professor" long before he even finished his degree. They treated him like someone to be reckoned with, so to come to a place where the opposite was true—Kyung can imagine the shock of it. He can see why his father always held himself to such impossibly high standards. Jin thought he had to be perfect. And Mae and Kyung and the house, they had to be perfect too. They were his extensions into the world, the things by which he was judged, and to hear it now, Kyung understands that people sometimes weren't kind. It makes sense, then, why the smallest things often mattered to Jin, why a burnt dinner or sullen expression or innocent mistake were all cause for a reaction. It makes sense that when the valve opened even slightly, the pressure building up inside needed a form of release. But why take his anger out on his wife instead of the people who mistreated them? This is where everything seizes up for Kyung, where his mind simply narrows and no amount of empathy can squeeze through to the other side.

"I don't understand what a price tag had to do with anything."

"Your mother was wearing it—she forgot to cut it off. That's why they were laughing at her." Jin winces, as if his embarrassment is days old, not decades. "The worst part was, she wasn't comfortable spending money back then, so instead of doing what I told her to do, she went out and bought something on sale. Her dress had been marked down so many times, there were bright orange stickers all over the tag."

"That's the worst thing you can think of? The stickers?" Kyung clutches the armrests of his chair. "That's the worst part of this story for you?"

"You don't know what it was like back then."

"But I was there, remember? Maybe not in the same room, but I was there. I heard what you did to her."

"No." Jin frowns, pinching the bridge of his nose. "I'm talking about the university, the town. It wasn't always like this, with blacks and Asians and Hispanics everywhere. Not in the '70s, it wasn't. I was the only one on campus for years, and people never let me forget that. They went out of their way to make me feel like nothing."

Kyung tries to imagine his father as a young man, a newly minted Ph.D. coming to America with a woman he didn't want to marry, a woman whose parents simply outbid the family of the other girl he wanted more. He's willing to accept the possibility that life was as hard as Jin claims, being the only non-white person to walk into a classroom or an office building. He has memories of his own to confirm this, faded memories of stares and snickers and nicknames that he didn't want, fights in the school yard that he could never win. He never mentioned these indignities to his parents; he assumed he suffered them alone. Kyung knows that he and his mother were a burden to Jin, especially during those early years when they relied on him for everything. What he doesn't understand is who blinked first—if his father was cruel to Mae because she couldn't help him cope, or if she didn't try to help because he was cruel.

"So are you done with your questions now?"

"No, not yet. Tell me about Mom's cousin. The one you actually wanted to marry."

"Why?"

"Because I want to know if things would have been different with her."

Jin stirs his drink with his finger. "She died young. In her forties, I think. Cancer."

"I'm not asking what would have been different. I'm asking if *you* would have been different."

"You have a Ph.D.," Jin says, lobbing the first grenade. "Act like you earned it. Say what you really want to say."

Kyung nods. "Fine, then. If you'd married this other woman, do you think you would have hit her too?"

The expression on Jin's face is smug at first. Then it settles into something that almost resembles a smile. "I probably would have hit her more."

It's not the response Kyung expected. He wanted Jin to say that things would have turned out differently, that the absence of love in their present was caused by an absence of love from the start. To hear him admit that nothing would have changed erases any last trace of doubt. There's no alternate version of history in which he and his family live happily, untouched by violence. They were always going to end up this way because of Jin. Until now, Kyung was able to sit calmly in his seat and just listen, but Jin's expression continues to taunt him.

"You're proud of hitting women?" he asks, drawing his hands into fists. "You think this is funny?"

"No. I'm not proud at all. I'm just being honest. You asked me a question, so I answered it. Your mother's cousin was a beautiful girl, but the people she came from . . . they were farmers. Look how much trouble your mother gave me, and she supposedly came from a good family." He tries to make quotation marks with his fingers as he says "good," spilling some of his drink on the sofa. "Your mother couldn't even read a book for the first three years we lived here. She was always trying to steal your schoolbooks to look at the pictures, as if reading and looking were the same thing. Do you know what it was like, taking my illiterate wife to dinner at my dean's house, praying that no one would notice how stupid she was?"

The second grenade. Something isn't right here. It hasn't felt right for a while. Jin rarely talks this much, and now it seems like he's saying the most hateful things he can, whether he means them or not. Kyung feels like he's being baited, forced to react before he's ready.

"I was hard on your mother. Too hard in the beginning. I understand that. And then you turned on me and told the reverend our secrets. You took her side."

"I took the right side."

"You took her side," he repeats. "So I tried to make it up to her. I did exactly what Reverend Sung told me to do. I put my wife on a pedestal. I worked day and night to give her this house and the kind of life we came to this country for. Anything she laid her eyes on, I gave it to her. Art, jewelry, a house at the beach. If she wanted to remodel the bathroom a year after she'd just remodeled it, I kept my mouth shut and opened my wallet. I let her spend entire paychecks on those antiques of hers. And you know what she finally said to me after thirty-six years of marriage, after I'd spent nearly half of them trying to make up for what I did? She said she was leaving. She was going to work—ha!—she was going to work for that friend of hers. She was planning to give up this house to live in a storeroom, a *storeroom,* somewhere in Connecticut, and she never wanted to see me again."

Jin looks increasingly bewildered as he tells this story, as if he still doesn't understand why Mae would want to leave.

"I made my mistakes a long time ago. Almost twenty years ago. And I did everything I could to be a better husband after that. I even went to church, and she sat right next to me every damn week, nodding while the reverend talked about forgiveness and compassion, as if she even understood what those things were." Jin waves his glass in the air, dousing the rug with his drink. "You know what she actually said to me that day? She said she never forgave me for any of it. Never."

"So you heard that and just went back to doing the exact same thing she couldn't forgive in the first place? Do you even understand what happened because of you?"

Jin exhales, and his face collapses like an old jack-o'-lantern. Tears squeeze out from his eyes as he shakes his head. "I never meant . . . those men . . ."

He's only seen his father cry once before, on the night that Reverend Sung came to their house. He felt no more pity for him then than he does now. Kyung's hands are about to break, clenched purple at the thought of what's missing from all of this.

"What about me?" he asks. "You never tried to make it up to me. Not once did you ever try. All this time, I've been watching you with Ethan, wondering why you seem like a completely different person with him."

"You know what it's like spending your entire life trying to make up for something you can't take back?"

"That's not an answer."

"I was different with Ethan because he let me be."

"*I* would have let you."

"You." Jin swats the air with his hand. "You were a lost cause. I saw the way you looked at me. You were never going to forgive me for any of it. You had hate in your eyes when you were a boy, and you still have hate in your eyes now." He slams his glass on the table and gets down on his knees, stretching his arms out to the sides. "So just do it already. Do what you came here to do. Hit me. Kill me. I don't care anymore." He strikes himself on the side of the head. "Make this go away." He strikes himself again, harder this time. "Make me stop seeing it. Make me stop seeing what they did to her."

Kyung gets out of his chair as Jin reaches for his leg. He stands in front of the fireplace, his hands shaking as he scans the objects on the mantel. There was once a globe on the left, a heavy marble globe attached to an iron pedestal. He studied it so often as a teenager that he eventually forgot to look for it, assuming his weapon of choice would be there when the time finally came. He didn't notice it was gone until now, replaced by an antique clock.

"Please make it stop."

In the mirror above the mantel, he sees Jin kneeling on the rug behind him, still begging to be hit. Kyung sizes up the clock, estimating the weight of its metal guts and case. As he reaches for it, he imagines what it would feel like to release all of his rage at once. It would only take one swing, one perfect swing, to end this. He inches his fingers closer, steeling himself to do what he came here to do, what his father keeps screaming at him to do. But as he touches the edge of the clock, he hears it again. The crack of the jar as it lands on the back of Connie's head. He flinches at the sound of it, like the sharp thwack of a bat connecting with a ball. The act of raising a hand to someone, it's the worst thing Kyung has ever done, the worst thing he's ever felt. And the power that surged through him in that moment—it made him feel like he had some semblance of control, but it lasted no longer than an instant before he lost it again. What if he hits his father and the rage inside him doesn't go away? Or what if it does go, only to be replaced by something else he can't live with?

"Why are you just standing there?" Jin shouts, hitting himself again. "This is what you want to do, so just do it already."

He came here because of a promise, a choice to make good on a promise that altered the entire trajectory of his life. But not once did Kyung stop to think about his life in the seconds and hours, the days and years afterward. All of that comes rushing at him now. With both of his parents gone, he knows he'll inherit their hopelessness, the same hopelessness that sent his mother headfirst into a tree, that has his father kneeling on the floor, begging for his own life to end. He'll never experience another moment in which change seems possible. He'll never have a reason to believe in his capacity to be better than what he is. Kyung looks at the mantel again, and he understands there's a different choice to be made. Pick up the clock, and he'll never escape this darkness. Leave it, and he still has a chance.

"Stop standing there. Do something."

Jin's reflection in the mirror is tortured. His skin is crimson; his expression, pitiful. It's all lines and creases and pain, such pain, the volume of which Kyung never saw until now. Jin held on to it for so long, hiding it under his wealth, feeding it with success and status and possessions, all the things Kyung wanted for himself. Kyung assumed they'd make him happy; he assumed they made Jin happy. But the happiest he ever saw his father was when he was with Ethan, someone who never knew him as he was before, who simply accepted the person he was trying to be. Jin wasn't acting then, he thinks. He was just being kind to Ethan, returning the very thing that everyone else had denied him. Kyung steps back from the mantel, aware that inflicting more pain won't lessen his own. It didn't work for his father. It won't work for him.

"I'm not going to hit you."

He sits down on the edge of the rug and brings his knees to his chest. He's tired again, so incredibly tired. The exhaustion catches up with him, settling deep into the hollows of his bones. He turns his head from side to side, listening to the gristly crack and pop of his neck. Jin studies him carefully, confused perhaps by his posture. He remains on his knees, hesitant and watchful, as if he expects Kyung to change his mind. When he doesn't, Jin lowers himself to the floor. They sit across from each other without speaking, their hands idle and limp.

"I see it too," Kyung finally says.

"What?"

"I see what they did to her. And then I see what you did to her, and what she did to me." He pauses. "I don't know how to make it stop either."

Jin stares at him, his eyes clouding over and filling with tears. He seems wounded, unable to stay upright. When he lies on his side, curled up like a ball on the rug, the tears slide down his face in long, diagonal streaks.

"I'm sorry," he says.

Kyung stares back, startled by the words despite how quietly they were spoken.

"I'm sorry," he says again.

He doesn't say what he's sorry for, but Kyung can tell from the look on Jin's face, from the way he keeps repeating himself, that the apology is an accumulation for all the things they haven't been able to forget. On and on, he goes. I'm sorry, I'm sorry, I'm sorry—so many times that it's impossible not to hear. Kyung considers telling him that everything will be all right as Connie did, but instead, he simply listens, trying to accept the unfamiliar for what it is. Minutes pass, and Jin begins to slur his words, softer and slower until he lets out a faint whistle, drifting off into a steady rhythm of sleep.

Kyung watches him, desperate to rest as he does, to be peaceful for the first time in so long. He crawls toward the center of the rug and lies down on his side, carefully fitting his body against the inner curve of his father's. He adjusts himself until they fit like puzzle pieces, pressed together with his head in the crook of Jin's arm. Slowly, he releases his weight, letting all of his muscles go slack. Outside, the sun is starting to rise above the trees, casting a single warm strip of light on the floor beneath the window. Every time Kyung looks at it, he thinks it's getting closer. If they wait here long enough, morning will finally reach them.

ACKNOWLEDGMENTS

After years of writing this work of fiction, it seems only fitting to end it with a few pages of truth. And the truth is, I've been incredibly fortunate, and I didn't get here alone.

The M.F.A. program at the University of Massachusetts Amherst reoriented my life in ways that I couldn't fully imagine when I first decided to apply. I'm grateful to my former classmates and the dedicated faculty—Noy Holland, Valerie Martin, Sam Michel, and Sabina Murray—whose many lessons continue to serve me well.

Brian Baldi, Chip Brantley, Deborah Carlin, Laura Dickerman, Elizabeth Hughey, Cecily Iddings, Valerie Martin, and Boomer Pinches took time out of their busy lives to read earlier versions of this manuscript and provide much-needed feedback. They were the best possible readers anyone could ever ask for—generous, clear-eyed, and unflinchingly honest.

Paul LeClerc and Marshall Rose hired me at the New York Public Library, the place where my childhood love of writing reignited. Mary Deane Sorcinelli created the rare kind of work–life balance that allowed me to pursue other passions outside of the office. Mira Bartók served as a constant source of encouragement. And the Massachusetts Cultural Council provided the gift of financial support and recognition at a time when I needed it most.

My devoted agent, Jennifer Gates, and her colleagues at Zachary Shuster Harmsworth, particularly Lane Zachary and Esmond Harmsworth, believed in the story I wanted to tell. I will forever be grateful to Jen for opening the door, and to Elizabeth Bruce, my wonderful editor at Picador, for ushering me in. The thoughtfulness and care that Elizabeth, Jen, and their colleagues invested in my work far surpassed every reasonable hope or expectation, and this book has safely reached your hands because of their collective efforts.

Last, but not least, thank you to the Yuns, the Andersons, and my extended family of friends for the constancy of their love and support over the years. I am especially thankful to my husband, Joel Anderson, to whom this book is dedicated. In addition to being the very first reader of these pages, Joel believed when I didn't, pushed when I couldn't, and never let me forget that this was a story that deserved to be told.